The

Whore's Companion

Ed Harvey

The Whore's Companion
Copyright © Ed Harvey 2011

All rights reserved
ISBN: 978-0-9568207-0-9

Imprint: Ed Harvey

Printed by www.createspace.com

Dedicated to Mike Macpherson

Stolen from us when our backs were turned

Acknowledgments

With thanks to my darling Sue for her love, patience and support, Tony Carter, Linda Karlson, Helen Harvey, Jean Macpherson and Humph Wills for their critical suggestions, Freda Lightfoot for her editorial advice, Dave Tadd for his forensic expertise, and Michael Muskett for his help with the cover.

And for all those family and friends who have asked, 'How's the book?' Thanks for your encouragement. I hope you enjoy reading The Whore's Companion.

Day One

Thursday 18th June 2009

Andalucia, Southern Spain.

For much of the morning, Juan Gonzales sat in the shadows of his small terrace. The doctors had told him that this would be his last summer but, at eighty-three, he was thankful to have the opportunity to kill one last time.

He'd been up long before the rooster's strangled call and had felt faint and light-headed, but at least the vomiting was no worse than usual. He sat and smoked, looking beyond the church and the terracotta roofs of whitewashed cottages to the maze of alleyways and narrow streets, watching the few men who still had work as they climbed into their white vans or took to the fields.

At eleven, he took his rifle and its ammunition from a secret chamber he'd built behind the long-defunct, wood-burning stove. The rifle was one of the few trophies his father had brought back from the Civil War and Juan treasured it, cradling it in his lap, cleaning and caressing it. He'd had to wait ten long years after the war but, as soon as he was old enough, he became one of the General's most dedicated assassins - nineteen men and four women, enemies of the General's new regime, their names recorded on the role of shame in the city of Salamanca, hunted down and disposed of.

He had no doubt that the rifle would still work, but, as a precaution, he took a handgun from behind the wooden lintel above the front door and filled its magazine.

As the sun rose higher in the sky and the heat baked the earth dry, he knew the streets would be deserted, the villagers gathering in their homes to eat before the siesta. He knew where his victims would be. Knew he wouldn't be disturbed.

He loaded five rounds into the rifle's magazine, wrapped it in the old rug, and pushed the handgun into his waistband, covering it with his blue cotton shirt. He stood before the fading photograph of his wife who'd died giving birth to their son in that very room, over fifty years ago. He took red wine he'd bottled last year and broke bread he'd bought yesterday - a final Communion, a simple prayer of thanks and to ask for strength for the task ahead.

Finally, Juan Gonzales covered his head with an old, black cap and stepped out into the blistering sun.

*

Antonio Fernández sat on a stool in one of the oldest bars in the historic quarter of Almeria. He sipped his beer and glanced intermittently at the football being screened on the large TV in the corner.

This was his local and few things entertained him more than watching men unwind at the end of the day. Like a fly on the wall, his eyes skipped from one group to another, watching their reactions to the game, amused by the intensity of their concentration and the asides they made to anyone within earshot.

Bars like this attracted very few women. Occasionally daughters would be sent to extricate their fathers, or tourists would be drawn by the bar's reputation. The walls were plastered with images that summoned the passions of many Spanish men: bullfighting, flamenco, hunting, and football. Alongside the public phone in the corner, the telephone number of the local taxi firm was pinned next to the contact details of several brothels.

He smiled as two men argued over a referee's decision. He didn't pretend to understand the psychology of distractions such as sport, the camaraderie of a bar, and a few beers, but in tough times he suspected that it was the simple things that could mean the difference between coping and going under. Most families would have been seriously affected by the deepening recession: men and women scratching a living by turning to anything on offer, cash-in-hand, no questions asked.

Fernández ordered another beer, glanced at the TV screen and noticed a familiar face agonising over a missed chance on goal. 'José Castaño still playing for the reserves?' he asked the bartender.

'Yeah, he's making a comeback after breaking his leg last year, but he's on the fringes of the first team. He was born in Los Mineros, wasn't he?'

'I think so,' Fernández said. A small lie. He'd known José well and had dated his sister, Ana-Marie, for three years. He'd heard she'd married, but wasn't sure if she'd moved out of the village.

The bartender placed his drink in front of him. 'You're early this evening, Inspector.'

'My first break for months. Been a long time coming. Three days - nothing planned except the family matanza on Sunday.' He ran his hand over a two-day stubble, pushed his long, dishevelled hair off his forehead, rubbed the back of his neck, and glanced at the face that stared back at him from the mirror behind the bar - eyes red rimmed, underscored by dark rings that betrayed his need for sleep.

'I'll give you a good price for any part of the pig you can pass my way.'

'No chance. It'll be divided amongst the family, as always.'

The barman nodded, as though knowing there was no point arguing. 'She well? Your mother?'

Fernández hesitated. He hadn't seen his mother for several weeks. Work meant he rarely had time to be with her.

'I wouldn't like to try and take the knife off her.' He smiled, got up and slid his hand into the hip pocket of his jeans. He'd left his wallet in his car. 'Add this to my tab?'

'Yeah, but you'll all have to settle up soon: the bank manager's breathing down my neck. Have this on me, but don't leave it too long.' The bartender poured him a complimentary brandy and, as he placed it in front of him, the men in the bar bellowed in celebration. Malaga had scored, cancelling out José Castaño's earlier goal for Real Madrid's reserves.

Several other men came into the bar, ordering their drinks with a nod towards the bartender and, as they settled down to watch the match, the shrill of Fernández's mobile phone cut through the air. He sighed, stepped outside and crushed his cigarette on the cobblestones. It was early and the light was still strong. Shops had reopened and pavements were alive with families strolling and enjoying the cool shadows cast by the city centre's ancient buildings.

'Yes?'

It was Cabo Leo Medina, a recent recruit to the Policia Nacional's plain-clothes division. 'Sorry to disturb you, Sir.'

'What is it, Leo?'

'A Major Incident, Sir. In our local village.'

'Los Mineros? Look I'm off duty. There must be someone else available.' His annoyance was nothing to do with missing out on a few days leave - murder didn't have the decency to keep office hours and he rarely planned to be out of reach – but an investigation in the village where he'd been born was the last thing he needed.

'The Comandante specifically asked for you, Sir.'

'Oh, really?' Fernández struggled to stifle his sarcasm and resigned himself to this unwelcome addition to his caseload. He lit another cigarette and said, 'Tell me.'

'There are four corpses…'

'Four?'

'Yeah. Looks like three were murdered and the gunman committed suicide.'

'Where are you?'

'At the crime scene. A building site in the campo behind the village.'

'You've shut everything down?'

'And I've contacted Cientifica. The white suits are on their way but I'm having difficulty locating the duty pathologist.'

'Try the bar or the brothel,' Fernández said as turned his back on the busy square. 'OK. Secure the area until I get there. Who reported the bodies?'

'Klaus Dagmar, an ex-pat. He called the local boys and they contacted us.'

'What time?'

'Sir?'

'What time did Dagmar phone in?'

'About four thirty.'

'Did he say what he was doing, snooping around a building site?'

'His dog died yesterday. Used to walk her across the campo - same time everyday. You know what these ex-pats are like? Treat their animals like one of the family.'

Fernández shook his head, took a drag, and exhaled forcefully. 'OK. Hold him there. Assume he's a suspect and don't prime him by asking questions.'

He ended the call and walked back into the bar just as the teams were leaving the field for halftime. He downed the brandy and checked the handgun stowed beneath his crumpled linen jacket.

His Seat was parked three blocks away – the lack of convenient parking one of the few disadvantages of buying an apartment in Almeria's old quarter. He'd chosen to live in the city preferring the anonymity it provided, its relative sophistication, and the edge he felt each time he looked at the anti-fascist, anti-state graffiti scribbled on walls – his favourite proclaiming a simple message: *'Policia! No!'*

He drove north towards Los Mineros, the road winding across the coastal plain before it sliced through a valley and rose steeply into the outlying hills near the village. He passed his mother's cortijo - the smallholding she'd managed single-handedly since his father's death and resolved to try to stop by and see her later.

Los Mineros had retained much of its natural beauty. Crescent-shaped, it nestled on the lower slopes of a hill and was protected from the prevailing winds. It enjoyed stunning views north to the high peaks of the Sierra Nevada and south across the vast plains that swept towards the golden beaches of the Mediterranean. It had garnered a reputation as a picture-postcard village. The villagers took pride in their humble houses with their white walls and terracotta roofs, the vines and bougainvillea that clambered up from the narrow flagstone and cobbled streets. Even the church, with its crumbling façade, still attracted a modest congregation to Sunday services.

As he approached the outskirts of the village, Fernández lost concentration momentarily when he saw the village carpenter working on a pergola at the entrance to one of a rash of villas that pockmarked the hillsides. Distracted, he rounded a blind bend and headed straight for a stream of goats that were crossing the empty road. He slammed on his brakes. The Seat veered violently and careered towards a ditch, stopping just in time.

'Shit!' He reversed and sat back, watching as the large herd ambled past, unhurried despite the attention of two mangy dogs scurrying back and forth, snapping at their hind legs. He drummed on the steering wheel, knowing that there was nothing on God's earth that would hasten this most biblical of scenes. He almost expected to see the goatherd dressed in a blue gandoura, carrying his staff, his feet shod in sandals. But, instead, Pepe appeared in stout black working boots, brown corduroy trousers and a white shirt buttoned to the neck. He carried a small bamboo cane, using it to prod the last of the goats as it scurried across the road.

Fernández forced a smile. As a child, he'd listened with a mixture of fascination and revulsion to the story of how 'simple' Pepe had had his tongue cut out by Fascist soldiers, and he'd often wondered what, if anything, went through the goatherd's mind as he tended his flock in the hills around the village.

10

Pepe stood his ground in the middle of the road for several moments, his eyes boring through the Seat's windscreen. He began to gesticulate wildly, stabbing his cane at the road that led to the top of the village and then at the Inspector's car.

Fernández shrugged exaggeratedly, lent out of the window and shouted, 'For God's sake, Pepe, I'm in a hurry.'

Again, Pepe pointed towards the top of the village, his eyes wide, as though desperate to be heard but having no way of making clear what he had to tell. And, then, quite suddenly, he gave up, shook his fist and clambered over the bank to catch up with his goats.

Fernández sat, holding on to the steering wheel for a moment, impatient, irritated by the delay. 'Poor bastard,' he muttered, and then drove into the village and parked on a grass verge near the football pitch. He clambered out and checked the damage. One of the headlights would need replacing but it would have to wait. The first few hours after a homicide were crucial and he was impatient to get started. The village was settling into the rhythm of the evening, the sun slipping behind the hills. It was only a matter of time before word would get round.

He exhaled forcefully, climbed over an old stonewall and made his way across the campo, towards the construction site.

Cabo Leo Medina was leaning against the door jam of the new-build, dressed in a black jacket, a dark polo shirt and beige chinos. When he saw the Inspector, he stooped to ease his way through the doorframe and walked down the gravel path to meet him. Born in Los Mineros, Medina had never strayed far, marrying a local girl and buying a dilapidated, two-storey house that he'd spent a couple of years restoring before joining the police force. Despite his lopsided grin, he cut an imposing figure beneath short, military styled hair. At six-four, he towered over most and had a reputation for a fiery temper, storing his passion, powder-keg-dry, just below the surface of a thin skin. Early signs suggested he would make the grade, but only if he could curb his tongue and channel his aggression.

'Very quiet, Leo? No press, no locals?'

'It's been kept under wraps, Sir. The local police decided to escort Dagmar back to his home.'

'Did they? I thought I made it quite clear that I wanted him kept away from the village.'

'They thought it best.'

'Oh, really?' Fernández pulled a pack of cigarettes from inside his jacket and took his time lighting up. This was Leo Medina's first big case – having a senior officer jump down his throat could make him defensive and kill any future initiative.

'I think I know when it happened.'

'The shooting?'

'Several shots must have been fired. We'd have heard them. Sound travels. You can't have an argument with the wife without the whole village knowing about it. I was at home, both my boys, Roz and me, sitting down for lunch when a whole load of rockets exploded around us.'

'Rockets?'

'Fireworks.'

'Felipe Romero risking life and limb again?'

'Thing is, Sir, the fiesta's not 'til tomorrow.'

'And rockets normally remind everyone.'

'On the day, not before.'

'What time was this?'

'About two.'

'And you're suggesting, what? That there was some sort of collusion between Juan Gonzales and Felipe?'

'God knows.'

'It's our job to know, Leo. We'll chase Felipe later; see what he has to say for himself. Probably a coincidence.' He took a drag, wincing when the smoke stung his eyes. 'OK. Contact uniform; tell them to bring Dagmar here. They're to keep everyone else away. Understand? We may already be too late.' He waited as Medina put in a call and used the lull to survey the carnage. He recognised each of the dead men, knew their names.

'Three from the same family,' Medina said, standing behind him. 'The grandfather, Alberto Ramos, his son, Bartolomé, and his grandson…'

'Matias,' Fernández said, understanding exactly why the Comandante had assigned him to the case.

'Two weapons. Both pretty ancient. The rifle's a Mauser 98 and the handgun's a Walther P38.'

'Really?'

Medina grinned. 'Games we played as kids. Became a bit of a hobby: that and bullfighting. Oh, and it looks like Juan Gonzales used the handgun on himself.'

'One of Franco's assassins.'

'Yeah. Could be some history between the two families.'

'Possibly.' Fernández knew Juan Gonzales had been detested for his part in Franco's purges after the Civil War, but this early in the investigation he was reluctant to drag up the past. He looked over at the SOCOs in their white suits and asked. 'Is this is all that Cientifica could manage?'

'Yes, Sir. They're waiting for your word. I thought you'd want to examine the area yourself before they stamped their size forty-eights all over it.'

'Did you track down the pathologist?'

'Yeah, they're sending his replacement. Seems he ignored the advice of his doctor to lose weight, stop smoking and lay off the hard liquor. Took a heart attack. The funeral's scheduled for Saturday.'

'Along with four others.' Fernández shook his head and dragged smoke deep into his lungs. 'What a fucking mess.'

'In a hurry to put this one to bed, Inspector?' A woman's voice cut through the sultry air. She was tall and casually dressed in black jeans and a white blouse, her long auburn hair tied tightly into a ponytail. She placed a large black case on the ground and held out her hand. 'Doctor Julieta Santiago, duty pathologist.' She pulled the cigarette from his mouth. 'Don't want our boys back at the lab adding you to the list of suspects, do we?' She smiled. 'Shall we suit up?'

13

Fernández was thrown by her directness and words failed him momentarily. He followed her over to the SOCOs who were quick to extinguish their cigarettes. He removed his jacket, adjusted his gun holster and pulled on a white forensic suit, finding the ritual as irritating as ever.

Doctor Santiago passed him a facemask. He didn't put it on immediately, but held it by his side as she stepped through the doorframe at the entrance to the new-build and surveyed the bloodbath. She moved silently, making hurried assessments as she stopped at each lifeless body before rejoining him at the door.

'So, what do you think?' she asked.

'Cabo Medina thinks it's open and shut. Happened during siesta. Unfinished business between the two old men.'

'And you?'

'It's possible, but it's never that simple, is it?' He turned his back on her and concentrated on the four bodies that lay strewn across the floor. 'On the face of it, my Comandante will probably want this wrapped up quickly. The kids will be on holiday in a few weeks and the whole area will be flooded with tourists. The last thing he'll want is this splashed over the front pages.'

'Unfortunately, the timing couldn't be worse,' Doctor Santiago said. 'This year marks the seventieth anniversary of the end of the Civil War and the start of Franco's dictatorship. The press will be all over it. We'd better make a start before we lose the light.'

'Sir?' Medina said. 'Klaus Dagmar? The ex-pat who found them? He's here.'

'Suit him up and bring him in,' Santiago said.

Medina glanced at Fernández who raised an eyebrow, shrugged and nodded.

'Is there a problem?' Santiago asked.

'My team usually run everything past me. They'd assume that this is my investigation and my crime scene.'

'Oh, I see.'

She hesitated.

She didn't know if he was posturing, but in her experience Spanish men didn't relate easily to assertive women - *women with balls*, as her mother would say. She knew she came over as tough and resilient, and that that didn't endear her to everyone, but the truth was that she'd been as nervous as always as she'd driven from the hospital in Almeria.

'Then I'll have to ensure there are no misunderstandings in future, won't I?' she said. 'Now, if you don't mind, we have work to do.'

She walked to where Matias had fallen and began examining his wounds. She then spent several minutes with the body of his father, Bartolomé, before checking his grandfather, Alberto.

Fernández took his time untangling the strapping of his facemask. He pulled a pack of cigarettes out and put one between his lips, looking up in time to see one of the SOCOs wag a finger at him. He shook his head and replaced the cigarette, pulled on his mask and crossed to where Doctor Santiago was standing over the crumpled corpse of Juan Gonzales.

She'd sidestepped blood coagulating in a large pool and knelt down. She lifted Gonzales' head, brushed away several flies and examined the bullet's exit wound. She then concentrated on the star-shaped laceration and the muzzle impression on his right temple where the bullet had entered.

Klaus Dagmar was brought to the doorframe.

'You found them like this?' Santiago stood up.

'Yes. Yes, of course, exactly as you see them. I knew it would be wrong to touch anything.'

'And you were sure they were dead?'

'Yes.'

'You didn't bother to check?'

'Well, it was pretty obvious they weren't going to get up,' Dagmar said. 'I'm sorry, it was such a shock.'

Santiago walked over to him. 'I know how distressing this must be for you, but if this goes to court, contaminated evidence would destroy the prosecution case. If you have compromised the scene of the crime in any way it could make the difference between catching whoever is responsible and...'

'But I heard that young detective say the old man probably committed suicide.'

'That's precisely my point.' She appeared to take a couple of moments to compose herself. 'I'm sorry, but we won't know exactly what happened here if you don't tell me the truth.'

Dagmar shifted from one foot to the other, finally confessing, 'I did move him.' He pointed at Bartolomé. 'I found him curled up, on his side.'

'That's it?'

'I rolled him onto his back. I wanted to make sure he was dead. I mean...'

'Yes, we know what you mean,' Fernández said, removing his mask. 'I'm sorry to hear about your dog.'

'Old age. Had her put down.'

'You'll have to stay away from here. No more sentimental journeys. Understand?' He smiled. 'Oh, and keep your mouth shut. We'll need time to inform the next of kin. I'd really hate them to hear it from anyone else.'

Before he handed Dagmar over to Medina he took the young detective to one side. 'Detail one of the SOCOs to process him - finger prints, gunshot residue. Tomorrow morning run a background check. It's unlikely, but we can't dismiss the possibility that he killed all four men.'

He watched as Medina went over and spoke to one of the forensic scientists and they escorted Dagmar into a large tent that served as a field laboratory. He turned to Doctor Santiago. 'I'll also need a couple of SOCOs to check Gonzales's home.'

'Fine, as long as you don't leave me short handed.' She glanced round at the handful of men from Cientifica. 'I'll be here for most of the night. So I'll need a generator, lights, and a full forensic team. We'll carry out a thorough search of the

16

immediate area tomorrow morning.' She paused. 'So, you want to tell me what you think happened here?'

Fernández pulled on his mask, walked to the other side of the room and stood between the corpses of Matias and Bartolomé, looking down at discarded orange peel, tins of tuna and a half-empty water container. He hesitated. Insecurity wasn't a familiar sensation, but she'd unsettled him and he found himself oddly reluctant to put himself on the line. 'Early days, obviously,' he began, 'but it looks like they had lunch and settled down for the siesta. If we assume that Juan Gonzales shot Matias and Bartolomé with the Mauser and used the P38 to kill Alberto…'

'It looks like he may also have used the handgun on Bartolomé.'

'But why shoot him twice?'

'Presumably, because he wasn't dead.'

Fernández heard one of the SOCOs snigger. He glanced round and the man melted into the brickwork. He moved over to the body of Bartolomé to examine the wounds to his throat and forehead.

Santiago replaced her mask and joined him. She took the dead man's head and eased it carefully off the floor. She turned the head gently, revealing a small, gaping crater with a distorted rim encrusted with subcutaneous tissue, splinters of bone and hair matted with drying blood. 'There are two exit wounds here. The first shot was fired into his throat, shattering the cervical vertebrae and the spinal chord. Any higher, exiting at the base of the skull, and it would have killed him instantly, but he may have survived, at least until the second shot through the forehead.'

She moved over to Juan Gonzales and spent several moments examining the handgun that lay just out of reach of the old man's right hand. She concentrated on where the bullet had entered. 'This is a contact-range gunshot wound.' She looked at Fernández. 'He could have taken his own life. We'll lift fingerprints from the rifle and handgun and get ballistics to check the striations on any bullets we recover, as well as firing pin

17

indentations on spent shells. It'll be important to match the bullets to the guns - we don't want to stand up in court to find that these weren't the weapons used, do we?'

'Gunshot residue? Ferrozine?' He was impressed by her meticulous approach.

'Yes. Good idea.'

He felt she was looking at him like a schoolteacher pleased that the pigheaded boy at the back of the class had volunteered something. He was beginning to warm to her.

'We'll take swabs from each of the victim's hands. It'll also be worth running ferrozine tests to check for traces of metal absorbed into the skin.' She stood up and removed her mask, discarding it into her bag and taking a fresh one. 'That's probably it, for now. Rigor mortis is advanced enough to suggest your Cabo might be right: sometime during siesta. I'll know more by the morning, but if I don't get the bodies back to the lab in Almeria they'll be pretty high come sun-up.'

'I'll let you get on, but I will need a video record of the scene and as many photographs as possible.' He stepped outside the shell of the new building and removed his forensic suit.

'I hope your department's got deep pockets, Inspector. Forensics, ballistics, fingerprint specialists, video, DNA samples – they don't come cheap and the recession's left gaping holes in our budget.'

Fernández shrugged. 'Balancing the books has never been part of my game. You'll let me know as soon as you have anything?'

'Drop by the morgue tomorrow, late morning, and I'll bring you up to date.' She paused. 'Anything else?'

He hesitated. They'd be spending the best part of several weeks working together and he wasn't sure how that prospect sat with her, but he had to admit that she was refreshingly different from other medics he'd crossed swords with. 'No, no thanks.' He lit a cigarette, drawing deep and exhaling forcefully. 'Now I get to carry out my favourite part of the job – breaking the news to three women who are waiting for their men folk to come home.'

18

Ana-Marie Castaño couldn't help but smile as she sauntered down the narrow alleyway where she'd played as a child; alongside the whitewashed walls that seemed so familiar and yet seemed so far removed from the life she and Paul had created together; light years from the humble, hand-to-mouth existence of the three women she'd spent the afternoon with, laughing, the taste of coffee and chocolate cake lingering in her mouth.

A carbon copy of her mother at the same age, Ana-Marie was tall, with full breasts accentuated by a close fitting dress that hugged her waist and billowed over her wide hips. Her dark hair fell below her shoulders and framed her sun-kissed face and hazel eyes.

Ahead, she saw her father, Enrique, as he trudged up from the fields, and she paused, giving him time as he sat down wearily outside the family cottage and removed his hat and boots before relighting the stub of a cigarette he'd brought with him from the field. He was short and stocky, his powerful arms and broad chest testimony to a lifetime's toil on the iron-hard land he'd inherited. She waited, hiding like a guilty child, watching him draw a last gasp of nicotine before snubbing the fag end between his powerful fingers, hauling himself to his feet and hustling his way past the heavy front door.

She made her way down and stopped outside, her hand resting on the metal latch, savouring those final moments of peace, before she stooped and pushed her way in. She stumbled over the granite sill that had been set in place over two centuries ago, cursed as she removed her high heels, and then smiled as she heard her mother, Inocenta, reproach her sister…

'Sofia, wait for Ana-Marie.'

'But I'm hungry.'

'Let her be, woman,' she heard her father say. 'She's a child. Let her eat like a child and give us all some peace.'

'Sorry I'm late,' Ana-Marie said, walking through to the kitchen where the table had been laid for supper.

Sofia ran towards Ana-Marie who lifted her high in the air, making her squeal with delight. At six years old, Sofia Castaño was slight, smaller than most girls of her age, and her unruly, dark hair fell across her face.

'Is it a fiesta? Did you hear Felipe's rockets?' Sofia asked.

'How could anyone not hear them? That man ought to be lynched for disturbing the siesta,' Enrique grumbled.

Ana-Marie looked over at her mother. 'Well, something smells good.'

'Chicken and chorizo. It was always your favourite. Come on, let's eat.'

They sat around the roughly hewn wooden table and, after Enrique had filled his plate, Inocenta spooned out the rest of the casserole. After a few moments Sofia asked, 'Will you take me to the fiesta?'

'It's not until tomorrow,' Ana-Marie said gently. 'The shops will be closed and everyone will go to the village square late in the evening to celebrate the summer solstice: the longest day of the year.'

'But will you be here?'

'Of course. I'll stay the night, if mama and papa don't mind.' She turned to her mother and said. 'I'm meeting Paul in Almeria this evening. I'll drive the Mercedes back on my own. He can use the Landcruiser to pick up the groceries and the laundry. He'll probably stay over at the apartment.' She sighed and shrugged, turned to her mother and said. 'He's put in a bid for the regeneration project in Almeria. Keep your fingers crossed. Things are getting pretty desperate. This damn recession is driving everyone out of business.'

'What does *damn* mean?' Sofia asked.

'It means we'll have to be very careful with our money. If we're lucky, we'll make a lot of money and we'll be able to buy mama and papa a car, and a new dress for you.' She took a piece of bread, dipped it in olive oil and offered it to Sofia, catching her big brown eyes, wide with expectation and trust.

Sofia looked at her mother and pushed the bread wilfully into her mouth.

Ana-Marie knew Inocenta had learned to pick her battles with Sofia, and guessed that this was one time she'd save her energy for later.

Inocenta looked across at her first-born. 'Did they enjoy the cake?'

'Of course. We talked, drank coffee and had a slice each. Chocolate cake never fails, does it? Everyone came back for more. They even asked for the recipe.'

Both women laughed before Inocenta said, 'Thanks for standing in for me.'

'It was nothing. They're good people.'

'You were there a long time.'

'We had lunch, a couple of glasses of wine. I took my siesta and then caught up with all the gossip. Madalena and Matias are trying for a family.'

'But that's wonderful. Bartolomé will be so chuffed, a grandchild. And Alberto, a great grandfather. Imagine the fuss they'll make of it.'

'He's doing well, isn't he, Alberto? There can't be too many men his age still working.'

'I'm not sure he contributes much these days – unless it's to give advice.' Mother and daughter laughed again before Ana-Marie turned to Sofia and said, 'Laura will be here for the fiesta.'

'When are they getting married?'

'Sofia.' Ana-Marie shook her head playfully. 'José and Laura have only been going out a few months. You must give these things time. Maybe, one day, they'll decide to get married and you'll make a beautiful bridesmaid.'

Enrique put his fork down and sighed heavily. He spoke gently, but with concern. 'That woman has the devil in her.'

'Papa!' Ana-Marie protested. 'Laura is my closest friend and could be your daughter-in-law soon.'

'She has an eye for your man.'

'Paul? Nonsense.'

'I've seen the way she looks at him.'

There was a long silence and Inocenta began to clear the table, carrying the dirty dishes to the sink. Ana-Marie rose to help her.

'What's so important that you have to be in Almeria this evening?' Inocenta said, slipping an apron round her waist.

'I've got another check-up at the hospital.'

'The hospital? Are you sick, woman?'

'Papa, not long ago, I was sick most mornings.' Ana-Marie smiled and looked at her mother.

'You'd better tell him, Ana-Marie, he'll worry me to death if you don't.'

'If God smiles on us, papa, you'll be a grandfather, come November.'

Enrique Castaño looked at the two women grinning at him, Ana-Marie blushing as she did when he challenged her as a teenager.

''Bout time,' he said, moving through to the front room, slumping heavily onto the soft cushions of the couch, swinging his legs over the end and closing his eyes. A thin smile flickered at the corner of his mouth and he mumbled, 'Didn't think he had it in him.'

Ana-Marie joined Inocenta at the sink and took a tea towel to dry the dishes, Sofia trailing behind.

'I was afraid when I heard Felipe's rockets. Bang! Bang!' Sofia screwed up her face.

Ana-Marie took her hand and walked her to the bedroom where she lay with her, comforting her, until, just before sleep overtook her, Sofia muttered, 'I saw Gloria today, playing hide-and-seek with that old man.'

'Gloria?'

'You know.' Sofia looked imploringly into her big sister's eyes. '*Gloria.*'

Ana-Marie shook her head, trying to recall Sofia's friend. She smiled indulgently, stroked hair from her eyes and whispered gently, 'Hush, nena. Go to sleep.'

Day Two

Friday 19th June 2009

Early, before the sun had time to chase the light summer dew from the ground, Fernández returned to where the bodies had been found and, trying to reconstruct the killings, he walked the most likely route Juan Gonzales had taken. He looked across at the houses that skirted the campo, wondering if anyone had caught sight of the old man. He slipped under the crime scene tape, stepped inside the shell of the new-build, glanced up through the void where the roof would be, and sat on a pile of cement bags covered in polythene.

Subject to confirmation from Doctor Julieta Santiago, he could be pretty confident that they had established the modus operandi. The weapons used in the killings had been dusted, bagged, and handed over to ballistics. There seemed little doubt that Juan Gonzales had killed all three men.

What nagged at him was motive. Why? Why had Juan Gonzales shot three men and then turned the gun on himself? He'd grown up without ever being aware of the *pact of silence* that had denied successive generations access to the truth about the appalling atrocities of the Civil War and Franco's reign. The media had exercised a level of self-restraint that amounted to suppression and schools had turned their backs on the past, modifying the curriculum so that most people had no idea what had happened.

The Comandante had given him until the end of the month, twelve days away and counting, the senior officer's passing shot a terse, 'Wrap it up quickly, Inspector, and don't make a meal of it.' And he couldn't argue with that. It looked cut and dry, but he'd learned to mistrust anything that was too easy and had already decided to set up an Incident Room in the village Town Hall and ask for administrative backup: Valencia Ramoz top of his list.

Without refrigeration facilities locally, the bodies had been taken to the hospital in Almeria. The Coroner had been put on stand by and warned that after the autopsies had been completed he'd have four bodies to sign over for cremation.

As the church clock struck nine forty-five, he eased himself from the stack of cement bags. He strolled back across the campo and deep into the village where he came upon an expectant crowd that had gathered, thirsty for information, outside the three cottages that had been home to the men who had been slaughtered less than twenty-four hours before.

He took a final drag, stubbed out his cigarette, knocked and eased open the front door.

Consuela Ramos sat on the large sofa that dominated the cramped sitting room. The family's matriarch was flanked by her daughter-in-law, Juanita, and her grandson's wife, Madalena - three widows before their time, staring blankly at the fireplace, family portraits occupying every shelf-space and flat surface, each woman toying absentmindedly with rosary beads and a crucifix.

He sat in the only other chair and waited a few moments, giving the women time to acknowledge his return. When he spoke, he did so gently, calmly, each sentence measured and punctuated by pauses that hung in the still air.

'I'm deeply sorry for your loss.'

The women remained impassive.

'Your bereavement has touched us all.'

There was little more than a flicker from the youngest, Madalena, as her fingers hesitated over the rosary beads.

'I cannot begin to imagine what you're going through.'

Consuela Ramos held her head high and looked at him through small, grey eyes that had retreated beneath her furrowed brow. 'They were good men,' she said, her voice cracked and fragile.

'Men who were respected by everyone in the village,' Fernández said.

'The man who did this?' Juanita moved her hand across to hold her mother-in-law's arm. 'He is dead?'

'Yes.'

'More's the pity. Fascist bastard. They should have killed him years ago when he returned to the village. The only reason he came back was to avenge the murder of his parents.' She fell silent.

'And you think Alberto had something to do with their murder?'

'If he had killed them, it would have been with good reason.' Consuela showed no emotion as she said; 'But if my husband did kill the them, he's kept it from me.'

'May I attend the funerals?'

All three women began to rock gently as though suddenly realising that their nightmare was set to continue - coffins paraded through the narrow streets on Saturday morning, the service in the church and the cremation, the ashes placed in the small cemetery behind tall, white walls at the entrance to the village.

'Why not?' Juanita said, sadness sweeping across her face. 'Most of the village will be there.'

'Inspector,' Consuela said quietly, 'why are you here?'

'I came to offer...'

'Yes, yes. We know that. But you are a police officer. You did your duty last night, when you came to...' she struggled to find the words, 'when you came to tell us what had happened. I presume you're back in your official capacity?'

'Yes.'

'Then there are things you are still investigating?'

'Questions that need answers. Juan Gonzales may have been his father's son, but I need your help to understand why this has happened. Your men deserve that.'

Silence filled the room and hushed voices from the crowd outside filtered through an open window. Somewhere a donkey brayed and the church clock struck ten.

Tears trickled down Madalena's face. 'They would have stopped for breakfast now,' she said. 'It would have been my turn to be with them today.' She turned to Juanita. 'It was your turn at lunchtime yesterday, wasn't it? But you didn't go, did you? None of us did. If we had...' She began to sob uncontrollably and collapsed into Consuela's frail arms. Juanita stood and pulled Madalena gently from the old lady's lap and led her upstairs.

Consuela was left alone, her small frame swallowed by the sofa. Fernández eased himself out of the fireside chair and sat next to her. She looked up and laid her hand gently alongside the Inspector's face, tracing a small scar high on his cheek. 'I remember the day you were born, Antonio. Your papa was so proud. He was drunk for a week.' She tried to laugh, but couldn't summon the strength. 'And then he was taken from you, and your mama has been without him all these years.' Her hand caressed his cheek. 'We have missed you, Antonio. How long has it been?'

'Ten years. Ten years since I moved out of the village.'

His words slipped through the open window and they sat in silence for a few moments until Consuela said, 'You will need to watch your back - you, and anyone who helps you.' She hesitated and wiped away a tear. 'There are those who might try to stop you. The village has grown silent over the years, but the silence only masks the legacy of the Civil War and Franco's barbarity. We may have to accept that my husband, my son and my grandson have been the latest casualties.' Her hand dropped, as though her arm could no longer support the weight of her despondency. 'You could be next.'

Fernández took her hands and, in them, saw his own mother's long, slender fingers, deeply veined skin delicate and fragile like ancient parchment upon which a lifetime had been recorded. He spoke gently. 'I hear what you say, Consuela, and I will be careful. But, if you can tell me what happened yesterday morning - every detail, no matter how insignificant, could be vital.' He realised she'd need prompting. 'Madalena mentioned it was Juanita's turn to take lunch to the men. Is that something you would do every day?'

'Most days.'

'So what kept Juanita away from them yesterday?'

Consuela sighed. 'A cup of coffee and a piece of homemade chocolate cake.'

'A cup of coffee…I'm sorry, I don't understand.'

She wiped her eyes once more. 'Ana-Marie Castaño brought a cake, fresh from her mother's oven. We had coffee, Ana-Marie stayed for lunch, and then she and Madalena spent a couple of hours chatting.' She looked up at him, her hand returning to his cheek. 'You know she's married, don't you?'

'Ana-Marie? Yes, I'd heard.'

'She broke your heart, didn't she, Antonio? Ana-Marie. Ten years ago.'

He left Consuela and drove back to Almeria, the despair of the three widows intermingling incongruously with impressions of his time with Ana-Marie. A day rarely passed without her face, her smile and her vitality intruding. It had been ten years, but his sub-conscious had never let him forget.

He made his way to the morgue, but was redirected by a technician to a local square where Doctor Julieta Santiago was taking her first break for several hours.

The market was in full swing and, as bargain-hunting crowds streamed past, he saw her sitting at a table outside a bar. He didn't know whether she lived locally, but he'd never seen her before Thursday's crime scene. He felt sure he would have noticed her.

As he walked crossed the square towards her, he saw an elderly woman hurry to the table with a young girl in-tow. He watched as the girl threw her arms around Santiago and they embraced tenderly. The elderly woman and the girl sat at the table, and Santiago caught the attention of the waitress.

Fernández made his way inside the bar, where he ordered a black coffee. 'I'll cover their tab.'

The barman smiled. 'She's a beauty, no?'

'A professional colleague.'

'Yeah, right.'

Fernández watched Santiago listening attentively to the excited chatter of the young girl and smiled as she performed a clumsy pirouette. It didn't tax his skills of deduction to conclude that they were mother and daughter: same auburn hair, wide, generous mouth, and long, slender legs. The bartender had been right: Julieta Santiago was a beauty.

'She local?' he asked.

'Nah. Been here a couple of months at the most. She's some sort of medic, judging by the white coat.' The barman turned, took a bottle of Soberano off the shelf and offered him a slug.

Fernández forced a smile, but declined the brandy. He took his coffee, walked out to the pavement and sat at a table as far away from the crowds as possible.

Santiago pulled the young girl onto her lap and cuddled her. Moments later, she looked up and saw him, said something to the elderly woman, handed over the young girl and they left, swallowed by the throng of the market.

She walked over to join him.

'Your daughter?' he asked.

'Yes. That's my Holly.'

'She wants to be a dancer?'

'Like her mother: still learning the finer points of flamenco.'

'Flamenco?'

'Come and see for yourself. Tomorrow evening. Eight o'clock. El Morato. I'm dancing with your friend, Ana-Marie.'

Moments before, he'd been watching her from the safe haven of the bar, but now he felt exposed, awkward, like a lover who'd been found out in a lie, as if he had been asked 'what are you staring at?' and, trying to dismiss the image of Ana-Marie from his mind, he had replied 'nothing'. He couldn't deny he found her attractive, but began to wonder how he would feel watching her dance alongside Ana-Marie.

He didn't respond immediately. He lit a cigarette and scuffed his feet on the ground.

'Well,' Santiago said, as though puzzled by his reticence, 'the invitation's on the table. Come if you want to.'

'Yes. Thanks. I'll see how things pan out.'

She shrugged and sipped her coffee. 'So, how's your day been?'

'I went back this morning - never gets any easier - three women who'd woken up yesterday without a care in the world and spent the day gossiping over homemade cake, only find themselves condemned to sleep in empty beds.' He rubbed his eyes, dragged his hands down his face and said, 'What time did you get away?'

'I had the bodies removed at about one this morning and came back here, to the lab.'

'You look tired.'

'You don't look too good yourself.' She leaned forward. 'But, you'll be interested to know that you were right to reserve judgement at the crime scene.' She stood up. 'Come on, I've got something to show you.'

She didn't wait for him, but walked ahead, down several narrow streets. She paused outside large double doors and punched an entry code into a security pad before pushing her way in. She ignored the lift and walked down three flights of stairs into the pre-op room. Here, they scrubbed up and dressed in blue protective suits.

The lab was an acre of scrubbed stainless steel. Wall-to-wall sinks, cupboards, and work surfaces lined with trays of surgical instruments surrounded the two height-adjustable operating tables in the centre of the room.

A mortuary technician removed two corpses from the refrigerator and then left them to it.

'I haven't completed the autopsies yet,' she said, pulling back one of the sheets and uncovering Bartolomé Ramos, 'but I thought you'd be interested in some of the work we've been doing over night.' She slipped on a pair of latex gloves, pulled up her facemask and used a stainless steel probe to trace the tour of his injuries. 'The first bullet was fired from the rifle, at a distance of about three meters, smashing through the cervical vertebrae and exiting here, at the back of the neck. The second bullet was fired from the handgun, within a meter, entering the forehead and exiting here, high on the back of the head.'

'So, he must have survived the first bullet.'

'Looks that way, doesn't it?' She covered Bartolomé with the cotton sheet and turned to uncover Juan Gonzales. 'When I opened him up, I found signs of excessive bleeding from an aggressively malignant brain tumour. You'll need to check his medical history with his doctor.' She turned the head to one side and pointed at the star-shaped laceration on the right temple 'This is a close-contact entry wound. And, this,' she pointed at a conspicuous circular imprint, 'is caused by super-heated gases burning an impression of the muzzle into his temple when the handgun was fired.'

'Which would confirm that Juan Gonzales did commit suicide.'

'I doubt it.'

'You doubt it?'

'There are two complications.' She pulled the sheet further down the body and took Juan Gonzales' right hand, turning it palm upwards. 'We used ferrozine spray to detect traces of metal absorbed into the skin. When a revolver is used in a suicide, it's quite common for the ferrozine to reveal metal deposits on the thumb of the hand used to hold the weapon. It's assumed that the victim hesitates and primes the handgun several times before actually pulling the trigger.' She paused. 'The handgun was found by Gonzales' right hand, but there were no metal deposits on his right thumb.'

'So, he didn't hesitate. He just put the gun to his head and pulled the trigger.'

'That's what I assumed at first, but the tests showed significant traces of metal on the palm and trigger finger of his left hand.'

'He held the handgun in his left hand?'

'The evidence points that way, yes. At least when he shot Alberto and Bartolomé.'

'Then why switch the gun to his right hand to commit suicide?'

'We don't know, but if you were going to commit suicide would you trust your non-dominant hand to pull the trigger?' Santiago let the question hang. 'That's not all.' She held gun-shaped fingers against her own temple and asked, 'If I put a gun to my head and pull the trigger, where would you expect to find the exit wound?'

Fernández stood before her, momentarily unsettled by the mock suicide, and then touched her head on the opposite side.

'Yes. More or less parallel, maybe slightly higher.' She rolled Juan Gonzales' head to expose the exit wound, just below the cheekbone on the left side of his face. 'This exit wound is much lower than we'd expect. The bullet would not have followed that trajectory if Gonzales had shot himself.'

'So where does that leave us?'

'You're the detective. But, it's not difficult, is it?'

Fernández stalled as the only real option surfaced. 'Someone else was there? Someone who shot him and tried to make it look like suicide?'

'It's a possibility.'

*

Usually, an evening's fiesta doesn't spark into life much before eleven. Any earlier and the villagers might gather, sink a few beers and wait for the music to begin. But this evening few had any appetite for a fiesta. Four men were dead. They had known the victims and the man who'd slaughtered them, and they understood the tensions that lay beneath the gentle facade of

31

a village. It would take more than a few glasses of beer to lift spirits.

Soon after ten, several children had dragged their parents to the square outside the Town Hall. They'd spent a few euros at sideshows or street vendors and had watched the itinerant jugglers and a fire-eater. Most of the women sat on plastic chairs; widows wore black, some covering their head in remembrance. Younger women, loaded with the next generation in their arms, supped wine, grateful for the respite when friends or neighbours took their child from them and rocked it gently to sleep. Men stood at the makeshift bar and drank beer.

Soon after mid-night, the band had completed their sound checks and were ready to play. But the villagers sat silently as Inspector Antonio Fernández, Cabo Leo Medina and officers from the Guardia Civil, Policia Local and the Policia Nacional moved among them, hoping someone would come forward with information.

Sofia Castaño skipped between Ana-Marie and Laura, dwarfed by their striking height. She was proud of her big sister and her big sister's best friend. Ana-Marie had married a rich man from England who was going to buy a new dress for Sofia. And Sofia longed for a new dress. With a new dress, she'd be the most beautiful bridesmaid at her brother's wedding to Laura. Sofia loved Laura. Laura made her laugh until her tummy hurt and they shared secrets - secrets Sofia had promised to keep, but was bursting to tell.

As the three of them walked across the square, Ana-Marie smiled at friends she had known all her life. Friends she had left behind when she went to live in the villa overlooking the beach. Friends who might be pleased for her or resented her good fortune - she might never know and was past caring. When Laura went to buy a couple of glasses of wine, Ana-Marie stopped to talk to a friend who had just given birth to her second child and already seemed contentedly middle-aged. She looked down at Sofia and smiled, and then glanced across at Laura standing at the bar, sharing a joke with one of the men, her father's words still stinging... '*She has an eye for your man.*'

Sofia slipped away and went over to a group of men who had gathered at the bar. She stood, listening to them and staring at faces that were full of anger and pain. The men were arguing, but their words and defiant gestures were not accompanied by the smiles of friends who were setting the world to rights. Sofia could feel the tension in their bodies and she became frightened.

One of the police officers came over to join them. He was a giant, taller than anyone else at the bar. Sofia heard the giant ask the men several questions before he struck the counter with his clenched fist and shouted, 'There must be someone in the village that saw the old man, for God's sake!' The giant glowered down at the men as, one by one, they returned to their beer.

The giant shook his head, turned and made his way down a steep, narrow alleyway that led towards the small square where the doctor held his surgery each day. There, he fished out a packet of cigarettes from his shirt pocket and lit up.

Sofia chased after him.

Ana-Marie turned and found Sofia missing. Laura smiled and pressed her forearm reassuringly. 'Don't worry she's down by the old olive press, talking to Leo Medina. I'll fetch her.'

She took her time, enjoying the few moments of peace and reflecting on the afternoon's diversion, a broad smile breaking across her face.

As she approached, she heard Sofia telling him that she'd seen an old man.

'Go back up to the square, Sofia. Go back to your sister.' Leo Medina took a drag from his cigarette and drank in Laura's long legs, short skirt, come-to-bed blue eyes, and fabulous golden hair that was unusual enough in this part of Spain to make her even more striking.

'You with Elliot, back there?' Laura laughed, pointing towards Inspector Fernández.

'Elliot?'

33

'Leo, we watched the movie together, remember? Elliot Ness, the FBI guy who tracked down Al Capone?'

Medina shook his head, his memory racing back to their youth, when he and Laura had been close and had taken the first, awkward steps into an adult world that they were never destined to share. He remembered a lot of things they'd done together but watching movies didn't rank any higher than washing dishes.

'I saw an old man,' Sofia insisted, tugging at Medina's sleeve. 'I saw an old man and Gloria. They were playing hide-and-seek.'

'Ignore her, Leo.' Laura smiled. 'She's got such an imagination.'

'How are you?' He asked. She flashed her engagement ring.

'So, it's true.'

'Yes, but this time it's for real.' She took Sophia's hand. 'It'll be the biggest wedding this village has seen for years.'

'And I'm going to have a new dress,' Sofia said.

Both adults laughed.

'Let's hope the mood's a little lighter by then.'

'I'd better get back.'

'Yes. Of course.' Medina pushed himself away from the wall, watching as Laura pulled Sofia after her. 'Congratulations, by the way...' he called.

Just before they entered the square, Laura's mobile phone trilled at the arrival of a text message. She stopped and pulled the phone from her belt, opening the message.

'Sofia,' she said, 'it's a message from your brother.' She read it and punched in a reply.

'I saw an old man.' Sofia stood and folded her arms. 'But no-one wants to listen to me. I saw an old man, and Gloria was playing hide-and-seek with him.'

Laura stowed her mobile and knelt down in front of Sofia. 'Gloria?'

'Yes. You know. *Gloria*.'

'Where did you see them, nena?'

34

'In the campo, when Felipe fired his rockets. I was on the terrace. I saw them.'

'When was this?'

'Yesterday.'

'You're sure it was Gloria?'

'Yes!' Sofia stamped on the cobblestones.

'And the old man? Was it Señor Gonzales?'

'Yes. He was carrying an old carpet under his arm. I think they were going to sit on it when they had their lunch. Why doesn't anyone believe me?'

Laura pulled Sofia to her breast and calmed her, stroking her long dark hair and rubbing her back gently, whispering, 'I believe you, Sofia.' She paused and held her at arms length before adding, 'But you must keep it a secret. You can keep a secret, can't you?'

'Of course I can. I'm nearly six and a half, and mama says I'm very grown up.'

Laura's laugh was contrived. 'Yes you are, and you're a very good girl, but I want you to promise me that you will never tell anyone that you saw Gloria.'

'Why?'

'It's a very special secret. You remember? He'd kill me if he found out.'

'Kill you?'

'No, not really.' Laura laughed again, anxious to keep the exchange as light-hearted as possible. 'But he wouldn't like it if he found out I'd given him a girl's nickname, would he? It's a bit like one of the horrible kids at school calling you Diego or Bernardo.'

Sofia giggled.

'And the game they were playing...' Laura said.

'Hide-and-seek.'

'I expect Gloria wanted to surprise the old man. And, if you tell anyone, it won't be a surprise anymore, will it?'

'I 'spose not,' Sofia said, confused.

35

'Listen.' Laura squeezed her arms gently, intensifying the significance of what she was about to say, her voice edged with seriousness. 'You must promise. Promise not to tell anyone and I'll buy you something very special to go with your bridesmaid's dress. Promise me, Sofia.'

'OK, I promise.'

Laura kissed her forehead and stood up, unclipped her mobile again and began to punch in another text message, a longer one this time, sending it moments later. She turned to Sofia and took her hand. 'Now, come on. Let's find Ana-Marie. I've got some great news to tell her.'

'What is it? I can keep a secret, you know.'

'I know you can, but this is not about Gloria or Señor Gonzales, this is something I want to share with the whole world.'

They found Ana-Marie and stood breathlessly before her.

'What is it?' Ana-Marie asked.

'José's just sent a text. He was pulled off at half time in last night's reserve game. He's made the first team squad for Sunday's exhibition match.'

'But that's fantastic!'

'I know. He wants me to fly up to Madrid to be with him.' The two women hugged. 'I must go home and pack. I'm booked on the early flight tomorrow morning.'

'I'll give you a lift to the airport.'

'No,' Laura said. 'No, no it's ok. I'll make my own way.' She recovered her composure and smiled, nodding towards Sofia. 'You have enough on your hands.' She knelt down and looked into the young child's eyes. 'Be a good girl won't you, Sofia? Ask your mama if you can watch the match on Sunday and you'll see your brother playing for Real Madrid.'

As she stood up, Laura saw Medina standing nearby.

'Crack open a beer on Sunday, Leo, and I'll wave to you from the Director's box.'

Day Three

Saturday 20th June 2009

Back at his apartment, Fernández dragged a lung full of smoke from his cigarette. It had been thirty-six hours since the discovery of the bodies and enquiries during the fiesta had produced nothing concrete. As expected, the men in the village had thrown a wall of silence around events and would want to deal with what had happened in their own way, in their own time. The women had shrugged and turned their backs, deferring to the village's tradition, knowing that Juan Gonzales' death had robbed the men of the chance to put things right.

He was coming under pressure. Soon, kids would be enjoying the first day of a long summer break. July and August meant that everything would begin to shut down and all officers would be needed to police the beachfront. As far as his superiors in Almeria were concerned, an old man had killed three members of the same family in a fit of revenge before turning the gun on himself.

The autopsies had been completed, DNA and fingerprint samples taken and stored. The bodies of the Ramos men had been handed over to funeral directors in preparation for today's service and cremation. Juan Gonzales' body had been collected by his son and would be cremated elsewhere.

But for Fernández things still didn't add up. He'd been a cop for too long, and although domestic disputes and bungled burglaries still counted for a substantial part of his business, the infiltration of drug dealers and organised crime into this booming area of the Costas had been accompanied by an exponential increase in ruthless and callous crimes.

But these had not been contract killings. They not only lacked the hallmarks of a professional hit, but hired gunmen weren't exactly renowned for executing their targets and then turning the gun on themselves.

So, what had driven Juan Gonzales to kill three men and then blow his brains out? Or was Doctor Julieta Santiago right? Someone else had been there.

The background checks on Klaus Dagmar, the ex-pat who'd raised the alarm, hadn't come through and Fernández hadn't ruled him out. It wouldn't be the first time a killer was drawn back to the scene, taking perverse delight in watching as the investigation unfolded. Had Dagmar orchestrated the killings and then turned the gun on Juan Gonzales, covering his tracks, making the old man's death look like suicide?

He still hadn't checked with the rocket man, and needed to wait for the ballistic and forensic reports, but unless he could find someone who was prepared to talk he knew he might never find the answer to his questions. If he was lucky, one of the Ramos women might remember something, but today their minds would be elsewhere.

Leo Medina had mentioned the exchange he'd had with Ana-Marie's six-year-old sister, Sofia. She was the only person in the village who'd said they'd seen an old man. But which old man had she seen? The village was full of them. When had she seen him? Where? And who the hell was Gloria? Playing hide-and-seek, a kid's game.

He looked at his watch. It was four o'clock. The sun wasn't up yet. He'd get his head down for a few hours, then go back to the village in time for the funeral and see if he could shake things up.

It was just after noon and, as the bells summoned villagers to share in the muted celebration of three lives cut short so brutally, he stood across from the flight of steps that led down to the small square outside the church.

For Antonio Fernández the church held bittersweet memories, but long before he had moved out of the village he'd lost his faith, turning his back on the pomp and ceremony, unable to reconcile the Church's message with the stories he'd heard of its past.

38

Today he stood like a stranger, with eyes that searched for clues, for someone, for anything that would uncover the truth about the murders that had rocked this small community to its very foundations.

The funeral procession started at the Town Hall, with nearly two hundred villagers following behind the Mayor and other members of the Ayuntamiento, its path well worn, snaking up towards the top of the village, along the narrow streets, past mourners standing at doorways throwing flowers onto the coffins, and then down, past the bakers and the post-office, towards the church square.

The coffins were carried on the broad shoulders of men closest to the deceased. The three widows clung to each other and stared ahead, unable to acknowledge those who had lined the narrow streets to pay their last respects.

The cortège passed between the huge oak doors at the church's entrance and the young, peripatetic Priest, Father Gabriel, welcomed the mourners, his face grave and sincere as he shook hands and exchanged words of comfort. He was hoping that, for once, the men who usually took their place on the steps outside the church, refusing to enter, would join in the service. But, by the time most of the mourners were inside, a dozen men had stepped aside, as resolute as ever to mark their protest and wait outside the church.

Father Gabriel nodded at Fernández and smiled, beckoning him inside. The Inspector cast his eyes towards the men assembled on the steps and shrugged his apology - not today, Father.

The church organ fell silent and Fernández watched as the last of the procession passed through the church doors. Several women, already late, hurried across the square, dressed in their Sunday best. Among them were Ana-Marie and her mother, Inocenta Castaño.

Ana-Marie had been a restless, volatile and temperamental child whose wild teens were littered with discarded suitors. Then, as they hit twenty-two, Antonio

39

Fernández and Ana-Marie had become an item, inseparable and destined for the altar. But her restlessness returned, heightened by a determination to escape and, as she grew into an arrestingly beautiful and voluptuous woman, she'd found no one in the village able to match up to her ambition. She'd elected, instead, to marry a wealthy Englishman, ten years her senior, and had cast Antonio Fernández onto the scrap heap.

Ana-Marie broke away from her mother when she saw him. 'Antonio.' She seemed genuinely pleased to see him and her wide mouth broke into the most disarming of smiles. 'It's been a such long time.' She kissed him on both cheeks.

'You're looking well.'

'Thank you.'

'Life's good?'

'But for this awful tragedy. You're here for the funeral?'

'I'm on duty.'

'Ah.'

'You'd brought them chocolate cake.'

She looked confused momentarily, then nodded. 'Sofia was playing up. Mama asked me to take it round. Is that when it happened?'

'Yes.' He paused and lit a cigarette, knowing he'd have to question her further, knowing that this was not the right time. 'Your husband's not with you?'

'Paul's in Almeria on business.'

'And doing well for himself.'

'He works hard,' she said, tilting her head to one side and smiling.

'The word is he's up for the regeneration project in Almeria.'

'A Godsend for everyone he'll employ if his tender's successful.'

'The recession biting deep?'

She sighed. 'Most construction companies are struggling or have gone under. If Paul does secure the Almeria contract it'll not only see us through the worst of the downturn, but it'll put

40

serious money in the bank.' She turned and pointed at the scaffolding along the south side of the church. 'He's also doing his bit for the community, of course, supervising the church renovation.'

The church bell tolled.

'Look, I'd better...' She lent forward and pressed his forearm. 'It's really good to see you again. I hope your investigation goes well.' She hesitated, as though remembering something. 'Oh, by the way, I'm dancing at the El Morato. Tonight. You must come. Please say you will.'

Fernández hesitated, uncertain, inexplicably cautious about telling her that Julieta Santiago had already invited him. 'I'm not sure I'll be able to.'

She held her fingers like a gun and pointed it towards him. 'Eight o'clock. This evening. Be there, Inspector.' She laughed, straightened her skirt, and then hurried over to the church.

He watched as she disappeared inside; his sudden sense of emptiness amplified by the final discord of the church bells. She was as beautiful as ever, more beautiful perhaps, if that was possible. Whilst the evening's flamenco might stir painful memories, he begrudgingly admitted to himself that watching both Ana-Marie and Julieta Santiago, together, could prove irresistible.

As the service began, he walked across the small square and stood before the men on the steps. He lit another cigarette and offered them around, but there were no takers.

'Most of you will know me and know why I'm here.' He took time to look at each of them. Some of them had seemed ancient when he'd been no taller than the handrail they stood against. Others were barely out of their teens. 'I only wish circumstances could have been different,' he said. But they didn't respond. He tried again. 'I grew up with many of you. I stole fruit from your orchards, helped you at harvest, and stood alongside you in the bar.' His voice trailed off and he sought respite in his cigarette, dragging on it, giving them time to realise he wasn't

41

going away. 'I understand the traditions and the customs we all grew up with. I think I understand why you wish to remain silent and to find your own way to deal with this tragedy.'

'Then you'll understand to keep your nose out of our business,' an old man said as he pushed himself away from the youngster who'd escorted him into the square.

Fernández shook his head as he exhaled.

'Unfortunately, my friend, it is as much my business as it is yours. I want to find out why we are burying three men today and why Juan Gonzales took away their lives in such a brutal, premeditated way.'

'Because he's a fascist bastard,' the old man said.

Fernández switched tack. 'I understand something of the history and the dreadful atrocities that this village suffered many years ago.'

'You know nothing,' another man shouted, his face suffused with anger, his fury breaching the dam.

'That bastard was born with violence in him.'

'Yeah, his father was no better.'

'They killed hundreds, for God's sake.'

'And bragged about the executions they'd carried out, how many innocent men, women, and children they'd murdered.'

'Fucking bastards!'

The bitter words hung in the air until Eduardo Gomez spoke, his voice barely above a whisper but commanding the respect that age, and three tours as Mayor, had earned. 'You'd be too young to remember, Antonio. The Civil War tore our country apart and for forty years Franco made the people of Andalucia pay a high price for backing the wrong side.' Gomez paused, drew on his cigarette and looked at Fernández through small, moist eyes. 'Juan Gonzales inherited his father's thirst for violence.'

His words did not cauterise the diatribe and others joined in the condemnation.

Fernández could have chosen to curb his impatience, but he wanted to provoke them, desperate to prise the door open still

42

further. 'So, what you're telling me,' he said, 'is that Juan Gonzales lived in the village for thirty-five years and then woke up on Thursday morning and decided that that was the day he'd avenge his parents?'

His sarcasm struck home and, as the men looked at one another, he could sense their smouldering resentment about to erupt in a violent back draft. They began to shout and curse at him, their faces contorting with their disgust, until one of the women hurried from the church and demanded their silence.

In the uneasy respite, Fernández walked towards Eduardo Gomez, intent on finding common ground. 'You're right to say that I have no memory of those times. Most of us rely on those of you who do remember. But, I don't believe that Thursday's appalling tragedy can be explained away by history. Yes, Juan Gonzales may have been driven to act because of the murder of his parents…'

'They got what they deserved. His parents and the Priest.'

Fernández stubbed out his cigarette and took several paces back, turning to face them. 'I'm more interested in why Gonzales chose that moment to set off across the campo, at the very time that one of their women should have been delivering lunch. Can you explain that to me? Can you explain how Juan Gonzales knew that the men would be alone?'

'If the woman had been there, he'd have killed her as well.' The old man cleared his throat and spat on the floor.

Eduardo Gomez held up his hand and the men fell silent as he asked, 'And what makes you think that this has been anything other than a cruel act of revenge?'

'I'm waiting for reports from the pathologist and the scene of crime officers.' He paused. 'You may not like what I have to say, but if my suspicions are correct, Juan Gonzales did not kill himself. Someone else pulled the trigger.'

'Please God, it had been me!' someone shouted and the men applauded.

Fernández called above them, 'And the killer may still be living among you.'

'He'd be welcome at my house, anytime.'

This sentiment was greeted with almost universal approval and the men fell into a raucous denunciation of everything Juan Gonzales had stood for.

'Inspector?' A strong, calm voice came from behind him. Fernández turned and recognised Rodrigo Perpiñán. Short, slightly built and wiry, Perpiñán's face was swamped by a large bushy moustache that would have been fashionable years ago and was still sported by many men in the village as a measure of pride and resilience. Perpiñán was twelve years older than Fernández and had built a reputation as an expert on Andalucian history. He spoke with measured intelligence. 'You will tread a very lonely path if you cannot curb your tongue. We have all lived in world of silent denial for many years. You're not going to shake them out of that. Your main suspect blew his brains out. That alone has denied them a chance to face the truth.'

Fernández stared over Perpiñán's shoulder at the men who had turned away and were arguing forcefully with one another. He whispered, 'You seem in no doubt that Juan Gonzales pulled the trigger. That he shot three men and then turned the gun on himself.'

'You have another explanation?'

'I will find out.'

'If you look under too many rocks, you may find more than you bargained for.'

'Not if I have you to turn them over for me.' Fernández stubbed out his cigarette. 'I need your help. I need you to tell me what happened here around the time that I was born and why these men still stand outside the church in protest. I want to know why Juan Gonzales came back to this village, revenge burning inside him, and then waited thirty-five years before carrying out this massacre.'

Rodrigo Perpiñán sighed heavily. 'It would be so much easier for everyone if these murders were the work of a lunatic,

44

unrelated to our past.' He hesitated and looked around at the men who had fallen into an awkward silence. 'Look we can't talk here, not now. Meet me tonight, at twelve, in the church.'

'I don't like wasting time, chasing shadows.'

'You will not be wasting time or chasing shadows, Inspector. I can tell you now that Juan Gonzales did not wait thirty-five years before avenging his parents.'

'What do you mean, he didn't wait?'

'Oh, for God's sake, Antonio. You don't know, do you?' Perpiñán hesitated, as though struggling to find the words. 'Thursday's killing spree started thirty-five years ago and your father was caught up in it.'

*

With Rodrigo Perpiñán's words ringing in his ears, Fernández stood outside the church and watched as the mourners dispersed. The square emptied and fell eerily silent, and he found himself struggling with his own impatience, desperate to know what part his father had played in the murder of Juan Gonzales's parents and the village Priest. He grabbed a coffee at the village bar and then decided to return to the scene of Thursday's murders.

The area was still cordoned off, a dozen forensic technicians diligently searching the area around the site, a uniformed police officer guarding the entrance to the new-build.

He went inside and stood in what would, one day, be someone's lounge. The chalk outlines of the four bodies were still visible.

After several minutes he heard footfalls on the gravel. He stepped back into the shadows and waited as the steps drew nearer. There was a moment's hesitation and a few hushed words before a tall, middle-aged woman, her head covered by a black lace shawl, stood in the doorframe and looked cautiously about the room. The uniformed officer led her to two of the chalk outlines, identifying each before withdrawing.

Juanita Ramos held three white Madonna lilies to her breast. He watched as she drew back her veil and moved forward to place one of the lilies against the wall where her son had fallen. She stood in silent prayer, her head bowed, before making the sign of the cross and moving over to the empty hearth. Here, she placed a second white lily for her husband and looked down at where he had collapsed, fighting for his life, before a second bullet had ended it. Her body began to tremble and she appeared to be fighting back tears. She wore a crucifix on a gold chain around her neck and she clasped at it, brought it to her lips and kissed it gently.

As she turned, trying to locate the place her father-in-law had fallen, she saw a figure in the shadows. 'Jesus, you startled me.'

'I am sorry to intrude upon your grief,' Fernández said.

'I came here to say goodbye. The funeral was so impersonal. I felt I wanted to say something in private. Besides, I couldn't face the wake. I just needed to be alone.' She looked across at the wall where she'd laid the first lily. 'That was for my son,' she said, and then nodded towards the fireplace. 'For my husband.' She searched amongst the rubble that was strewn across the floor.

'We found Alberto here.' He showed her where her father-in-law had fallen and stood to one side as she knelt to place the third lily and offer up a solitary prayer. She lifted the crucifix and kissed it gently.

'Thank you,' she said, looking up at him, tears in her eyes. She managed a weak smile. 'Has it helped? Being here?'

'It's been good to talk to you.' Of the three widows, it was Juanita who had shown the most anger and bitterness and who would, he hoped, be ready to offer an insight into the tragedy.

'It doesn't take a genius to know what happened.' She looked at him, anger returning to her face, her voice growing stronger. 'That fascist bastard murdered my father-in-law, my

46

husband and my son. And then the coward turned the gun on himself. What more do you want?'

'The truth. We know when, where and how. But we don't know why.' He moved closer to her. 'I need your help, Juanita. I need to know everything about the men in your family. Their friends, any problems with neighbours, which bars they drank in, what business they had with Juan Gonzales.'

Juanita laughed hollowly. 'They'd have nothing to do with him.'

'But you knew him?'

'We all knew him.'

'But you didn't speak to him, pass the time of day?'

'No.'

'Do you know anyone in the village who would have spent time with him?'

'Inspector. That man was the butcher of innocent people. He may have lived among us, but no-one I know would have had anything to do with him.'

'No one?' He allowed the question to hang in the air and watched her face.

'Oh, God, I don't know. Maybe someone new to the village. Foreigners. Kids. Kids of foreigners who know nothing of our history. The Scottish lass, maybe.' She breathed out heavily and then said, 'I need a few moments alone. Do you mind?'

'No. No, of course not.'

He stepped out into the blazing sun and lit a cigarette. He began to stroll back across the campo when he saw Sofia Castaño waving at him from their terrace. He waved back and smiled. She'd been conceived about seven years ago - a shock for parents who thought they'd done with rearing. He heard her call out and watched as her mother hurried on to the terrace to see what was exciting the child. Sofia waved again, Inocenta standing behind her and then bundling her inside.

He shrugged and scanned the rest of the village. Most homes faced away from the hill, preferring the views towards the sea and the mountains in the distance. Very few of them had terraces that overlooked the campo - but the Castaño home did, and Sofia had said she'd seen an old man.

He escorted Juanita to the edge of the village and left her to make her own way back home, hoping she wouldn't have to run the gauntlet of too many well-meaning friends and neighbours.

He returned to his apartment in Almeria and sat on the balcony, impatient for the hours to pass. He needed to tackle Rodrigo Perpiñán about his assertion that Thursday's deaths had began thirty-five years ago and that his father had been involved.

He'd taken down the photograph of his parent's wedding and looked at it, wondering why the hell was he feeling so anxious and apprehensive. He'd never known his father: he'd been killed a year after he'd been born. He looked more closely at the photograph than he had at any time and wondered if he was looking at the face of a murderer: *a man who had killed a priest, for Christ's sake, as well as a man and a woman*. He wondered if anyone else had been involved and had helped his father - if they were still alive, still living in the village? He wondered how many people knew of his father's involvement and why his mother hadn't told him.

Suddenly, he felt sick as he realised that he'd assumed that his father *had* killed that night, thirty-five years ago. He wondered why he'd jumped so readily to that conclusion?

In contrast to his anxiety, the evening was unfolding without urgency and, from his vantage point on his balcony, he saw several old men make their way unhurriedly across the square, each from a different direction. They converged towards two benches under a huge ficus tree that had been trimmed into the shape of an annular and resembled a bullring. One of the men carried a newspaper tucked under his arm, whilst another stopped to light his pipe. A third wore a fading red scarf around his neck and Fernández watched as the men greeted one another with a barely-disguised Republican salute that reminded him of a less exuberant high-five. They exchanged simple greetings and sat in silence as though words were no longer a valued currency.

He wondered if they'd ever known his father.

As the Town Hall clock chimed seven, he retreated inside his apartment, poured himself a glass of red wine, slumped onto the couch and tried to relax. He'd left the wooden shutters open, allowing the sounds of the evening to drift into his apartment. He sighed heavily and stared at the ceiling fan.

An hour later, he woke with a start and checked the time, still undecided about whether he would drive to the north of the city and watch Ana-Marie and Julieta Santiago dance. It would be worth the effort, he tried to convince himself - watching Ana-Marie dance flamenco was one of the most sensual experiences he, or any man, could have. But did he really want to open up old wounds? They'd had something special, for sure, but she'd dumped him and they'd drifted apart. Today's funeral was the first time he'd seen her in nearly ten years and tonight she'd be going home with her husband, lying in his arms, making love with him.

Why, he asked himself, was he even thinking of going? Whilst he'd always enjoyed flamenco at village fiestas and concerts, he preferred a lonely beach, with a small group of friends, a few beers, the air filled with a lone voice and a soulful guitar, and the rhythmic body of one of the girls swaying in the moonlight. He wondered if Ana-Marie still danced on the beach and found himself asking the same question of Doctor Julieta Santiago - had she ever danced beneath the moonlight, on a deserted beach somewhere, accompanied by a lone voice and a soulful guitar?

He looked at his watch again and shrugged, shaved, took a shower, and stopped off in his local bar for a shot of brandy, then drove across town and parked as close as he could to El Morato.

El Morato is one of Almeria's most authentic flamenco venues and, set in a natural cave, the passion of the music is trapped beneath its low ceiling, an intimacy that's hard to beat, with the audience never far from the performers.

Fernández picked up a programme from a trestle table at the entrance and crossed to the side of the cavern as the full house applauded dancers on to the stage for one of the last items on the evening's schedule. He glanced at the audience and recognised Holly, Julieta Santiago's daughter. She was standing on a chair at the end of the third row from the front, holding the hand of another young girl who stood on the chair next to her. The elderly woman he'd seen at the bar sat next to them. Neither of the girls could contain her excitement, giggling and pointing, whispering to each other, animated and swept away by the urgency of the music. Several times the elderly woman raised her forefinger to her lips to silence them.

The other child was Sofia Castaño. Her mother, Inocenta, sat nearby but seemed to be trying to ignore the girl's antics, concentrating instead on the performance.

He watched a man, probably in his mid-forties, move quietly to the end of the row and place Sofia on his lap. He whispered to her, calming her as the *fandango* reached its climax, and clapping with her as the performers bowed.

Then, two women took to the stage: Ana-Marie wearing a cream Sevillana dress that contrasted well with her dark hair, Julieta Santiago in midnight blue. They shook their dresses and waited for the audience to settle. The difference between the two women was marked. Ana-Marie's full breasts were accentuated by the décolleté of the dress. Her large, fiery eyes, shone in defiance as she thrust her rounded hips provocatively to the side. She smiled that same, self-assured smile he'd seen outside the church that morning. Santiago, by contrast, was tall and slight. Her auburn hair hung like a velvet curtain as she reclined her head and looked self-consciously over the heads of the audience.

Fernández did what most men would have done - he found himself comparing them, but, as he did, he felt concerned that Julieta Santiago would not be able to hold her own in the company of a woman who knew every trick in the book and

50

could command a man's attention with the slightest movement of her head.

Out of the corner of his eye he saw the man who had moved to sit with Sofia, get up, scoop both of the girls into his arms and carry them to the side of the cave. From there, they watched in silence as Julieta and Ana-Marie danced to a classic lament, a *petenera,* telling the story of a beautiful girl who brings tragedy to herself and her village. Although their slow, lyrical movements contrasted with the heady exuberance of the rest of the programme, Fernández sensed the audience was enjoying the sensitivity of the piece and its gentle emotions. There was no doubt who was the more sensual, but Julieta's vulnerability gave her an edge —as though, at any moment, she would falter or forget which way to turn - and he spent most of the performance willing her to come through, willing her to succeed.

Their performance was distilled into a final tableau, the cave resounded with applause and Ana-Marie and Julieta embraced. They were joined on stage by the rest of the performers for the finale – *a fandangos grandes*.

He left the cave, walked towards the water's edge, lit a cigarette and waited for the audience to file out.

'Antonio.' Julieta Santiago waved from behind the crowd as it eased through the double doors, Holly skipping at her side. 'Why didn't you tell me Ana-Marie had invited you? Were you in time to see us dance?'

'Yes, of course.'

'And? What did you think?'

He didn't answer, but stubbed his cigarette out and knelt down, eye-to-eye with Holly who'd slipped behind her mother, hiding from the man with the scar on his face.

'What do you think? Not bad, eh?'

'My mama was beautiful,' Holly said, burying herself in Santiago's Sevillana.

He smiled at her. 'I agree. The dancing was pretty good, as well.'

'Pretty good?' Ana-Marie called as she joined them, her voice raised in good humour. 'Antonio Fernandez, how could you tease Julieta and Holly like that? We were sensational.' She placed an arm around Santiago's shoulder and hugged her. 'Knocked 'em dead, didn't we?'

'We surely did.'

'There should have been three of us, of course. *Scarpetta*, Laura and myself...'

'Scarpetta?' Fernández said.

'Laura's got a thing about nicknames,' Santiago said. 'Mine's Scarpetta: The pathologist in Patricia Cornwall's books? It's a harmless bit of fun, but Laura doesn't tell everyone what their nickname is, does she Ana-Marie?'

'She hasn't told me and I don't want to know.' Ana-Marie laughed and turned to Fernández. 'You're Elliot, by the way. Elliot Ness? He put Scarface Capone away.'

'But Laura couldn't make it tonight?'

'She's flown up to Madrid to watch José make his first team debut.'

'Well, the two of you did just fine without her.' The voice came from behind them.

Santiago introduced the older woman who'd been at the bar earlier in the day. 'This is my mother, Pedra.'

'You have a very talented daughter,'

'You seem surprised.'

'Mama. Behave. Antonio is a colleague of mine and a friend of Ana-Marie's.'

'He's a man, isn't he?'

'Mama!' Santiago wagged her finger at her and laughed just as Sofia appeared, carried aloft on the shoulders of the man who'd swept both of the girls into his arms. 'Holly,' Santiago said to her daughter, 'why don't you take Sofia and play in the square?'

'Do you want to play?'

'Yes, please. She's my best friend.'

'Come on, let's play chase!'

'Don't go outside the square,' Ana-Marie called, then turned to Fernández. 'You'll remember my mother?'

'Of course. It's good to see you again, Inocenta. It's been a long time.'

She looked older; more than the ten years that had passed.

'You look a mess, Antonio. You need a good woman to sort you out.'

'If only you weren't spoken for.' Fernández took her hand and kissed it. 'Sofia must be a joy to you.'

'She runs rings round me, but I wouldn't be without her.'

'And, this is my husband,' Ana-Marie said. 'Paul. Paul Turnbull.' He was fractionally taller than Fernández, his broad shoulders suggesting that he was used to manual labour, his receding hairline accentuating his furrowed forehead.

Fernández shook his hand and said, 'You seem to have a way with Sofia.'

'She's a good girl.' Turnbull smiled, watching the girls chase each other. 'Ana-Marie tells me you've been busy with the deaths in the campo. An easy one to wrap up, I guess, with the murderer blowing his own brains out.'

'Colourful, but inaccurate. My money's on murder, on all four counts.' He didn't usually take an instant dislike to someone, but, given the circumstances, he sensed he'd be making an exception. He wondered if Ana-Marie had told her husband about their relationship and guessed she hadn't, but experience had taught him that the signs were always there if you knew where to look. 'Is your business always straightforward?' he asked.

'Construction and property development are never straightforward in Spain, Inspector, especially during a recession. There are too many hogs with their snouts in the trough. But, everything I'm involved in is legitimate and above board.'

Fernández held his tongue.

'I deal with reputable companies and suppliers.'

Fernández dragged on his cigarette.

'Let's not talk shop all evening,' Ana-Marie said. 'Besides, we've got some good news.' She pulled Turnbull towards her. 'We'll be starting our own family soon, won't we darling?'

Fernández found himself saying, 'Congratulations.' He wasn't sure whether he was jealous, envious or apprehensive. He'd known what it meant - to be with Ana-Marie. They'd even talked of kids and starting a family of their own.

He looked away, searching for a distraction.

He watched Sofia cover her eyes and count to ten, Holly hiding behind a palm tree, Leo Medina's words jangling in his head: Sofia Castaño had seen *an old man carrying a carpet*...

Julieta Santiago called after the two girls and they came hurrying over. Inocenta took Sofia's hand and led her towards a Landcruiser parked on the pavement.

Ana-Marie smiled. 'We must do this again sometime. Perhaps we could have dinner at our villa. We have a terrace overlooking the beach. What do you say?' She looked from Santiago, to Fernández, and to her husband.

'Yes. Yes, of course,' Turnbull said.

'I know,' Ana-Marie laughed, 'work permitting.' She took his arm and they started to walk towards the car. 'Julieta,' she called, 'give me a ring tomorrow.'

'I'll try.'

Holly took her mother's hand and they watched as the car pulled into the evening traffic.

'It was good of you to come tonight, Antonio,' Santiago said. 'I'm sure Ana-Marie really appreciated you being here.'

He nodded, awkward, unsure what she expected him to say.

'You like cake?' Holly asked him.

'Not particularly.'

'I think Holly is inviting you for tea, tomorrow. Her idea, not mine.'

'I can't.'

'No, of course not.'

54

'No, no. That's not what I meant. I can't tomorrow. It's a family thing. A matanza.'

'The slaughter of a pig?'

'Sounds gross,' said Holly. 'Can I watch?'

'She takes after her mother.' Santiago smiled. 'Eight years old and already fascinated by the macabre.'

'You could come, if you want to. Everyone starts arriving at about four. It's a bit short notice, I know.'

Holly looked up at her mother, eyes pleading, almost unable to contain herself.

'It would seem there is a rare gap in our social diary. We'd love to be there.'

'Good.'

'And, we'll suspend hostilities for the afternoon?'

'Yes. Yes, of course. I…'

'I'm kidding, Antonio.'

'Oh. Good. That's settled then.'

'Good.'

Holly pulled at her mother's arm. 'Bye. See you tomorrow.'

*

Rodrigo Perpiñán had suggested they meet in the church, long after the setting of the sun, once the village had withdrawn for the night. It was late, just before mid-night. The bar had closed and a few stragglers filtered through the narrow streets having had a skin-full and an update on the gossip surrounding the investigation.

Fernández arrived early and took time to enjoy the tranquility the church offered - cool and quiet, dark and faintly perfumed by the infusion of incense. Although he had struggled with his own faith since adolescence, he found a special solace in a church. He stared at the simple alter in the middle of the Chancel, the figure of Christ on the cross dominating the semi-circular apse behind, the pulpit to the left. He lifted his head to the high, vaulted ceilings. Time to talk to God? He wasn't sure. Time to ask that his mother, his sisters and their families should enjoy good health. Time to hope that the families of the bereaved would find comfort in one another. Prayers of a sort.

He lit a candle and stood at the entrance to the vestibule, between the choir stalls and the pulpit.

'For your father?' Perpiñán's voice filled the church as he walked down the central nave. 'The candle? For your father?'

'Yes. I never knew him.'

'He was a good man, Antonio. My father counted himself lucky to have him as a friend: a man he could trust.'

'A product of their times, perhaps?' He shook the scholar's hand warmly and they sat on an ancient wooden pew in the side chapel. Yellow streetlights filtered through the stain glass, casting strange shadows across their faces.

'I hear the restoration is proceeding well,' Perpiñán said, peering about him, 'although Father Gabriel tells me that Paul Turnbull believes the foundations are suspect.'

'Paul Turnbull. Ana-Marie's husband?'

'Yes. Pouring money into the project, apparently.'

'Change out of his back pocket.'

'Someone's back pocket,' Perpiñán agreed. 'Oiling wheels-within-wheels, no doubt. He has bigger fish to fry: hoping to get a slice of the Almeria regeneration project. Angling for those who will take a back-hander.'

Both men seemed to welcome this light-hearted prelude, but then Perpiñán said, 'Outside the church today, I told you that your father was caught up in a killing spree that started thirty-five years ago?'

'I had no idea.'

'You'd only just been born.'

'But, my mother...'

'Should have told you?'

'Why wouldn't she?'

'Perhaps if I give you some background, it might help explain what happened, why it happened and how our fathers got involved?'

'Our fathers?'

'Your father wasn't alone...' Perpiñán drew air, filled his lungs, and exhaled forcefully before saying, 'I asked you to meet me here because you need to understand the significance of this church and its Priest, Father Emanuel.'

'Father Emanuel, the Priest, thirty-five years ago?'

'Yes. You'll know, of course, that for centuries the clergy sided with landowners and exploited the landless poor. The Priest lived in the big house at the top of the village and each morning he'd walk down to the square accompanied by the landowner and those who managed the mines. They'd select the labourers who'd work that day...'

'Deciding who would eat and who would go hungry.'

'A pattern that was repeated across much of Spain. It was only a matter of time before frustrations and resentment erupted into violence. And when the landowners and Priests sided with the Fascists in 1936...'

'The poor backed the Republicans.'

'The tragedy of the Civil War is that it tore families and communities apart. It's not as simple as rich against poor.' Perpiñán tilted his head to one side. 'But if a man is watching his family die of starvation, and you offer him an opportunity to redistribute wealth, what would you expect his response to be?'

'Was there much bloodshed here?'

'Yes, but compared with many areas of Spain the village was spared the worst of Franco's purges. Apart from minor skirmishes, there's only one date that need concern your investigation - January 1974.'

'But that was long after Franco's death squads had finished mopping-up opposition to his regime.'

Perpiñán's face hardened, he smiled weakly, his thin features cloaked in shadows. Fernández offered water from a bottle he'd carried with him and Perpiñán sipped at it, distracted, distant. 'You're right, after the Civil War, Franco set about crushing any opposition. His early reprisals were on a massive and terrifying scale. A list was drawn up in Salamanca of all known Republican sympathizers and they were hunted down and executed, often with little more than a summary trial. Accurate figures have been difficult to come by, but former prisoners of war were incarcerated in concentration camps, political dissidents in labour camps, whilst homosexuals and other 'deviants' were locked up mental asylums. The Jews suffered here just as they did elsewhere in Europe – six thousand names handed over to Heinrich Himmler. Estimates vary, but the overall death toll probably ran to hundreds of thousands. To this day, mass graves are still being uncovered.'

'And Juan Gonzales was part of that tyranny?'

'Once he was old enough he became one of Franco's assassins.' As the church clock struck twelve-thirty, Perpiñán said, 'You asked me if there was much bloodshed here?'

'Yes.'

'There are clues to atrocities throughout the village, but today few would understand their significance.' The scholar paused. 'And then, in the winter of 1974, something dreadful happened - an incident you can use not only to judge our fathers, but also to understand what drove Juan Gonzales to shoot three men last Thursday.'

'Judge our fathers?'

Perpiñán sat and stared out at the blackness of the night. The village streetlights had been turned out and most homes were in darkness. Only the scream of cats fighting or a lone dog barking cut through the still air. 'By the early nineteen-fifties, most of the organized resistance against Franco had been wiped out. Throughout the nineteen-sixties Spain prospered as tourists poured into the Costas.' Perpiñán sighed. 'And then, in December 1973, Admiral Carrero Blanco was assassinated by ETA. He'd been Prime Minister for less than six months and would have succeeded Franco'

'Operation Orgo?'

'Some would say the Basque separatists' most successful action. Five of them spent months excavating a tunnel under the street Admiral Blanco used to drive to Mass. The blast catapulted the vehicle over the church and onto a second floor balcony on the other side.'

'Spain's first astronaut,' Fernández said, recalling reports he'd read: the black humour of a nation weary of the Dictator's tyranny and repression.

'Yes, Spain's first astronaut.' Perpiñán smiled ruefully, echoing the bitter epitaph.

'ETA enjoying popular support for their stand against the Dictator.'

'Franco's response appeared to be uncharacteristically restrained and many commentators interpreted this as a sign of his frailty and the beginning of the end of his authority. But, he wasn't going to go quietly. The assassination prompted some of his most violent reprisals. He was determined to hunt down those responsible and unleashed his death squads throughout Spain and across the boarder into France. Hundreds were tortured and killed. In January 1974, news reached us that a death squad was closing in on two ETA fugitives. As it neared, anyone considered a likely target was hidden in a safe house. We watched the military convoy as it snaked across the plain. When they arrived in the village, they searched every house and barn. One man was lucky to escape serious injury when they beat him for not returning the Nazis salute Franco had adopted. Pepe, the goatherd, was no more than a teenager but they cut his tongue out when they mistook his stupidity for insolence.'

Perpiñán paused again. 'And then we saw the Priest, Father Emanuel, and Jésus Gonzales, Juan's father. Both were Francoists and, in hindsight, what they did next should not have shocked us. But, it did. Father Emanuel and Jésus Gonzales led a group of soldiers to a safe house where we'd hidden two fugitives.'

'They'd been responsible for the assassination?'

'No, but they were well known Republican sympathisers, leading members of the Resistance. The men had slipped away, but the widow who lived there, her son and a neighbour were taken to the square outside the Town Hall. They were forced to kneel and when they refused to tell the soldiers where the fugitives were, they were shot in the back of the head, gunned down like dogs, their bodies left as a warning to us all.'

Perpiñán sipped at the water. 'That evening, after the death squad had left, three men from the village attended Mass and, after the service, they waited until the church emptied. They followed the Priest home and broke into his house. Two of the men took Father Emanuel 'for a stroll', high into the hills beyond the village, tying him up alongside a disused mineshaft. They slit his throat, left him there to die and went back for Jésus Gonzales. They took Jésus and his wife, Teresa, to where they'd secured the Priest. They slit their throats as well and threw all three bodies down the mineshaft.'

'Our fathers did this?'

'Yes.'

'But how can you be sure?'

'I was ten years old, Antonio. I followed them. I saw everything that happened that night. I watched my father kill Father Emanuel and Teresa Gonzales, and I watched your father kill Jésus Gonzales.'

They sat in silence, Fernández unable to stop the mixture of emotions surging through his body. His breath was shallow and rapid as he struggled to justify what his father had done. Everything he'd stood for was crumbling before him: the distain he'd felt for anyone who took another's life; the dedication he'd shown in tracking down those guilty of murder; his inability to countenance any justification and his contempt for bleeding-heart excuses. But he *could* justify what his father had done that night, couldn't he? *Jésus Gonzales had betrayed his neighbours, for Christ's sake. Three innocent people had died, the back of their heads blown off. And what sort of Priest is it who sends his own flock to slaughter? They'd deserved everything they got.* But then

60

he pictured the terrified face of Teresa Gonzales, dragged from her home, shocked and bewildered, unable to comprehend what was happening, only to watch as her husband was slaughtered in front of her. *Did she deserve to die?* He found himself gulping in air as arguments raged inside.

It was several minutes before he lifted his head and looked at Roderigo Perpiñán. 'You said there were three men involved that night?'

'Three men, Antonio. Your father, my father and...'

'Alberto Ramos?'

'Yes. His involvement had been shrouded in secrecy for thirty-five years until...'

'Someone found out and told Juan Gonzales.' He hesitated; realising there must be more. 'That wasn't the end of it, was it? There were reprisals? More bloodshed?'

Perpiñán looked at him. 'When we spoke outside the church at the funeral earlier today, I told you that last Thursday's killing spree started over thirty years ago.'

'Yes.'

'My father was murdered a year after they'd killed the Priest and Gonzales' parents. That was in 1975. He was found in an outbuilding on our land. His throat had been slit. And your father...'

'Died in 1976. A hit-and-run accident.'

'Your father wasn't killed by a car, Antonio. You were probably told that to hide the truth from you. His throat was slit.'

'My God.' He shook his head. 'Why would my mother lie to me? She must have known I'd find out. Eventually.'

'And then what? You go after Juan Gonzales and the cycle of violence continues? It could not have been easy for her, faced with her husband's murder, three children to fend for – alone.'

'And Alberto?'

'Would have been next on his list. He was in his mid-thirties at the time and had just been elected Mayor.'

'And as Mayor he could have arrested Juan Gonzales for the murder of your father, of my father...'

'And implicate himself in the death of a priest? And besides, Alberto knew that if Juan Gonzales found out he'd been involved he would have come after him.'

'But, he survived.'

'There were five people who knew what happened that night. Two were dead. The other three were Alberto. Me. And a young girl: the Priest's whore. She was with Father Emanuel, in his bed, when our fathers burst in and took him away. Alberto stayed with the girl.'

'And wasn't actually involved in...' Fernández sat in silence for several minutes. 'I'll assume Juan Gonzales didn't know about you?'

'No, but I suppose there could have been someone who'd attended Mass that evening, or had seen our fathers drag the three of them off.'

'Villagers who knew something, but have remained silent...'

'But someone told him and, after thirty-five years, he didn't hesitate, did he?'

They left the oppressive confines of the church and crossed the village to Perpiñán's home where they sat on the terrace and opened a new bottle of Soberano brandy, sank a shot and recharged their glasses, Fernández lost in thought, trying to come to terms with his father's part in the slaughter of three people.

After several minutes, Perpiñán said, 'We're assuming someone betrayed Alberto.'

'The Priest's whore?'

'After Mass, Father Emanuel came back to his house, unaware that our fathers and Alberto were in pursuit. I followed them, using shadows for cover. I climbed a tree and saw her, naked, in the Priest's bed, waiting for him.'

'She knew what our fathers had done?'

'She was not a witness, as such. Alberto stayed with her. She didn't actually see what happened.'

'But?'

62

'It was rumoured that a few months after the Priest was killed not only did she marry a local man, but was carrying the Priest's child.'

'She was pregnant?'

'It was rumoured but, just as Alberto's involvement was hushed up, so was her identity.'

'But you saw her that evening? You know who she is?'

'It was dark, the room lit by candlelight. Her back was turned towards me as I watched the Priest being dragged from her arms…'

'And, presumably, the man she married was unaware that she was carrying someone else's child?'

'Probably. But suppose, after all this time, someone found out and threatened to blow her cover? Threatened to tell her husband that the child he'd cared for all these years was not his own? Threatened to tell the child that the man she thinks of as her father, isn't really her father? Suppose someone threatened to tell the child that her real father was a Priest who'd betrayed innocent people and had been executed – that his throat had been slit and he had been left to bleed to death before being thrown down a mineshaft?'

'You said, *she*. The child was a girl?'

'I believe so. Find the Priest's whore and the Priest's child, Antonio, and you may begin to unravel this tragedy.'

Day Four

Sunday 21st June 2009

Fernández drove home in the small hours and after several fitful hours he gave up trying to sleep. He poured himself a brandy, sat out on his balcony and watched the day unfold. But the sounds of the city were distant and vague, his body sluggish and inert, his mind numb and impassive. He no longer felt anything. He was no longer shocked, ashamed, confused, or angry. Just so dog-tired that all he wanted to do was curl up and sleep. Except that he knew he wouldn't be able to, even if he tried.

As the chill morning air wrapped around him he shuddered and withdrew to the sofa in his lounge. He lay there, staring at the ceiling, his mind melting in the confusion of images that staged repeat performances each time he tried to close his eyes.

At nine he drove to the village, parked his car, crossed the road and, leaning heavily on the door, pushed his way into a packed bar. The cascade of conversation trickled to nothing, as though a dam had been installed above a waterfall.

He looked across the poorly lit room at the long, wood-panelled bar. A glass fronted cabinet on top of the bar displayed a range of homemade tapas, the floor was strewn with discarded cigarette butts and paper serviettes, and men stood with one foot on the metal rest, the other firmly planted on the wooden floor, sipping coffee, anise or brandy. The tables, wooden and square, and the chairs, uncomfortable with high slatted backs, were exactly as he remembered them. The cigarette machine, the one-armed bandit, TV and pool table appeared to be the only additions to the drab decor.

As everyone returned to their breakfast, he walked over to the bar, lit a cigarette and ordered a double espresso.

He glanced at the display of old village photographs on the wall – miners with blackened faces stepping into the daylight, donkeys carrying water or salted fish, a goatherd cradling a new born kid, proud villagers dressed-to-the-nines in their Sunday best. Above the cigarette machine, a poster featured several images of a bullfight at The Plaza de la Maestranza in Seville. Next to the large-screen television, the handsome face of José Castaño in his Real Madrid strip smiled self-assuredly from a publicity photograph. His father, Enrique Castaño, was standing at the far end of the bar, making light work of several tapas.

Fernández watched a group of Brits who'd congregated around several tables they'd pushed together. He supposed they lived in the village or in one of the villas on the surrounding hills, and came to the bar to pass the time of day and to gossip. He had no doubt that they would see themselves as card carrying, tax paying, voting members of the community, but he knew the locals would not so generous, referring to them as *guiris* - a term of contempt, the meaning of which had long disappeared, but any dictionary would define simply as *foreigner*. He decided the Brits would keep, but knew he'd have to get back to them sooner or later, if only because Klaus Dagmar, the man who had reported the bodies, was sitting mid-way down on the far side and seemed to be the focus of their undivided attention.

The barmen began to enlist help to rearrange the furniture for the afternoon's big match. Fernández asked one of the men what all the fuss was about and was told that José Castaño was playing in a close-season, exhibition match - Real Madrid v's an all-star South American line up. This was seen as an opportunity for José to state his case for a regular place in Madrid's first team.

He finished his brandy, left the bar, and walked into the village where he found a teenage girl sitting on the doorstep of the general store, stroking a dog that had been barred from entering. The dog appeared to appreciate her attention and had rolled over to expose his tummy, inviting her to tickle him. She obliged but Fernández could see her heart wasn't in it. She appeared bored, resentful and sullen.

He wasn't to know, of course, but her world had fallen apart six months ago when her parents had decided that they'd had enough of each other and she'd found herself sitting next to her tearful mother on a budget flight to 'sunny' Spain. She would like Spain; her mother had tried to reassure her. She would be able to swim in the sea, learn a new language and make new friends. Trouble was all she wanted to do was stay with her friends in Edinburgh, sit her dance exams and snog Mickey, her first serious boyfriend. As if the wrench hadn't been enough, she'd been deposited in a local Spanish school where she couldn't understand a word the teacher or her classmates were saying. To compound her misery even more, her mother hooked up with Danny, a tattooed plumber who had moved into their cramped accommodation and began lording it over both of them. Life was not sweet. The dog had it better. At least he got his tummy rubbed.

She sat, her chin resting on the palm of her left hand, mouth glum, eyes glazed and her mind back in Scotland, where she'd be snogging Mickey.

It had been Juanita Ramos's suggestion that he speak to the young lass from Scotland.

'Mind if I join you?' he asked in his heavily accented English and sat next to her.

She shuffled away from him, resting against the door jam.

'Your dog?'

'I wish,' she said. 'Our apartment's too small. Would nay be fair to keep a dog, so Danny says. Me mum don't argue. So that's that.'

'School out?'

'Yeah. Thank God.'

He looked at her big blue eyes and fair, freckled skin. 'What is it they say? School, the happiest days of your life.'

She snorted. 'School sucks.'

66

'Yes. I know what you mean.'

'At least you can speak the language.'

Fernández laughed. 'I've had to work hard to lose the local dialect. Even visitors from other parts of Spain can't understand a word the locals say.'

She smiled and looked at him for the first time. 'I know how they feel.'

'New to the village?'

'Aye. It's like wearing new shoes.' She looked at him. 'It's what my gran used to say. Painful.'

'What did your gran call you?'

'Aimee, when she was sober.'

'You know who I am?'

'You're the cop who's investigating them murders.'

'And what have you heard?'

'Only what I make out from the few friends I have in the village.' She paused. 'The old man shot three men from the same family and then blew his own brains out, right?'

'Something like that. You knew the old man?'

'Señor Gonzales? Aye, s'pose so. Most of the kids in the village used to shout obscenities at him. But he was OK.'

'He didn't have too many friends in the village?'

'He was OK,' Aimee repeated. 'I'd feed his cats and his chickens. His English was crap, so we didn't talk much - all sign language and the odd word, you know?' She paused, looking down at the dog at her feet. 'I'd do his dishes and he'd teach me how to care for his canaries. He liked to play games.'

'Like?'

'Board games, cards, dominoes.'

'And which hand did he use to throw the dice or pick up a card?'

'Left, I think.' She hesitated. 'Aye. He'd make a real show of rattling the dice before he threw. I'm pretty sure he was left-handed.'

Fernández lent forward and rubbed the dog's tummy, before saying, 'Thank you for talking to me.'

'I was nay rushed off me feet, Inspector.'

He stood up. 'I've no doubt your mama's a good woman, Aimee. Give her a break and maybe you'll start enjoying your time here.'

'It can't get any worse.'

He began to walk away, then turned and said. 'You know a kid called Gloria?'

'Gloria? Here, in the village?'

'Yes, probably a young girl, about six years old. I'm not sure.'

'She part of your investigation, then?'

'She's a friend of Sofia Castaño's.'

'I know little Sofia, but I've not seen her pal. *Gloria*, you say?' Aimee pursed her lips and shook her head. 'It's no good. I dunnay know the wee lass. They witnesses or summat?'

'I'm not sure.'

'You're not sure about a lot of things, are ye?'

'You like jigsaws?'

'That's what you do then, is it? Put all the pieces together before it makes sense?'

He laughed. 'Yes, something like that. Look, if you do come across Gloria, you'll let me know?'

'Aye, if you think it'll help.'

*

Fernández found the cottage near the top of the village.

He ducked under the crime scene tape and opened a wooden gate onto a terrace. It splintered away from its top hinge and crashed onto the flagstone floor. Several cats scurried for cover as he entered a wooden lean-to that doubled as a chicken coop and toilet. He sensed that this was one of the few homes that had been by-passed when mains water and sewage were installed in the village. Over time, effluent had nowhere else to go but to seep into the surrounding hillside.

68

The smell inside the lean-to was almost unbearable. The corpses of several chickens, probably the victims of a fox, lay strewn across the dirt floor, whilst others continued to scurry and scratch out their meager existence. On top of a long table, caged canaries screamed with alarm, demanding to be fed, struggling from one side of their cage to the other. It had been three days since Juan Gonzales had left home to execute three men. Three days and, after SOCOs had finished, no one had thought to check on his animals.

He unlatched the door leading into the kitchen and was greeted by the stench of rubbish rotting in the bin next to the sink. He pushed the bin's pedal and the top flipped open, releasing flies and wasps that were gorging on chicken giblets and discarded cat food. He took out his handkerchief, covered his nose, moved over to drawers under the work surface and rummaged through them. There was nothing to confirm that Juan Gonzales was left-handed.

He moved into the sitting room with its low, beamed ceiling and stonewalls. He was surprised by its order and neatness, the home of man who had been meticulous and precise. The room narrowed significantly where the open hearth and chimneybreast jutted into the room. There were two pieces of furniture - a leather armchair in the corner and a small, drop-leaf table. Abandoned on top of the table was a lined note pad and fountain pen.

He picked up the beautifully crafted, gold inlay pen. He imagined it had been stolen from someone Juan Gonzales had executed during one of his missions. He cracked open the case of the pen, unscrewing the two parts until he was able to apply light pressure to the bladder inside. A small droplet of ink oozed onto the nib and dropped onto the table. He reassembled the pen and began to write his name on the pad. The nib caught and scratched the surface of the paper. It was a left-handed nib.

Julieta Santiago's assertion was beginning to look irrefutable. Juan Gonzales did not turn the handgun on himself. Someone else was there.

He pulled his Beretta from its holster and felt its weight, switching it from his left hand to his right, and back again. He repeated this several times and moved over to stand in front of the mirror over the fireplace. Using his left hand, he raised the handgun to his left temple and held it there. His hand trembled slightly, as though the muscles in the wrist were struggling to manage the gun's weight. He lowered the gun, passing it to his right hand, and raised it to his right temple. In his right hand, the gun felt so much easier to handle, so much more natural. This was how he would blow his brains out - holding the gun in his dominant hand - and, in that moment, he knew there could no doubt that he was heading a murder inquiry.

*

Adelina Fernández lived in a rambling, white-walled cortijo that over the centuries had been farmed by labourers paid 'in kind' when money was short. Since her husband's death, she'd scaled down the extent and diversity of the farm and, in spite of poor health, remained almost self-sufficient. She tended her goats, pigs and chickens and was able to grow enough fruit and vegetables to provide for herself.

Twice a year, in mid-December and around the summer solstice, the whole family gathered and it was Adelina who presided over the matanza. The slaughter would provide food for several weeks, with every part of the carcass used, the choicest cuts hung to produce the leanest hams, whilst the rest made soups, stews and sausages. Everything was used - flesh, bone, blood, trotters, head, offal. Nothing was wasted.

New regulations had been introduced in the name of health and safety, making it illegal for the slaughter to be carried out by anyone other than a designated official. But the rules were widely ignored, although a small portion of meat would be taken to the vet in the morning after the slaughter. The vet would test the meat and, if found healthy, he'd gratefully accept his 'cut' and the family's feast could begin.

Adelina shuffled from her front door, stooped, frail, weary, but overjoyed to see her son as Fernández parked his car. She would often boast that he was the 'chief of police'. She held up long, slender arms and pulled him firmly into her body.

'Mama,' Fernández said, gently, 'you're looking well.'

'And you've never been able to lie, Antonio. So don't start now.' They held each other tenderly.

'Are Inez and Olivia here?' he asked.

'Of course. And my grandchildren.' She rarely missed the opportunity to remind him that time was running out for her. 'You're late, as always.' Adelina looked at her son and brushed the thick, dark hair away from his eyes. 'You look tired. You work too hard. You'll make yourself ill.' She paused and smiled, pulling him to her once again.

As they embraced, another car pulled up and parked.

'Mama,' Fernández said, as Santiago and her daughter walked hand-in-hand towards them, 'this is Julieta.'

Momentarily, Adelina looked confused and Fernández instantly regretted not warning her - it had been a long time since he'd brought someone home. His mother looked at the tall, graceful woman with her long, auburn hair and green eyes and said, 'You look like you could do with a good meal inside you.'

'Mama.'

'What? The woman's a bag of bones.'

'Mama, Julieta is a colleague and my guest.'

'No, you're right,' Santiago smiled. 'I haven't been taking as much care of myself as I should. This is Holly.' She eased her daughter gently in front of her, placing her hands on her chest. 'We're very pleased to be here, aren't we Holly?'

Holly pushed herself away and walked tentatively towards the woman who looked as ancient as any she'd ever seen. Holly held out her hand and said, 'I am very pleased to meet you.' Adelina chuckled, raised both her hands, framed Holly's face, brushed her copper hair to one side and looked deep into her eyes as she said, 'You're very beautiful, like your mother.'

71

'Thank you. Are you very old?'

'Am I very old?' Adelina cried with delight. 'I would say I'm the oldest woman in the whole of Spain.'

'Really?'

'I have been on this earth for over two hundred years.'

Holly giggled as Adelina stroked her cheek with the back of her hand and said, 'You'll need to stay out of the sun. Your skin is too fair and the sun too fierce. Come with me. I have a hat for you to wear.' She led Holly into the house.

Santiago looked across at Fernández, 'How does she do that? People fall in love with her everywhere we go.'

'Well, it can't be genetic, can it?' He said, raising an eyebrow and titling his head slightly.

'A truce, remember?'

'A ceasefire, as negotiated.' He smiled. 'Holly has an accent. Your Spanish is flawless, but you weren't born here were you?'

'My mother's Spanish. My father's English. A physician. I was born in London.'

'And Holly's father?'

'A holiday romance that turned sour. I should have known better. It lasted three years. He left without knowing I was pregnant. Hasn't been in touch since.' She smiled ruefully. 'Come on, introduce me to the rest of your tribe.'

They walked round to the back of the house. His sisters stood talking - an art they had taken to astonishing heights, practising as they did for many hours each day. Their husbands were drinking beer - stomachs testifying to their dedication.

A pig foraged, unperturbed, in a large holding-pen built onto the side of the cortijo.

Children were playing chase among the small outcrop of olive and almond trees. 'Uncle Antonio,' they cried as they hurried to him, bounding around him like puppies and badgering him until he produced the shiny euro coins he always brought, a token offering for his long absences.

He shook hands with his brothers-in-law and kissed his sisters tenderly on the cheek. He introduced Santiago and within seconds she'd been dragged off into the secret cabal that characterized his sister's social gatherings. He smiled, grateful for his sisters' instant hospitality.

'These murders. A sorry business, Antonio,' Julio, the eldest of the two husbands said, his face serious.

'Yes, indeed.'

'But not something that will tax your powers of deduction, eh?' Carlos mumbled, wiping beer froth from his moustache. 'Open and shut's what I hear.'

'Then your sources are better than mine,' Fernández said. 'Is that beer cold?' He took a can from the icebox and pulled at the ring. 'Salud.'

'You'll stay for supper, this time, Antonio?' his sister Inez asked, as she strolled over to join them.

'Of course, but I can't stay long. I need to get back to work. I'm sorry.'

'You must find more time for mama. She will not always be with us.'

Adelina came from the kitchen with Holly in tow, a straw hat, edged with a full brim, shading the young girl's face. The old woman called her grandchildren to her. They gathered round and looked at the stranger clinging to their grandmother's arm. Then the eldest girl walked over, held out a hand and said, 'Come on. Don't be shy.' Holly didn't need a second invitation and it wasn't long before her shrieks rivaled those of her newfound friends.

Others began to arrive - friends, neighbours, and more relatives from the extensive family network and soon the yard was full and noisy.

The men prepared to drag the pig onto the table where the slaughter would take place. Without a cellar or a barn, they would subdue the pig and then stand in line, forming a barrier, shielding the moment of slaughter.

Weighing in at fifty kilos, more or less, and with a temper to match, this saddleback was built like a rhino and did not take kindly to being manhandled. As they started to chase it round the pen, it became obvious to everyone that this pig's sacrifice was going to be hard-won and, after Carlos had been upended and Julio had tumbled onto his backside, Fernández and two other men were drafted in. It was this part of the ceremony that dignified the pig's death - allowing it the opportunity to fight back - but it wasn't long before the men ran out of steam and patience.

The pig was wrestled to the table where the combined weight of it captors pinned it down, eventually subduing it.

As the men rolled the pig on to its side and pulled its head back to expose its throat, Adelina motioned to Inez and Olivia to place a stainless steel bowl on the floor under the pig's head and drew a long bladed knife from its sheath.

She stepped forward, but was not looking at the pig, staring instead at the hills beyond, and Fernández saw something in her face that he had not expected: a tranquility and serenity, a gentleness and compassion that he'd only ever seen reserved for those she loved, as though this ritual was her private, personal way of commemorating his father's death; her way of confronting the horror that she'd had to live with over so many years, as though she owed that much to the man she'd loved – to carry on, to remain steadfast, to take his place.

Even so, he couldn't help wondering what went through her mind each time she held a knife, and cut a pig's throat and watched the blood flow.

He joined the other men subduing the pig, wondering if her strike would be swift and deep enough; if she still had the strength and the power to make it clean. But, he need not have worried. As though summoning all her strength, she sank the sharp blade into the pig's neck, plunging through the jugular and the carotid artery. As the thyroid cartilage was severed, the pigs vocal cords vented in a scream that would live in the nightmares of anyone who was susceptible.

74

The men stepped away, leaving Adelina, alone.

She dropped the knife and stood for several seconds, her head bowed, then lifted her crucifix, kissed it, and walked slowly towards the back door and into her home.

The death of a pig, slaughtered in this way, is never instantaneous. It suffers, life draining from it, squirming hopelessly as its hind legs are tethered and it is hauled upside down, allowing each heartbeat to pump blood from it.

As it drifted into death, the pig's body began to spasm, as though its muscles were reluctant to give way as its brain surrendered control.

Finally, there was a calm and stillness as the final drops of blood dripped into the bowl.

There was no lament at the pig's passing. This was the way it had always been. The cicadas came alive and most of the kids tore off into the garden to continue their game of chase, leaving the adults to drink their wine.

'Don't be sad,' the child's voice startled him. 'It's only a pig.'

Fernández turned and found Holly looking anxiously at him. He turned away from her momentarily; his breath snatched from his throat by overwhelming sorrow, unable to shake the image of his father, his throat slit, hanging on to life as it ebbed away from him. 'Yes. You're right. It's only a pig,' he muttered. 'You wouldn't treat a person like that, would you?' He summoned a smile from somewhere, and then hesitated, suddenly out of his depth, not sure how to counter her innocence. Instead he asked, 'Where's your mother?'

'Right behind you.' Julieta Santiago smiled and, taking Holly's hand, she said, 'I thought you'd be playing chase with the other girls.'

'I was. I wanted a drink and I saw him looking very sad.'

'That's very thoughtful, my darling, but go on, off you go.' They watched as Holly joined the other children. 'She's very perceptive,' Santiago said.

'She'd make a good cop,' he said, fumbling to light a cigarette.

'You OK?'

'There's something I need to tell you.'

'Need to tell me?'

'Yes.' He lifted his head and stared directly at her. 'But not here. Not tonight.'

He stayed for an hour into the meal and, as he prepared to leave, his mother took his hand and led him towards his car.

As they embraced, she held on to him, stroking the back of his neck.

'Mama.'

She held him at arms length. 'What is it?'

'Juan Gonzales.'

'He is dead.'

'Yes.'

'Then you know?'

'Yes.' He hesitated. 'And Inez and Olivia?'

'I'd prefer it if they didn't know the truth.'

They held each other, as though neither wanted to allow the moment to pass, until Adelina stepped back, caressed his face and said, 'You have your father's eyes. You're not as good-looking as he was, of course. And you've put on weight.' She hesitated before adding, 'He was very proud of you, Antonio. He'd be very proud of you now, our chief of police.' She smiled, but the smile faded quickly. 'Don't leave it too long before you come and see me again.'

On his way home, he pulled over into an almond grove and turned off the car's engine. He held onto the steering wheel, gripping it as though he needed to stop the world from spinning. He looked up at the flood of light from a full moon and the gaunt silhouettes of the almond trees.

And it was there, in the stillness of the night, that the tears came.

Day Five

Monday 30th July 2009

Sometime after midnight Fernández turned the ignition key, eased his car out of the almond grove and drove back to his apartment. That would, he resolved, be the last time he'd succumb to the confusion of emotions that had raged inside him since he'd come face-to-face with the tragedy of his father's last years.

At ten he showered, changed and grabbed a coffee at his local bar. He settled his bill and picked up a pile of washing from the family-owned laundry next door.

He spent the next hour sitting on his balcony. He phoned Valencia Ramoz, his administrator at the Incident Room, brought her up to date with his lines of enquiry and checked on the support she was getting from headquarters in Almeria. She was primarily concerned about the growing media interest. Press and TV were camped near the police cordon at the building site where Juan Gonzales had exacted his revenge. There was growing speculation that the murders were linked to past terrorist activities in the village and that an unknown assailant was still at large.

He phoned Leo Medina and asked him to ruffle a few feathers in the village, see if anyone would open up and tell him anything that might take them forward - anything about the Ramos men, about Juan Gonzales, about the fascist's parents, or about the Priest and his fifteen-year-old whore.

'Doctor Santiago come down yet?' Medina asked.

'From what?'

'Her high horse. Throwing her weight around when she first arrived at the crime scene the other day; taking control without so much as nod in your direction. She was out of order, if you ask me.'

'No one's asking you. Besides, I'm not sure I handled it as well as I could have done.'

'Bloody typical: woman like that.'

'I didn't have you down as a misogynist, Leo.'

'She just pissed me off, that's all.'

'I think there's more to Doctor Santiago than meets the eye. First impressions can be very misleading.'

'If you say so, Sir.'

'I do. Now go rattle a few cages and see what you can come up with.'

At twelve, he drove back to the village, parked outside the bar and walked to the cottage where he knew he'd find Felipe Romero. The torrential rain had stopped as suddenly as it had started and the sun had already washed away any standing water.

Romero was asleep in the shade of a fig tree that grew in a rubbish-strewn ginnel between two houses, an empty red wine bottle lying among the weeds around the tree's exposed roots. Fernández sat on the ground beside him and waited, taking the time to look across the valley towards the mountains in the distance and the sea beyond the plains.

It wasn't long before Romero stirred and scowled at him through a mouth full of decay and neglect. 'What d'you want with me?'

'I didn't see you at the funeral on Saturday.'

'So?'

'There are three more widows in the village, Felipe. Widows before their time.'

'I pray for them.'

Fernández looked at him, barely out of his forties, ravaged by drink, robbed of his youth, his skin sallow, jaundiced, hollow cheeks jutting beneath sunken eyes, hair thin, sparse, matted to his head, his mouth hosting festering sores and broken teeth. 'But, they need answers to the same questions as I do. Without them, they will not be able to rest.'

Romero's dog pushed its way past Fernández and sat at its master's feet. Romero laid a gnarled hand on the animal's coat and smoothed it, nipping a tick from the fur and flicking it away.

'Last Thursday, during siesta,' Fernández said, 'how many rockets did you fire?'

'I don't remember.'

'You'd be lynched for disturbing the siesta.'

'Another case for you to solve, then.'

'You're sure?'

'If I fired rockets, or I'd be lynched?'

'You heard the gun fire?'

'Fuck knows.' Romero wiped his eyes on the back of his sleeve. 'Sound travels. It echoes.'

The church clock struck one and Fernández stood up.

'Launch one for me.'

'A rocket? What now, days after the fiesta? You really do want to get me lynched, don't you?'

'They'll forgive you. Just one.'

Romero shrugged, struggled to his feet uneasily and disappeared into his home. Moments later he returned with a rocket in his hand. He moved away from his front door and checked for obstructions overhead. With the fingertips of his left hand he grasped the body of the rocket and held it level with his eyes. He took the cigarette from his mouth and used it to light the blue touch-paper, turning his head away at the last moment. Within seconds, the missile had launched from his hand and exploded over the village.

Romero forced a smile.

'I'm told you set off several on Thursday, around the time the Ramos men were murdered. You must have been well prepared. But then you had plenty of time to plan the display, didn't you?'

Romero took his time, counting the fingers on both hands. 'Ten. Ten fingers. No accidents.' He looked at Fernández. 'That's the way I like it. Pays to be careful. That be all, Inspector?'

'For now. You don't have plans to leave town, I suppose?' He began to retrace his steps up the ginnel when he turned and asked, 'Oh, by the way, do you remember the fifteen year old girl the fascist Priest was fucking?'

'What?'

'The Priest who was killed, back in 1974.'

'Murdered.' Romero spat the word out. 'Father Emanuel was murdered.'

Fernández felt a rush of anger: anger he'd swore he'd control; anger he'd have to suppress time and time again if he was to make any sort of progress in the investigation. He knew that Romero wasn't provoking or goading him, just telling it as he saw it, but he found himself trying to justify his father's actions. 'Father Emanuel was responsible for the death of three innocent villagers - shot by fascist soldiers who were searching for those who blew the Prime Minister to bits.'

'Bloody terrorists.'

Fernández persisted. 'The Priest was having an affair with a young girl. Difficult to ignore, if it's true.'

'I don't know and I don't care. It was a long time ago. I was only a kid.'

'It may have been a long time ago, Felipe, but no matter how much wine you've drunk it seems inconceivable that you would forget. Was she a whore from the brothel, or self-employed, making a bit of pocket money? Or was she one of his parishioners? A girl from the village? What happened to her? Is she still alive? Does she still live in the village?'

'Fuck your questions and fuck you!' Romero fell silent and then mumbled, 'It was a long time ago. I was kid.'

'How old were you?'

'I don't know.'

'Oh, come on. 1974. How old were you?'

'Fifteen, I think.'

'Same age as the Priest's whore.'

'If you say so.'

'Did she sit next to you at school? At church? A girl from the village? Your age?'

There was silence. Romero sat on his haunches, picked up a stick and began to draw absentmindedly in the dust. Fernández guessed he was struggling with the images of the past, misty in an alcoholic fog, and said, 'There was a child.'

'A child?'

'A girl, born to the Priest's whore.'

'You're making this up.'

'Born within eight months of the Priest's death.' Fernández retreated into the shade and sat close enough to smell the wine that seemed to seep from every pore of Romero's parched skin.

'Your telling me the Priest fathered a child?'

'A girl.'

'A girl?' Romero continued to carve random designs in the earth.

'Do you know where they are now?'

'How would I know?' His eyes had lost their focus and he appeared to be grappling with his recall of events thirty-five years ago. 'I've told you all I know. I don't remember.'

Fernández grabbed him by the lapels and pulled him close. 'Don't remember, or won't remember? Which is it, Felipe?' He held him there for several moments before he loosened his grip and pushed Romero back to the ground. 'I'll leave you to think things over, but I'll be back.'

As he turned to go, he fished a five-euro note from his pocket and threw it on the floor in front of Romero. 'I expect to hear more from you, my friend.'

'I don't need your charity,' Romero said as he staggered to his feet and stumbled into the blazing sun. 'Don't insult me.' He picked up the five-euro note and threw it after Fernández, shouting, 'You won't buy me with that.'

Fernández turned, watching the note flutter to the floor and said, 'Then, how much will I need? How much before you tell me what I want to know? What price the truth, Felipe? What price, peace of mind for three widows?'

*

He found Rodrigo Perpiñán in his study, pouring over a set of photographs donated to him in the will of one of the village's oldest inhabitants.

'How goes it?' Perpiñán asked without looking up from a print that he was studying through a large magnifying glass.

'I could murder a coffee.'

'An unfortunate turn of phrase.' Perpiñán smiled as he rose wearily from his desk and ambled into his small kitchen. He filled the kettle, placed it on the range and spooned several heaps of coffee into a Pyrex cafeteria. 'You still driving from the city each day?' he called.

'What option do I have? It's where I live.'

'Well, if it makes it any easier, you can always crash here anytime you need to.'

'Thanks.'

They took the coffee onto the terrace and sat on white plastic chairs, taking a few moments to enjoy the tranquility, knowing that their time together would be laden with the tragedy of the past and the horror of the present.

As he finished his first cup, Perpiñán said, 'Juan Gonzales was murdered?'

'It looks like it. He was left-handed. The gun was found near his right hand. The bullet entered his right temple but exited through his lower jaw. Difficult, if not impossible, to self-inflict.'

'If he'd not been murdered, had it occurred to you that he may have turned his gun on us?'

'It crossed my mind but it's not an issue now, is it?'

'No, I suppose not, although who ever murdered *him*…'

'You want me to arrange protection?'

'No.'

82

'Even so, watch your back.' Fernández poured himself another coffee and stared absentmindedly towards the sea. 'I'm finding it difficult to accept that my father, our fathers, were responsible for such a...'

'What are you going to call it, Antonio? Wicked? Evil? Immoral?' Rodrigo Perpiñán's eyes flared suddenly. 'You think you can compare the desperation of those times with today? For God's sake, how would you feel if your mother or your sisters had been dragged through the streets, made to kneel and beg for mercy before they had the back of their heads blown off?'

Fernández nodded, but was unable to let it rest.

'Doesn't make it right, what they did. Does it?'

Perpiñán hauled himself out of the chair. 'You asked for my help. But if you want to solve these murders, you must cast aside all sentiment, all emotion, anything that will stop you seeing the truth for what it is. Yes, our fathers killed the Priest and Gonzales' parents, but given similar circumstances you and I might have done the same.'

Perpiñán's anger and passion were suddenly displaced by coldness. 'Juan Gonzales killed Alberto because he was with our fathers that night, but to think of your father, or of my father, as no better than terrorists is to deny the age in which they lived.'

The two men sat in silence, but after several minutes Perpiñán couldn't hide his impatience. 'If it had been us, you and me, we'd have reacted in the same way as they did. We'd have been at the forefront of the Resistance, no matter what the cost. You know it as well as I do.'

Fernández knew there was some truth in his friend's words: some wisdom, even. He'd grown up in a Spain struggling with its new democracy, and was part of the unsophisticated machine that was easing its people away from the horrors of Civil War and the tyranny of the Dictator towards the rule of law. And yet there had been times when he'd been called to investigate acts of violence triggered by revenge or retaliation when he'd found himself empathizing with the perpetrator – if it had been his mother or either of his sisters who had been executed by the death squad, God knows what he might have been capable of.

Perpiñán put his coffee down and wiped traces from his moustache. 'In time,' he said, his voice moderated, calm, 'you'll be able to put the barbarity of the past into some sort of perspective.'

Fernández didn't react immediately. He dragged air into his lungs, puffed out his cheeks, lifted his head and looked at his friend. 'You must have found it difficult as a child, knowing what your father had done, witnessing the slaughter. How did you cope?'

'I didn't at first. I couldn't speak to him. I withdrew, happy only when I was roaming the hills or reading. I don't mind admitting that I cried, always alone, more often at night when the nightmares returned and I saw my father slaughtering the Priest and Teresa Gonzales. But, when he was murdered, the tears dried up and I turned all my guilt and anger into caring for my mother and two younger brothers. I've dedicated my life to trying to understand what drove my father to act so…' He hesitated, and then smiled. 'And the more I know, the less I understand. You were right when you said they were products of their time. Thank God those days are behind us.'

Fernández looked at his friend. 'I spent time with my family yesterday. Mama's frail. She knows I know.'

'She's probably relieved. Feels lighter for it.'

'I left soon after I'd told her. On the way home I had difficulty holding it together.'

'Crying's not a sign of weakness, Antonio.'

'Yes, I know.' He breathed out heavily. 'Once they'd started, I couldn't stop. I was exhausted by the time it was all over.' He paused. 'Trouble was, I didn't know whether the tears were for papa, for mama, or…'

'For yourself.'

'Sounds pathetic, doesn't it?'

'Yes.'

He looked up. Rodrigo Perpiñán was grinning.

84

'You bastard.'

Perpiñán retreated to the kitchen. 'So, where do we begin?' he called.

Fernández sat silently for a few moments and then joined him. 'With the Priest's whore.'

'I was ten when our fathers killed Father Emanuel. He had always surrounded himself with youngsters from the village. He heard our confessions, encouraged us in our faith and spent time with us. I think he must have enjoyed our company.'

'And that's all he enjoyed?'

'Abuse? No, I don't think so, or rather, I don't know. Those were days of innocence, Antonio. Days when an eleven year old had no more knowledge of life than a six year old today. No one in the village had a television. Few read newspapers, or could read at all. Radios were so big they would fill a sideboard, and batteries had to be sent to the local garage to be recharged each week. Programmes, of course, were controlled by the State and listening to pirate or foreign channels was punishable by imprisonment. The only movies we saw were newsreels provided by Franco's propaganda machine. Father Emanuel made no secret of his political loyalties and Franco made sure that the church was restored to the heart of village affairs. Everyone had to go to church on Sundays and no one could marry unless they'd been baptized.' He paused. 'They called her the Priest's whore. Unfair, given her age.'

'Could they have been in love?'

'Is it important?'

Fernández began to pace the small, white-walled kitchen. 'It might be. If there was an attachment that went beyond lust or infatuation and if there was a child, we may have motive for the murder of our fathers and the execution of three men last week.' He stopped and stared down toward the vast plains that stretched towards the sea. 'You say she was fifteen?'

'More or less.'

'I need to look at every photograph you have.'

'All of them?' Perpiñán laughed. 'Then you'd better make a start.'

The wind picked up and threatened to wipe out an afternoon's work as Fernández looked at the photographs that lay on the table before him - black and white, sepia, and colour, coincidentally charting the development of photography since its earliest days.

He'd been methodical, resisting the temptation to scrutinize each image in turn, cataloguing them so that he could begin to make sense of the history each one told and the era it recorded. He was ruthless in his selection, discarding anything that didn't fit his criteria: Los Mineros, 1939 to1975.

Rodrigo Perpiñán helped him gather the prints together as the wind whipped across the campo and they retreated inside, clearing the dining table and placing each stack of photographs in some semblance of chronological order.

Perpiñán fetched a bottle of brandy and two tumblers, and a second magnifying glass. 'The brandy will help us concentrate.' He smiled and poured the first shot.

They worked into the evening and, by the time the brandy bottle was half empty, they had sorted the images into several groups: families in their Sunday best, the gathering of the harvest, proud miners and their machinery, fiestas, football teams, church services, and the slaughter of a pig.

The wind brought more heavy clouds and the heavens opened, sending torrents into the narrow streets, washing litter through the ginnels and drenching the lower meadows and orchards. As the evening drew in and a chill air nipped at their bare arms, they sat and stared at five photographs, each of which they'd placed under the magnifying glass time and time again.

The first photograph was of Pedro Perpiñán, Rodrigo's father, with his arm draped casually over the shoulder of two friends, circa1948. They were in their early twenties, eyes full of mischief, cloth caps at rakish angles, collarless shirts and braces holding up loose-fitting trousers.

The second, Pedro Fernández, circa1973, at forty-seven, holding his infant son outside their home, his wife, Adelina, straight-backed by his side.

The third was of Jésus Gonzales, circa1963, wearing a blue shirt, standing at the bar, a beer glass in one hand and what might have been a propaganda broadsheet in the other. The photograph showed the bar was full, but most of the men had turned their backs on him, whilst others stared contemptuously at the fascist agitator.

Perpiñán snatched the photograph and spat on it.

'Careful, my friend,' Fernández said. 'I may need that as evidence.'

Perpiñán was staring intently at the photograph through his magnifying glass when he said, 'Good God!'

'What is it?'

'Who's that?'

Fernández took the print from him. 'Juan Gonzales?'

'The same fascist shirt, the same arrogant expression and the same light shining from his backside.' Perpiñán poured another brandy. 'Salud, Inspector. We have our murderer, aged, what, thirty-six, thirty-seven?'

They sat in silence and enjoyed the sensation of the brandy as it warmed and befuddled them. They felt they were making progress and it felt good. Most importantly, they had two other photographs that could prove invaluable in their search for the Priest's whore.

Their contentment was cut short by the shrill of Fernández's mobile phone.

It was Leo Medina, phoning from the Town Hall. 'We've got a problem, Sir.'

'What is it Leo?'

'Uniforms are searching for a seven year old boy, Joaquin Alvarez. He didn't return home after school. He's been missing now for at least eight hours, possibly longer.' Medina sketched in the detail, adding, 'There's another kid involved. Ricardo Castro.'

'Missing?'

'No, Ricardo returned home just after four this afternoon. Soaked to the skin, his clothes torn, limping from a bad cut, one trainer missing. It was Ricardo's aunt who called us after seeing the appeal for Joaquin Alvarez on the six-thirty local news.'

'So why have we been dragged into this? The local uniform should be able to sort it out.'

'The Comandante wanted a senior officer. And since you're already in the area…'

Fernández exhaled forcefully. 'So, what time did they leave school?'

'We're checking.'

'And what's Ricardo's story?'

'He's not said a word. There's concern that he may be traumatised. The child protection team's been called in.'

'Do we have time for this?'

'It's complicated working with kids, Sir. It's late, late for a kid of seven, anyway. They're both in my eldest boy's class.'

'Ok,' Fernandez struggled to clear his head. He looked across at Perpiñán and covered the phone, saying, 'I could do with a coffee.' He returned to Leo Medina. 'Contact the Comandante and explain the situation to him. Ask him for additional bodies on the ground. Get Valencia Ramoz into the Incident Room and pull in a team from Almeria. Tell her to fire up the computers, collate information as it comes in and keep tabs on the search teams and voluntary groups, including any villagers who offer to help. Ask her to make sure every barn and out-house is searched, as well as the disused railway track and old mine workings. And ask her to contact the Policia Local and get them to conduct door-to-door enquiries. We may need the coast guard helicopter and dog handlers.' Fernandez paused as Perpiñán placed a coffee in front of him, and then asked Medina, 'What else do we know about Ricardo Castro?'

Medina gave a summary of statements taken from the staff at the primary school, a few of his classmates, neighbours, and his aunt. 'My boy says he's ok.' Medina paused. 'Where are you, sir? Do you need a lift?'

'No. I'll leave you to handle it. I'll contact Doctor Santiago. If the missing kid's dead, we'll need her on site. I'll join you as soon as I can. Start with Ricardo. Get him to talk.'

*

The terraced cottage was on the lower fringes of the village.

Leo Medina made his way towards the uniformed officer who was guarding the front door and then followed him into a small entrance hall. A narrow corridor led to a kitchen, where several skinned rabbits hung from hooks.

A stairway led to a small landing, where a door opened and a pretty woman, with tear-stained eyes and her hair pulled hard off her face, hurried down to greet them.

'Any news?' she asked.

'Mrs. Castro?'

'Her sister. Ricardo's aunt.' She gave a flustered rundown of Ricardo's background and the reasons for his arrival on her doorstep a few months ago. 'Have they found Joaquin yet?'

'I'm afraid not. Where's Ricardo?'

'Upstairs, in his bedroom. There's a policewoman with him.'

'There's a social worker on her way.'

'Perhaps we ought to wait until she arrives?'

'A child's life is at stake,' Medina said calmly. 'Any delay could mean the difference between finding Joaquin alive and being too late.'

'Perhaps I should be with you?'

'Kids tend to play adults off against one another.' Medina could sense time slipping away. 'Ricardo knows one of my boys. They're in the same class at school. It might trigger something if I speak to him.' He could sense she was wavering, as though unsure what her sister would want her to do. He began to climb the stairs. 'It'll be fine,' he said. 'Put the kettle on. We could be in for a long night.'

The police officer stood as Medina entered Ricardo's room. 'We don't seem to be getting very far, I'm afraid,' she said.

'Stay with us.' He looked about the room. A few toys were scattered on the floor; Tintin and Asterix annuals, translated from the original French, on a small bedside table.

'Hey. How y'doing?' Medina said.

Ricardo had had a bath and was dressed in striped pyjamas. He smelt clean and fresh, and was ready for bed. He was sitting up, resting on two pillows, the duvet pulled up under his chin, mouth set in defiance.

'You know why we're here?' Medina kept his voice quiet and soft.

Nothing.

'We need you to help us.'

Nothing.

'You're not in trouble.' Medina smiled and sat at the foot of Ricardo's bed, towering above him. 'We need your help to find Joaquin Alvarez.'

Nothing: stillness in the room. Medina wondered what might be going through Ricardo's mind - abandoned by his mother, taken in by an aunt a million miles from the slums of Barcelona - wondering if he'd taken a beating in the past, or been abused, wondering how resilient he was.

He sat silently for several moments and then asked,

'You know my son, Pablo?'

Ricardo stirred.

'Pablo Medina. He's in your class at school. You give the girls a hard time, from what I hear.' Medina smiled, picking up one of the Tintin annuals. 'He often talks about you. You're his best mate, he says. You swap comics and play football together on the way home. Pablo says you're a bit tasty.'

Ricardo stirred, his legs curled up under his chin.

90

'Pablo reckons Joaquin Alvarez is a bit of a wimp.'

Ricardo snorted.

'Not one of your friends.'

'As if.'

'Doesn't even play football,' Medina laughed.

'He's crap.'

'Clever though.'

Ricardo looked up. 'Yeah, 'spose so - gets everything right in the tests Miss gives us.'

'Pablo says you're pretty smart. You keep getting better marks than him in everything.'

''Cept in maths. Your Pablo's bloody good at maths.' Ricardo stifled a laugh. 'S'why I sit next to him if Miss don't spot us and move me next to some stupid girl.' He looked at Medina as he added, 'Your Pablo's a big bugger, like you. He can handle himself. He's a good friend.' Tears welled up in his eyes, ''Spose you'll tell him we can't go round together?'

'And why would I do that?'

''Cause!' he shouted. ''Cause you think I did it on purpose.'

'Did what?'

'Joaquin followed me. I didn't want him to come. He hangs round me like a fly round shit.'

'So, that makes you the shit?' Medina smiled.

'You know what I mean.' Ricardo's face cracked for a moment, a hint of a smile.

Medina sat quietly watching the turmoil on his face. Ricardo sniffed, wiped his nose and eyes on the duvet cover, and rested his chin on his knees, staring down at a point midway between him and Medina. 'I didn't kill him,' he muttered.

'He may not be dead, but we won't know until we find him.'

'I didn't kill him. He fell.'

'Where was this?'

'In that old mine. We climbed down this ladder and went exploring. We thought we'd found treasure. But it wasn't. It was…'

'What? What did you find down there Ricardo?'

'I tried to help him but he fell.'

Medina moved closer and spoke quietly. 'Joaquin may still be alive. You can help us. Will you do that, Ricardo? Will you show me where you went?'

'I'll have to get dressed first.' Ricardo began to get out of bed, easing the duvet down and swinging his legs onto the floor. 'Can you get me aunt?'

'Of course.'

Medina's smile faded as Ricardo said, 'Joaquin ain't the only one down there. We found someone else.'

*

Sofia Castaño was sitting in a neighbour's doorway stroking a cat when she saw an old woman talking to the Mayor. She watched as the Mayor listened intently and then hurried away from the Town Hall. She felt sure that his urgency could mean only one thing - something exciting was happening. She left the cat and scampered after him.

By the time she'd reached the Plaza de la Libertad she was fighting for breath. She rested her hands on her knees and dragged muggy air into her lungs, and then scurried onto a terrace overlooking the village. From there, she saw the Mayor down near the cemetery, hurrying towards a group of older kids who were checking out a flash-looking car. She watched the Mayor speak to them and watched them disperse.

When most of the kids had gone, Sofia could see the car with its snarling, big-cat-grill and knew instantly who it belonged to. She couldn't wait to get home to tell mama that her brother José had driven down from Madrid and was in the village.

*

The collapse in the demand for iron ore and its plunging market value hastened the demise of the mining industry around Los Mineros, but it was the succession of accidental explosions and cave-ins during the last years of the mine's working life that proved to be its death-knell, throwing men and their families out onto the street.

Every child in the village had been told a thousand times not to play in or near the abandoned mine workings or trample across the campo and risk falling into unmarked, vertical mine shafts. But after what he'd been told about his background, Leo Medina wasn't surprised that Ricardo Castro had chosen to ignore the warnings and skip school earlier that day.

With dark clouds rumbling above them and the first drops of heavy rain splashing to the ground, Medina held Ricardo's hand as they made their way over a carpet of thick gorse that covered an old spoil-heap. Stark against the backdrop of the hillside, the mine's ruins appeared sombre and dejected, whilst wind that accompanied the rain howled among the ruins, as though lamenting the dereliction. As they approached the entrance to the mining complex, the rain became more insistent, sheet lightning rent the sky and thunder rumbled about them. Two huge wooden doors, sagging on rusting hinges, had been pushed open and rusting cart rails disappeared into the darkness of the mine.

He placed a hand on Ricardo's shoulder and smiled reassuringly as the young boy looked up at him, eyes wide and fearful. They made their way into the tunnel, arc lights blazing where Ricardo's torch had shone earlier that day, and retraced the route they'd taken, stopping at the top of a ladder. 'He's down there,' he said, tears staining his face.

Several uniformed officers clambered down the ladder, followed by a medical team.

'Is Joaquin alright?' Ricardo said. 'Is he dead?'

'No, I don't think so. The doctors are doing everything they can to keep him alive.' Medina took his hand. 'You mustn't blame yourself. Understand? It was not your fault. It was an accident.'

Ricardo nodded, but his head dropped. Medina knelt down; his eyes level with Ricardo's face. 'You said there was someone else down here.'

'Yes.' Ricardo moved to the top of the ladder.

'You want to show me?'

At the bottom of the ladder, Ricardo led him into the darkness, glancing backwards and stumbling as he tried to see what was happening to his classmate.

As they approached the mouth of a large chamber, Ricardo hesitated, pointing towards a roll of polythene on a raised platform lit by diffused light from a vertical shaft.

Medina felt his pulse quicken, wondering what the boys had been doing in the mine and what they might have seen hidden beneath the shroud of polythene. 'Let's get you out of here.'

He handed Ricardo over to a uniformed police officer, watched him climb the ladder, and then glanced over at Fernandez and Doctor Santiago who had just arrived and were listening to the paramedic's initial diagnosis of Joaquin's condition. 'He's probably sustained multiple fractures from the fall and lost a lot of blood from a wound to the back of his head. We'll need to secure him and evacuate to hospital.'

'There's a helicopter on standby,' Medina heard Fernandez say and then waited as the Inspector and Doctor Santiago made their way into the chamber and across to the raised platform.

Part of the polythene had come away and a cotton sheet had been exposed to rain funnelling down the vertical shaft, making it translucent. Santiago cut away the remaining polythene, looked at Fernandez and took a deep breath before peeling back the cotton.

The young woman's head rolled to face them, her eyes open, staring, her mouth locked in a hideous grin, her lower jaw

94

gaping to one side, her skin pale and grey, her matted blond hair stained dark.

Medina recognised her instantly.

Santiago began an abridged examination in light provided by a hand-held tungsten torch. 'She's female. Caucasian. Her throat's been cut. There's damage to the structure of the face.' She pointed at bruising to cheek and forehead. 'Probably a man's fist. Several teeth are missing, although there's enough to cross check with her dental records. The jaw's dislocated. I won't know until after I've carried out an autopsy whether the knife wound to the throat was fatal, or whether it was post-mortem.'

She knelt beside the platform to examine the arm and forefinger of the right hand. 'We'll take nail clippings and scrapings. If she put up a struggle, we maybe lucky, but don't hold your breath: DNA from under the nails can produce misleading profiles.' She stood up, took a pair of scissors from her black bag and cut away the polythene, easing the white sheet away from the body and providing a commentary. 'Although the body appears relatively fresh, bacteria will have broken out of the intestine and started digesting internal organs. Flies would have been attracted to her body from the moment she died, laying eggs around any open wounds as well as the mouth, nose, eyes, anus, and genitalia. I'll get a entomologist to check the rate and progress of infestation.'

'Approximate time of death?'

'Sometime between the last time she was seen and when the body was discovered.' She looked at him. 'This isn't a TV cop drama, Inspector. I'll know more after I've carried out my tests. Even then, pin-pointing the time of death won't be easy.'

'Did she die down here?'

'It's possible but unlikely.' Santiago spent several more minutes examining the body before she said, 'She was probably killed elsewhere, then dumped down here. You know her?'

'No.'

She covered the body and stood up as Leo Medina joined them. 'Let's get her out of here,' she said. 'I'll know more by tomorrow. If she's local, dental and finger-print records will help provide a positive ID.'

'She's local,' Medina said, his voice strangled by emotions that pitched up from his gut, tears welling. He moved forward and looked intently at the face of a woman he'd known all his life. 'It's Laura. Laura Domingo.'

Day Six

Tuesday 23rd June 2009

Fernández made sure that Julieta Santiago had all she needed and that the crime scene was secure. It was two o'clock in the morning before he got away, cutting a lonely figure as he walked through the deserted streets towards Perpiñán's cottage.

He pushed through a half open door, apologized and slumped into the fireside chair.

'Trouble?'

'Bank manager's son's had a serious accident. He and another boy were playing in the old mine.'

'God, how many times do they have to be told?'

Fernández sucked in air and exhaled forcefully.

'Antonio?'

'We've found the body of Laura Domingo. Carlos's daughter.'

'Engaged to José Castaño?'

'Her throat's been slit.'

'Oh, Jesus.'

'Sound familiar?'

Soon after the church clock struck four-thirty, another thunderstorm broke and torrential rain cascaded off the roof and on to the terrace. Fernández woke with a start to find his friend proffering a cup of coffee.

They sat out the storm, drank more coffee and put the small hours to good use, studying two photographs they hoped would hold the key to last Thursday's murders.

The first photograph was a group portrait of a dozen or more teenagers, dressed in pantomime clothing and standing beside a billboard outside the village hall. The billboard heralded their interpretation of La Cenicienta, based on the story of Cinderella, the dates of the performances clearly visible.

'Three nights only!' The 6th, 7th and 8th of December 1973, a white sash, *'Sold out'* draped across the billboard.

The youngsters appeared to be embarrassed by all the fuss. Buttons stood sheepishly at the end of the row in his tight-fitting pageboy costume and pillbox hat. The fairy godmother's tutu displayed her ample legs and thighs, and was clearly several sizes too small. The Prince stood in the middle, his face up-turned, appearing disdainful of everyone around him. The two ugly sisters, gaudy in their layers of thickly applied make up, made sure the camera recorded their wickedness, creating impromptu grimaces that belonged more to Halloween than the spirit of the season. Cinders smiled sweetly beneath a dislodged tiara. Her soft, round face framed by long dark-hair, her large eyes shining at the camera. The rest of the cast huddled around the central characters, grinning playfully.

Fernández knew that adolescence could re-draw faces, altering features as an artist might rework a portrait. The inexpertly applied stage make-up disguised rather than enhanced faces in the pantomime photograph, making it difficult to match all eight of the teenagers with those who appeared in the second photograph.

It had been taken in May, earlier the same year. The group was standing outside the massive oak doors at the entrance to the village church, smiling proudly, carrying bibles or prayer books. The four boys looked awkward in dark suits and white shirts. The girls appeared demure in long, white dresses, white socks, black shiny shoes and white bonnets.

In both photographs, the village Priest stood behind one of the girls - the same girl. In the photograph of the pantomime, lost but for the power of Rodrigo's magnifying glass, the Priest's right arm had slipped behind her back, his hand resting on her hip.

As the storm abated and the church clock struck eight-fifteen, Fernández made his way to the doctor's surgery. When he'd settled on a seat in the corner of the crowded waiting room, he took the photographs, magnifying glass and calculator out of a document case he'd borrowed from Perpiñán.

It wasn't long before questions began demanding answers: could Cinders have been the Priest's whore? Had the photograph caught them at a moment of shared intimacy, or was the Priest simply pulling her into the frame? If she had been fifteen at the time the photograph, she'd be in her early fifties now. If she'd been pregnant at the time, her child would be in her mid-thirties.

He stared at the photographs, wary of being presumptive: he couldn't even be certain that it was the Priest who'd fathered the child.

An hour later, the doctor beckoned him into his room.

Javier Guzmán was a locum covering for the village doctor who had been indisposed for the last three months, suffering from a severe bout of gout. Young, handsome, and immaculately dressed in light trousers and green shirt with a white collar, Guzmán looked incongruous in the stark, sparse surroundings of the village surgery.

He took a file out of the cabinet in the corner of the room, confirmed that he had been on duty when the couple had brought Juan Gonzales to the surgery a month ago, and then used his notes to remind himself of the salient details:

The old man had collapsed and was unconscious when they'd found him. He'd been sent for a scan at the public hospital in Almeria and had been diagnosed with a malignant primary brain tumour at an advanced stage. Treatments, including steroids, the implant of a shunt to relieve intracranial pressure, surgery, radiology, and chemotherapy had been discussed with the patient. He had been warned that the symptoms he'd been experiencing - vomiting, headaches, problems with vision - would become more severe. The type of seizure he'd experienced when he'd collapsed would become more frequent and life threatening. He would suffer problems with coordination,

99

balance and speech, as well as the ability to carry out fine motor activities such as writing. If the tumour spread into both lobes, his temperament and personality would also be affected.

In short, unless anyone was prepared to administer the palliative care he needed, Juan Gonzales would die, alone and wretched. And, in any case, if he refused treatment, he'd probably succumb before summer was out.

Juan Gonzales had rejected all medical care, returned home and had not visited the doctor again.

Dr. Guzmán closed the file. 'I understand he blew his brains out last week, after murdering three men.'

'It's not as simple as that, I'm afraid. I'd like a copy of his medical history.'

'Do you have a court order?'

'That would take time.'

'Nonetheless…'

'Time I don't have.'

Guzmán sighed and shook his head. 'Very well, if you think it's absolutely necessary.'

'Thank you. Grateful for your cooperation.' Fernández glanced down at the tubular bandage extending from just below the elbow and covering much of the doctor's right hand. 'You look like you've been in the wars yourself.'

'A precaution. I sprained it during a fishing trip last week. I need to be fit for a golf tournament in a few days.' He hesitated. 'Look, Inspector, if there's nothing more, I really am very busy.'

'Tell me about the good Samaritans who brought him to you.'

'There's not a lot to tell. I hadn't seen them before. My visits to the village are irregular and neither of them had attended surgery whilst I'd been on duty. For all I know, they may live in the village, or could have been passing through. If it helps, the woman spoke with an Andalucian accent. By that I mean…'

'I know what you mean, doctor.'

'Yes, I'm sure you do.'

Fernández let the condescension slide. 'The couple? Can you describe them for me?'

'The woman was middle aged, silver hair tied back in a chignon, matronly, not unlike many Spanish women of her age.'

'That's it?'

'What do you expect? I was trying to save a man's life.'

'So nothing that would help you pick her out in an identity parade?'

Guzmán laughed and shook his head. 'You don't honestly think she had anything to do with the old man's death, do you?'

'But you'd recognise her again?'

'Possibly, but I wouldn't bet on it. She'd probably have been quite attractive - handsome face, large eyes - but she'd let herself go.'

'And the man?'

'Her companion?'

'Her companion? They weren't married?'

'No, I don't think so. He'd carried Juan Gonzales into the surgery but didn't say a great deal. He was younger than the woman. Ten years, maybe less.' Guzmán pushed errant strands of pale, thin hair from his forehead. 'They left soon after I'd stabilised the old man.' He shuffled several folders on his desk, tidying them into a plastic tray and looked at his watch. 'If that's all, Inspector, close the door on your way out.'

Being dismissed didn't sit well. He sat on the edge of the doctor's desk, lit a cigarette and blew a lungful of smoke into the air. 'You can make a copy of that medical report now. I'll wait.'

*

In the stark, stainless steel confines of the climate-controlled laboratory deep in the basement of Almeria's public hospital, Doctor Julieta Santiago was not relishing the challenge presented by the body of Laura Domingo. In the early stages of decay, it was always difficult to be precise about the time of death, despite the calculations she had already made.

After Laura's clothing had been stripped away, the extent of her injuries was clearly evident. She hadn't died in the mine. The telltale purple-blue tinge to the skin in the lower abdomen and thigh confirmed that during the first few hours of death she had been lying on her side. She'd sustained injuries, post-mortem, to the head, legs and spinal column when she'd been dropped down the shaft.

'You OK?' she asked her technician.

'Yes,' he said, 'as long as I don't think of her as a young woman in the prime of her life.' He turned his face away from her and back to the corpse lying on the cold slab.

'She deserves our very best attention and that's what's she'd going to get, eh?' She examined the deep cut in Laura's neck that had nearly severed the cervical vertebrae, then prepared for surgery. 'Let's see what other tales she has to tell us, shall we?'

The body had been through a complete cycle of rigor mortis, indicating that death had occurred more than two days ago. Core temperature, confirmed on-site, was close to the mine's ambient temperature, eighteen degrees, although the insulation provided by the cotton sheet and polythene could have delayed the decrease.

DNA and fingerprint samples had been sent to the Policia Nacional headquarters to be cross-referenced on the national database and through Interpol.

A specialist forensic entomologist had checked the progress and extent of infestation and had confirmed that eggs, laid by flies in the first few hours of death, had hatched and larvae had begun to pupate, indicating that they were over forty-eight hours old.

Santiago settled on an approximate time of death, the furthest she was prepared to stick her neck out at this stage: more than two days, less than three.

They worked methodically for several hours, before she left her technician to finish up and, checking the time, she went to her office and drew breath before calling Antonio Fernandez.

Fernández had waited for a copy of Juan Gonzales's medical records and then made his way to the bar.

The Brits had colonised the white plastic seats on the terrace next to the road and were lost in strident conversation, barely noticing as he passed and went into the bar.

Inside, men stood silently, picking at their tapas, their despondency contrasting sharply with the bright sunshine glistening on surface water left behind by the early morning storm. The news of Joaquin's accident and the discovery of a body in the mine had hit home, compounding the shock and the trauma of the deaths of the three Ramos men. The sorrow of those in the bar was palpable, threatening to suffocate their natural optimism - untimely deaths, deaths on their own doorstep, too close to home.

In the eyes of those who hadn't turned their backs on him, Fernández thought he detected a shift in demeanour and he hoped they might begin to open up.

He ordered an expresso, placed the document case on the top of the bar and savoured the first sip of strong coffee as it roasted the back of this throat. He took a serviette from the dispenser on the bar, scribbled his name and the contact details of the Incident Room at the Town Hall and announced, 'If you think of anything, there'll be someone to take your call. Day or night.'

He took his coffee outside, pulling up a chair at the Brits' table. 'Mind if I join you?' They nodded, shuffled to make room for him and fell silent. Fernández smiled. It wasn't the first time his presence had sent conversation into freefall.

'I was hoping you'd be a little more forthcoming.'

'It's such a sad business,' an elderly woman said.

'Heartbreaking,' said the woman next to her.

They fell silent and returned to their coffee and toast.

'But the boy's alright. I mean, he'll live, won't he?' a man asked from the other end of the table.

'Touch and go. It's too early to tell,' Fernández said.

'If there's anything we can do.'

'We know the family, of course.'

'The boy's father manages the village bank.'

'I think they'd prefer to be left alone.'

'But it was an accident?'

'Yes.'

'Is it true? A woman's body's been found?'

'Yes, but you'll appreciate that until she's been formally identified I can't comment further.'

'We'd heard, but just couldn't believe it,' said a thin-lipped, thin-faced man, his eyes darting back and forth as he screwed up a serviette. 'I've lived here for over twenty years. I wouldn't swap it for the world, but when something like this happens, it shakes you.'

'I agree.' Adam Wells, a well-known local artist, pushed hair from his forehead.'But there have been tensions in the village for years. It's such a small community; you can't sneeze without everyone catching a cold. Keeps the local press busy, reporting disputes between neighbours over boundaries, water cut off after an argument, homes bull-dozed to the ground.'

Klaus Dagmar put down his toast and wiped his mouth. 'Tensions lie much deeper - way back in the past. The Civil War tore this country apart and Franco did nothing to heel the wounds. Corruption and nepotism are still endemic. Establishing the Rule of Law remains one of Spain's greatest challenges.' He sat back and folded his arms.

Fernández rested his elbows on the white tabletop and his chin on his fists. It would have been easy for him to dismiss their observations as ill informed, but they were not far off the mark: there were still those in Spain who refused to accept that the Law applied to everyone.

He looked down the length of the table, scanning each face, settling on Klaus Dagmar's for a moment before saying, 'We've set up an Incident Room at the Town Hall. We're treating the events of the past few days as three separate investigations: the murder of a young woman; last Thursday's execution of three men; and the murder of the man who killed them.'

'It was murder then? He didn't commit suicide?' Dagmar said. 'Presumably you're looking for someone in the village?'

Fernández hesitated, raising his head as a cobra might before it strikes. 'I may not have to look any further than this table.'

'Now, look here, Inspector, you're not suggesting...'

He got up, lit a cigarette and said, 'Juan Gonzales was murdered. Whoever pulled the trigger had not done his homework - an amateur who thought he'd committed the perfect murder, but forgot to check which hand his victim used to wipe his backside. The woman found in the mine last night was probably dumped a few days ago and the man who threw her body down the shaft assumed that it would be months, if not years, before she was found - and he may have been right, but for two young boys.' He paused before he turned on Klaus Dagmar. 'You're right. I won't be looking very far from the village, but it would be a mistake to think that my investigation will be restricted to local Spanish.' He threw a euro onto the table to cover his coffee. 'Have nice day.'

*

Ana-Marie checked her reflection in the full-length mirror, her white cotton robe falling casually open, the bump just beginning to show. She clamped the phone between her shoulder and neck and began towel-drying her hair 'Mama? I got your message. Is José with you?'

'No, he's not here. Why didn't you call back last night? I've spent the whole night worrying.'

'Oh, come on mama! José's a big boy now. He probably drove Laura back from Madrid after the match on Sunday and they're making up for lost time.'

'If that relationship's based on lust, it'll not last.'

'I'm sure they're very much in love. You'll remember

105

what it was like, in those early days, you and Papa? You probably couldn't keep your hands off each other.'

'We was both very young...'

'And oh, so innocent, Inocenta?' Ana-Marie laughed, glancing out at the beach and the calm sea sipping at golden sand.

'You shouldn't tease me like that. You'll see me into an early grave. Sofia's always wandering off, José's in Madrid, and you're putting my grandchild at risk. You shouldn't drink, you know, not when you're pregnant.'

'Mama, your grandson will be fine.'

'It's a boy then?'

'The scan confirmed it. I even saw his little penis.'

'Ana-Marie!' They both laughed.

Ana-Marie walked into her dressing room and saw her full-time maid changing the bed. She watched her for a few moments as she struggled with the weight of the mattress and then returned to her phone call. 'I've got to run a few errands, but then I'll drive over to see you. Where did you say Sofia saw José's car?'

'Near the cemetery.'

'The Mayor hasn't impounded it, or towed it away?'

'I've no idea. Probably been vandalised by now.'

The maid knocked on the door, apologised for disturbing her and asked for clean sheets.

'They're where they always are.'

'I'm sorry Ma'am, but I can't find them.'

'Then use a new set. They're in the airing cupboard.'

'Yes, ma'am. Thank you ma'am.'

Ana-Marie sighed and shook her head. She would talk to Paul about replacing her. Maybe they ought to employ a proper housekeeper and let her sort out all the domestic arrangements. It would cost more, but if Paul landed the Almeria regeneration project they'd be able to afford a dozen housekeepers.

She pressed the speaker button on the phone, began to apply her make-up and tried to reassure her mother.

'Paul's in the village this morning, supervising the restoration of the church. He's off to England tomorrow. He said he was going to pop in and see you. I'll drive over. We'll come for lunch. Anyway, stop worrying. José and Laura will turn up.'

*

Back at the Incident Room, Fernández sought somewhere he could draw breath as the morning's civilian support began to filter in. He grabbed a coffee and escaped onto a small balcony at the rear of the Town Hall. A collapsible chair had been propped up in the corner and he wrestled with it impatiently before managing to open it. He sat down, took a deep breath and shut his eyes.

Ten minutes later, Jacinta Estrada stepped out onto the balcony to light up her first cigarette of the day. 'Good morning, Sir.'

'Let's hope so,' he said, easing out of the chair.

Estrada was smiling at him like a young mother at a lazy child. The daughter of Ecuadorian immigrants, she was short, with dark skin, dark eyes and jet-black hair platted into a braid. Her eyes seemed to light up whenever she found anything remotely amusing and her enthusiasm for her job was infectious, but anyone thinking she'd be a soft touch would be in for a shock. She'd been promoted after several years in Barcelona, working for the vice squad and then training for an elite firearms response team. In her spare time, she taught self-defence to women who'd been abused. Since she'd been transferred to his patch, Fernández had taken personal interest in the career of Sargento Jacinta Estrada and he was delighted to have her on board.

He followed her into the Incident Room.

Shots of Laura Domingo were displayed on one of the white boards, and scene-of-crime photographs of Juan Gonzales, as well as Alberto, Bartolomé and Matias Ramos, had been pinned to another. Fernández watched the officers and support staff bustling about their business. He hated the profligate circus of a large investigation – computers, civilian staff, meetings, superiors to update, and the media. He would have preferred to work alone, but his designation as Senior Investigating Officer meant he was a reluctant ringmaster.

He'd already delegated the running of the Incident Room to Jacinta Estrada and she brought him up to speed. With Joaquin Alvarez on life support and Laura Domingo's body awaiting autopsy, Fernández's superiors had begun to throw resources his way. More computer and technical back up had been made available; Estrada and Leo Medina drafted in full-time. Staff had worked through the night, firing up computers, storing information gleaned so far in each of the cases, and installing software that enabled them to exchange information with forces throughout Europe.

Leo Medina came in and threw himself into a chair opposite the Inspector.

'OK?' Fernández said.

'Been better.'

'I'm sorry about Laura.'

'Such a fucking waste.'

'Just make sure we catch the bastard, right?'

'Yeah.' Medina's breath seemed to catch in his throat, and it was clear he was struggling.

'You did well with Joaquin.'

'Thanks. I went to his home, took the parents to see him in hospital. He's in Intensive Care. The next forty-eight hours are crucial. Mother collapsed at his bedside, needed sedation. Father seems bent on pointing the finger and probably won't be happy until someone's head's on the block.'

'Not our problem, thank God.' Fernández paused. 'I'm waiting to hear from Dr. Santiago. Laura's autopsy.'

Medina shrugged, hauled himself out of the chair and went to make a coffee.

Estrada came over and sat on the edge of the Inspector's desk. 'I've been reviewing missing person case files of over the last couple of weeks. We're awaiting confirmation of a couple of items found on her. I thought it would be better to be absolutely sure before going to see her father.'

'It is Laura,' Medina said, a flash of anger in his voice. 'She...' He hesitated. 'We dated, way back, no more than kids.'

'Has anyone reported her missing?' Fernández asked.

'Nothing in the records, Sir.'

'I saw her on Friday night, at the fiesta,' Medina said. 'She was with Sofia, Ana-Marie's little sister. Sofia was prattling on about a game of hide-and-seek.'

'With Gloria?' Fernández said.

'Yeah. Laura took her back to Ana-Marie. I followed, caught the tail-end of the excitement caused by a text message Laura received from Ana-Marie's brother.'

'José? Played for Real Madrid reserves, Thursday evening?'

'He was pulled off at half-time, made his first team debut in an exhibition match on Sunday. That's what all the fuss was about. Laura left the fiesta soon after receiving the text. She was going to fly up to Madrid on Saturday morning.'

'Makes sense. She was due to dance flamenco at El Morato on Saturday evening. She didn't turn up.'

'It takes an hour, at most, to get to the airport,' Estrada said. 'So, where was she between midnight on Friday and the time she should have boarded the flight?'

'Check out the flight manifests and the airport CCTV. Ask the Madrid police to pull José Castaño in for questioning. Let me know when they've located him.' Fernández paused before adding, 'Contact the Public Prosecutor's Office. Ask the judge to issue a search warrant for tomorrow morning – we'll pay our friend Felipe Romero another visit.' He turned to Medina. 'You feel up to seeing Laura's father?'

'Yeah. I'd like to be there. It'll probably kill him. Poor bastard.'

The phone rang and Fernández lent wearily across his desk. 'Yes?'

'I hope I didn't wake you, Inspector?'

'Doctor Santiago. What've you got for me?'

'An update on Laura Domingo's autopsy. We may never know for certain but it looks as though she'd been killed elsewhere and thrown down the mineshaft. She was knocked unconscious by repeated blows to the head and body and then someone then slit her throat. The knife was sharp, long bladed. She bled to death, was wrapped in a cotton sheet and polythene, and then dumped. She did not go quietly. If tissue found under her nails doesn't match her gene profile, it might help you secure a conviction. If you want to drop by at about six this evening, I might have more for you.' Santiago paused and he sensed she had something else to share with him.

'Doctor?'

'When you're considering motives for such a brutal attack, you should include impending paternity. Laura Domingo was pregnant.'

*

Carlos Domingo used to like mornings.

In the summer, he would have been up at daybreak and put in several hours before grilling bacon and enjoying a toasted sandwich washed down by strong coffee. The winter months had always been slower, the days shorter. The olive crop would ripen, be harvested and taken to the local cooperative press. As April got into its stride, he would check on his orchard of apple, orange and lemon trees. In May and throughout the summer, he used to take on itinerant help from South America or from Eastern Europe, not knowing or caring if the immigrants were illegal.

But he hadn't found a buyer for the fruit, or the cauliflower, broccoli and potatoes he'd planted hoping they'd be snapped up by big-chain supermarkets.

The recession had put paid to the good times, and now the farm was a one-man show, his days were long, grindingly hard, and every penny was ploughed back into the business. Two

110

months ago the bank manager had called him in and told him they could no longer extend his credit. The farm and all he had worked for was at risk.

Carlos's health was also failing. He had an appointment to see Dr. Javier Guzmán sometime soon.

If only Marta was here. God hadn't given them enough time for the number of kids they'd planned in the early days of their courtship. When Marta died soon after giving birth to Laura, Carlos had poured all of his anger, passion, grief and love into nurturing his baby girl.

Laura took to school and did well, but couldn't wait for her father's mud-splattered, series-one Defender to pull up outside the school gates so that she could lend a hand with the chores on the farm. She'd helped at harvest time and learned to use his twelve bore to kill the foxes that ate chickens and attacked lambs. She'd grown up around animals, had watched them mate and helped when they had their young. She blossomed into the most beautiful of teenagers, driving him mad with her stubbornness and her ardent defense of her independence. When she left school, she went on to the University in Almeria and had just finished her final exams after three years. She'd brought friends home - young men with ridiculous goatee beards and young women who seemed strangely at odds with Laura, their faces plastered with heavy make-up, hair streaked with gaudy colours. She would encourage them to help out when the farm got busy. They would drink cheap wine and make music, kidding themselves that they could be the next 'big thing'. They'd even cut a demo disc, sent it to recording company and waited for the call that never came.

And then, three days ago, Laura had disappeared.

Carlos had been over it a thousand times. She'd come home from the fiesta, earlier than he'd expected. She had packed, leaving him a note on the kitchen table:

Off 2 Madrid! José in RM's 1st team! Luv. L xx

He'd heard a car pull up in the small hours - two o'clock, maybe. He'd managed to clamber out of bed, assuming she'd ordered a taxi, but was too late to see which firm she'd used. It had not occurred to him until a few hours later that she had left much earlier than would have been necessary to catch a flight to Madrid.

Later that morning, he'd tried to phone the airport, but got a recorded message asking him to 'choose from the following options'. He'd given up after getting confused.

Fernández pulled over at the gate that barred entry into Domingo Farm. Medina got out, pushed it open and was greeted by half a dozen geese, led by a much larger gander hissing and screaming, flapping its wings and threatening to attack. Two German Shepherds barked and snarled, baring their teeth.

Suddenly, a human voice railed above them and Carlos Domingo filled the doorjamb of the farmhouse door. 'What's your business?' he said, cradling an axe he'd been sharpening.

'We're police officers, Señor Domingo.' He flashed his ID and introduced Medina. The gander had positioned itself between them and the farmhouse and was advancing.

'Best come in then,' Carlos said. 'Don't mind them. You'll come to no harm, unless they smell fear, then I can't be held responsible for what they might do.' He disappeared inside and Fernández looked across at Medina.

Medina strolled briskly across the yard, mud oozing from beneath the soles of his shoes as he headed straight for the steps leading up to the wooden door that was lodged half open. As Fernandez followed, the dogs continued to rail against their presence and when he misplaced a foot on the bottom of the three steps, the gander attacked, knocking him off balance. He fell awkwardly and the other geese moved in, their noise intensifying as they sensed his panic. Medina pulled Fernández to his feet, kicked out at the gaggle's ringleader and bundled him inside.

'Always got to show them who's boss,' Carlos said as he took the kettle off the range and poured hot water onto the instant coffee he'd spooned into three mugs. 'Sit down. Help yourselves to milk and sugar.'

As Medina slid one of the heavy wooden chairs from under the table, the farmer said, 'Do I know you?'

'Yes. Laura and I,' Medina hesitated, the crushing enormity of their visit pounding in his chest. 'We were close for a while. A long time ago.' He tried to smile but failed, averting his eyes downwards.

Fernández took a mug off the table and glanced around the kitchen. Logs were piled to one side of the open fireplace, ready for winter. The range had blackened by years of use. Photographs clustered together on the long oak mantelpiece above the hearth. Two were of young women, both remarkably alike, but the age of the photographs suggested that the one taken in the orchard was that of Laura's mother, and the other, sitting on the top step outside the farmhouse door, was of Laura. Other photographs were of Laura with groups of friends - mucking out the pigs, riding on the back of an open truck, at a party, a fiesta, and on a field trip as part of her University course.

'This must be Laura,' Fernández said. 'May I?'

Carlos shrugged.

'And your wife?' He held both photographs, his heart shredding at the sight of the two beautiful women with their strong jaw line, long blond hair, open-faces and blue eyes that shone with love and youthful vitality.

'This ain't a social call, so if you've got something to say, you'd best be out with it.'

He replaced the photographs. 'Yesterday afternoon, during the search for a missing boy, the body of a young woman was found in the old mine workings outside the village.'

Carlos's eyes narrowed and he looked at Fernández.

'We have reason to believe that the young woman is your daughter, Laura.'

Carlos looked down at the flagstone floor. 'No.' He shook his head slowly, his voice barely above a whisper. 'No.'

'We've recovered a few items that may have been hers.' Fernández paused. 'The initial examination suggests that she died about three days ago.'

Carlos began to rock back and forth, slowly. 'Saturday,' he said. 'The morning she left home and didn't come back.' He moved over to the hearth and placed his hands on the mantelpiece, leaning forward, his head bowed, fighting for breath, powerful arms trembling as his body began to convulse.

'We'll need to take a statement from you.'

'Can I see her?'

'Yes. Yes, of course. We'll need you to identify her before we can be certain.'

'I want to be left alone with her,' he said, his voice no more than a whisper.

'I'm afraid that's not going to be possible…' Fernández began, not anticipating the farmer's reaction. Carlos charged at him, catching him on the side of his head and knocking him to the ground.

'I will spend time with her!' He screamed as he stood over Fernández.

Medina pulled at the farmer's massive shoulders, tearing him away, pushing him back against the mantelpiece and standing between him and Fernández. 'She's at peace,' he said, calmly. 'No more harm can come to her. I'll take you to see her. But, we need your help for the formal identification.'

Carlos Domingo fell silent. He pushed past Medina and slumped into the fireside chair, unable to stop the tears as his life crumbled around him. Minutes passed before he stood up and turned on Fernández again. 'You're sure it's her?'

'Yes, I'm sorry. If I could make this go away, believe me I would.'

*

114

Throughout the day, local and National TV ran special news bulletins that carried updates on Joaquin Alvarez's progress - still in a coma, still on life support.

Soon after Carlos Domingo had confirmed that the body at the morgue was his daughter, a press statement was issued and a recent photograph of Laura appeared on TV - her beautiful, blond hair cascading onto her shoulders, her blue eyes full of the excitement of youth and her confident, infectious smile beaming out at the viewer. Maps pinpointing the location of the mine and diagrams illustrating the layout of the complex of tunnels pinpointed where Joaquin and Laura had been found.

The final feature of the day's news was reserved for a profile on Real Madrid's latest rising star - shots of José Castaño waving to the crowd as he ran onto the hallowed turf at the San Bernabeu, Sunday's match his first outing in the all-white strip in front of the passionate Madrid fans, playing alongside Los Galácticos. After the game, the press had hounded him for an impromptu interview and José had stood, acknowledging the adulation of the crowd, as he shouted into half-a-dozen microphones.

*

The chill of the church was a welcome relief for Ana-Marie as she pushed open the heavy oak door and stepped reverently towards the top of the nave. She crossed herself and genuflected, lifting her eyes from the cold stone floor and staring at the crucifixion. She spent a few moments, lost in a short prayer, and then crossed herself again before pushing herself upright. It would be more difficult, she knew, as time went on, but if she maintained her fitness, ate well and cut down on the booze, she would soon regain her figure after the baby boy was born.

It was the first time she had been to the church since the renovation had begun. She hadn't expected it to be so quiet and, as she moved down the nave towards the altar she called, 'Hallo!'

She stood before the font. They hadn't agreed on a name, but now that they knew it was a boy she'd settled on Enrique, after her father.

'Hallo?' she tried again and walked over to the massive tarpaulin draped over the chancel screen and across the entrance to the Lady Chapel, shielding worshippers from the latest phase of the renovation. She eased the tarpaulin back and peered into the dank gloom. The stairwell to the crypt had been demolished and a concrete ramp installed to facilitate access to the catacomb below.

She walked a few paces down the ramp and paused to listen. 'Hallo?' she called once more, then noticed a plastic cable, with a switch on one end fastened to the ancient granite wall. She flicked the switch and the cavern below was bathed in harsh florescent light.

'Hallo.' Her voice sounded shrill, disappearing into the numerous passages and burial chambers that had been unearthed recently. Amid the rubble, there was a small Bobcat digger with its shovel suspended in mid-air like a praying mantis, the slurry of its feeding frenzy strewn across the floor - stones, earth, blocks torn from tombs and the remnants of a pillar. Five boreholes, each excavated recently, had been filled with rubble, two more with fresh concrete.

The silence of the church had tracked Ana-Marie into the crypt, cloaking her in a numbness that chilled and frightened her, making her shudder. She turned to make her way back up the concrete ramp, when she stopped and retraced her steps to the edge of one of the boreholes. Something on the floor, glinting in the fluorescent light, had caught her eye. She knelt down and dusted it free, lifting to examine it and recognising it instantly. It was a gold pendant, fashioned into the image of a stick man with his arms arched above his head. An *Indalo Man,* a symbol that had become synonymous with the area, especially in tourist shops.

'You're lucky I didn't lock you in.'

'Jesus Christ, you startled me!'

116

'I gave the boys the day off.' Paul Turnbull glanced around at the excavation work. 'Thought they'd appreciate a long weekend. Schools have shut up shop. It'll give them a chance to get the kids settled at home.'

Ana-Marie recovered her composure and said, 'Mama called. She was worried about José. His car was found near the cemetery yesterday.'

'I thought he'd be celebrating his two-goal debut, ordering room service in some swank hotel in Madrid and getting Laura legless.'

'So, what's his car doing here, parked outside the cemetery?'

'You're sure it's his?'

'Well, Sofia saw it and...'

Turnbull laughed. 'Sofia? Sofia wouldn't know a car from a dustcart. Have you tried phoning his mobile?'

'Yes, of course, several times, but I haven't been able to get through. It's as though his phone's dead.'

'He's probably forgotten to charge it. I didn't leave my mobile at home this morning, did I? I can't find it anywhere.'

'You'll have to get yourself a new one.'

'Maybe a Godsend, anyway. The Almeria regeneration contract should be given the go ahead in the next couple of days and I could do with upgrading. I fancy an iPhone.'

'Have you packed?'

'No. There's no hurry. I don't go until tomorrow. I'll drive down to the airport after lunch, tie things up in the UK and fly back on Friday afternoon.' Turnbull moved towards her and threw a protective arm around her. 'You shouldn't be down here on your own. It's dangerous. What if you'd slipped and hit your head? You could lie here for days before someone found you.' He kissed her forehead and led her back up the ramp, pausing to switch off the light. 'No more adventures. Promise?' He paused and ran his hand over her stomach. 'How's junior?'

'Enrique. I thought we could call him Enrique, after my father. What do you think?'

Turnbull pulled open the heavy oak door and harsh sunlight stung their eyes. 'Your father?' he said.

'Yes. He'd be so pleased.' Ana-Marie detected reservation in him. 'There's no hurry. It was just a thought. We can talk about it later.'

'And what are you trying to hide from me?'

'What do you mean?'

'In your hand.'

'Oh. Oh, that. I found it on the floor, in the crypt.'

He took the pendant from her. 'And now you've gone and spoilt my surprise.' He lent forward, slipped it round her neck, fastened the clasp and kissed her gently on the lips. 'I bought it in Almeria on Saturday when you were sleeping off the fiesta. I wanted to give you something to show you how much I love you and how much having a child means to me.' He paused and kissed her again. 'I must have dropped it yesterday.'

'It's beautiful,' Ana-Marie said, lifting her face towards him.

'And so are you, my darling. Now, stop worrying. José'll turn up in his own good time, with the lovely Laura on his arm. Come on. Inocenta will be wondering where we've got to.'

'You think she's lovely? Laura?'

'Not when she stands next to you.'

She slipped her arm through his, pulling his strong forearm into her side and they strolled from the church to her childhood home.

As they stepped into the living room, Inocenta Castaño turned from the television set, her face streaked with tears.

'Mama?' Ana-Marie hurried over and sat down next to her. 'Mama, what's wrong? What's happened?'

Inocenta's was trembling, her hands shaking uncontrollably, tears flowing.

'Where's Sofia?' Ana-Marie looked round, suddenly fearful. 'Mama, is it Sofia? Has something happened to Sofia?'

Inocenta looked up and said, 'It's Laura. She's been murdered.'

*

Fernández drove back from Domingo farm, dropped Leo Medina and Carlos close to the doctor's surgery and then made his way up to the busy Incident Room. He sat heavily in his chair, switched on his computer and glanced over at the display boards.

'You alright, Sir?' Valencia Ramoz looked up from her monitor. 'Need a coffee?'

'Yes, thanks Val.'

'You might like to check the database,' she called as she spooned instant coffee into a mug.

'What's new?'

'The SOCOs and forensics have erected a tent inside the mine and are sifting through years of rubbish tossed into the shaft. No joy yet.'

'No hand-luggage? Mobile phone?'

'Nothing.' She passed him his coffee. 'You can strike Klaus Dagmar off your list. Forensics have cleared him from any involvement in Thursday's murders.'

'Was never going to be that easy, was it?'

'Not entirely without a result though. Interpol picked up the request for information and contacted the German authorities. Extradition's only a matter of time: Klaus Dagmar owes the German taxman a substantial sum of money.'

'Better than nothing, I suppose.' He sipped his coffee. 'Has José Castaño been located?'

'No, not yet. I'll chase the Madrid police.' Ramoz checked through reports that had come in over night. 'Oh, yesterday, an Aston Martin was found abandoned near the cemetery.'

'An Aston? Here, in Los Mineros? Did someone come up on the lottery?'

'It's got a Madrid number plate.'

'Probably a tourist with a skin-full, got a lift back to their hotel.' Fernández looked across at Ramoz. 'Any feedback from taxi firms? Anyone remember picking up Laura?'

119

'Nothing yet, Sir. Oh, last thing you want to hear but there have been demands for an enquiry into the security arrangements at Joaquin Alvarez's school. The press have been demanding a statement.'

'Contact the Comandante in Almeria and ask him to send up someone from PR.'

'We could rope in the Mayor. Give him something to get his teeth into,' Ramoz suggested.

'Vincente Cabrera's a politician, for God's sake.' Fernández forced a smile. 'Yes, ok. See if he'll play ball and keep the press of our backs.'

'How's Carlos?'

'No better than you'd expect.' He looked across at her, sighed and leaned forward. 'Better start running background checks on both Carlos and Laura.'

'You can't think that Carlos...'

'I don't know what to think at the moment, but I do want to know everything about both of them. What they grow, where their markets are, how they finance the farm, bank statements. How serious her relationship was with José Castaño. Other men in her life, past and present - anyone who could hold a grudge or had a score to settle.' He paused, the image of Laura's shattered face at the forefront of his mind. 'No, of course I don't think Carlos had anything to do with his daughter's death, but he is part of her story, and I've a feeling we're only on page one.'

*

Leo Medina accompanied Carlos Domingo to the doctor's surgery near the old olive press. Carlos found the uneven surface of the cobbled streets difficult to negotiate and welcomed the arm offered by the detective. He remembered Medina as the young man who'd dated Laura, but hadn't said anything to him when he'd taken him to the morgue. Medina had sat with him and broken all the rules when he'd left Carlos alone with Laura to say his goodbyes. Then he'd helped him complete the paper work and had driven him home. They'd stopped at the cemetery just outside the village and Carlos had spent time at his wife's graveside.

Mercifully, the evening surgery was quiet and they only had to wait a few minutes.

'How have you been, Carlos?' Dr. Javier Guzmán glanced up from his desk and put his pen down.

'How d'you think?'

'I'm really very sorry.'

'That's what everyone says. Don't bring her back, does it?'

'I'll prescribe something to help you sleep.'

'Got me twelve bore. That's all I need.'

'Don't talk like that, Carlos. It's not what Laura would want to hear, is it?'

'You talk of her as though she's going walk through that door, right as rain. She ain't coming back y'know.'

'I know, Carlos. I know.'

'You had them results back yet?'

Dr. Guzmán had the results locked away in the filing cabinet. It wasn't good news. He chose to wait. A few more days wouldn't make any difference. Nothing would make any difference. Carlos Domingo was on borrowed time.

'Not yet,' Guzmán lied as he finished scribbling a prescription. 'Pop into the chemist and pick up some of these. They'll give you a chance to recover.'

'I don't need drugs,' Carlos paused. 'I want to be around when they find the bastard that's done this. They will, you know, now they've found her. They'll find clues, evidence, and I'll be there. I'll be there when they find him.'

'Take the prescription. Just in case. Now, unbutton your shirt and sit on the couch. This shouldn't take long.'

'How is he?' Medina asked as Dr. Guzmán closed the surgery door behind him.

121

'He's a very sick man. No more than a couple of months at most. He has an advanced and extremely virulent form of prostate cancer. It's infected several other major organs in the body.'

'Does he know?'

'No. No. It's the last thing he needs to hear. The test results only came through on Friday and, what with Laura...' Guzmán paused, appearing to stumble over the next few words. 'You, you knew she was pregnant?'

'Yeah. The autopsy report.' There was something in the doctor's voice Medina couldn't place. It wasn't embarrassment, but it was as though he was nervous - like one of his kids when they'd done something wrong and wanted to hide it. The detective took a stab, asking, 'How long had you known Laura?'

'As a patient? For over the past six months, but only as a locum.'

'As a patient?'

'Yes, I qualified in Madrid and then spent six months as an intern at a hospital in Los Angeles. I came back here to put my parent's holiday apartment on the market. Selling it has taken longer than I'd anticipated and I got roped into helping out here.'

'But you said that you'd known Laura as a patient for six months?'

'Yes. Look, where's this going?'

'I'm interest in your relationship with her. You said *as a patient*. How else would you have known her?'

Guzmán laughed, but there was something synthetic about its ring. 'OK. OK. There's no point trying to hide anything. You'll find out soon enough. We dated a couple of times after we met at a bar on the beach.'

'I spent a couple of hours with Carlos after we left the morgue. He mentioned her relationship with several other men. Friends, nothing serious.'

'Doesn't surprise me. Laura was very beautiful. But I had no long-term expectations of my relationship with her. I'm

122

returning to the States. My fiancée has completed her studies and we're due to be married in the fall.'

'You were engaged when you dated Laura?'

'As if it's any of your business?'

'You used her.'

'Oh, grow up. No one got hurt. She knew my situation, right from the start. Beside, she didn't waste much time finding someone else, did she? If anyone knew what Laura was up to it would be her fiancé, don't you think?'

'But you continued to see her as a patient,' Medina said, 'despite your relationship with her?'

'It was Laura's choice.' Guzmán started to pace around the waiting room, tidying away magazines and newspapers scattered by patients. 'She could have backed out at any time. Believe me, I'm as shocked and as upset as anyone by her death, but don't try to pin Laura's murder on me.'

'Could have been you.'

'If that's a joke, it's in bad taste.'

'I don't hear anybody laughing, Doctor.' Medina said calmly, and then paused before asking, 'Did she say who the father was?'

'The father? Oh, for God's sake, I would have thought that was obvious.'

'José Castaño?' Medina looked into Guzmán's face, trying to read it. 'Could be yours.'

'That's a long-shot, Detective. You're clutching at straws.'

'But it could be yours.'

'If she was as promiscuous as you say,' Guzmán eyes flashed in anger, his mouth distorting as saliva seeped from the corners, 'she may not have known who the father was.'

'A simple DNA test should clarify things.' Medina stood up. 'Next time you phone your fiancée, you might like to tell her that you're helping us with a murder enquiry.'

'You leave her out of this!'

'But she ought to know the sort of man she's involved with, don't you think?' Medina opened the surgery door. 'I'll wait for Carlos outside,' he said, adding, 'I hope you're not thinking of leaving us soon. We need to talk some more, you and me. I'll be in touch.'

*

Fernández drove back to Almeria and parked three blocks from the hospital. He stopped at a local fruit stall and then caught the fresh bake of the afternoon, dropping the oranges and two sticks of bread off at his apartment.

It was six thirty. He was already late, but he took time to splash cold water on his face, before running a comb through his hair.

He took the narrow, cobbled alleyways to the rear entrance of the hospital where he punched in the security code and made his way down to the morgue. He found Santiago sitting at a small table.

'Sorry I'm late...'

'Don't be,' she said, without looking up. 'It's given me a chance to catch up with some paper work. Besides, I don't have anything new to tell you.' She paused, signing off at the bottom of a form. 'If you want to wait, there's a coffee machine outside in the corridor. It takes a Euro. You may have to kick it to get any response.' She sighed, pulled her hair away from her eyes and collected another form from off the top of the pile. She looked up at him, 'I'll be through in about ten minutes. Make yourself comfortable.'

'I can come back.'

'Whatever.'

'You ok?'

'Fine. Grab a coffee and I'll join you when I can.'

124

He retreated to the claustrophobia of the narrow corridor outside the morgue and decided to forgo the coffee. He trudged up to street level, crossed to the square below his apartment, nodded at the old men sitting beneath a ficus tree and chose a bench near them.

He lit a cigarette and stared down at the two photographs he had taken from Rodrigo Perpiñán's collection. He realised he couldn't see the detail without the scholar's magnifying glass and cursed.

One of the old men sat down next to him and slipped a pair of cheap bifocals into his hand. 'Comes to us all, Inspector.' The old man smiled, teeth stained by a thousand cigarettes, breath sweetened by an early evening brandy. He leaned over and peered at the photographs. 'That's not you,' he said, confidently.

'1973.'

'No more than a twinkle in your father's eye. Same year Admiral Blanco was assassinated. You know,' the old man said, his eyes lighting up, 'The bomb was so huge it blew a massive crater in the road and his car sailed over the roof of the church.'

'Spain's first astronaut.'

'Yes!' the old man cried. 'One more pot hole, one less arsehole!' He fell silent as though reflecting on Franco's brutal response to the Prime Minister's death. 'His assassination sparked a wave of reprisals.'

'Yes, I know. The village where I grew up suffered at the hands of a death squad. Three innocent people were executed. A bullet to the back of the head.'

'Los Mineros?'

'Yes.'

'Where those photos were taken?'

'Yes.'

'Not the end of the story, though, was it?' the old man said. 'The Priest and the man who'd betrayed the villagers were killed.'

'And his wife.'

'I remember.'

125

'My own father was caught up in it.'

'Killed?'

'Throat slit.' This was the first time he had uttered the words outside Rodrigo Perpiñán's home and he felt naked suddenly, as though people were staring at him, pointing and telling others that his father had been a murderer, and that he was the son of a murderer.

'It was a long time ago,' the old man said, taking back his glasses. 'You're too young for these. You just need to get your head down for a few hours.' He slipped the glasses onto the end of his nose, took the photographs, and studied them for several minutes, nodding repeatedly. 'I'd recognize the church anywhere,' he tapped the Confirmation photograph. 'Time was, we'd drive out to see friends, sink a few beers at a fiesta, stay over for New Year to drink Cava and eat grapes in the church square at midnight. I was no more than your age when this photograph was taken.'

'Then you'll know Alberto Ramos?'

'Yes, we go back a long way.' The old man laughed and then caught the shift in the Inspector's demeanour. 'Why, what's the old bugger been up to?'

Fernández outlined the murder of Alberto, Bartolomé and Matias, and filled in the background. The old man was clearly shocked and took several moments to compose himself before asking, 'And you're sure Juan Gonzales was murdered?'

'Yes.'

'When you catch the man who pulled the trigger, tell him he would have been last in line if any of us had been there.'

'And I may well have been at the front,' Fernández said, forcing a smile, picturing the photograph on his mother's mantelpiece, his father holding his newborn son.

'You know why Juan Gonzales killed Alberto, his son, and his grandson?' the old man asked.

'Alberto, yes...' His voice trailed off. 'Maybe they were just in the wrong place at the wrong time.'

'Possibly, but some of us old-timers see things

126

differently.' The old man paused. 'The family is the most important thing in a man's life. You'd agree?'

'Of course.'

'He will do everything he can to make sure that his children's future is secure, especially now that they have a future to look forward to?'

'Of course,' Fernández repeated, unsure where this was going.

'It's why, in any dispute, no matter how serious, many families will involve all generations.' The old man smiled. 'Let's say, for example, my neighbour's dog craps on the step at my front door? This goes on for sometime and I speak to my neighbour about it, but the dog doesn't stop shitting. The next time my son and his family, arrive for lunch, I take down my hunting rifle and we walk across to the boundary. I call to my neighbour and then, in front of my son and my grandson, I tell my neighbour that if his dog comes onto my land once more I'll shoot it. It's a trivial example, I know, but the point is that all generations would be involved. The dog owner would know that, even if something happened to me, there would always be my son, and my son's son. That's why Juan Gonzales had to kill all three men - the younger men would have come after him.'

It made sense, particularly if Juan Gonzales had not planned to commit suicide. But it wasn't the whole story. It didn't explain why someone had killed Juan Gonzales.

He pulled his mobile from his jacket pocket and scrolled through the presets. He nodded and smiled at the old man as Rodrigo Perpiñán answered. 'Can I catch you early tomorrow morning?'

'At home before ten, yes. Otherwise I'll be in the bar.'

'I need to know who else has shown an interest in your photographs over the past twelve months. It could be important.'

Fernández cut the call and lifted the photographs from his lap. He turned to the old man. 'I'm sorry, I don't know your name.'

The old man smiled. 'Pedro. Just like your father.'

127

'You knew him?'

'No. I'm sorry. If I had I'm sure I'd have counted him among my friends, but I'm not going to lie to you.'

'Do you recognise anyone in these photographs?'

The old man took them from him once more and, removing his glasses, he pulled them close to his face. 'I may have seen the Priest around, but can't be sure. Cinderella has something about her, don't you think?' He laughed. 'I can only put a name to one of them. He was probably a bit older than the rest, couple of years maybe, and as-stupid-as-a-donkey, if you know what I mean?' The old man fell silent. He took a handkerchief from his breast pocket and dabbed moist eyes. 'You said there was a fascist raid, about the same time as this photo was taken? I remember. They cut out his tongue.'

'Pepe?'

'Yes.'

'Excuse me.' Fernández took out his mobile and pressed one of the presets. Jacinta Estrada answered. 'Has the judge issued that warrant?'

'Yes, Sir.'

'OK. Arrange for a dozen officers from the Policia Local to be on standby tomorrow at ten, and see if you can track down Pepe, the goatherd. Call everyone in for a meeting tomorrow at nine. Make sure the Mayor's there.'

'Will do,' Estrada said and then told him, 'Ana-Marie Castaño came in this afternoon. Distraught's putting it mildly. She was accompanied by her husband. She wanted to talk to you about Laura and her brother, José. She was insistent - it had to be you. She wouldn't talk to any one else.'

'Ring her. Set up a meeting for tomorrow at eleven thirty. Has José surfaced yet?'

'No, but the Madrid police have contacted us. He hasn't shown up for training since Sunday's match.'

'Probably nursing a hangover and sleeping it off somewhere.'

'I said much the same, but apparently he's tea-total.'

128

'OK, keep me posted.'

He ended the call and turned to see Julieta Santiago walking up the lane towards the square, her fine hair dancing as the breeze picked up.

'Always thought you were a lazy bastard, sitting on your balcony for hours on end,' the old man said, grinning at him.

'You don't miss much, do you?'

'If you'd spent a lifetime looking over your shoulder, Inspector, you'd know where each part of the puzzle fits.'

'How did you know I was a cop?'

He lent forward, his face close to Fernández's jacket, and sniffed several times. 'I can smell a cop a mile away. Unmistakable.' He laughed. 'Time was; if you'd been Guardia, I'd have spat on you. But that was a long time ago. And this,' he nodded towards Julieta Santiago, 'is who you've really come to see. Tell me I'm wrong.' He grinned and patted the Inspector's knee, but before he got up to rejoin his friends, his face softened. 'Don't be too hard on your father. Those were desperate times.'

He introduced Julieta Santiago and Pedro took her hand, kissed it and told her she shouldn't waste her time on a washed-up police Inspector. She smiled at him, told him she would think about it and asked him if he'd care to make her a better offer.

'Twenty years ago, maybe,' he said, grinning. 'But, if he doesn't measure up, you know where to find me.'

They took their leave, found a table outside a bar and ordered a bottle of red wine. Santiago sat, lightheaded and weary. She propped her elbow on the arm of the chair, dropped her forehead in the palm of her hand and closed her eyes.

Fernández sat in silence.

Around them, the city was alive and the drum of humanity echoed across the square. He picked out an elderly couple, impressed by the effort they'd made to get ready, and watched them walking side by side, without a word passing between them, their dignity more eloquent than a thousand words. She was dressed in a calf-length black skirt, a long

129

woolen jumper, and sensible black shoes with a small heel. Her hair was tied back in a bun and her mouth was pinched and stoical. Her husband had put on a crisply ironed shirt, open at the neck, and a dark waistcoat. His shoes had been polished and his moustache trimmed and lightly waxed. In their faces, Fernández saw, just for an instant, the faces of his mother and father growing old together and, as they passed, he imagined they stopped and smiled at him before turning and walking away. If they'd been holding hands, he might have believed it was them. His parents, he felt sure, would always have held hands.

'Sir?' he heard a woman's voice. It broke the spell.

The waitress had brought a bottle of red wine and two glasses to their table. She smiled at Santiago, probably appreciating what it was to be exhausted, and readied to uncork the bottle. Fernández shook his head, put his index finger to his lips and took the bottle from her.

Santiago had turned away from him, her face in profile, her hair folding gently onto her shoulders. As she dozed, he found himself studying her, looking for the first time at her slender neck, the light freckling on the pale skin of her cheeks, her long eyelashes curving gracefully, faint laughter lines at the corner of her eye. He glanced down at the training shoes she'd discarded as she sat down - new, tied carelessly, the laces flopping to the floor. She'd told him why she wore them– the hours of standing during an autopsy playing havoc with her back. He looked down, at a small red rose she'd had tattooed just above the anklebone of her right foot. He wondered if it was symbol of a rebellious youth or a passionate love affair.

He was unaware that she had stirred and was watching him, until he looked up. 'I'm sorry,' she said. 'I must have dozed off.'

'I was just admiring the scenery.'

'So I noticed.' She smiled.

'Drink?' He opened the bottle.

'Thanks. I'm sorry about earlier.'

'I was late.'

'You didn't deserve the tongue lashing though.' She paused and sipped at the wine. 'When I'm tired I get grumpy.'

'Don't we all?'

'Yes, I suppose so.'

'It can't be easy holding down a career and bringing up Holly.'

'Thousands of women do. My mother's a godsend.'

They sat in silence for several minutes; sipping their wine and watching the world go by. 'Death doesn't keep convenient hours, does it?' she said, turning to face him. 'Is that why you've never married?'

'No. I'm not sure. Never had time, I suppose.'

'Ana-Marie's a lot to live up to, for any woman.'

'It was a long time ago.'

They fell silent again. He topped his wine glass up and offered her a refill. She put her hand over the top of the glass and shook her head.

She looked at him, studying his face. 'I didn't thank you for inviting us to your family's matanza.'

'Holly didn't…' He was searching for the right words. 'Have nightmares afterwards?'

'No, she's tough as old boots. It's in the genes.'

'What time did you get away?'

'Not long after you left. Your mother was very generous.'

He stumbled over this next few words: 'My family took to you.'

'Took to Holly, more like.'

He looked across the square, the words *I took to you* forming in his head, but he hesitated long enough for them to tiptoe from the tip of his tongue and vanish.

Santiago sipped her wine and said nothing, then placed the glass on the table, still half full. 'I'd better be going,' she said.

'I'll walk you home.'

She smiled, stood and slipped her jacket onto her

shoulders. 'I'm sorry, Antonio, but…'

'I didn't mean…'

'No. No, I know you didn't, but I have a daughter to get home to. Good night.'

*

Leo Medina held onto to his two boys just a little longer than usual that evening.

They asked him if they could pray to Jésus; so they could ask Him to look after Joaquin and make him get better soon. Leo's wife, Roz, joined them and they sat on the rug in front of the hearth, the youngest sitting on her lap.

Medina's prayer was for his boys' safety - dreading their next adventure into the big wide world at the dawn of a new day, and the day after, until one day…

His boys were allowed to stay up an extra ten minutes and Medina watched as they played together, filling the house with laughter and their wild imagination, so innocent behind those mischievous eyes.

'You ok?' Roz asked.

'Yeah.' He sighed deeply. 'I guess so.'

'You want to talk about her?'

'Laura? No.' Medina hesitated. 'I don't know. I just can't believe…'

'Seems such a waste.'

'She was engaged.'

'José?'

'Yes.' Medina paused. 'She was pregnant.'

'Oh, dear God. Does Carlos know?'

'No, no he doesn't.' He looked down, his right thumb rubbing the knuckles of his left hand. 'He only has a few weeks at most. Cancer.'

Roz took his hand.

'I love you.' Medina said, turning to face her.

'Yes, I know you do. But, I want you to be careful.'

132

'Afraid I might do something stupid?'

'Wouldn't be the first time.' She paused before adding, 'Catch the man who did this and let the courts deal with it.'

'Yeah,' he replied, looking over at his two boys.

'For their sake. And for my mine. I don't want to be a widow just yet.'

Day Seven

Wednesday 24th June 2009

The clock in the tower of the village church struck seven-thirty, bee-eaters vied with swallows and swifts for an early morning breakfast, and the sun streamed through the window, already hot, heralding another daylong assault.

Rodrigo Perpiñán was dressed in nothing more than his shorts when he unlatched the door. He looked tired. 'Coffee's on,' he said. 'Help yourself.' He wandered across the small lounge and up the stairs.

Fernández stood at the sink in the kitchen and waited for the kettle to boil. He heard Perpiñán above the noise of the shower, singing. There was a rap on the door. He opened it and a stick of bread, three croissant, and two pastries had been left on the step.

'Thought you'd need something before your day starts,' Perpiñán said, running a towel over his head. 'Help yourself. There's eggs in the pantry.'

'The Danish look good.'

'The widow García drops them off every day.'

'In return for?'

'Man cannot live by bread alone.' Perpiñán smiled. 'How's tricks with your favourite pathologist?'

'It's complicated.'

Perpiñán took the kettle from the stove. 'It always is with you. You watch her dance, you invite her to your mother's home, and now you tell me it's complicated?'

'We have more important things on our minds.'

'Yeah, right. You still have a soft spot for Ana-Marie, don't you? I saw the way you looked at her outside the church. She's a bit beyond reach, I'd say: married, wealthy husband, kid on the way.' Perpiñán couldn't resist twisting the knife. 'Admittedly, the good doctor carries excess baggage, but she's

134

smart, successful, beautiful…She scares the pants off you, doesn't she? It's been a long time, hasn't it, Antonio? Ten years since Ana-Marie dumped you. How many women have you nailed since then?'

Fernández broke a Danish in half and took a cup of coffee onto the terrace.

Perpiñán followed him. 'It's like riding a bike, you know. Comes back with practice. Besides, I'm sure you'll be in very good hands.'

Fernández sat heavily on one of the patio chairs. 'Can we get on with it?'

'If you insist.' Perpiñán smiled and pulled a file towards him. 'I have the list you asked for: those who'd bought photographs from me over the past year.' He handed Fernández a copy. 'I've been keeping a record of each purchase for tax purposes. I got stung for IVA a couple of year's ago. They assumed I'd been ripping them off for years and threw the book at me.'

'Poetic justice,' Fernández mumbled as he scanned the list. 'Anyone we know?'

'Most are tourists. A couple of Brits – Adam Wells, the artist, wanted to use the photos to provide inspiration for his next series of paintings. The Mayor sent his clerk down to buy half a dozen of my books, and a copy of all photographs showing buildings in the village, for a display in the Cultural Centre. Paul Turnbull bought copies of photographs of the church for the restoration. Javier Guzmán bought two copies of my latest pictorial history.'

'Doctor Guzmán?'

'One for his mother in Madrid and one for his fiancée in the States.'

'What do you make of him?'

'Needs to work on his bedside manner, but otherwise…' Perpiñán shrugged. 'Why?'

'He told Leo Medina he'd dated Laura just before she took up with José Castaño.'

'So, Guzmán could be the father of her child?'

'It's possible, but we won't know that until we run DNA tests. The smart money's on José. When we find him we'll be able to match his DNA with the foetus removed from Laura's womb.'

'Presumably that's José's car outside the cemetery?' Perpiñán paused. 'You don't need José, of course. Ana-Marie's his sister. They'll have the same DNA. Might save time, 'til you find him.'

'Maybe worth a shot. I'm seeing Ana-Marie later this morning.' He got up and made for the front door.

'Oh, and the Priest, Father Gabriel,' Perpiñán called. 'He's on the list. Came to see me about three months ago.'

'Did he say why?'

'No. But he went through the entire collection and bought copies of at least two dozen photographs, including the ones you're interested in.'

*

The civilian night shift had clocked-off at eight and the day shift were familiarising themselves with information that had come in over night. Fernandez glanced across at Leo Medina sifting through evidence-bags laid out on trestle tables below the three incident-boards. He grabbed a coffee and Valencia Ramoz brought him up to speed with the latest developments: Julieta Santiago had emailed the main findings of Laura Domingo's autopsy; Madrid police had asked for assistance in tracing José Castaño; Joaquin Alvarez was still on life support - there was concern he might be permanently brain damaged; Ana-Marie Turnbull would meet with him at eleven-thirty, but her husband had been called to a planning meeting in Almeria and would be flying to the UK after lunch, so he wouldn't be there; the Comandante had requested detailed information about each investigation in time for a press conference at nine that morning.

136

He sat on the edge of her desk and drained his coffee.

'Val, I may need you to head up things here. I want Jacinta and Leo out on the streets for the next couple of days.'

'As long as I have you at the end of a mobile.'

'Of course.'

'It's not my arse they'll be after if things go belly-up.'

'Don't worry. Just keep on top of things.'

They both looked around as the door opened and the Mayor walked in.

Vincente Cabrera had been elected for a second term, representing the socialist PSOE. He was in his early fifties, short and barrel-chested, with a face that was dominated by a full moustache. He'd worked hard to cultivate an image as an *incorruptible,* making it clear he would never succumb to temptation and accept backhanders or actively manipulate applications for construction developments to line his own pockets - temptations that had proved irresistible to countless other local administrations throughout Spain, resulting in thousands of illegal buildings across the country. He had campaigned for a clean up, laws had been tightened and more Guardia officers specializing in fraud had been appointed. Now developers, local politicians, lawyers and notaries all knew that, at the whiff of a scandal, the spotlight would be turned on them.

Fernández shook the Mayor's hand and brought him up to date with the investigations.

'So, what do you want from me?' Vincente Cabrera asked, his voice high-pitched and irritatingly abrasive. He accepted a cigarette but declined a coffee.

'Access to the Town Halls records. Details of all residents, locals, guiris and immigrants; births, deaths and marriages; building applications, especially those involving the Ramos family; crime statistics; disputes between neighbours; maps identifying the location of mining works in the area and any diagrams of the internal structure of the underground layout. I'll assign an officer to liaise with you. There may be other records we need to access as the investigations proceed.'

137

'How far have you got?'

'We're making progress.'

Cabrera pursed his lips. 'Don't patronise me, Inspector. I can open doors for you. You're up against it. You have no idea who murdered Juan Gonzales, you have no idea who killed Laura Domingo, you have no idea where José Castaño is, and you've managed to upset most villagers you've come into contact with, including the Brits for God's sake.'

'Then I'll need certain assurances from you.'

'You'll want me to guarantee that whatever happens in these four walls, stays in these four walls, right?'

'I want nothing leaked to the press.'

'By that, I presume, you mean nothing that will damage your investigation.'

'The flow of information must be restricted and controlled.'

'But, if it's in the public interest?'

'I'll be the judge of that,' Fernández said. 'As long as we understand each other. I'll expect you to attend all meetings and carry out any requests we make of you in the course of the investigations. I'll also expect you to keep the media off our backs.'

'Easier said than done.'

'That's the deal.'

Jacinta Estrada came in carrying a bundle of files. She smiled at Fernández and the Mayor, stood at her desk and fired up her computer. Fernández pulled her to one side and told her about his decision to hand the day-to-day running of the incident room to Valencia Ramoz.

'Makes sense,' Estrada said. 'It's your call.'

'You'll be more of an asset at the sharp end than sitting behind a desk, but I want you to head up any meetings.'

'Including this one?'

He tilted his head.

'Let's not waste anymore time, then, shall we?' She stood before the whiteboards and said, 'OK let's get started.' She

138

waited for everyone to settle and welcomed Vincente Cabrera. She reviewed the progress made in both investigations and then turned to Leo Medina.

Medina stayed at his desk, his chair reversed, sitting astride the seat, his face glum, conscious of the eyes bearing down on him. He dragged a tray in front of him. 'We know Laura didn't check in. These items were found on or near her body.' He hesitated as he held up several plastics bags - her leather belt and jacket, her jeans, and a pair of trainers – stripped from her body. He took a deep breath and continued, faltering several times as he explained that other debris was being examined, forensics hoping to have their analysis with them by lunchtime tomorrow.

'Hand luggage, camera, mobile phone?'

'No, Sir. Uniformed officers will sweep the area around the top of the mineshaft today.'

'Tell Uniform to ring Laura's mobile.' Estrada said. 'It's worth a try. Batteries have a long stand-by life. If it was ditched, someone might hear it.' She turned back to the meeting. 'The database will be maintained round the clock. Additional support staff have been drafted in and they're crosschecking information. Exhibits will be displayed here.'

She walked over to the trestle tables near the whiteboards. 'Of particular interest,' she said, 'is this.' She held up a gold pendant that had been found around Laura Domingo's neck. 'Something you'll all be familiar with. It's an *Indalo Man*.' She pointed at the enlarged photocopy that had been pinned up and asked if anyone could throw some light on the origins of this local talisman.

Medina put his coffee down, walked over and took the gold pendant from her. 'I helped my eldest research this for a project at school. I got an A-plus from the teacher,' he said, his smile weak. He paused, clearing his throat. 'Anyway. A team of archeologists found a cave painting in the late 1860's. They named it after San Indalecio, one of the Saints who converted Spain to Christianity. It was forgotten about until the hippies invaded this area after the Second World War. They were regarded as evil and many local families painted the image of Indalo Man on the walls of their homes for protection.' He was just about to sit down when he turned and asked, 'Where's Carlos, Sir?'

'At home, I guess. Why?'

'I'm not sure. But, when we went to tell him about...' He paused, obviously struggling, and cleared his throat. 'When we went to tell him about Laura, I thought I saw a similar pendant in one of the photos on his mantelpiece.'

'We'll pay him another visit later.' Fernández turned to Estrada. 'Anything else?'

'Yes. Laura's DNA. Samples were taken from the foetus she was carrying, as well as tissue found under her nails. The results will be available later today - a rush job, the lab boys on over time. It may be that her attacker was the father, or we may be looking for two different men. We need to start identifying possible suspects.'

'I'll give you a name,' Medina said. 'Guzmán.'

'Doctor Javier Guzmán?'

'Laura and her father were both patients. Carlos has terminal cancer.' Medina dropped his head, unable to hide his bitterness. 'Guzmán dated Laura.'

'One of several, Leo,' Estrada said.

'But the bastard's engaged. His fiancée lives in the States.'

'Immoral, maybe, but not illegal.' Fernández turned to Valencia Ramoz. 'Bank accounts?'

Ramoz pulled a file from a tray on her desk. 'These are copies obtained from the bank. Carlos has a large overdraft. The farm's been running at a loss for several years and he's up to his neck in debt. He'd borrowed to try to stay afloat, but has been refused any further loans.'

'Where's this going?' Medina asked.

'Laura's bank account is typical of many students: overdrawn. But she opened a separate saving's account two weeks ago. Two deposits have been made. Both for twenty-grand. The first was made by Doctor Javier Guzmán, a week ago.' Ramoz paused and raised her eyebrows, waiting for the shock to dissipate. 'And, then, two days before she was killed, Adam Wells deposited the same amount.'

'Blackmail?'

'Why not? Laura's inheritance is disappearing as Carlos' debts finally catch up with him. She's pregnant and is casting around for potential surrogates – doesn't have to be the real father, just someone she'd been with.'

'Oh, for God's sake!'

'Someone who'd rather their little secret wasn't leaked and had plenty of cash.'

'Her father told us that Laura played the field,' Fernández said, looking directly at Medina, knowing he was finding the going tough. 'Since Christmas, she'd probably brought home a few boyfriends. God knows how many she didn't. But, for the last three months, she seemed to have met her match in José Castaño. José is the brother of Laura's closest friend, Anna-Marie, who's married to Paul Turnbull.' He paused, waiting for the information to be assimilated.

'Hasn't Turnbull been tipped for the Almeria regeneration project, or the docks, or something?'

'He's in the running for both.' Fernández turned to Jacinta Estrada.

'We know,' she said, 'that Dr. Guzmán dated Laura a few times. So, let's imagine Laura visits the surgery. Guzmán confirms she's pregnant and she tells him that he's the father. She offers a deal. And, if it worked with him, why not try someone else she'd known? Adam Wells: all alone in his studio; surrounded by his make-believe world; a wife who'd take him to the cleaners.' She hurried over to the whiteboard and scribbled both names. 'Two men. Two suspects. Both with motive. Neat.'

'Too neat,' Fernández said. He slipped from the desk and stood in front of them. 'Jacinta, check out Adam Wells, then call on the Ramos women. I want to know more about their coffee morning with Ana-Marie. Leo, see if you can prise anything else from our two-timing doctor. Go easy. When you're done we'll go and see Carlos.'

'But, I don't understand. If they'd already paid up, why kill her?' Medina said.

'Maybe she went back for more,' Estrada offered.

'Let's not be too hasty,' Fernández said. 'We need to establish if both Guzmán and Wells have alibis and check them out. Forty-grand may be a lot of money but it wouldn't cover Carlos Domingo's debts. Maybe Laura did go back for more.' He turned to Valencia Ramoz. 'Val, as soon as the DNA results come in, let me know. We'll also need a DNA sample from both Wells and Guzmán to establish paternity or rule them out.'

'Or their guilt,' Estrada said. 'They may not be the father but one of them could have attacked her.'

'There is one other possibility, Sir,' Valencia Ramoz said. 'I don't want to speak ill of the dead, but Laura may have tried to extort money from another man.'

'Someone else she'd been shagging, I suppose.' Medina could no longer hide his anger as the denigration continued.

'Why not?' Estrada insisted. 'These days, it's not unheard off for young women to have several different sexual partners on the go.' She paused. 'Look, she knows her old man is in deep shit financially. She blackmails Guzmán and Wells. Thinks back through other conquests or targets someone who'd have the necessary readies.'

'José Castaño?' Valencia Ramoz asked. 'Laura's latest?'

Fernandez rubbed the back of his neck and, after a moment, said, 'Val, you said Laura's bank account only showed two deposits?'

'Yes, Sir.'

He walked over to the whiteboard and added a name: *José Castaño.*

'Let's find him and bring him in.'

*

142

Carlos Domingo hated Almeria, hated towns and cities, but wanted to talk to the funeral director about arrangements for Saturday. A neighbour gave him a lift and he spent an hour with a nice man who had talked him through everything that would happen, making a note of any requests or suggestions. He'd taken one of Laura's most beautiful dresses and a photograph of his wife with Laura as a babe in arms. He asked if they could be placed in the coffin.

When everything was settled, he left the funeral directors and found a chemist, where he handed over the prescription Dr. Guzmán had given him. The pharmacist's assistant apologized, said there would be a delay of about fifteen minutes, and asked if he would wait or if he preferred to come back later? Carlos told her he would come back.

He ambled aimlessly along the wide pavement, away from the port and harbour, up the Paseo de Almeria towards the Puerta de Purchena. He sat and ordered a coffee at one of the pavement cafés, and watched pedestrians as they passed by. He tried to focus, but all he could see in every woman was Laura: tall, blond, her corpse lying on the pathologist's trolley. Leo Medina had shown him her belt, jeans, blouse, and trainers. The pathologist's assistant had taken him by the arm and led him over to Laura's body, lying under a white shroud. The assistant had pulled back the sheet and Carlos had stood for several moments unable to take in what he saw – his beautiful little girl, still and lifeless. He'd tried desperately to compose himself, snatching at his breath, his chest threatening to burst with grief. Medina had asked him to confirm that it was his daughter. He'd nodded and said, 'Yes.' Medina had then taken the assistant to one side and, for a few precious moments, Carlos was left alone with his daughter.

He would never forget Medina's kindness. Never.

The town teemed with tourists, shoppers and those hurrying to work. Carlos left his coffee and walked along a side street where he paused outside an electrical store. He looked at the bewildering array of TV screens and other gadgets on offer.

143

Anything technical left him cold. It was Laura who'd installed computer software for the business. It was Laura who kept the accounts and printed out a statement for him each month. It was Laura who had warned him that the years of plenty were about to end and they would have to pull their horns in. They had laughed at that, 'pulling in horns', on a farm. They had laughed a lot. She'd been so full of life.

He walked into the shop and glanced at the bank of television screens blazing across an entire wall, each tuned to the same local news channel. He stood and watched the updates on the condition of Joaquin Alvarez, the young boy who'd been found near Laura.

One of the shop's assistants came over and asked him if he could be of any help.

'Do they have sound on them televisions? I can't hear anything.'

'Each of these sets has the very latest digital surround sound system, sir.'

'Then let me listen to what they're saying.'

The feature included aerial shots of the village and the campo near where the murders had taken place last Thursday. He watched as the news helicopter swooped across the hills and zoomed in on the disused mining complex where Laura had been found. He studied the campo from the helicopter's vantage and turned to the shop assistant. 'Can you stop the picture?'

'You mean freeze it, sir? Yes, of course. We have the very latest, hard-disk multi-channel-tuners.'

'Then freeze it,' Carlos said, unable to tear his eyes away from the screen.

The assistant took a remote control and pointed it towards a slim, silver machine below the bank of TVs. The aerial shot froze above the hills surrounding the village and Carlos moved closer to study the detail.

After several moments, he turned to the shop assistant and said, 'Thank you. Thank you very much.'

*

'I'm concerned,' Vincente Cabrera said as they hurried after the group of local police who'd been drafted in. They'd left the briefing at the Town Hall and were on their way to the homes of Juan Gonzales and Felipe Romero. 'You've identified two suspects, Javier Guzmán and Adam Wells, and then made the evidence you have fit their profile. I'd call that a stitch-up.'

'We have to start somewhere,' Fernández said. 'The elimination of suspects is an important part of the process. They're our first real lead. Who knows? We could strike lucky,'

'You're just keeping your troops occupied, giving them a sense of purpose.'

'Time will tell, Vincente. Meanwhile, we have a couple of homes to search.'

They stood to one side as a crocodile of young children headed down towards lush vegetation, nourished by an underground stream, that had been turned into a nature area for kids to study mini-beasts, plants and trees. School was out, and this was summer camp, run by volunteers and oversubscribed each year. The kids were noisy, chatting, laughing, conspiring and giggling, seemingly without a care in the world. At the back, head down, sullen, his hand held by stern faced adult, Ricardo Castro had distanced himself from the rest of his classmates. They would probably have been told not to talk to Ricardo about what happened down the mine, but to involve him in their games, not to blame him, and to remember that it had been an accident. Fernández wondered if it was too early for him to be back in the mainstream, but had no doubt that everyone would be praying for good news from the hospital and hoping that Joaquin Alvarez would be back at school soon.

They watched them disappear and made their way to Juan Gonzales's cottage, where Fernández left half a dozen officers to bag anything they thought might throw some light on why three men had been shot, and then led the remaining officers to Felipe Romero's.

His dog had been asleep in the sun by the front door and was quick to vent its anger at being disturbed, barking furiously. Romero came to the door - a grubby, white t-shirt and black, nylon shorts, covering his scrawny body. His spindly legs seemed hardly able to support his weight. His feet were bare and filthy.

Fernández stepped forward and said, 'You fired rockets during the siesta last Thursday at the time the three Ramos men were being shot.'

'So, what?'

'The Mayor hadn't asked you to disturb the siesta, had he?' Fernández looked at Cabrera, who shrugged, exaggerating the gesture. 'So, I ask myself, what made Felipe risk the wrath of the villagers?'

'I must have lost track of time. Easily done.'

'But something you've never done before,' the Mayor said.

'I ain't done nothing wrong.'

'Then you won't mind if we take a look around inside.' Fernández handed him the search warrant and nodded at the uniformed officers.

As they pushed past Romero, Fernández pulled several photographs from an envelope. 'You were quite a thespian, way back,' he began, holding up the photograph of the group celebrating the success of the Cinderella production. 'Did they type-cast you as an Ugly Sister?' He handed Romero the photograph. 'Enjoy treading the boards, did you? Acting. Cinders carry off the butter-wouldn't-melt-in-my-mouth role, did she? Or were you all sniggering behind the scenery at the Priest's whore?'

'Oh, for God's sake. I've already told you, I've no idea who the Priest was fucking.'

Fernández showed him a second photograph. 'And here you are again, standing outside the church in all your finery. Your first Communion, I'd say. Cinders is radiant, isn't she? She was pregnant and they say carrying a child gives a woman the

146

warmest of glows.'

'I wouldn't know.'

'She needed to cast around for a father, especially after Emanuel was killed.'

'I've no idea what you're talking about.'

'You still turn your *'face to the sun'*?'

'Do I do what?'

'You'll know the words to the *Cara al Sol*? You'd have sung them often enough. You were a member of the fascist youth movement; the *Little Arrows*.' Fernández passed him a third photograph. It was early 1973 and a middle-aged Jésus Gonzales had clambered up onto a table in the bar, bottle in hand, and appeared to be berating the men, most of whom had turned their backs on him. Jésus was heavy, with an obvious beer gut. He was dressed in a dark blue shirt and clumsy trousers. Juan Gonzales must have been home from one of his missions and was dressed casually in white shirt and flared cords. Felipe Romero was standing at the door to the bar, his right arm raised in what could have been a fascist salute.

'God, you must be desperate - dragging up photos of a drunken old man. You say this was taken in 1973? The war ended in 1939, for God's sake.'

'For many, my friend, 1939 was just the beginning.' Fernández produced the magnifying glass. 'Would you like to look more carefully? See the expression on your face? What is that – adulation?'

'There you go again, hiding behind your long words. You may have the education, Inspector, but you don't have a fucking clue.'

'Here's another one of my big words. Collusion in the planning and execution of a murder.'

'I told you, I've done nothing wrong.'

'You're looking at a long stretch in prison. You want to spend the rest of your life behind bars?' Fernández moved close enough to smell the wine that Romero had drunk that morning and whispered, 'It's time for you to sing, my friend.'

One of the uniformed officers came out holding a plastic supermarket bag, folded neatly. He handed it to Fernández. 'You want to tell me what this is?'

'Me savings. I don't trust banks. Greedy bastards. Look at the mess they've got us in to. There's no law against keeping money in me house.'

Fernández handed the bag to Vincente Cabrera and he began to count out the bank notes stuffed at the bottom. 'There must be one and a half, two thousand euros here. Where the hell would you get this sort of money?'

Romero said nothing, shrugged and turned away.

'A small price to pay for your silence,' Fernández said.

Uniformed officers began to emerge from the cottage, carrying bulging black plastic bin liners. Romero watched as his world was carted off.

'Don't make things worse for yourself, Felipe,' Vincente Cabrera said. 'If you know anything about last Thursday, you must tell us.'

'Think about it, Felipe,' Fernández said. 'Someone's taken you for a sucker and you'll go to prison because of them. You want to tell me who?'

*

Jacinta Estrada glanced around the studio. Adam Wells was clearly a prolific and very accomplished artist, although she didn't care much for paintings that simply represented a subject without telling a story. Cameras could that, so why spend hours copying a landscape or a bowl of fruit? But these, she thought, were exceptional. She walked over to an unfinished work that was propped up on one of three easels. The canvas had been washed and an outline had been sketched in. She glanced around at the other paintings. 'To my untrained eye, these look good.'

'They are,' he said without a hint of modesty, 'but I don't use acrylic very often. The paint dries too quickly in this climate, but the students in my class wanted to explore the medium, so I

148

thought I'd throw something together to demonstrate the main techniques.'

'You have many students?'

'My classes are always oversubscribed. Mainly Brits. Mainly women.'

'But no-one with your talent?'

He laughed. 'Are you trying to flatter me, detective?'

'The thought wouldn't have crossed my mind.'

Adam Wells had turned fifty and had a full head of dark hair that looked as though it had been dyed. His face was tanned and creased warmly when he smiled. Estrada grudgingly admitted that she could see why some women, most women probably, certainly those of a certain age, would find him attractive.

'You know why I'm here?' she asked.

'I assume it's routine. You're interviewing everyone who may have some insight into the dreadful events of the past week.'

'And you have an insight?'

'Only what I told the Inspector when he joined us at the bar yesterday. He upset quite a few folk, I can tell you. As if we'd be involved.'

'Does your art sell?'

'It used to. I've had exhibitions in London, Paris, and Madrid. These days there are fewer people around able to afford them. My books keep the wolf from the door.' He paused. 'What's this all about?'

'Do you ever lend money?'

'We have done. My wife is very generous. She likes to support good causes.'

'And, would she count your mistress among the good causes she'd be likely to support?'

'Mistress?'

'Your pregnant, young mistress: Laura Domingo?'

The blood drained from Adam Wells' face and his eyes darted from Estrada to the studio door, as if to check his wife hadn't come back with the tea. 'Good God,' he stammered, 'you

149

can't seriously think that I had anything to do with Laura's death?'

Estrada pulled a sheaf of papers from her document case.

'This is a copy of Laura's bank statement. Twenty thousand is very generous. Your wife must have had a very good reason for supporting Laura like that.'

'My wife...'

'Doesn't know. Of course she doesn't. You'd be out on your ear, if she did.' She waved the bank statement in his face. 'Are you going to tell me what this is all about?'

*

A week ago, the Incident Room in the Town Hall had been just that, one room, set up in the main reception area. Now it occupied most of the rooms on the ground floor. The building dated back to the middle of the nineteenth century and still retained many of its original features, including ornate cornices and roses, as well as a tile-clad wrought-iron fireplace fashioned by the village blacksmith. The reception area served as the hub of the investigation, whilst smaller rooms enabled police officers to conduct interviews, provide storage, and process those arrested. The doors of two rooms had been reinforced to provide lock-up facilities. DNA swabs, blood, urine or hair samples could be collected in the bathroom: not ideal, but the best they could do under the circumstances.

Ana-Marie had been shown into one of the interview rooms and given a cup of coffee. A uniformed woman police officer was waiting with her. As Fernández entered, Ana-Marie rushed over to him and fell into his arms. She held onto him for several moments and pulled him tight to her. He encircled her with his arms, his hands resting gently on her back. She began to sob, her body trembling. He felt her softness, inhaling the subtle scent of her perfume and the fragrance of her shampoo.

As he remembered it, she had been the one with more experience when they'd first met. He'd moved out of his mother's home, rented a studio apartment in Almeria and Ana-

Marie had packed her bags to join him. Those heady days had lasted two full summers, but she had grown tired of the demands of his work and its meager wage packet. He would never forget the evening, almost ten years ago, when they'd sat in a café, and she'd caught the eye of a young man who had parked his convertible sports car in a bay in front of them. The driver had smiled at her. She had no interest in him and had feigned modesty, but in that instant a world of possibilities opened up before her and the young, flat-broke Antonio Fernández was confined to history.

They stood in the interview room, holding on to each other for several moments, Ana-Marie seemingly unable to pull away, Fernández not wanting her to. The outpouring of sorrow over Laura's death had taken its toll and dark rings underscored her eyes, accentuating her pain, but not diminishing the beauty of her eyes or their impact.

At last, she moved away from him and took another tissue from the box on the table. 'I'm sorry,' she whispered, her voice weak.

'Don't be. Those who are left behind never find enough answers.'

'But murder?'

'Would it have been any easier if she'd died in the plane on her way to see José?'

'At least we'd be able to understand why. Oh, Antonio, what has happened? How could anyone want to harm Laura? She was so beautiful, so full of life, so...'

'You look tired,' he said, pulling a chair out from underneath the table and steering her into it. 'Can I get you anything?'

'No, no. I'm ok.'

'I'm sorry I wasn't here yesterday.'

'It's probably for the best. I was a wreck. I'm sure I don't look much better now.' She managed a thin smile but it soon faded.

'Do you feel up to making a statement?'

151

'A statement?'

'Routine, but you were one of the last to see Laura alive, other than…'

Ana-Marie dragged air into her lungs as though fighting for composure. After a few moments she said quietly. 'She was with us at the fiesta. Leo Medina was chatting to her. She'd just received a text message from José. He'd made Madrid's first team.'

'Sunday. Played well, apparently.'

'Did you see the match?'

'No. I was busy.'

'I caught some of it. Sofia couldn't sit through it all.'

'I'll need to talk to Sofia. Leo said she was with Laura moments before she left.'

'Sofia?'

'The investigation into the murders last Thursday is not making much headway and Sofia did report seeing an old man carrying a carpet. An old carpet was used to conceal the weapons.'

'She probably overheard the men talking at the bar, or Leo questioning them, and repeated what she heard.'

'Maybe.' He offered her a cigarette, but she declined. 'I'd like to talk to her and her friend, Gloria.'

'I'll talk to Inocenta.' Ana-Marie shuddered. 'And Laura?' she asked. 'What's happening?'

'Tell me about their relationship.'

'Well, they've known each other for years, of course. Went to school in the village, same class I think. Leo knew them both. They're all about the same age. José signed professional for Real on his sixteenth birthday and has been in Madrid for the past nine years, making his way through the youth and reserve teams. He had a setback last year when he broke his leg. He spent a few weeks at home, met up with Laura, they had a fling and he went back to Madrid. That was that until about three months ago. He was playing in the Madrid reserves against Almeria. A group of us went to support him. He was substituted at halftime and came into the stands to watch the rest of the match with us. He and Laura clicked, I guess. They've been an item ever since.'

'But you haven't seen José recently?'

'No.'

'Or spoken to him?'

'No. I've tried his mobile several times. His car's parked outside the cemetery.'

'The Aston Martin? Forensics have towed it away.'

'You can't think my brother had anything to do with Laura's death?'

'We know she left the fiesta early, went home to pack and was scheduled to catch the morning flight to Madrid. We know that she didn't check-in at the airport. We can only assume that José tried to contact her, and then drove down to find out why she hadn't turned up.' Fernández hesitated; knowing the next few questions would be painful. 'Laura's father has told us about her other boyfriends.'

'She was an attractive woman. Men found her irresistible. But she wouldn't have risked her relationship with José.'

'You knew she was pregnant?'

'José was going to be a father?'

'We haven't been able to establish that yet.'

'But it would be his.'

'It would help if you'd allow us to take a sample of your DNA. Until we find your brother…'

'Are you suggesting there may be someone else?'

'We have a couple of names.'

'Men she may have..?'

'Our investigation is on-going.' He looked across the table at a gold pendant resting high between her breasts. 'Do you mind if I have a look at that? We found something similar on Laura.'

She fumbled with the clasp behind her neck, managed to undo it, but hesitated before handing the pendant over to him.

153

'Paul wanted it to be a surprise, but he must have dropped it. I found it in the rubble when I went to see him at the church yesterday.' She ran her fingers over it absentmindedly. 'I remember Laura was wearing hers on Friday evening. She and José had bought one for each other. She never took it off.' She passed it to him, her tears returning and she wept silently.

Fernández glanced at the pendant and waited. He offered another coffee. She shook her head.

'Ana-Marie,' he said, sitting on the edge of the table and taking her left hand, holding it gently, conscious of her wedding and engagement rings, 'I need you to tell me everything you remember about Friday evening at the fiesta and,' he hesitated. 'I also need to know why you chose to visit Consuela, Juanita, and Madalena last Thursday.'

She looked at him. 'I went because mama had baked a chocolate cake. She's known Juanita for...well forever, really.'

'They're friends?'

'Yes.'

'Why didn't she take the cake herself?'

'Antonio, what is this? Is it a criminal offense to share cake and coffee with neighbours?'

'I don't know,' he said, 'but three men carried their own lunches into the field that day and, as you were enjoying your cake and coffee, they were murdered.'

*

Dr. Javier Guzmán had just reached the ninth hole when he caught sight of Leo Medina striding down the fairway.

The morning's four-balls had gone well. Guzmán and his partner were three up, looking forward to pressing home their advantage on the back nine and enjoying a few drinks, courtesy of their vanquished opponents. He lent over his club and after several phantom strokes he struck the ball firmly. It skirted the rim of the cup and settled about two meters away. He stood back, cursed quietly, shook his head and watched as his opponent's ball disappeared into the hole, cutting their lead by one shot.

'At least you went for it,' Medina called, as he strode onto the green. 'Nothing I hate more than those who wimp out and pull up short.'

'What is it, detective?'

'We need to talk.'

'Can't it wait?'

'If it could, I wouldn't be here, would I?'

Guzmán stowed his putter and carried the full set over to an electric buggy, where his golfing buddies were waiting. 'I'll be with you as soon as the wooden top's done,' Medina heard him say and watched him dump his clubs in the back before it moved off to the next tee.

Guzmán turned slowly and strolled towards Medina.

'So, what is it that's so important that you have to disrupt my only day off?'

'We need to know Laura's due date.'

'And, by simple calculation, the date of conception?'

'It would help.'

'You still think I killed her, don't you?'

'You're in the frame.'

'Now, ask yourself, why would I do that? We had an affair, yes. It ended around the time she conceived, yes. I didn't want any complications, agreed. But murder?'

'You'd have access to a sharp bladed knife – not a scalpel, too clinical, more like a knife you'd use for gutting a fish or slitting a pig's throat.'

'Oh, come on!' Guzmán's temper began to surface, just as Medina had seen it bubble during their exchange at the surgery the day before.

'You'd know how to slit her throat so death was a certainty. You'd know how long it would take for her to bleed to death. You wrapped her body in a sheet and then in polythene to prevent your 4x4 from being soiled. You bundled her into the boot and threw her down the mineshaft.'

'Oh, for God's sake. I really don't have to put up with this.' Guzmán moved towards Medina and stabbed a finger at his

155

chest. 'You're way off the mark, detective.' He hesitated, his anger making him stumble over his words. 'I'm sick to death of your, of your accusations. I'll say it once more. I did not kill Laura.'

'You'll need a lift home.' Medina nodded towards the doctor's car being winched onto the back of a break down truck.

'This is outrageous!'

'Not if you've got nothing to hide. It's amazing how forensic science has advanced. Do you watch any of those documentaries on satellite TV? Amazing.' Medina's voice trailed off as he opened an envelope. 'Whoever murdered Laura hadn't expected her to be found. The mines have been closed for years and…'

'Oh, spare me the history lesson.'

'But then two little boys decided they'd skip school and we have a murder enquiry on our hands. An enquiry that will strip away every layer of the victim's life, personal and private - those parts of their life that are already in the public domain and those they'd rather have kept under wraps. Except, of course, the victim isn't able to complain about the invasion of privacy, is she? Her human rights have already been taken from her and we're left to represent her.'

'Jesus. You're beginning to sound pompous.' Guzmán shook his head and began to stride towards the next tee, shouting, 'Now, if you've done harassing me, I do have a round of golf to complete.'

Medina sensed Guzmán's composure was about to evaporate and he couldn't resist baiting him once more, calling out, 'We could do this back at the Town Hall in a nice, cosy interview room. We'll lay on coffee and you can have your lawyer sitting by your side, holding your hand.' He waited as Guzmán approached the tee, his golfing buddies within earshot, before he waved a sheet of paper he'd taken from the envelope and shouted, 'And, you'll be able to tell us why you paid twenty-thousand euros into Laura Domingo's bank account and where you were in the small hours of Saturday morning.'

156

*

Carlos Domingo sat silently in the passenger seat of his neighbour's truck during the journey back from Almeria. He asked to be dropped off outside the village bank and stood gazing through the window at the solitary teller behind the counter. The bank manager had refused his last request for more time and more money and Carlos couldn't decide whether it was worth going cap-in-hand again, whether it was worth carrying on, keeping the farm going. His doctor had lied to him. The test results were on his desk. Carlos didn't understand most of it, but he knew what *terminal* meant.

He hesitated, rested his head on the bank's display window and rocked slowly, his forehead hitting the glass.

'Carlos.' The bank teller came out. 'You'll do yourself a mischief.' She smiled and went over to him, taking his arm. 'Have you come to see me?'

'I've come to see him.'

'Mr. Alvarez is very busy at the moment.'

'He'll see me.'

'Not without an appointment.'

'Then I'll wait.'

'Can I help you?'

He looked at her pretty face and said, 'You'd be about her age.'

'Laura was very beautiful, and popular with everyone. We were in the same class all the way through high school.' The teller dropped her voice. 'We'll all miss her, dreadfully.'

'Can I see him now?'

She sighed, trying to be patient. 'No, I'm sorry. It's all a bit difficult today, what with his son being so ill after that dreadful fall in the mine. I'll call you tomorrow with an appointment.'

'I said I'll wait.'

'Tomorrow. I promise.'

Suddenly a voice interrupted them. 'Carlos?' Fernández got out of his car, took him by the arm and steered him away

157

from the entrance to the bank.

'You caught him yet?'

'We've narrowed the search down to three possible suspects. My officers have been conducting interviews with two of them this morning. Come on. Let's get you home.' He opened the rear door of his car, waited until the farmer got in and then climbed into the driver's seat.

Carlos stared out of the window. 'I was on me way to see you.'

'What about?'

'Can you get copies of the stuff they show on the news?'

'Newsreel footage? I would imagine so. Why?'

'Can you get them shots of the campo they showed this morning? From a helicopter. Shots of the mineshaft and the hills where them three men was killed.'

'You going to tell me why?'

'I was watching the news in a shop in Almeria this morning. I think I saw someone who could have seen them murders. What do you call it? A witness? Yes, a witness to them murders.'

'A witness to the murders on Thursday?'

'He could have seen what happened to my Laura, as well. But he'll won't be able to tell you.'

'Carlos, you're beginning to talk in riddles. You want to tell me who he is?'

'Pepe. The goatherd. He ain't got no tongue, so he can't talk. But he could've seen what happened.'

'You're sure about this?'

'Not 'til I see the…'

'Newsreel footage?'

'Could help you though, couldn't it, if someone sees them doing it?'

'It could indeed, Carlos. It could indeed.' Fernandez took his mobile from his jacket pocket and dialled one of the presets. He passed on Carlos' request for the newsreel footage to Valencia Ramoz. She had some good news for him - Laura's

DNA results were in. 'OK. Thanks,' he said. 'Get some coffee on. Did Ana-Marie leave a blood sample?'

'Yes. You can pick it up and take it over to the lab on your way home tonight.'

'I'll call in and see Doctor Santiago.'

'Thought you might.'

'I don't pay you to think, Val.' He smiled as he cut the call and glanced in the rear view mirror as Jacinta Estrada turned the corner. He lent over and opened the front passenger door for her. She slid in beside him, turning to say, 'Morning, Carlos. How've you been?'

He didn't answer.

Estrada looked across at Fernandez who shook his head slightly and then passed a small plastic evidence bag to her. 'See what he makes of this. Then take him home. You may have to run the press gauntlet when you get there.'

'No worries. I was going to call the troops together tomorrow morning, nine o'clock. Thought we should establish a routine - check in each day and plan the next step.'

'Sounds good. And now I'm going to church. I need to have a chat with Father Gabriel.' He got out of the car.

Carlos rolled down the car window and said, 'When they going to let me take her home? I'd like her home one more time before she's put to rest.'

'I'll arrange for a funeral director to talk you,' Fernandez said.

'I've already been to see him. This morning.'

'Perhaps we can arrange something later. The officer will take you home now. Don't go setting those geese on the newshounds camped outside your farm, will you?' He nodded at Jacinta Estrada who clambered into the driver's seat and turned the ignition key.

As he watched the car round a bend, his mobile rang.

'Yes?'

'Well, good morning Inspector.'

'Doctor Santiago. Did the walk last night clear your head?'

'It helped. I have the results of the DNA and other tests, including the cotton and polythene sheets Laura was wrapped in. Can you come over this afternoon?'

'About four? I'll try not to be late.'

She laughed. 'I should be finished by then.'

'I'll have Ana-Marie's DNA sample with me.'

'Really? And who suggested you take a sample from her?'

He hesitated, catching the edge in her voice. 'Well, she's José's sister. We thought we could cut a few corners, run a check on the foetus Laura was carrying.'

'That's not what I asked you.' Her tone had changed, dropping several degrees.

'Is there a problem?'

'Yes, for Christ's sake. I can't keep track of the forensic evidence if I'm not kept in the loop.' She paused. 'The forensics are very much my shout, Inspector. Who the hell had the temerity to suggest you take a sample from Ana-Marie? And, more to the point, who the hell authorised the procedure?'

Fernandez heard something in her voice he hadn't heard before and hadn't even considered it might be an issue. It was the way she said *Ana-Marie*, as though resentful of her and, if not resentful, then what? Threatened by her, jealous of her? He wasn't sure, but whatever Santiago's agenda he wasn't going to admit taking medical advice from Rodrigo Perpiñán. 'I'll see you at four,' he said. 'We can talk then.'

*

Estrada drove down the two-kilometre hill into the valley and then swung onto the dirt track that climbed towards Domingo Farm. Before they got to the farm, she pulled over into the entrance to a field, turned the engine off and took the evidence bag that Fernandez had given her from the glove compartment. She broke the seal and took out the gold Indalo Man pendant. She passed it over to Carlos. 'This was found on Laura,' she said.

160

He turned the figure in his hands. 'She wore it round her neck.'

'You know what it is?'

'Indalo Man,' he answered. 'Something to do with a cave painting, as far as I know.'

'Leo Medina said he remembered seeing someone else wearing something similar in one of the photographs you had on your mantelpiece. Do you mind if I take a look when we get you home?'

'Why should I mind?'

'This is gold, Carlos. Expensive. Do you know where Laura bought it?'

'She didn't.'

Estrada sensed he might not be able to hold it together for much longer. 'Carlos?'

'Laura had lots of friends. They'd come and stay, sleep out in the barn, drink themselves silly, she'd play her guitar and they'd sing songs.' He paused. 'They used to record themselves on a machine, in the barn.'

'They made a demo?'

'I helped them. I used to press the button on the machine they had.' He sighed heavily, struggling with the recall. 'They'd count: one, two three, and I'd press the button.' He looked at Estrada. 'They'd work on me farm, some of them did, come summer. I often wonder if they had homes of their own to go to. But they was happy, if you know what I mean?'

'I think I do, Carlos.'

'She had lots of boys after her.' He used the sleeve of his shirt to wipe away his tears. 'No-one serious.'

Estrada realised that he had no idea that Laura was pregnant. Any contact with the media would probably have been accidental. He didn't have TV, and newspapers probably left him cold or challenged his ability to read. She asked, 'Did Laura ever mention Dr. Guzmán?'

'He was her doctor. They went out a few times, as far as I know.'

161

'Did she know a man called Adam Wells?'

'I never heard that one's name before.' Carlos paused. 'Besides, it all stopped a few months ago.'

'What do you mean?'

'The man wearing that thing round his neck in the photo you're on about?' He broke off, as tears began to flow. 'He's a boy from the village. José Castaño. They fell in love. They was getting married. Bought each other that Indalo Man. Sort of engagement, I s'pose.'

He started to sob and she realised this could have been the first time he'd cried since the news of Laura's murder. She stepped out of the driver's seat, opened the rear door and slid next to him. She offered tissues and pulled him into her, holding him, as his body shook with grief. He resisted at first, as though unused to the comfort of a woman, but, once he had surrendered to her, she held him and waited. Laura had been all he had. Now he had no one.

'I'm sorry,' he said eventually, taking a handkerchief, blowing his nose and looking at her through tear stained eyes.

'Don't be, Carlos. You've been through a lot.'

'It was that pendant that set me off.' He took the figure from her. 'Indalo Man. He's holding a rainbow above his head.' He paused, as though fighting to regain his composure. 'It's meant to protect the person that wears it and bring them good luck.'

*

Fernández found Father Gabriel in the church fussing over the mess being made by the contractors. Shoring up the foundations in the crypt had delayed the completion of the renovation and, no matter how well the entrance to the ramp was screened, dust continued to leak into the main body of the church. The sound of the Bobcat clawing away resonated through the church as a procession of men carried buckets full of rubble through a side door and dumped their loads into a skip.

162

'They do the best they can, I suppose,' Father Gabriel said as he pushed his spectacles back up the bridge of his nose. 'I was just going to check on progress. Would you like to join me, Inspector?'

He walked uneasily down the ramp, his hand searching the wall for purchase.

The basement of the church spread under most of its footprint, supported by massive stone columns that sectioned the cavernous area into a honeycomb of chambers. The floor was cratered with fresh diggings, some of which had been left gaping, whilst others had been filled with rubble or concrete. Additional metal joists had been brought in to shore up the walls and ceiling. The air was thick with dust.

Father Gabriel stepped cautiously through the rubble. He stopped at one side of the Bobcat and signalled to the driver. Within moments the machine's engine died and Paul Turnbull clambered out of the cab. He removed his helmet and mask and cast them to one side.

'Father,' Turnbull said, looking over at Fernández and nodding, 'I hope these aren't the reinforcements you promised me.'

'I wanted to satisfy myself that things are on schedule.'

'As far as possible. One of my drivers is off sick today so I've had to step in.'

'That's good of you.'

'I can't stay long. I've got a meeting in Almeria and a plane to catch. But this remedial work can't be delayed much longer.' He looked at Fernández. 'The church was built on weak foundations. Cracks began to appear in the walls as the building shifted.'

'Subsidence?'

'The original foundations were laid over a thousand years ago on old Roman mine workings. The problems weren't detected when they rebuilt in the sixteenth century.'

'But the work you are doing will remedy that?'

163

'We're drilling boreholes and filling with concrete. Have the funds been agreed, by the way?'

'I'm still waiting for confirmation.'

'Any delay could prove costly.' Turnbull climbed back into the Bobcat. He smiled at Fernández, 'Good to see you again, Antonio.'

The Bobcat's engine gunned into life and Fernández followed Father Gabriel back up the ramp.

As they left the church and walked up the main road towards the heart of the village, the Priest said, 'You wanted to see me?'

'I wondered why you'd want so many photographs of the village, particularly from the early nineteen seventies?'

'You've been to see Rodrigo Perpiñán.'

'He gave me a list of everyone who'd shown an interest in the last twelve months.'

'And, how's your investigation going, Inspector?'

'That's what I need to talk to you about. There was an incident around the end of 1973, beginning of 1974.'

The Priest stepped up onto the small viewing platform that overlooked the plains and mountains. He sat on a wooden bench and patted the seat beside him. 'You know why the men still refuse to enter the church?'

'Rome withdrew the village's full-time Priest after Father Emanuel was killed.'

'He was murdered and I think you're aware of the part your father played during events that dreadful night.'

Fernández held his tongue, blood pounding in his head, struggling with the accusation and its veracity.

'The murder of Father Emanuel, a man of the cloth, shocked Rome, particularly because it happened so many years after the terrible events of the Civil War.' Father Gabriel paused and looked at Fernández. 'Juan Gonzales was one of the few in the village who would talk to me about that night.'

'You knew he was going to kill Alberto Ramos?'

'No, of course not, but after what he did last Thursday, you cannot doubt the depth of despair and anger he felt when he heard that both his father and his mother had been slaughtered.' He paused again. 'The assassination of the Prime Minister, Luis Blanco, in December1973 is still regarded as one of the first acts of modern terrorism. Those who plotted his death, those who carried out the attack, and those who harboured the perpetrators were, effectively, part of the same terrorist organisation.'

'You're saying my father was a terrorist.'

'That's what today's newspapers would say, wouldn't they? I can just imagine the headlines: *The hunt for the terrorists who killed the Prime Minister*'. What else would you expect those responsible to be called? Freedom fighters? ETA is still active today; still committing acts of terrorism, still killing innocent people.' Father Gabriel paused and looked over his glasses. 'To take another man's life is no more excusable in war than it is under the circumstances faced by your father. No matter how much we might argue that the cause was just.'

'But it was Franco's death squad who killed innocent people that night. And that was down to Father Emanuel and Jésus Gonzales.'

'And Teresa Gonzales? What part did she play? Did she deserve to die?'

Fernández turned away, his anger threatening to spill over. He was still struggling to justify what his father had done and wondered if he'd ever be able to come to terms with the barbarity of his actions.

'After Father Emanuel had been killed,' Father Gabriel continued, 'the Vatican decided that the village should no longer be entitled to its own Priest.' He stared down at the sandals on his feet, his face drawn in seriousness. 'I needed copies of the photographs because I am charged with undertaking an investigation of my own. I need to know everything about that evening in January 1974 when Father Emanuel was murdered. If I can uncover the truth then it's possible that we can kick-start a process of reconciliation.'

'And the village would get its Priest back, full time?'

'But only if I learn all there is to know. And that means exposing the part played by your father and his accomplices.'

'Accomplices?' The word stung.

Father Gabriel tilted his head slightly.

'And, and your report will be made public?'

'That is for Rome to decide, but these days it is difficult to suppress matters that are deemed to be in the public interest. But, I will see what I can do and with your help, who knows what miracles we can perform, eh?'

'I'll see to it that you have access to the information our investigation uncovers once it no longer sub judice.'

'Thank you. I also need to know if there is any truth in the rumour that he fathered a child. I need to find the woman known by those closest to Father Emanuel as the Priest's whore. And, I think you might be able to point me in the right direction, Inspector.'

He left Father Gabriel and made his way towards the Town Hall where he'd parked his car.

As he entered the square the old mayor, Eduardo Gomez, called after him. 'Antonio. Can you spare me a moment of your precious time?'

'What can I do for you, Eduardo?'

'It's more a case of what we can do for you.'

'We?'

'Things have moved apace since we last spoke at the funerals of Alberto, Bartolomé and Matias.'

'I'm forgiven then?'

'Passions were running high, but you should close the book on their deaths and concentrate on finding who killed Laura Domingo.'

'You must know I won't do that?'

The old mayor was silent for a moment and dropped his head, shuffling his feet, clearly debating with himself.

'That's as we expected.'

'You keep saying *we*.'

'Saturday seems an age away but, since the funerals, many of the men in the village have been talking. Well, arguing, more like. We know Rodrigo Perpiñán has been working with you. We know that you've questioned Felipe Romero and taken things from his home. For most of us, nothing adds up.'

'Then, let's hope my arithmetic is superior.'

'Come on, Inspector, I'm throwing you a lifeline. We can help you.'

Fernández waited, taking out a cigarette and offering one across. He knew Gomez's offer was tempting and he'd be stupid not to take it. This was a sign that the men in the village had seen sense at last and their co-operation, no matter how begrudgingly given, was exactly what he'd hoped for.

'It was Laura's murder that changed everything,' Gomez said, accepting a cigarette and pausing as he cupped his hands around the lighter's weak flame. 'We want to help.'

'You must know I won't tolerate any vigilante gangs cutting loose on my patch.'

'Yes, of course. But, you don't have the manpower to cover everything. You have the press breathing down your neck. José Castaño is still missing and his fiancée's in the city morgue.' Gomez paused as he drew deeply on his cigarette. 'I'm offering to help, in any way we can.'

'You think the men can be trusted not to step outside the boundaries I lay down?'

'You have my personal assurance.'

'It's not your head on the block, is it?' Fernández needed to channel the men's anger, their frustration and their fear, and not allow it to run rampant, unchecked. He had felt their volatility during the funerals and knew that this was something that could blow up in his face if he didn't seize it by the throat.

He turned back and faced the man who, for the best part of a decade, had once been 'the law' in this community. If anyone could exert the control needed to keep a tight reign, it would be Eduardo Gomez.

He stubbed out his cigarette. 'You're serious?'

'Yes.'

'Then you'll need to report to the Incident Room at the Town Hall each morning at nine. You'll form part of the civilian support team and take instructions from Sargento Jacinta Estrada. Go there now and she'll brief you.'

'I knew you'd see the sense of it,' Gomez said, and held out his hand. 'You won't regret this, Antonio. You'll see.'

As he walked towards his car, Aimee Douglas called after him. 'Hey, Inspector, wait up.' She began to run, encouraging a stray dog to follow her. 'You got a moment?' she asked. 'I've been thinking about what you said, about girls in the village who'd play with little Sofia.'

'You've found Gloria?'

'Not yet. Most kids that age go to school, so I may have missed her. Maybe she doesn't exist? Now, there'd be a real mystery for you, Inspector.' Aimee chuckled. She seemed happier than the last time he saw her. 'There isn't a Gloria in the village, as far as I know. Least ways, I haven't come across her. Could be an imaginary friend. I had a word with Sofia.'

Fernández stopped abruptly. 'And?'

'Nothing. That's what's so odd. Most kids create a whole world for their imaginary friend. I used to tell everyone I was training a horse for dressage competitions. I'd tell them about mucking him out each morning, grooming him, feeding him, taking him for a canter.' She smiled as she reminisced. 'A pack of lies, of course, but there you go.'

'But with Sofia?'

'She said she had a secret she'd promised never to tell.'

'Promised who?' Fernández felt his pulse quicken. 'Did she mention anyone, anyone at all?'

'No. Like I said, she told me she knew a secret. It was as though she was desperate to tell someone but was afraid to.'

'Afraid?'

'You know what it's like when you're a kid and you're

168

worried because you've done something wrong?' Aimee looked at him, her face serious and worried. 'I'm not a trick-cyclist but that girl's got some serious stuff going on in her head. She was always so carefree - wild, I suppose - always giggling, up to mischief. You know what I mean?'

'But?'

'The village is alive with rumours, you know? So much has happened. Sofia's brother's gone missing. His car's been left outside the cemetery and his girl friend's been murdered. Sofia's mother's upset, crying an' stuff. And those men were murdered a stone's throw from her home. All that's gotta do little Sofia's head in, don't you think?'

*

Leo Medina was the first to arrive back at the Incident Room and set about completing outstanding paper work, which he would pass over to Valencia Ramoz to process.

'Things hotting up?' Ramoz said.

'Yeah.' He seemed despondent.

'You ok?'

'Yeah.' He turned back to his computer.

'Kids glad to be out of school?'

'The youngest's waited until he's on holiday to go down with flu and the eldest has a hacking cough that suggests he's up to forty-a-day.'

'Best get them to the doctor's.'

'Roz'll give it a couple of days, see if they get any better.'

'You've told her about Dr. Guzmán and Laura?'

'She doesn't need me to keep her up to date. Gossip doesn't take long to do the rounds, does it?'

'Roz coping?'

'Yeah, her mum's staying with us for the summer.'

'How did your interview with Dr. Guzmán go?'

'I'm not sure, but do you know what really pisses me off?' Medina paused. 'He showed no sign of sadness or loss.'

'You think he killed Laura?'

'Maybe. The only thing I'm sure about is that he's a piece of shit.'

'Does he have an alibi?'

'He says he was at a Lodge meeting on Friday evening and then toured the bars on the beach until the small hours.'

'I'll send uniform down to the front, see if anyone can remember seeing him. Did he consent to giving a DNA sample?'

'Yeah. Said he'd drop by before surgery this evening. He didn't seem overly concerned. If he was the father, he's not going to have to worry about maintenance payments is he?'

Jacinta Estrada breezed in.

'Eduardo Gomez is waiting for you - interview room one,' Ramoz told her.

'Thanks, Val. The Inspector called me to say Eduardo would be dropping by. Do me a favour and give him a coffee. I'll sort him out after I've had lunch.'

'No problem. How's Carlos?'

'In a mess. He tried to see the bank manager. I took him home. We were greeted by press boys who'd been waiting all day.'

'I hope he set his dogs on them.' Medina muttered.

'No, but he did discharge both barrels of his shotgun at them.'

'You're joking.'

'Nope. We pulled up outside the gates of the farm. Carlos called his dogs over. They held the press boys at bay whilst we retreated inside. Then, before I knew it, he'd taken a loaded twelve bore outside and fired above their heads. By the time I got there, he'd given them a piece of his mind and seen them off.'

'Probably did him a power of good.'

'We may have to make a show of taking action against him. Cover our backs.' Estrada removed her jacket and tossed it

170

onto the back of her chair. 'I'll follow it up later.'

'And Adam Wells?' Ramoz handed her a cup of coffee.

'Another piece of shit,' muttered Medina.

'He'll have some explaining to do when his wife puts two and two together.'

'Alibi?'

'Says they went to the fiesta on Friday night, stayed until it was pretty obvious the band had set up for nothing and went home about one. He'll drop by before his art class this evening and give whatever DNA samples we need. He's hoping his cooperation will buy our discretion.'

'Any idea what time he's likely to be here?' Ramoz asked. 'It's my little one's birthday.'

'You go. I'll hold the fort. Just don't forget my piece of cake tomorrow morning.' Estrada smiled thinly, and then pulled several evidence bags from a hold all and looked across at Medina. 'You were right, Leo - the photos you saw at the farm - Laura with José, both wearing Indalo Man pendants.' She looked through the clear plastic at the faces of the young lovers, needing to ensure that Medina stayed focused. 'See if anything useful's been found in the bags taken from the homes of Juan Gonzales and Felipe Romero. Let me know what's turned up.' She watched him haul himself to his feet and trudge out of the room before turning to Ramoz. 'Keep an eye on him.'

'Of course. It's not surprising he's finding it difficult: too close to home. Not sure if I'd cope half as well.'

'You and me.' Estrada hesitated and then passed the photos of Laura and José to Ramoz. 'Process these and put them with everything else we've found so far. And don't forget that coffee for Eduardo Gomez. I can't spend too long with him. I need to catch up with our three widows.'

*

Julieta Santiago saw Fernández sitting in the corridor with his eyes closed, head bowed, arms folded, the fingers of his right hand drumming on a coolsafe. His face was tight with concentration and his forehead furrowed. She decided she'd leave him too it.

She left her mortuary technician to finish up and retrieved the recording she'd made earlier during an autopsy on a suspected heart attack - a young man, twenty-three years old. She had arranged to see the family, to explain that he'd had a congenital heart defect and could have gone at any time. She had trouble getting away, pouring out more energy than she could afford, soaking up the family's anguish. In the end, the only way she felt she could survive was to leave them to it and walk away.

She grabbed a couple of files from the lab, tucked them under her arm and filled a paper cup with cold water from a dispenser. She walked down the corridor and nudged the Inspector's toecap.

He woke with a start.

'Have you brought her sample?'

'Yes.' He handed over the cool-safe containing Ana-Marie's DNA. 'How'd it go? The family.'

'Hang me out to dry. I'm not sure how anyone copes with such tragedy. He was no more than a kid playing football on the beach, for God's sake.' Santiago sat next to him, opened the coolsafe and toyed with the tubes in the micro centrifuge. 'Did you authorize this?'

'Yes.'

She sighed and threw her head back, blowing a lungful of air up towards the ceiling.

'Is there a problem?'

'Yes. Yes there's a problem, Antonio. To stand a chance of conviction, the forensics will have to be watertight. I've seen too many lawyers drive a chasm between the prosecution case and the truth. I don't want to lose this one. And besides, samples like this are usually a waste of time. Ana-Marie is José's sister and, if he is the father, Ana-Marie would be the child's aunt.

There may not be a sufficient match for the DNA to be used in court. I'll get the sample processed but don't hold your breath.'

He broke open a new packet of cigarettes.

'Not down here. Come up to my office.'

She led him up two floors. The room was sunny and a large vase of flowers had been placed in the centre of a table. 'Coffee?' She threw the files on the table and removed her lab coat. She picked up a kettle and disappeared into an adjoining room that served as a kitchen and storeroom. 'Ashtray's on the table. Browse the files if you want.'

'I'd prefer the edited highlights.' He walked over to the window, lit a cigarette and looked down at the hospital car park. She was right, of course: if the forensics were compromised, there'd be no conviction.

Santiago carried a tray with two mugs, a cafeteria and a box of chocolates to the table. 'Help yourself.'

'I'll pass.' He dragged on his cigarette and watched her bury herself in one of the files. 'Did you ever have an imaginary friend?' he asked, as he pulled up a chair next to her.

'Yes. It's a phase most kids go through. They can be very real and any suggestion to the contrary can provoke a strong reaction: big pout, the sulks, and a scornful affirmation of the adult's stupidity. Holly and Sofia share an imaginary friend.'

'Gloria?'

'Yes, how did you..?' She stopped and looked at the concern in his face. 'What is it, Antonio?'

'I don't think Gloria is part of Sofia's make believe. I think Gloria is real and may even have been involved in the murder of four men last Thursday. I just haven't worked out how, yet.'

'Let's see if this helps.' She opened one of the files she'd carried from the mortuary, and helped herself to another chocolate. 'We have three different types of DNA - Laura's, her unborn child's, and the deposits found under her fingernails. The child's DNA will help us identify the father.'

173

'We've got two men volunteering samples. We're waiting to interview Laura's fiancé, José Castaño.'

'Still missing?'

'He hasn't come forward or made contact with his family. It's possible that he was the last person to see Laura alive.'

She sipped her coffee, took the other file and flipped it open, scanning it quickly. 'The sheet in which Laura's body was wrapped is fine Egyptian cotton. Not unusual in itself, although when I say fine I mean expensive. There'll be a limited number of outlets selling quality sheets like this, even in Almeria. The killer must have worked quickly or in poor lighting. He overlooked a dry cleaning ticket that was stapled to one of the corners of the sheet. There's no company name, address, or telephone number. It's simply a ticket with a number on it, like a raffle ticket, purchased in any stationers. But it does have a secret. We've immersed it in Ninhydrin and lifted a fingerprint. It's unlikely to be the killer's, but if you can match the print with someone at the laundry they might be able to identify the customer.'

'I'll ask Jacinta Estrada to organize a sweep of all dry cleaners and high-end retailers in Almeria.'

'It's a long shot.'

'We only need one hit.'

'The sheet had traces of Laura's blood, hair, and fibres from her clothing, as well as particles of sand. We also found sea water that had dried into the fabric, leaving salt deposits.'

'A beach?'

'Most probably. The small amount of blood found on the sheet suggests that she bled to death before she'd been rolled up in it.'

'So, he took her to the beach...' Fernández hesitated before asking, 'Were there signs of sexual intercourse or rape?'

'No.'

'They argued and he hit her.'

'Repeatedly.'

'Then slit her throat.'

'Why would he do that? Why not break her neck or use a rock to smash her skull?' Santiago's face darkened. She stood and walked over to the second filing cabinet and pulled a box of tissues from the top drawer.

Fernández watched as she composed herself and waited. She looked exhausted. She'd worked long hours on Laura and had operated on the body of a young man that afternoon. Only she would know why she chose such a vocation and only she would know the toll it took on her, day in, and day out.

'We've lifted several sets of fingerprints from the polythene,' she said.

'We'll run checks'

'We also found traces of cement, sand, and lime. The polythene could have been used to cover a collection of building materials to protect them against rain. If you're lucky, there'll be traces in the car used to transport the body from the beach to the mineshaft. But, even if you matched the fingerprints and the car contained traces, you'll never be able to make it stick in court. Either of your main suspects could have picked up the polythene from any building site. Finding her blood would help, of course.' Santiago tried to smile as she looked at him. 'You still haven't told me why you think he slit her throat.'

Fernández sighed heavily. 'I don't know. It may be his calling card or a local man used to slitting the pig's throat at a matanza. He could have acted instinctively or during the frenzy of the kill. He may have wanted to protect his car by draining all the blood into the sand and let the high tide wash it away - no trace, no evidence.' He hesitated. 'It's too easy to accept the most obvious reason for the attack - she was pregnant and was extorting money. But, what if it wasn't that simple? What if Laura knew something far more threatening?'

'Like what?'

'I'm not sure.' He paused. 'I'm still wrestling with the murders in the campo last Thursday.'

'But we're getting closer to the truth.'

175

'Yes, but we still don't know who shot Juan Gonzales and tried to fake his suicide, or why Bártolome was finished off.' He got up and walked over to the window overlooking the car park.

'You ok?' She asked.

'Not really.' He continued to stare out of the window.

'What is it, Antonio? What's wrong?'

He dragged air into his lungs, determined not to renege on his resolution and succumb to his emotions, but he wanted to tell her.

When he'd finished, Santiago joined him at the window, linked an arm though his and said gently, 'I wish you'd told me before.'

'The timing has never been right, has it? It's why I found Sunday so difficult, after mama had slaughtered the pig.' He hesitated. 'I'm sorry for keeping you out of this particular loop.'

She closed her eyes and shuddered. He took his jacket off and slipped it over her shoulders. 'Thanks,' she said, and pulled the coat tighter into her. 'And thanks for telling me about your father.'

They stood for several moments, arm in arm, as though hypnotised by the mundane activity of the car park below. She pulled him to her and he tightened his grip on her, acknowledging the reassurance. 'We should get back to work,' he said, eventually.

'Yes.'

He brushed away hair that had fallen onto his forehead, unsure how she would react to his next request. 'I need to talk to Holly.'

'About?'

'What Sofia told her.'

'You think Sofia saw something, don't you?'

'I'm up against a wall of silence. I haven't heard anything from the Ramos women and I was sure that Juanita would come through.'

'They've had a lot on their minds, Antonio.'

176

'Yes, I know. Jacinta Estrada's been to see Juanita today. She may have something for me. I'll know tomorrow morning.' He paused and then added, 'Ana-Marie thinks Sofia made it up or overheard it.'

'Highly likely, given her age.' Santiago returned to the table and gathered up the files. 'You can talk to Holly but I want to be present.'

'Of course.'

She stood beside him at the window. Her arm brushed against him and he caught her stale perfume, testimony to her long hours. 'You must be shattered,' he said.

'Nothing a long walk or hot shower won't remedy.'

'Would you mind if I joined you?'

'In the shower?' She looked at him and there was a moment's hesitation before they both tumbled into laughter, hesitant at first, as though neither could let go, and then, as though throwing caution to the wind, they both succumbed, and each time one of them tried to stifle the laughter they burst out laughing again until their sides ached and their eyes watered.

'God those endorphins are better than any drug,' she said as she fought for breath. 'If we could bottle them we'd make a fortune.'

He looked at her - her face alive with joy – his mind sidetracked by the thought of joining her in the shower. 'I meant,' he said, 'for a walk.'

'Don't apologise, Antonio. I know what you meant. Just couldn't resist teasing you.'

'Look,' he said, 'I may have stepped out of line when I authorized Ana-Marie's DNA sample, but I thought it was for the best.'

'I know. We're on the same side. Just keep me in the loop in future. Please.' She glanced at him. 'Come on, let's take that walk.'

They made their way down the Paseo de Almeria and across the busy intersection to the harbour.

He glanced across the quiet quayside at the huge container ships, cargo boats, barges, tugs, and pilot launches. Most craft were tied up for the night, probably manned by a skeleton crew, as seamen took well-earned shore leave.

'I love it here,' she said.'Gives me a sense of perspective. I come down whenever I can, sometimes alone, usually with Holly. I spend most of my days in the confines of a windowless morgue, but here we have ships registered in Panama, Luxembourg, Madeira, Japan, France, and Norway. Each with multinational crews, sailing to the far corners of the world, visiting countries I've only ever dreamed of. If I wasn't so knackered, I'd steal up a rope ladder, stow away and wake up in Rio.' They passed a gangplank of a large container ship. It creaked with the gentle rhythm of the water lapping against the side of the quay. 'Another day, perhaps.'

'There's nothing to stop you walking the plank right now,' he said, as he retraced the few steps. 'Go on. What's the worst that could happen?'

She turned sharply and began to haul herself up a steep gangplank. 'I could be arrested and spend the night in a cell,' she called. She slowed as she neared the gaping entrance to the ship's cargo hold. As she neared the top, she stopped, threw her arms into the air and screamed, her joyous cry punching through the air. Then, she sat down, pulled her knees up to her chest and buried her head in her arms, looking for all the world like a small, vulnerable child.

He'd taken a few steps up the gangplank when someone opened the door to the Harbour Master's office and shouted, ''Ere, what's going on?' The uniformed guard moved from the light of the doorway, his eyes set on Santiago's figure hunched near the entrance to the cargo hold.

Fernández hurried over to him, fished out his police ID card and whispered, 'I'm with the Policia Judicial. This is a police affair. Leave it with me.'

'You want me to call for back-up?'

'No. No, I can handle it.'

'Cos I don't want no trouble on my watch.'

'You could cover me.'

Before the official could take up station on the balcony overlooking the harbour, Fernández made his way up the gangplank. He sat next to Santiago and was tempted to put his arm around her, but hesitated. She looked up at him, her eyes full, tears streaming down her face. He took a handkerchief from his jacket pocket and handed it to her. She blew her nose, took several deep breaths and looked at him, grinning broadly. She offered to return the handkerchief.

'Keep it.' He smiled. 'You ok?'

'Yes. Yes, I'm fine. It's stupid, I know, but that's the first time I've done something impulsive for years and it feels so good.'

'You want to walk?'

'No, I want to stay here forever.' She laughed and he felt her brush against him as she rocked with the gentle rhythm of the ship at anchor. 'If Holly could see me now. The number of times she's wanted to do this, to scramble up a gangplank and pretend to stow away, and I've forbidden it.' She laughed again, but her laughter died, her face suddenly etched with pain. 'She's missed out on so much.' She chewed on her lower lip as she admitted, 'Towards the end, my relationship with Holly's father was pretty acrimonious. She's confused and blames herself for his disappearance, despite the fact she never knew him.' She stood in front of Fernández and looked earnestly into his eyes. 'She's a child who needs a lot of affection and doesn't want to share her mother with anyone. She just needs time, I suppose.'

'Same could be said for her mother,' he said, and this time he did put his arm round her. She sank into his embrace as tears began to defy her. He held her as she wept, stroking her hair as he imagined she would stroke her daughter's after she'd woken from a nightmare.

He glanced across at the officer standing on the Harbour Master's balcony and signalled that all was well. He watched as ships moved eerily across the harbour and seagulls settled in for

179

the night, perching on the high ledges of buildings that skirted the wharf.

After several minutes he said gently, 'Holly's not the only one who needs time.'

'She comes as part of the package.'

'I know.' He tilted her chin upwards and kissed her gently on the lips.

She lent forward and returned his kiss, tender, light, and warm, and then rested her forehead on his, catching her breath. 'So this is what happens when we call a truce?' She smiled awkwardly. 'It's been a long time.'

'You and me, both.'

'Is it Ana-Marie?' she asked without pulling away.

'Is what Ana-Marie?'

'We met at Flamenco and when I told her I was a pathologist she asked if I'd come across you, in the line of duty. Of course, I didn't know you from Adam, but she told me all about the mad thing you had together. She's still very fond of you.' Santiago hesitated and brushed hair from his forehead. 'She meant a lot to you, didn't she?'

He puffed out his cheeks and sighed heavily. 'At the time, yes. I thought we'd be together forever. It never crossed my mind...' He laughed, hollowly. 'Now, there's arrogance for you. I didn't believe she'd dump me.'

'Are you still in love with her?'

'It was a long time ago.'

'Doesn't answer my question.'

'Do you still love Holly's father?'

'That's not fair.'

'Of course it is.'

'So, you do still love her?'

He stood up, pulled her to her feet and they walked back down the gangplank. When they'd settled on the quayside, he said, 'I won't deny that when I saw her at the funeral on Saturday, I thought she looked as attractive as ever. But,' he said, hesitating, unsure whether what he was about to say was the

180

whole truth. 'Whatever I felt for Ana-Marie died a long time ago.'

Suddenly, the shrill tone of his mobile phone cut through the air.

'I'm sorry,' he said. 'There are times when I really hate this job...' He snapped open the mobile. It was Leo Medina.

'There's been an accident, Sir. A car's over-turned on the coastal track near one of the local nudist beaches.'

'Then get Trafico out.'

'Thing is Sir, Sargento Estrada's already there. She's called out SOCO and forensics. She thinks she's found where Laura was killed.'

Day Eight

Thursday 25th June 2009

It was twenty past midnight when he drew up behind police cars that blocked the narrow track leading to the naturist beach. Santiago had insisted on accompanying him and they'd stopped off at the hospital to collect her field bag and leave a note for her assistant. He'd used the short delay to contact Jacinta Estrada, who updated him:

The emergency services had received a call from a young man. His girlfriend had been taken to hospital with a fractured pelvis, a broken leg, and multiple lacerations to her face and hands after being thrown through the windscreen of the car she was driving.

Uniformed officers had been first to arrive at the scene and the girl's boyfriend had insisted on handing over a mobile phone. The boyfriend had given Estrada an account of the events that led up to the discovery of the mobile and had been taken to see his girlfriend in hospital.

Estrada had called out reinforcements from Trafico and Policia Local and had already sealed off access to the beach where the mobile was found. An incident van and forensic team were on the way, and tents had been erected to provide a rudimentary lab, a kitchen and somewhere for officers to rest up before sunrise.

At first light, they would be ready to start combing the area. In the meantime, nothing was to be disturbed.

They walked away from the wrecked car and found Jacinta Estrada and Leo Medina waiting for them outside one of the tents.

'OK,' Estrada began, 'we may have our first real break-through.' She held an evidence bag between her thumb and forefinger. It contained the mobile phone. 'A teenage girl found it buried in the sand. According to her boyfriend, it rang several times. The caller wanted to speak to Laura.' She nodded at Medina.

'If this is where Laura was…' he hesitated. 'If this is where she was killed, we can establish an approximate timeline for her last…' Again he hesitated. 'I saw her leave the fiesta at just after midnight. She went home, packed and was picked up by a taxi just before sunrise…'

'We haven't established if it was a taxi,' Estrada said. 'Local firms have no record of a fare that matches.'

'I think we can assume whoever picked her up, killed her,' Fernández said.

'Laura was brought here,' Medina said, 'probably willingly, which would suggest she knew her killer and felt she had nothing to fear.'

'The sooner we begin the search, the better.' Santiago said, 'If she was killed above the tide line, SOCOs will need to search for blood absorbed into the sand. If the tide's washed away any trace…' She paused. 'Her body was wrapped in a sheet: Egyptian cotton, recently laundered. So, we're looking for a lightweight, plastic bag with the name of a dry-cleaners on it.'

Estrada turned to Fernández. 'You want me to stay here?'

He nodded. 'Yes. Thanks. Get your head down for a few hours. Make an early start at sun-up. You can update us at the scheduled meeting back at the Incident Room.'

'I'll stay as well,' Santiago said. 'Any evidence you find could be vital. I'd like to be on hand.'

'Fine by me.' Estrada smiled and then picked up where she'd left off. 'OK. Laura was killed and bundled into the trunk of a car, driven to the mineshaft and dumped.'

Medina moaned audibly. 'I'm sorry, but Laura was a friend, with her whole life ahead of her, and words like dumped, bundled…it's so fucking disrespectful.'

'Yes, you're right, I'm sorry.'

'It comes with the territory, Leo,' Santiago said.

'Doesn't make it any easier to listen to.'

The wind picked up as the night cooled and the tents began to flap. They retreated inside the mess tent, stood beneath a gas heater and accepted a coffee from a uniformed police cadet.

Estrada held up the mobile once again. 'Leo,' she said, 'you want to give them the really good news?'

'Yeah, sure. OK.' Medina paused, looking directly at Fernández. 'We've already established that there were several calls made before the car accident – a woman's voice, wanting to talk to Laura. I've been through the text messages and found these…' He scrolled through the sent messages and opened the one timed at ten past twelve, early on Saturday morning. 'Laura was at the fiesta. I'd been chatting to her. She got a text from José. He told her he'd been selected for Real's first team for Sunday. She sent him this message:

Congrats! Will ask Gloria 2 take me 2 airport.

'Gloria?'

'That's not all. Sofia told us she'd seen an old man and Gloria playing hide and seek. Laura took Sofia to one side, spoke to her, and then sent another text message to José.'

Got dirt on Gloria! Will use 2 get sharks off your back.

'Do we know where José Castaño was in the small hours of Saturday morning?' Fernández said. 'In an Aston Martin, he could probably do the drive from Madrid in under four-hours.'

'I've checked back through the phone's call log. There were two from a landline number in Madrid, traced to José's hotel.' Medina looked at Fernández. 'Both calls were between one and two on Saturday morning. He could have driven down, killed Laura and got back to Madrid before anyone missed him.'

'A long shot, on the eve of the most important match of his life…' Fernández hesitated. 'Question is, why would he want to harm her?'

184

Carlos Domingo had been restless all night. He was angry that the police hadn't contacted him about the newsreel footage he'd asked for. He thought at the very least Leo Medina would have chased things for him.

He'd given up trying to sleep and had sat in the high-winged chair by an unlit fire, catching his breath whenever he heard a sound, staring at the front door, his faltering imagination allowing him glimpses of Laura as she waltzed through the door, telling him she'd stopped over with friends, completely unaware of the worry he'd been through.

He had cried when the first rays of the sun broke the horizon far out at sea and reality dawned. Laura wasn't coming home. Not today. Not ever.

He knew he had a choice. He could sit in that chair and wait for the cancer to take him, or he could get up off his backside and do something. He got up, pulled on his heavy boots and slipped out the back door and stole silently across the campo.

The air was still. Early-morning swallows swept across the sky, excited by the promise of breakfast. As the sun's warmth began to bathe the land, Carlos headed towards the hills where the four men had been shot and where, over in the next valley, Laura had been found.

He knew the police would still be at both crime scenes and scientists would be sifting through evidence, helping detectives to piece together what had happened. He knew the media would be camped within striking distance. But it was Pepe, the goatherd, who Carlos wanted to find. The goats would be out there somewhere, high on the hills, searching for fresh pastures.

He caught sight of them as they ambled lazily over the sparse hillside, dogs yapping at their hindquarters, Pepe meandering slowly behind, using a makeshift staff to measure each footfall.

Carlos knew better than to surprise him and circled round to wait higher on the track. From there, he watched until he was within twenty meters

'Good morning, my friend. Do you mind if I walk with you?'

Pepe didn't acknowledge him, but walked straight past, his head bowed, his eyes fixed on the ground. Carlos caught up with him and said, 'You know who I am?'

Pepe did not respond.

'The young woman they found murdered, across the valley, in that old mineshaft? She was my daughter, Laura.' Carlos looked up at the steep path before them; the shorn backsides of the goats wandering inelegantly as each hoof found uneven footing. 'They say she had her throat cut, no better than a pig.'

Pepe tracked after his herd.

'She ain't coming back, I know that, but you can help me find him what did that to her.'

Still, Pepe appeared to ignore him.

Suddenly, he grabbed Pepe's arm and pulled him round to face him. 'I needs your help. I'm sorry but I ain't got much time. I want to find the man who did that to my little girl.' He prodded Pepe's chest. 'You gotta help me, my friend.'

Pepe's eyes widened, his mouth gaped open and a deep guttural noise rasped its way from the back of his throat. He turned onto the track and walked off, each footfall leaden and weary as though he carried a heavy burden.

Carlos watched him for a few moments then hurried after him, catching his shoulder and pulling him to face him. 'You can't walk away from this. I will not let you walk away from this. I need your help.'

Pepe shoved Carlos' hand away, screamed at him, turned and stomped after the goats.

'I was in Almeria,' Carlos shouted, 'and I passed one of them shops that sells TVs. They had the local news on, and that's when I saw you, with them goats, on this hillside.' He scurried after Pepe and caught up with him just as he reached the brow of the hill. The goats had hurried down the other side, driven by the sight of fresh vegetation. Both men fought for breath as they stood looking down towards the old mine workings and the SOCO tents that masked the entrance to the mine. 'You gotta help me,' Carlos said. 'I think you could have seen something. You could have seen the man who did that to my little girl, my Laura.'

Pepe turned on him, sounds streaming from the back of his throat, louder and more strident. He began to gesticulate, waving his arms angrily about him, shaking his fists at him. But Carlos persisted. 'I know you can't talk to me, but I thought we'd play a game, one of my little girl's favourites. You know how to play twenty questions?'

Pepe looked at him, dismissing him with a wave of his hand and starting back along the track. Carlos shouted after him, hurried to catch him, spinning him round and catching the collar of his shirt; pulling him close enough to smell the milk he'd drunk that morning. 'You nod if I get a question right. You shakes your head if I get it wrong.' Carlos looked deep into Pepe's eyes as he asked, 'Were you up here on the day my little girl was killed?'

Pepe shrugged.

'Yes, or no.'

Pepe shrugged and screamed once more, his face contorting with anger as he wrestled himself free. He tried to turn away but Carlos pulled him back to face him.

'Did you see him with her?' Carlos tightened his grip. 'You must tell me. You must tell me what you saw.'

Pepe wrenched himself free and lifted his staff, pointing it at Carlos, his eyes flaming with anger and frustration, aberrant sounds spilling from him, his body wired to strike. Suddenly, he lunged at Carlos, bringing the staff down heavily and striking him on the forearm. Again, Pepe struck and caught him on the side of the head.

Carlos stumbled backwards and lost his footing. He tumbled into the thick gorse and rolled uncontrollably down the steep slope of the hill until his head jerked backwards and hit a

187

rock. He lay motionless.

Pepe looked down, tears streaming. He raised both arms, his staff in his right hand, his left fist clenched, his whole body shaking.

His scream echoed across the valley.

*

Jacinta Estrada wondered if the aches and pains that accompanied every movement she made would ever ease. She'd slept fitfully on a thin bed of foam in a tent on the beach, conscious of a restless Julieta Santiago beside her, but at least they were able to begin the search as soon as the sun broke cover.

After several fruitless hours scouring the tidal shore, they'd driven back to the village, stopping off to grab a coffee and tostada at a bar on the main road, thankful for clean toilets and cold water to splash on their faces.

They arrived at the Town Hall just before nine-thirty to find Fernández and Leo Medina engrossed in conversation with Rodrigo Perpiñán, and Valencia Ramoz poring over documents with the Vincente Cabrera and Eduardo Gomez.

'Good to see a full house.' Estrada removed her crumpled jacket, rolled up the sleeves of her shirt and tidied her hair into a ponytail. 'I trust you all slept well.' She stood in front of the additional whiteboards installed to cope with developments in the investigations and looked across at Medina. 'Leo, any success with the items confiscated during the searches yesterday?'

'Apart from the stash of money, there wasn't a lot to write home about at Felipe Romano's, but I thought these might be of interest: several handwritten diaries belonging to Juan Gonzales.'

'OK. Good work. Have a word with one of the uniformed officers, ask him to go round to Felipe Romero's cottage and bring him here. I think it's time we turned the screw. Let's see how he copes without his daily ration of booze.'

188

She took the diaries and turned to Rodrigo Perpiñán. 'Something to keep you off the streets. Some light reading…' She placed the volumes on his lap. 'Let us know the moment you find anything.'

As Perpiñán left the room, she said, 'OK, first some good news - Joaquin Alvarez has recovered consciousness, he's been taken off life-support and has been moved into a general ward. His mother has been with him throughout the night and the doctors are optimistic he'll make a full recovery.' She smiled broadly as everyone applauded the news. 'Let's hope the rest of the day is as positive.'

She paused, checking agenda items she'd scribbled down over breakfast. 'We have documentation provided by the Mayor. Thank you, Vincente. This will be fed into the computer's database. We're still trying to locate Gloria, although Laura's texts suggest that Gloria is an adult. Technicians are still analyzing the messages and calls, but I want you all to concentrate on the two she sent at the fiesta just after midnight on Saturday.' She pinned enlarged copies on the incident board:

Congrats! I'll ask Gloria 2 take me 2 airport.

Got dirt on Gloria! Will use 2 get sharks off your back.

'I've sent copies to the Madrid police handling José's disappearance. The Aston Martin found outside the village cemetery has been traced to a company in the capital. They have confirmed that this particular car was leased to Real Madrid. José Castaño took delivery of it two months ago. Forensics have been through it with a fine tooth comb and found nothing that takes us any further forward - no mobile, no letters, no sign of a struggle.' She looked across the room, inviting Julieta Santiago to take the floor.

'I've no doubt forensics will find traces of hair on the driver's headrest. This will provide a DNA profile, but we'll be unable to compare it with José's until we locate him. The

189

resources at our disposal are stretched to breaking point.'

'Why didn't anyone see him?' Leo Medina asked suddenly. 'How did he park up and walk into the village without anyone seeing him?'

'If he drove down on Saturday morning,' Fernández said, 'killed Laura and drove back, he wouldn't have come into the village. And if he drove down after the match on Sunday, he would have arrived after dark. It wouldn't have been too difficult to slip into the village.'

'But he'd go home, wouldn't he, to his parents, or to the farm to see Laura?'

'We can assume she was picked up early Saturday morning by Gloria and José went to see him as soon as he'd parked up.'

'Him?' Estrada looked doubtful.

'I'd put money on it.' Fernández paused. 'If José came down on Saturday, he killed her. But if he came down on Sunday, he's in the clear.'

'And that puts our two other suspects back in the frame.' Estrada shook her head. 'Leo, lean on the good doctor. See if he has anyone who can confirm his alibi.'

She turned to Fernández who moved over to one of the whiteboards and wrote *Gloria*. 'Has cropped up in both investigations. Sofia Castaño claims to have seen an old man playing hide-and-seek with Gloria...'

'But we can't be certain if her old man is our old man,' Estrada said. 'Gloria could be a friend.'

'It's a coincidence, then, that he was due to take Laura to the airport?'

'And Laura had *dirt* on him.'

Suddenly, the door to the Incident Room crashed open and a uniformed officer stood fighting for breath.

'You'd better come quick. It's Felipe Romero!'

*

'His neck's been snapped like a chicken's,' Julieta Santiago said. 'Not the most scientific of descriptions, but accurate enough. The bruising here and here indicates someone came up behind him, placed a forearm around his neck and twisted, pulling upwards at the same time. Not difficult given he's severely emaciated and would not have had the strength to resist a surprise attack.'

Felipe Romero's body was propped up in a white plastic chair, his head hanging to one side, his eyes vacant. Santiago removed her mask and inhaled odour lingering at his mouth. 'He'd been drinking. I'll carry out toxicology tests later, but he probably wasn't in a fit state to put up a fight.'

The area had been sealed off, but news of the murder had reached the few remaining reporters. They'd hurried down from the square and stood craning for a shot of the corpse or trying to glean information from uniformed officers who held them at bay.

'How long's he been dead?' Fernández asked.

'His poor muscle mass may complicate diagnosis and the heat may have accelerated the process, but I'd say he's been through the eighteen hour cycle of rigor mortis and it's on its way out.' Santiago checked the thermometer. 'Core temperature's stabilised around the ambient temperature. Lividity is fixed.' She pulled Romero's t-shirt up. 'This blue-green discolouration indicates the extent of decomposition - twenty-four hours, given the heat of the sun throughout yesterday, but certainly no more than thirty-six hours, otherwise we'd have marbling, bloating of the face...'

'But he was alive at ten yesterday. We were here, carrying out a search.'

'Anytime after that then.'

The Mayor, who'd been listening intently to her analysis, turned to Fernández. 'If you'd arrested him yesterday...'

'Hindsight's a wonderful thing, Vincente.'

'Nonetheless, when this is all over...'

'Anything we had yesterday,' Jacinta Estrada said, 'was pure supposition. We had nothing to go on.'

191

'We do now.' Fernández rifled through Romero's pockets, only to find them empty. 'Robbery seems unlikely and unless this was a random act of violence we must assume he's been silenced.' He looked up at the Mayor. 'When he was young, Romero was a fascist. Juan Gonzales was a fascist. It would have been easy enough to enlist Romero's help, especially for two thousand euros. But whoever killed Juan Gonzales knew that Romero could testify against him. As far as I'm concerned, his death confirms that Juan Gonzales was murdered by the same man who finished off Bartolomé Ramos.' He turned on Cabrera. 'It's an ugly game we're playing, Vincente. A game with no rules and no time out. If you want to make something of what's happened here, go ahead, but don't take the moral high ground with me.'

'But, a man is dead!'

Fernández pulled him to one side. 'And if we don't find his killer soon, there'll be more bodies littering your patch.' He raised his hand close to the Mayor's face, wanting to slap some sense into him, but withdrew it at the last moment, saying, 'I need you to stay focused, Vincente. I need you to keep the media off my back. I need you to help collate the information you've provided. Above all, I need you to help me find the key to this case.'

Estrada's mobile interrupted the standoff and she moved away from the reporters and waited until Fernández and Medina had joined her. 'The young woman who found Laura's mobile on the beach? Crashed her car? She's regained consciousness.'

'You want me to go?' Medina asked.

'No, I'll go. She might find it easier to open up to a woman, given what she went through last night. I'm not sure how much more she'll be able to tell us, but it's worth a shot.' She paused. 'That's not all. Carlos has been brought to the Town Hall.'

'What's he been up to this time?' Medina said.

'SOCOs at the mineshaft reported an incident in the hills above them - two men arguing. Carlos was found badly shaken.

A lump on the back of his head, the size of a golf ball, but otherwise he's all right. He refused any medical attention but insisted on speaking with you, Leo.'

'I'm on my way.' Medina muscled his way through the reporters and hurried towards the Town Hall.

Fernández crouched down and whispered to Santiago, 'Can you arrange for Holly to come over and play with Sofia this evening?'

'I'll be here for most of the day.'

'Could Pedra bring her? Inocenta may welcome her company. She's having a rough time. What do you say?'

'I want to be there, when you talk to the girls.'

'Yes. Yes, I know.' He broke off as his mobile phone rang.

It was Rodrigo Perpiñán. 'I have something for you.' He sounded tense. 'From the diaries.'

'Where are you?'

'At home.'

'Stay there. I'm sending a uniformed police officer round. Felipe Romero's been murdered. It looks like Consuela was right - anyone helping with our enquiries is at risk.'

'I don't need a minder, but you need to look at what I've found.'

'I've got to go and see Juanita, Bartolomé's wife. The coffee and cake story just doesn't add up and I want to know what she's not telling me. I'll be with you in an hour. Put the coffee on.' Fernández snapped the phone shut.

Julieta Santiago was looking at him earnestly. 'This had better be good, Antonio. They're both vulnerable young kids.'

'Yes, I know.' He looked around, checking that no one could overhear him and noticed Vincente Cabrera remonstrating with the pack of media hounds. 'The text message on Laura's phone did more than confirm that she knew her killer. We must assume that she was picked up by him.'

'Him?'

'Went to the beach with him and was killed there, before being dumped in the mine. It also provided us with her killer's motivation.'

'Because she was trying to extort money from him?'

'Possibly, but not because she was pregnant by him, but because she knew something else, something important enough to get her killed.'

'She knew he was Gloria?'

'I'd put serious money on it. She'd asked Gloria to take her to the airport. She had some dirt on him.'

'Used it to blackmail him - more money?'

'To get the sharks off José's back.'

'The same Gloria that Sofia saw playing hide-and-seek with Juan Gonzales.'

'Someone Laura knew well,' Fernández looked at Santiago. 'It could be a nickname - for a man she disliked or didn't respect, telling only those she could trust.'

'Like her fiancé?'

'And Sofia could have overheard Laura calling him Gloria.'

'Sofia's big secret…'

*

'Where is he?' Leo Medina asked as he bustled into the Incident Room.

'Carlos has gone.' Valencia Ramoz looked up from her the computer screen. 'He checked himself out, said he couldn't wait any longer.'

'He's OK, though?'

'Wouldn't talk about it. Asked if we'd got the newsreel footage. I told him it hadn't come through yet.'

'Shit.'

Adam Wells came in.

'And what can we do for you, today?' Ramoz said, failing to hide her contempt.

194

'I had a call, from the Sargento. She said there were more questions. She offered to send a car to pick me up, but I didn't want any fuss.'

'Sargento Estrada is not here.'

'I'll take him,' Medina said. 'This way, sir.'

He showed the artist into one of the interrogation rooms and suggested he sat down.

Adam Wells was quick off the mark. 'I just wanted to say how much I appreciate the discreet manner in which you are conducting your investigation.'

'You mean your wife hasn't sussed out what's going on yet?'

'I mean that I am happy to help in any way I can as long as my...' Wells hesitated, as though searching for the most appropriate word.

'Infidelity?' Medina suggested.

'My indiscretion...'

'Perhaps you'd prefer disloyalty or betrayal?'

'Look,' Wells attempted be sound defiant, 'I'm here at your invitation.'

Medina rounded on him, leaning across the table, towering above him. 'You're here because you're in the frame for murdering Laura Domingo.'

'That's preposterous.'

'You gave her twenty-thousand euros.'

'She posed for several portraits and nude studies. I'd completed at least five and had two more on the go. Laura said she was happy for me to exhibit and sell them. That was part of the deal.' He paused. 'Look, I've told Estrada this already.'

'Sargento Estrada.' Medina sat down, opening a folder in front of him. 'Twenty grand's a lot to pay someone to sit for you. Must have been a very special series of portraits.'

'They should sell well, especially now...'

'You're joking?'

'It was part of the deal.'

Medina looked up, unable to believe what he'd just

195

heard. He shook his head, struggling to control his temper. 'You knew she was engaged?'

'Yes.'

'But that didn't stop you fucking her.'

'You make it sound so coarse, so vulgar.'

'And when she told you she was pregnant, demanded more money and threatened to tell your wife, you panicked, drove her down to the beach...'

'Look,' Adam Wells leaned forward, 'we're both men of the world, you and me. You can't tell me that you don't fancy playing away from home occasionally, especially with someone as beautiful as Laura.'

Medina sprang from behind the desk and grabbed Wells by the collar. 'She's lying on a slab in the morgue. Her baby's dead. Her father's life's been shattered. Jesus Christ, I ought to rip you apart, you fucking piece of shit!' He pushed Adam Wells into his chair and watched as he toppled backwards, crashing onto the tiled floor.

Valencia Ramoz opened the door and stared down at Wells. 'What happened?'

'His center of gravity shifted and he fell backwards,' Medina said, standing over Wells like a prizefighter, willing him to get up so that he could have another shot at him.

'I'll get Dr. Guzmán,' Ramoz said.

'Don't bother.'

'It's no bother, Leo. He's already here.'

*

'It must have occurred to you, Cabo, that you're not only exceeding your authority, but also contravening the Penal Code.' Dr. Javier Guzmán rocked back on his chair. 'And locking another innocent man in a makeshift cell isn't going to endear you to your superiors. Your actions may even herald the end of a career that's hardly got off the ground. You'll probably find yourself working on a construction site this time next week.

Suspended from duty, pending an internal enquiry.' The doctor sat forward. 'Not looking good, is it Leo? It's only a matter of time before my lawyer gets here.'

Medina spun the chair opposite Guzmán and sat astride it, resting his arms on its high back and his chin on his hands. He looked at the man who had dated Laura, who had fucked her and who may yet prove to be the father of her child. Sargento Estrada had said that he should lean on the good doctor. He'd only be following orders...

He allowed the silence to linger, his eyes unflinching. His heart screamed for retribution, whilst his mind advised caution. He knew Adam Wells would be unlikely to press charges and risk his wife discovering what he'd been up to, but Dr. Javier Guzmán had trouble written all over his smug face.

Medina forced a smile. 'We've been unable to find anyone who can confirm your alibi for the early hours of Saturday morning, 20th June.'

'Then you need to work harder at it.'

'We've checked every bar, every restaurant, every nightclub on the beach. We've got over one hundred hours of CCTV footage to go through. We've spoken to your friends at the Lodge, circulated your car details to Trafico, but so far we've drawn a blank. No one saw you after you left the meeting. You must have had a quiet night.'

'Have you been down to the beachfront lately, on a weekend, in the small hours? Have you any idea the state people get into? Most wouldn't recognise their own grandmothers.' Guzmán's face had flushed, his anger simmering.

Medina allowed himself a slight smile. 'Your car,' he said.

'My parent's car.'

'Nice, new, gas guzzling, four-by-four. You'll remember it being towed away from outside the golf club? Yes, of course you would. Forensic report should be with us soon.'

'They're wasting their time. They'll find nothing.' Guzmán folded his arms and sat back in his chair. 'This is preposterous.'

'Interesting choice of word: preposterous. That's exactly what Adam Wells said.'

'You're not going to accuse us of conspiracy?'

'You're both in the frame, doctor.' Medina got up and walked around the table, perching on the edge, towering over Guzmán. 'You into home-improvement?'

'Why? Should I be?'

'Oh, I don't know. The odd extension, stone wall, patio.'

'There were a few outstanding jobs to finish before putting the apartment on the market.'

'Had cement in the back of your parent's car recently?'

'It's possible.'

'Sand?'

'Oh, for God's sake. Now you listen to me, charge me or let me go.'

'We could have up to seventy-two hours together and the clock hasn't started ticking yet, doctor. You came here voluntarily. You haven't been arrested, or charged. Just helping us with our enquiries.'

Guzmán stood up. 'Then I shall bid you good day. Enjoy what remains of your career.'

Medina stood and barred his way to the door. 'Sit down. I haven't finished with you yet.'

'But I've finished with this ridiculous charade.'

As Guzmán stepped forward Medina pushed him back into his chair, grabbing his shirt to prevent him tipping backwards. 'You have the motive. Laura was blackmailing you – threatening to tell your American fiancée of your affair and the child you'd fathered.'

'You'll have to substantiate that the child is mine.' Guzmán nearly choked as Medina's grip tightened.

'Doesn't matter one way or another, does it?' Medina lent forward, his face close enough to smell the doctor's subtle cologne. 'Once your fiancée finds out you've been fucking another woman...' He pulled him closer and whispered, 'Tell me

198

doctor, is it ethical to be screwing a patient?'

He released his grip and swung away, stretching the stiffness from his body, trying all the time to stop himself kicking the shit out of Guzmán. 'So, we can agree, I hope, that you had motive? Now, let's consider the opportunity...' Medina smiled as he recalled Guzmán's uncorroborated alibi. 'It was the seafront, wasn't it? Where you say you were? Wandering from bar to bar?' He moved away, perching on the other side of the desk, confident that he had the doctor's full attention. 'You rolled her up in an expensive cotton sheet; the sort I'm sure we'll find when we search your apartment. Wrapped her in polythene to protect your new car and took the scenic route to the old mine shaft, where you dumped her body.'

'I'm not saying anything else until my lawyer arrives.'

'Have something to hide?'

'I'm bored. Bored and irritated by your accusations. I've nothing more to say.' Guzmán got up and squared up to Medina. 'No comment.'

'No alibi, doctor. More to lose than anyone...' Medina grinned. 'As you say - not looking good, is it?'

*

Fernández found Juanita Ramos in the outhouse near the village water fountain, scrubbing a pale garment over a stone washboard and rinsing it in the fresh stream water that trickled from a lead pipe. She had placed a row of detergents on a ledge above the granite sink, using them as the cleaning routine progressed. The wooden rollers of an iron mangle appeared poised to crush the water from each item of clothing.

'It's like stepping back in time, ' he said, lighting a cigarette and watching her wring the water from a pair of trousers.

Juanita threw the trousers into a basket at her feet and wiped her brow, 'You going to stand there all day, Inspector, or earn your keep?'

He drew heavily on his cigarette, stubbed it out, and stood along side her waiting to wring the shirt she was rinsing.

'Washing machine broken?'

'This,' she said, slapping the shirt onto the stone washboard, 'is the shirt my husband was wearing on the day he was shot.' She pummeled it into the stone. 'This,' she explained, her breath shortening as her effort grew more violent, 'is how I used to wash all of our clothing when we were first married. There was no running water in the village, no sewerage, no electricity' She punctuated each phrase, rinsing and clouting the shirt.

She chose a vest from a carrier bag under the sink and repeated the washing cycle, taking the stain remover and unscrewing the lid. 'For the blood stains,' she explained as she splashed the cloth liberally. 'My husband's blood. The blood of the man I loved.' She pounded the vest against the stone washboard and then, lifting it above her head, she lashed it against the granite sink, as though flaying the life from it, again and again, and again. Tears fell from her cheeks and were absorbed into the soiled foam.

Fernández caught her shoulders, pulling her towards him, trying to stop her from damaging herself, but Juanita pushed him away. 'Don't touch me,' she sobbed. 'Just, don't touch me.'

He stepped back and watched her strength ebb as she fought to regain her breath. It took several minutes, but eventually she was calm. She rinsed the vest, ran it through the mangle and tidied, ready to leave.

'Your Sargento Estrada made no sense at all yesterday,' she said, standing before him, laundry basket tucked under her arm.

'Perhaps she wasn't meant to.'

'She kept asking us why we drank coffee and ate cake with Ana-Marie on the day our men were butchered.'

'Doesn't make a lot of sense, does it?'

'What do you mean?'

'It's troubled me from day one. Why did Ana-Marie

come to see you on that particular day? Why not the day before?'

'It was her mother who phoned to ask if we'd like to try her latest bake.'

'So why Ana-Marie?'

'What do you mean?'

'Why didn't Inocenta bring the cake round herself?'

'I have no idea. Maybe Sofia was unwell or playing up. Wouldn't be unusual.'

Fernández moved towards her and she backed away, a small movement, but one that he hadn't seen before. Something had changed. Something had happened to Juanita. Maybe Jacinta Estrada had touched a nerve. Maybe Juanita was beginning to realise that Bartolomé had been singled out and there was something he hadn't told her.

'Here,' he said, gently, 'let me take that for you.'

She relinquished the laundry basket and looked at him. 'What now, Inspector?'

'Now? We find somewhere quiet and you tell me everything there is to know about your husband, including those things you wish you'd buried with him.'

He spent an hour with Juanita at the business premises her husband had rented. They chatted and drank coffee, and he'd left with a promise that she would go through Bartolomé's papers to see if there was anything that might help.

When he arrived at Rodrigo Perpiñán's, freshly brewed coffee and a selection of pastries were laid out on the white plastic table. He helped himself and then closed his eyes for a moment, enjoying the sugar-rush from the Danish and the coffee.

'You ready for this?' Perpiñán asked.

'As I'll ever be.' Fernández sat upright, drew his hands across his face and rubbed his eyes.

Perpiñán placed the diaries on the table. 'You said these were taken from the home of Juan Gonzales?'

'Yes, yesterday morning.'

'There are eight hard-backed manuscripts in all, although

201

the last one remains incomplete. Each dairy covers five years, from 1936 to 1973.'

'Then Juan Gonzales could not have written them.'

'He didn't. The diaries are his mother's. Teresa Gonzales. From the outbreak of the Civil War up to, and including, the evening Teresa and Jésus Gonzales died.'

'It's all there?' Fernández sat forward.

'It's a personal account. Quite remarkable, given that most people couldn't read or write. She'd obviously been well educated. It's unreliable as a historical record but priceless as a testimony to the effect that national events have on the lives of ordinary people. This is an important find, for both of us, and I would beg you to allow me to add them to my archives once this is all over.'

'To do what?'

'I shall write a book, using these diaries as the basis of her story.'

'And glorify the fascist movement?'

'Is that likely?' Perpiñán said, taking several moments to calm down. 'I want to tell her tale. It has a resonance that deserves to be heard – a voice of the times in which our father's lived and died.'

Fernández let it go, anxious to know what the scholar had discovered hidden in the diaries. 'So, what relevance do they have to our investigations?'

Perpiñán took the last of the diaries from the bottom of the pile. He opened it with the reverence accorded to a museum piece of great antiquity. He slipped his reading glasses on and scanned the entries. 'This volume covers 1970 – 1975. The last two years are blank, for obvious reasons. I have photocopied several months during this period and highlighted particular entries, which I think you'll find interesting.' He handed over twenty A4 sheets. 'If you need to take these diaries for evidence, I must beg you to look after them.'

'I'll wear white gloves if it'll put your mind at rest. Just tell me what you're so excited about.'

202

'Look at the first photocopied page - February1972. I've highlighted the reference to a meeting attended by several of the main characters in your investigation: the author, her husband Jésus, her son Juan, and the Priest Father Emanuel.' He waited for Fernández to locate the section and began to read from the diary...

They seem to have settled on our house for their meetings. They read through the copy of the ABC the doctor passes to them each day and tune into radio broadcasts from Madrid. There are reports of unrest, especially in the Basque area of the north. The General is growing weaker. God bless Him and give Him the strength to carry on His great work. Jésus is drinking more than ever. He will be seventy next week and still refuses to guard his tongue. Juan is home for his son's birthday. He seems to be away such a lot. The General's work is never done, he says.

'If we skip to 21st December 1973 - page seven. This extract deals with the incident that brought the fascist death squad to our village...

Oh, Dear God, news has reached us of the assassination of the Prime Minister, Admiral Blanco. The reports say that the explosion was so big that the car was blown over the roof of the San Francisco de Borga where he'd just attended Mass. When we came together last night, everyone feared this would be the beginning of a new wave of anarchy and hoped the General's response would be as swift and as effective as ever. Father Emanuel is devastated. He has his own health to worry about, poor man. He's just returned from the sanatorium near Valencia. They managed to stop the bleeding, but he'll always have to be careful if he falls heavily or cuts himself badly. They say his condition could be life threatening.

'Father Emanuel was a haemophiliac?'
'Only males are at risk, apparently.'
'It's hereditary?'

203

'I've no idea. You'll have to ask Doctor Santiago.' Perpiñán grinned. 'How's it going, by the way?'

'What do you mean, how's it going? You make us sound like two love-sick kids.'

'So, it's still complicated then?'

'A work-in-progress.' Fernández looked at his friend and shook his head. 'I don't know. One pace forward, two back. Our personal and professional lives clash, and we don't seem to have control over either.'

'Well I doubt if your love-life's as complicated as our fascist Priest's.' Perpiñán glanced through the last of the diaries, carefully turning each page. 'Ah, here we are. Page fifteen. The date is 12th January, 1974.' He waited until Fernández had found the highlighted section. 'If nothing else, this confirms the existence of the Priest's whore...

She has her claws in him. Stole his heart months ago. The poor man doesn't know which way to turn. Cinderella in the kid's panto. Well, she seems to have found her prince charming! And, what a scandal, if the news ever got out. The Father is to be a father. Or is he? I wonder if Emanuel is aware he has a rival for her affections, who may yet be the father of the child she is carrying? Jésus calls her a whore, but that's unfair. A whore? She's just a kid. But, not so innocent.

'Her final entry...'

'Wait. I'm sorry. Just wait a minute.'

Fernández read through the last entry again, tracing each word. He sat back, his face ashen.

'You ok?'

'Yes, yes.'

'What is it?'

'Nothing. Go on. Her final entry...'

'Is on the morning of the 16th January 1974; the day the death squad arrived. It's on the last page...'

At last! Juan has sent word that Special Forces have orders to extend their search for the terrorists who assassinated the Prime Minister. Juan phoned to tell us that a military convoy will pass through the village later today. Jésus has called a meeting...

I have a heavy heart.

*

It took Carlos Domingo over an hour before he relocated Pepe. The goats had stumbled across a patch of lush vegetation and were stubbornly ignoring all efforts to move them on. Pepe had taken the soft option, an early lunch, and was hunched against a rock beneath the shade of an olive tree. He had just settled for a brief nap, when he became conscious of a shadow cast by someone standing over him. He raised a hand to block out the sun.

'This time I've come prepared,' Carlos said, the twin barrels of the shotgun aimed at the goatherd.

Pepe scrambled to his feet.

'I know you know something about what happened to my Laura, or them men who were killed in that new-build. I know you can't say much. I know everyone thinks you're stupid as well as dumb.' Carlos pulled back the shotgun's top firing hammer and placed his index finger alongside the trigger guard. 'But I need you to come with me and talk to them police officers.'

Pepe began to gesticulate wildly, pointing at the goats and his dogs. He shrugged and held out his hands, as though demanding to know what he was meant to do with his animals.

'You can bring them with us,' Carlos said and stood to one side, nudging the shotgun towards the path back down towards the village. 'Let's see how well trained you've got them dogs, shall we?'

*

Jacinta Estrada returned from the hospital empty handed.

The teenage girl had recovered consciousness but had no recollection of the events that had preceded the car crash. Estrada

205

asked the boyfriend what she was doing, driving his car. He'd told her they'd had a row.

Estrada smiled several times during the journey back to the Incident Room, glad the girl was out of danger and wondering what the row was about. They'd probably remember last night for the rest of the lives, though probably not for the reason that had brought them to the beach in the first place.

Her smile disappeared when Valencia Ramoz brought her up to date with Leo Medina's efforts to interview Adam Wells and Dr. Guzmán.

She paused outside the interview room and listened. Whatever Leo had done was down to her. She'd instructed him to lean on the good doctor. She would be more specific next time. If there was a next time. She didn't know whether she was more concerned about Adam Wells or Javier Guzmán. Both could cause serious trouble. Maybe the man whose art she'd seen yesterday did rock on his chair and tip over backwards. Maybe he had had a little help from the big, blundering Cabo. Maybe Leo should have been pulled off the case as soon as Laura's body had been found.

She tried the handle, but he door was locked. 'Leo, open up,' she called.

Within moments, the door cracked ajar. She pushed it open and watched as Medina returned to his seat.

'Ah, the cavalry!' Javier Guzmán beamed. 'Feel the noose tightening, Sargento?'

'Is there anything I can get you?'

'Out of here? My lawyer? Either way, you can't keep me here against my will.' Guzmán's voice was edged with tension.

'So, there is nothing I can get you that will make your detention more comfortable?'

'Charge me, or I walk.'

She smiled. 'Empty your pockets. I'll take your belt, your shoelaces and your tie. We don't want you topping yourself, do we?'

'I said charge me or let me go! You'll pay for this – both

206

of you! You'll be stacking supermarket shelves by the time I've finished with you!'

'That's quite a temper you've got on you, doctor. You've hidden that well, haven't you? Until provoked. Is that what happened? Laura threatened to tell your fiancée you'd been sleeping with her?'

'For God's sake!' Guzmán shoved his chair away, moved from behind the table and began to bear down on Estrada. Leo Medina was quick to react, placing himself between them. The two men stood staring at each other, Medina silently begging that Guzmán would attack and give him the excuse he needed.

'Leave us, Leo.' Estrada said, giving Guzmán time to weigh up his options.

'I'm not sure I should.'

'I don't think Doctor Guzmán is that stupid, are you doctor?' She waited as Medina walked reluctantly from the room and she heard the door click behind her before she said, 'Now, if you don't mind, your pockets, belt, tie and shoelaces.'

'I will make you pay for this.'

'So you said.' She stood her ground.

Guzmán unbuckled his belt and removed it. From his jacket he took his mobile, a wallet and a pocketknife.

Estrada took a handkerchief and lifted the knife, careful not to contaminate it.

He laughed. 'I would be that stupid, wouldn't I?'

'You know, there's one thing that's been bugging me since you first volunteered information about your affair with Laura – your total lack of sorrow, or shock, or sadness, or grief after such an appalling tragedy. For once, heartless, might be the most apposite of words - callous and heartless.' Estrada took the items he had discarded and added, 'But then, you weren't shocked when you heard that Laura was dead, were you?' She walked out of the room, locking the door behind her.

She stood for several moments, wondering what she would say to Leo Medina.

She found him slumped in a chair opposite Valencia Ramoz, toying with the gold pendant of the Indalo Man that had been found around Laura's neck. 'Val,' Estrada said. 'Take everyone out for an early lunch and get me a pastry from the bakery.'

'What and miss all the action?' Ramoz pouted.

'Val?'

'OK. You want anything, Leo?'

'Yeah. A thick slice of justice, with lashings of penal solitude for one of our guests.' He didn't look up from the gold pendant.

Estrada threw her jacket on the back of her chair and watched the day shift take an early lunch. When they were alone, she said, 'OK, Leo, in your own time. What happened with Adam Wells?'

'He should have listened more closely at school. The teachers were always telling us to sit with all four feet of the chair on the floor, else we'd topple backwards and crack our heads open.'

'So, that's your story?'

'Yep.'

'Leo, this could be a disciplinary matter.'

'Nah. He'll remember it just as I do.' Medina continued to study the pendent.

'And the good doctor?'

'Let him stew. Wait until his brief gets here. You said I should lean on him. I did and he's rattled.'

'Got a temper on him, for sure. But, listen, Leo, you can't go throwing that weight of yours around. We have to do things by the book. Even if you hit someone in self-defence, all hell would let loose.'

'Yeah, I get it. Don't worry.' Suddenly, Medina sprang out of his chair. 'Look at this.' He dangled the gold pendant of the Indalo Man before her. 'How much d'you think it's worth?'

She took it from him and examined it. It looked as though it was solid gold but she had no way of telling. 'Probably expensive. Didn't Carlos say Laura and José had bought them as a sort of symbol of their love?'

'Yeah, something like that. It's got a hallmark, so it's probably kosher. But, there's something else. See if you can find it.'

She ran the pendant through her fingers, flipping it over to check both sides, found the hallmark but nothing else, shrugged and handed it back. Medina held the pendant by its head and turned it upside down so that its feet pointed towards the ceiling. He grabbed the magnifying glass he'd been using and handed it to Estrada. She peered at the soles of the pendant's feet. On one foot was the letter L, and on the other, the letter D.

'Laura Domingo?'

'Could be, couldn't it?'

'So where does that take us?'

'I don't know. But, I'm guessing that the pendant José Castaño is wearing will be stamped JC.'

'Well we won't be able to check until he turns up, will we?'

There was an unusual stillness in the room, Medina sipping coffee, Estrada examining the pendant, but the tranquility didn't last long. The door crashed open and Carlos Domingo pushed Pepe into the Incident Room, his shotgun planted firmly in the goatherd's back.

'Carlos?'

'He can help you,' Carlos said, using the end of the barrel to prod Pepe. The goatherd's face was suffused with anger, his eyes indignant, his mouth snarling. Low guttural sounds mingled with spittle at the corners of his mouth.

Medina had not moved, his initial amusement turning to fear when he realized the gun was armed. He rose slowly, as though aware that any sudden movement might make Carlos trigger-happy.

Estrada tried to appear calm. 'You want to tell me what this is all about Carlos?'

'He needed a bit of persuasion to come and talk to you.'

209

'You don't need the gun, Carlos.' Estrada held out her hand.

Carlos suddenly screamed at her, turning the muzzle of the shotgun towards her. 'He knows what happened to my Laura!'

'Carlos,' Medina said. 'Don't do this.'

'He wouldn't listen to me. He saw what happened, but he wouldn't help.'

Estrada moved towards the man she'd held in her arms less than twenty-four hours before, soaking up his grief. 'I agree, we need to talk to him, but I can't do that with a shotgun aimed at my chest, can I?'

'Carlos,' Medina said quietly. 'Put the gun down.'

'You'll make him talk? You'll make him tell you what he saw?'

'Yes, I promise,' Estrada said.

'He knows what happened.' Carlos paused, lowered the gun. 'You want me to help you with him? He don't have no tongue, see. Cut out, it was. You have to play that kid's game with him.'

'Anything you can do. Anyway you can help us would be great. But I need you to give me the gun.' Estrada moved forward and held out her hands once again.

Suddenly, Carlos lunged forward and brought the butt of the shotgun down on top of Pepe's left shoulder, knocking him to the floor. Just as suddenly, Carlos held the shotgun at arms length towards Estrada but, as she moved to take the gun from him, he pulled it back and looked at her.

'You will talk to him?'

'You have my word.' She handed the shotgun to Medina. 'But, you have to understand that you can't keep interfering in our investigation like this.'

'When we catch someone, I'll rest easy.'

*

Estrada told Medina to take Carlos Domingo home, and insisted he took the rest of the day off, to spend some time with his family, to chill out and calm down.

Guzmán's lawyer arrived and spent ten minutes with his client before demanding his release. Estrada explained the circumstances of Guzmán's detention and his aggressive response to questioning, but knew in her heart that she'd have to release him. 'You've not heard the end of this.' She'd been assured, and sighed with relief as the two men pull out of the Town Hall Square in the lawyer's Mercedes.

'One down.' Valencia Ramoz said.

'He's still in the frame.'

'Not for much longer, I suspect.' Ramoz passed her a copy of an email that had just come through from Julieta Santiago.

Estrada scanned the information, got up, walked out of the main office, down the hallway, and unlocked the interrogation room where Adam Wells had been left kicking his heels.

'About bloody time, too,' he said as he gathered confiscated items and slipped his belt on. He hesitated before leaving. 'Look, I came here to help in your enquiries. That's all anyone needs to know, right?'

'What you tell your wife, is your affair. Now, get out before I change my mind.'

She watched him saunter across the square, took out her mobile and waited for Fernández to answer. She updated him on the morning's events and gave him edited highlights from information collated during the morning, adding, 'The DNA results for Adam Wells and Javier Guzmán have been emailed through. Neither matches the foetus carried by Laura Domingo.'

'Doesn't rule them out.'

'But the sooner we find José Castaño, or his sister's result's come through…' Estrada hesitated as Valencia Ramoz handed her two more pages of information. 'The Aston Martin's been given a clean bill of health and the hotel in Madrid has

211

confirmed that José ordered room service just after midnight, Saturday morning. He could have driven down from Madrid in time to kill Laura.'

'And driven back for the match?' Fernández said. 'Possibly. But his car was found on Monday. It's more likely he drove down on Sunday to find out why she didn't turn up.'

'Maybe *the sharks* got to her before they went after José?'

'Let's wait and see what the police in Madrid come up with. Anything else?'

'Oh, God, this is so sad.' Estrada paused. 'The mystery woman who'd phoned several times, when the phone was found on the beach?'

'Yes?'

'The calls were made by Laura's tutor at University to tell her she had passed her final exams, with distinction.'

*

They lay on their bed in the quiet of their village house, Roz sleeping peacefully in his arms, her head resting on his chest and her dark hair spilling over his arm. Medina stared at the ceiling as the drilling of the cicadas drifted through the open window and his boys stirred in the heat in the bedroom next door. He had come close to killing someone today. If he'd pushed Adam Wells with more force, or submitted to his detestation of Javier Guzmán, both could be lying on a slab in the morgue and he might never have been able to lie like this again, with his family around him, with the woman he loved in his arms.

In his gut, he knew the fuss caused by his 'inappropriate behaviour' would blow over and he assumed that Guzmán wouldn't press charges. But he didn't care if he'd stepped out of line. He didn't care if he lost his job and had to go back to labouring on building sites. He didn't care what Inspector Fernández, or Sargento Estrada, or Julieta Santiago, or Vincente

212

Cabrera, or what any of them thought.

And then he heard Roz mumble in her sleep and he realized that he did care. He understood suddenly what it would mean to be without her and the boys. His eyes filled as he pulled Roz to him, grasping the simplest of truths that, apart from his family, finding the man who killed Laura was the most important thing in his life. He'd have to behave. He'd have to keep his hands in his pockets and to do things by the book, as Estrada had insisted. But he would find the man who killed Laura and he hoped to God that someone would be there to stop him tearing the bastard apart.

*

Ana-Marie looked at her reflection in the hairdresser's mirror and wondered why salons used such harsh, unflattering lights? Even she looked pale. Maybe it was the black cloak they'd draped around her that drained her colour? But she trusted Eva to cut well and to make sure her hair always looked immaculate.

She took her mobile phone from the smoky glass shelf below the mirror, dialed a preset and studied her face whilst she waited for her mother to answer. She smiled as Sofia answered the call. 'Nena! How are you?'

'Mama says I've been a naughty girl.' Sofia's voice sounded flat.

'Why? What have you been up to?'

'Nothing.'

'Is mama there?' The phone fell silent and Ana-Marie waited as Eva fussed with the silver foil she'd used to add highlights.

'Ana-Marie? Is that you?'

'Mama? Is Sofia sick?'

'I don't think so, but I'm worried about her. She's not herself.'

'Any news of José?'

'The men have been out, searching everywhere. The police have taken his car away. You don't think anything awful's happened, do you?'

'No, give it time. He'll turn up.'

'Antonio Fernández wants to talk to Sofia.'

'He's not still going on about the old man she said she saw, is he? Does he never listen? I told him she'd probably overheard Leo Medina talking to the men during the fiesta. You know how imaginative she can be?'

'He's coming round this evening. Holly's grandmother's bringing her over; give the girls a chance to play together. Antonio seems to think Sofia may have told Holly something.'

'About what?'

'Can you both come over, this evening?'

'Paul's gone to England for a couple of days. The Almeria contract is all but signed, and he wants to make sure the UK side of the business can function without him for a few months.'

'But you'll be here this evening?'

'Of course I will. We can ask Antonio if they've had the results of the blood test - make sure Laura's baby was José's.'

'Of course the baby was his.' Both women fell silent. 'You mean it could be someone else's?'

'They're questioning two other men who knew Laura. They've taken DNA from both of them and used my blood because José's...'

'But they can't think Laura slept around, could they?'

The hair dryer had been wheeled into place and the hairdresser's assistant was waiting. 'They need to be sure, mama. I don't understand the science, but because José and I have the same mother and father, it should be possible to check the baby's DNA against mine.' Ana-Marie waited, expecting her mother to say something. 'Mama?' She hesitated. 'Mama, are you alright?'

*

214

Fernández hurried to the morgue where he found Julieta Santiago struggling through a pile of paper work.

'Help yourself to coffee,' she said without looking up at him.

He retreated to the corridor where he found an empty bench, rolled up his jacket to use as a pillow and stretched out, propping his feet up on the handrail at the other end. He stared up at the ceiling as the mortuary theatre door swung open and he caught the sound of a cutter being tested. He shuddered and closed his eyes. Perhaps it wasn't surprising that she didn't always have time for niceties.

An hour later, an orderly stopped a loaded trolley outside the lab doors, Santiago came out, unzipped the cadaver's shroud, checked the identity of the corpse, nodded and watched the orderly push the trolley into the lab. She turned to Fernández and they walked up to her office. 'How's it going?' she asked.

He brought her up to date and then added, 'Leo's struggling.'

'Laura's death's hit him hard.'

'Yes. Maybe I should pull him off the case.'

'If you do, you'll be denying him the opportunity for closure. Sitting on the sidelines is not going to help him, or you.'

'He could decide to take things into his own hands.'

She looked at him. 'No one else is likely to work harder than Leo to find Laura's killer.'

'I'll talk to him.' He dropped his head and rubbed the back of his neck. 'Do you have anything else for me?'

'There's another complication. Ana-Marie's DNA. As I suggested, the tests on the sample you collected are inconclusive. When a child is born, she inherits half of her DNA from the mother and half from the father. DNA tests produce a profile that looks a bit like a bar code. The stripes on one bar code can be compared to the stripes on someone else's. Matching a child's profile to its mother and father is usually straightforward.'

'Which is why it was easy to eliminate Adam Wells and Javier Guzmán?'

'Yes. If either of them had been the father there would have been a positive match.'

'And, when we find José?'

'It will be easy to establish if he is the father. Ana-Marie is the child's aunt. The match is inconclusive.'

'So, José may not be the father. Adam Wells will be in the clear if his wife corroborates his alibi. And that leaves Javier Guzmán with some explaining to do.'

'Even though he's not the father?'

'But Laura may have told him that he was. Why else would he cough up twenty-grand?'

Santiago hesitated. 'José could be the father.'

'But I thought we'd just established that he couldn't be, because the bar codes don't match?'

'They don't match sufficiently to be positive: to be absolutely sure.' She paused. 'There is another possibility. If José is the father, the only other explanation for the insufficient match between Ana-Marie's DNA and the child's, is that Ana-Marie and José are not brother and sister. At least,' she hesitated. 'They have different fathers.'

'So, Enrique…'

'May not be Ana-Marie's father.'

She made a small movement of resignation with her shoulders but hadn't finished. 'That's not all,' she said, quietly.

Fernández got up and opened a window, sounds of the city invading immediately. He watched as two men remonstrated with each other over a parking space. 'Go on.'

'The tests we carried out on Ana-Marie's blood sample showed she's a haemophiliac. At least, she's a carrier.'

He dropped his head as he recalled the extracts Rodrigo Perpiñán had highlighted from Teresa Gonzales's diaries.

'You OK?' Santiago asked.

'Just another piece of the jigsaw. Please, go on.'

'We can come back to it later.'

'No, no it's OK.'

'Haemophilia is inherited. If the man who fathered Ana-Marie was a haemophiliac, she would have inherited the condition.'

Fernández got up. 'I need some time.'

'We're meeting at Inocenta's later. You wanted to talk to Holly and Sofia.'

'Yes. Yes, I know.' He sighed heavily. 'I'm just not sure that now is the best time.'

'What is it, Antonio?'

'Rodrigo Perpiñán told me that if I looked under too many rocks, I'd find more than I bargained for.'

They sat in silence throughout the drive from Almeria, Fernández grateful for the chance to clear the images that tumbled through his mind.

The harshness of the afternoon sun had relented and a warm breeze swept off the sea. Fair-weather cumulus clouds scurried above the mountains, bathing the hills in a patchwork of shadows. As they approached the village, they saw a large herd of goats roaming the lower slopes of the hills and Fernández made a mental note to pull Pepe in for questioning.

He dropped Santiago near the Castaño home and watched as she disappeared among the labyrinth of narrow lanes.

He parked outside the cemetery and made his way to Rodrigo Perpiñán's cottage. As he approached, he noticed that the front door was open. The front room was deserted and Fernández stood and listened. He moved across the room and through the open doors onto the terrace, assuming his friend had fallen asleep. The two chairs had been pushed under the table. He heard the faintest of sounds from an upstairs window, eased the Beretta from beneath his jacket and slid the breechblock backwards, engaging a round of ammunition and setting the trigger mechanism. He retraced his steps into the sitting room and started to climb the narrow staircase that led to the only bedroom.

The door was closed. He stopped and listened, couldn't hear anything, placed his left hand on the brass doorknob, turned it slowly, raised his handgun, kicked the door open, and found himself looking down the twin barrels of a shotgun.

Perpiñán had sat upright, his arms extended, trembling with the weight of the firearm. 'For Christ's sake, Antonio, what the hell are you doing?'

Fernández lowered his handgun, rested against the doorframe and began to laugh, relief flooding through him like the surge of cool beer on a hot afternoon.

'Do you mind?' Perpiñán placed the shotgun on the bed beside him.

Fernández looked at the shape beneath the bedclothes, the mop of greying hair betraying Perpiñán's lover.

'Antonio!'

'I need to talk to you.'

'Now? Can't it wait?'

'I wish it could my friend.' He smiled. 'I'll be downstairs.'

'Oh, that's good of you.'

Whilst he waited, Fernández collected Teresa Gonzales's diaries and went out on to the terrace. He opened the first of the manuscripts and began to flip through it.

Ten minutes later he heard muffled exchanges and the front door close.

'The widow García, I presume?' he said, without looking up.

'None of your business. I should've let you have both barrels.' Perpiñán poured himself a brandy and offered the bottle to Fernández.

'Maybe later.'

'This had better be good.'

'I want to look at the diaries again.'

'Because you didn't want to face the truth first time round?' Perpiñán sipped his brandy. 'Oh, come on, Antonio! You've seen the photographs. The reference to the Priest's whore

218

in these diaries confirms her existence. The age profile fits. And, as if that wasn't enough, Teresa Gonzales didn't exactly disguise the whore's name, did she? '*Not so innocent*'. Your only problem is that you won't admit that Ana-Marie, the great love of your life, is the illegitimate child of a woman who'd been fucking the local Priest.' Perpiñán downed the brandy and poured another shot. 'Inocenta Castaño was the Priest's whore – a woman who married another man and passed the child off as his.'

'It's more complicated than that.'

'It always is with you. You're too personally involved. '

'Ana-Marie's DNA came back. The match was inconclusive.'

'Well, it would be, wouldn't it?'

'You've known all along? Then why suggest I take a sample from her?'

'Well, I knew you wouldn't listen to me, but you might listen to Doctor Santiago and her *irrefutable* evidence.' Perpiñán sat down and lowered his voice, as though concerned the walls had grown ears, or the warm air would carry their conversation beyond his home. 'I was there that night. Remember? Thirty-five years ago, I was there. I saw the Priest and his whore.'

'But not her face, you said she had her back to you.'

'Yes, but I recognized Inocenta in Cinderella the moment I saw the photograph - Father Emanuel's hand on her hip - but couldn't work out why you couldn't see it. Now, I know. You didn't want to see it. Or rather, you didn't want to *admit* Inocenta was the Priest's whore.' He paused, as though waiting for Fernández to accept the truth. Finally. Several moments passed before he added. 'It doesn't stretch the imagination too far to suggest that Inocenta Castaño may have been party to the murder of Alberto, Bartolomé, and Matias: that she didn't want the truth to be made public and may even have been involved in the attempted cover up.'

'The murder of Juan Gonzales?'

'Yes. So what are you waiting for?'

'I need to be sure.'

'Who the hell are you trying to protect?'

Fernández looked out at the campo as the village lights began to flicker into life. His head was swimming. He struggled to stay focused. 'The diaries suggest that Father Emanuel was a haemophiliac. Ana-Marie is a haemophiliac, or at least she's a carrier.'

'She inherited the condition from her father - the Priest, Father Emanuel.'

'Yes, but nothing we have, none of the evidence ties Inocenta to the murders. Identifying her as the Priest's whore, and Ana-Marie as the Priest's child, doesn't make Inocenta guilty of murder or conspiracy to murder.'

'You could pull her in and ask the questions that need asking.'

'And if she had nothing to do with what happened last week?' Fernández spun round and faced him. 'You want to ruin the lives of a whole family. Destroy their happiness and their reputation?' He paused. 'I need something more than a few faded photographs, an old woman's diaries, and the results of a blood test.'

'You're protecting Ana-Marie. You know it. I know it.'

Fernández rose heavily to his feet. 'I'm done here.'

'You can't run from the truth, you know, Antonio.'

His mobile phone rang.

Julieta Santiago. 'Holly and Sofia have disappeared!'

'What?'

'They were sitting out on the terrace. When Ana-Marie arrived, we went out to join them but they'd gone.'

'I'll be there as soon as I can. Phone Jacinta Estrada, tell her to get the local uniforms out.' He turned to Rodrigo Perpiñán. 'Get dressed and go down to the bar. See if Eduardo Gomez and his merry men are there. We need all the help we can get. Our primary witness just went AWOL.'

*

220

Leo Medina toyed with the empty glass in front of him and decided one more shot wouldn't hurt. He'd begun to feel mellow and enjoy the sensation of the warm, smooth brandy as it slipped down. He held up the glass, ordered another slug and noticed Enrique Castaño in somber conversation with Carlos Domingo at the far end of the bar. It wasn't hard for him to imagine what they would be talking about. Not wedding arrangements, for sure.

Medina looked at the publicity shots of José Castaño on the wall. 'And where the fuck are you, my friend?' He stared into the eyes of the young Real Madrid star and remembered the hours they'd spent together. They'd been best mates and it seemed that Laura had always been there to tease them, to flirt, to flash her knickers and to promise but never deliver…not, that is, until they were a bit older and José had moved on to the big-time - joining Real Madrid's youth squad - leaving the stage clear for the awkward adolescent that Medina had mushroomed into. Looking back, it was all so innocent, but even then Laura had had a bit of a reputation - making her all the more attractive to a seventeen year old.

'You went off and left us, didn't you?' Medina said, staring at José's poster as he sipped his refill. 'Off to the bright lights, the flash cars, the money…' He raised his glass and seemed to others in the bar to be toasting his friend. 'You were always such a lucky bastard. I was never in the same league, of course. And then you and Laura became an item.' He drained the glass. 'I didn't think it would last, to be honest.' His head dropped and tears began to muster in his eyes. 'And, it didn't, did it?' He stood up, unsteady on his feet and pointed at the face smiling at him from the publicity poster. 'You bastard! If you killed her, I'll fucking swing for you!' He threw the empty glass at the wall, shattering it and bringing the packed bar to a standstill.

Enrique Castaño was quick to react, but Carlos Domingo slapped a firm hand on his shoulder, restraining him, guiding him back to his bar stool and nodding towards Eduardo Gomez who had already crossed the room.

Gomez stood alongside Medina and folded his arms.

'Feel better for that?' he said. 'You've no proof that José had anything to do with Laura's death.' Gomez looked up at the big man who was visibly wrestling with the emotions raging inside him.

'Why would he?' Medina slumped back in his chair. 'Why would he destroy the one decent thing in his life?'

'Would another help?' Gomez picked up his brandy glass.

'I'll buy my own.'

Gomez didn't have time to respond. The bar door flew open and Rodrigo Perpiñán stood fighting for breath. He looked towards Enrique Castaño. 'It's Sofia. She's disappeared.'

Enrique knocked the stool over as he leapt to his feet and barged his way out, closely followed by Carlos Domingo.

'Eduardo,' Rodrigo Perpiñán shouted across at the old Mayor. 'We could do with your help.'

Eduardo Gomez turned to the bar tender. 'Pour a coffee down the plank-of-wood over there and get him over to the Castaño home'

*

Ana-Marie led Fernández onto the terrace and they scanned the campo, hoping to catch sight of the two girls. The light was fading and shadows played tricks, raising hopes and then dashing them as human shapes turned into a straggling bush or jagged cacti.

Julieta Santiago joined them. 'Inocenta and Pedra are out there. The girls must have climbed down the vine.'

Fernández turned to Ana-Marie. 'What were they doing on the terrace?'

'Mama said they'd been rummaging through Sofia's toy-box and seemed to be playing happily.'

'Sofia told Leo Medina that she saw an old man in the campo last Thursday.'

'Antonio,' Ana-Marie said, 'we've been over this a thousand times. She was listening to Leo talking to the men at the bar when we first arrived at the fiesta on Friday night. It was late. She was tired. She would have been confused and repeated what she heard.'

'She told Holly about Gloria,' Santiago said.

'Oh, my God,' Ana-Marie said suddenly, sinking onto a white plastic chair. 'Oh, my God, I'm so sorry.' She looked up at Fernández. 'She told me. Sofia told me. Just after lunch last Thursday. I'd taken her up to bed for siesta and she told me she'd seen Gloria playing hide-and-seek.'

'Can you remember exactly what Sofia said? Her exact words?'

'She just kept on insisting that I would know who Gloria was: *you know*, she said, *Gloria* - as if by repeating the name I'd understand.' She hesitated. 'You think Gloria killed Juan Gonzales, don't you? And you think Sofia may be able to identify him?'

'We think so, yes. We also believe that Laura was blackmailing him to help José.'

'José was in trouble?'

'We don't know yet.'

'But,' Santiago said, 'Sofia may be the only one who could tie Gloria to both investigations.'

'But you don't know who Gloria is.'

'We're assuming it's Laura's nickname for him.'

'Him?'

'Odds on.'

Enrique and Carlos burst into the room.

'Where is she?' Enrique demanded.

'We don't know. Inocenta's out there looking and…'

Before Fernández could finish, Sofia's father and Carlos Domingo pushed past him, clambered over the railings and down the vine.

Eduardo Gomez and several men arrived soon after, closely followed by uniformed officers scrambling from two

223

police cars, reporters snapping at their heels. Jacinta Estrada pushed through the press, herded the extra manpower into the Castaño sitting room, and began to organize the search.

'I can't just stand here and do nothing,' Ana-Marie said as she made for the door.

'It might be better if you stayed here,' Fernández called after her.

Julieta Santiago brushed past him and followed Ana-Marie. At the door she turned and said, 'You just don't get it, do you Antonio?'

*

The bar tender placed a coffee in front of Leo Medina, waited for the young Cabo to pay his tab, and then made a song and dance of sweeping up the shattered glass that littered the floor beneath the publicity shots of José Castaño.

Medina didn't need the coffee to sober up but drank it anyway. He called Roz, just to hear her voice and know that the boys were safely tucked up in bed. He told her he was heading down to the Castaño home to see what he could do to help.

He ended the call and stared at the poster depicting a montage of bull-fighting photographs taken at the *Plaza de la Maestranza* in Seville. Medina snorted, regret and disappointment jostling side by side. As a child he'd dreamt of growing up to be one of Spain's great bullfighters. His bedroom wall had been plastered with posters of his heroes, men who had risked their lives dressed in their *suit of lights*. Heroes and legends. The stuff of a little boy's dreams, cruelly shattered because he grew too tall, too heavy.

He tried to focus on the photographs: the entrance of the bull into the ring; the novice matadors taunting it with the *capote,* the large pink cape; the picadors on their armour-clad horses, piercing the bull's back with a blooded pike; and the star matador confusing and frustrating the enraged bull, turning it this way and that.

224

He stared at the last two photographs depicting the *pase de la Muerte*, the pass of death, turning the bull for the last time before the sword is driven between its withers and down into its heart. 'Oh, dear God.' He said, unable to believe his eyes, his heart hammering, his breath shortening. He took out his mobile and phoned Fernández.

'Yes, Leo. What is it?'

'Can you get to the bar?'

'You should be here, for Christ's sake. Two young girls are missing.'

'This is really important, Sir,' Medina said without taking his eyes off the title at the top of the bullfighting poster. 'I know who Gloria is.'

*

At the Castaño home Fernández pulled Jacinta Estrada to one side. 'Stay and coordinate the search from here. If the girls don't turn up within the hour, request permission to scramble an army rescue helicopter. Use search dogs and call out the Sierra Nevada mountain rescue team. Whatever you do, keep the media well away from the area.'

'That's not going to be easy. We can't seal off the whole hillside.'

'Do what you can,' he said, placing a hand on her forearm to reassure her. 'I'll be with Leo. If anything happens, let me know. OK?'

He opened the front door to be greeted by a flurry of flashguns, microphones and questions. He decided to make an impromptu statement. 'Two young girls have been missing for less than an hour. We are hopeful of finding them soon. When we have any news, we'll pass it on to you. I would ask that you do nothing that will hinder the search effort. Thank you.' He pushed his way through them, ignoring questions that tracked him past the police cars and up the road through the village.

He found Medina waiting impatiently alongside the cigarette machine in the bar. 'This had better be good, Leo.'

'Oh, it is. It's better than good.' Medina paused, as though trying to regulate his thoughts. 'Gloria's an adult. Right? Female? Unlikely, given the way she was killed. She gave everyone nicknames...'

'Scarpetta, Elliot Ness.'

'Exactly.' Medina turned to the photographs of the bullfight in Seville. 'Each of these photographs demonstrate how the bull is forced to turn and turn again, growing increasingly angry and frustrated with each pass.' He pointed at the matador holding the sword, ready to strike. Medina grinned at Fernández and then stabbed his hand at the top of the poster. 'Look at the title!'

'Pases de Gloria?'

'The Pases de Gloria. The turning of the bull!' Medina repeated, labouring each word. 'The turning of the bull!'

'Jesus.' Fernández stared at the photographs and the title. He pulled his mobile from his pocket and called Valencia Ramoz.

As he waited for the call to be answered he walked over and tapped on the bar. The bar tender poured a brandy, holding the bottle aloft, checking if Medina wanted another. He shook his head. Fernández sank the brandy and then arranged for SOCO, forensics and backup from the Guardia Civil to meet him at the village church.

He cut the call and turned to Medina. 'Go and find Father Gabriel. Get him over to the church. See if he has a magnifying glass. Wait for me outside the church. No one is to enter. No one. You understand?'

*

'Sofia!' Most of the search party could hear Inocenta's anguished cries carried across the campo by a stiffening breeze.

'Holly!' Pedra's voice was harsher, more severe.

Both women knew that the odds on finding the girls had reduced dramatically as darkness cut vision to a few feet, camouflaging undergrowth, disguising rocks and old mineshafts, putting everyone at risk. They also knew that no one would give up the search willingly, no matter how long it took to find the girls.

Enrique and Carlos had struck out on their own, outflanking the organized sweep, scrambling among the rocky outcrops that littered the higher slopes, stopping occasionally to bellow across the valley.

Jacinta Estrada was standing on the Castaño terrace, tracking progress through binoculars.

After an hour, she made the call and was told that the helicopter would be there in fifteen minutes. It would fly several passes, using its searchlight to try to locate the girls, but, without night vision, it would have to stand down until sun-up. If the girls had not been found, the search and rescue coordinator told her, they would probably survive, given it was summer and temperatures were high. Estrada didn't know how to respond to 'probably survive'. She tried to imagine what might be going through Inocenta and Julieta's minds, and what dangers the girls might be facing. Not only did they have the dark to contend with, but darkness also brought with it wild boar, snakes and scorpions, and hid mineshafts and deep crevasses. The girls could be huddling together, trying to be brave, listening to every sound, and growing more anxious, more terrified.

Estrada didn't have as much luck with her next call. The Mountain rescue teams were at full stretch responding to an accident high in the Sierra Nevada. They would get to Los Mineros as soon as possible. In the meantime, they advised pulling everybody off the hills. 'It's too dangerous,' the rescue coordinator told her. 'Weather could close in. Darkness brings its own set of problems.'

Three police dog-handlers turned up, their dogs yapping and eager, pulling on their leads.

An hour later, she made the most difficult of calls, ordering civilians off the hill.

The police officer who had assumed field control brought everyone together and explained what was about to happen - they would make a final sweep, double check all the ruins, outbuildings, orchards, gullies and thickets, before the search would be called off for the night.

'Yeah, right, as if that's going to happen,' One of men from the village echoed the sentiments of everyone involved.

'This is not up for debate. You'll clear the campo and start again at first light. You put yourself and others at risk.'

'There's two kids out there. You don't honestly expect us just to turn our backs?'

'My officers will continue the search throughout the night. A mountain rescue team is on its way and a helicopter has been scrambled.' The policeman stood his ground, but was relieved to see Antonio Fernández striding towards them.

'Eduardo,' Fernández called as he approached. 'Get a dozen men and meet me outside the church. I'll explain when I get there.' He looked around and smiled at Pedra who had her arm around Inocenta, warming her and consoling her, no doubt trying to find some comfort for herself. 'I know it must be difficult,' he said, gently, 'but leave the rest of the night to the police officers.'

'You think it'll take the rest of the night? They won't find them?' Inocenta said.

'They'll be all right. Now, go home. As soon as they've been found, we'll let you know. I promise.' He nodded at Pedra and watched as they joined the others, dragging their heels, hoping they had missed something, desperate for a result before they crossed the police line into the village.

He asked the police officer if he knew where Ana-Marie, Julieta, Enrique, and Carlos had gone?

'Last I saw them, they'd moved up the mountain to just below the escarpment. The women went off that way.' He pointed towards a building site.

'That's ok. I think I know where they'll be.' Fernández borrowed a torch and made his way over to the new-build, ducking under the crime scene tape as the moon slipped from behind a cloud.

He hesitated at the doorway, the image of the four bodies still etched in his mind, the area cleared of anything forensics might have found useful. He heard Ana-Marie's voice, drifting up from the basement as she called out, hoping to locate the girls. Then he heard Santiago's, softer, more fearful.

He stopped at the top of a skeleton-staircase leading to the basement and waited. Ana-Marie headed up the stairs, concentrating on each footstep, still calling Sofia's name. As she neared the top, she lifted her head, saw his silhouette and swore. She shone her torch in his face, strode up the last few steps and confronted him. 'Jesus, Antonio. You think that's funny?'

'I need you to come with me.'

'They've found them?' Santiago asked; her face drained of any color in the pale moonlight.

'Everyone's been pulled off for the night, except the police. A helicopter's on its way.'

'But the girls are still out there?'

'Yes.'

'And you expect us to just walk away?' Ana-Marie said.

Fernández knew they'd want to continue the search, but he needed Ana-Marie at the church. 'To walk away from the search may be the hardest thing you've ever done, but, I need your help. Ten minutes, that's all I ask. Then you can do whatever you feel is right.' He glanced down at the gold pendant of Indalo Man nestling on Ana-Marie's cleavage and, as he looked up, her eyes met his. He smiled awkwardly, knowing that the next few hours would be immeasurably more painful than anything Ana-Marie had ever been through, at any time of her life.

'I need you to show me exactly where you found that pendant,' he said.

'I told you; I found it in the church. Paul had dropped it.'

'Will you show me, please?'

'I don't understand.'

'Where's your husband?'

'He's in the UK. Flying back tomorrow. Why?'

'You must trust me. Come back to the church. Please.' Fernández turned and began to lead the way as a helicopter swooped down, lighting the campo with its searchlight.

'I'm sorry, Antonio, I'm not going anywhere until you tell me what's going on.' Ana-Marie stood firm. 'Sofia and Holly are out there somewhere, Laura's dead, José's missing, and my husband's out of the country. And all you seem interested in is a couple of ounces of gold.' She folded her arms, resolute.

'You can't expect her to quit, Antonio,' Santiago said. 'Doesn't Sofia's safety mean anything to you?'

Fernández ignored her, turned to Ana-Marie and said, 'I need you at the church. Now.'

'And I'm staying here until we find Holly and Sofia. For God's sake, Antonio, nothing can be more important than what's happening right here, right now. Can't it wait until the morning?'

'No, I'm sorry, it can't.' His voice had moderated but had lost none of its gravity. He looked at Ana-Marie. 'Not if we are to stand a chance of finding your brother alive.'

*

He knew that if they'd continued the search, they may well have stumbled across Holly and Sofia within minutes of leaving the new-build. Sunday papers often carried stories of searches being called off whilst victims were still alive, often no more than a few hundred meters from safety, or they'd be found days later, injured, close to starvation, having lived off the land.

230

But, there was another possibility that had nagged at him: the girls could have been abducted. Abducted by Paul Turnbull. Ana-Marie had just told him her husband had flown to the UK and would be back tomorrow. But, what if he hadn't got on the plane? What if he'd returned to the village, enticed Sofia and Holly from the terrace, bundled them into the back of his Landcruiser and was holding them somewhere? Or worse: he'd already silenced them.

The thought of two fragile bodies lying broken in a lonely grave tore at his heart as he led Ana-Marie through the village. He'd almost convinced himself that he wasn't dealing with abduction, that the girls had slipped away on some misguided adventure, and that the chances of the search party finding them tonight were good. He'd almost convinced himself, but not quite.

'You going to tell me what's happening?' Ana-Marie called after him. 'Antonio?' She stopped as they entered the church square. 'I need to know, Inspector. I need to know what's going on.' She stood, her hands resolutely on her hips, her chest heaving with exertion and emotion.

Fernández offered his hand. 'Come with me, please. I can't tell you here.'

The Guardia had been called in and were holding a dozen or more reporters at bay, unable to stop their flashguns tracking the two forlorn figures, huddled together, as they crossed the church square. Curious villagers pestered Eduardo Gomez for an update but he ignored them.

Father Gabriel was waiting impatiently by the huge doors at the church's entrance, Leo Medina by his side.

'You OK?' Fernández whispered to Ana-Marie.

She shuddered, her mind full of her father's words – '*she has an eye for your man.*' She stopped him in his tracks and looked up into his anxious face. 'Tell me what you want me to do.'

He led her down the side aisle and pulled back the tarpaulin protecting the nave from the renovation work in the crypt. He flicked on the light switch as he led her down the concrete ramp. They stood among the rubble in the crypt.

'Would you mind?' Fernández pointed at the pendant of the Indalo Man between her breasts. Silently, she undid the clasp behind her neck. He took the magnifying glass Medina had passed to him as they entered the church and studied the markings on the feet of the gold figure. The initials 'JC' were clearly visible.

'Can you show me exactly where you found this?'

'It's José's isn't it?'

'I think it may be. Yes.'

'Oh, my God, no.' She backed away from him. 'You can't mean?'

'I need to know where you found it.'

Ana-Marie scanned the crypt, her eyes settling on the fresco she'd been looking at just before she'd found the pendant, just before her husband arrived. She remembered that he'd asked her what she had in her hand, and had told her that he'd bought the pendant for her, that he'd mislaid it and wanted it to be a surprise. 'He lied to me.'

'Ana-Marie?'

'My husband lied to me. He lied to me and…'

'We think he may have killed Laura.'

'Oh, my God. Her baby was his?'

'We don't know.'

'But the blood sample you took from me?'

'Was inconclusive.'

'And José? Where's José?' Her voice had lost all strength and her eyes brimmed with tears. Suddenly, she dropped on to her knees and began to tear at the rubble that filled one of the drill holes. 'He's here, isn't he? He's here! Help me!' She continued to claw at the earth and rocks, shoveling debris to one side with her hands, frantic in her desperation, her accusations raining down on Fernández. 'You told me that if I left the search for the girls and helped you we'd be able to save José's life...'

'There still a chance.'

'You lied to me. You knew he was dead.'

'We won't know that, until we find him.'

'You know he's dead. I know you do!'

Alarmed by her screams, Father Gabriel ordered the Guardia to keep everyone out and led Leo Medina down the ramp. They paused at the entrance to the crypt and watched as Fernández knelt down and took Ana-Marie into his arms.

They sat there, amid the rubble, rocking back and forth, until he nodded at Father Gabriel. The Priest moved forward and led Ana-Marie out of the crypt, back up the ramp, to one of the pews near the altar.

'Leo, get SOCO and forensics down here,' Fernández said. 'Tell Eduardo to be ready to help clear the rubble. Find the Mayor and tell him to keep the press off our backs here and outside the Castaño home. Phone Valencia Ramoz – get her to contact the airlines. We need to know if Paul Turnbull flew to the UK yesterday and, if he did, what time he's due to land here tomorrow. Tell her to call Guardia headquarters in Almeria and arrange a welcoming committee. Make sure they board the plane before anyone has a chance to disembark. I don't want any cock-ups.'

He cut the call and accompanied Medina back up the ramp, pushed the tarpaulin to one side and saw Father Gabriel talking to Ana-Marie.

'You'd better go and see Carlos Domingo,' he said to Medina. 'Tell him he won't be able to bury Laura on Saturday.'

His mobile brought everything to a standstill, everyone hoping for good news – the girls had been found, safe and well.

Ana-Marie lifted her head from Father Gabriel's shoulder, tears dragging mascara down her cheeks.

'Yes?'

It was Juanita Ramos. He shook his head and turned away to take the call.

'How's the search for Sofia and her little friend going?'

233

'Nothing yet.'

'Can we meet?'

'Now's not a good time.'

'Tomorrow morning, then?'

'What is it, Juanita?'

'I've been through Bartolomé's papers. I think I know why my husband was killed and who pulled the trigger.'

Day Nine

Friday 26th June 2009

By three in the morning, the painstaking work of clearing the rubble had produced nothing. They'd hit two meters without a trace of José Castaño and started to excavate two other bore holes that had also been temporarily filled with rubble.

Valencia Ramoz had contacted Fernández to confirm that Paul Turnbull had flown from Almeria on Wednesday and was booked to return on a British Airways flight, today, leaving Heathrow at nine. He would stop off in Madrid and transfer to a scheduled Air Nostrum flight for the one-hour trip to Almeria. Travelling business class on the first leg, Turnbull would have access to the lounge in Madrid and time for duty free shopping. What Turnbull wouldn't know was that, throughout the journey, he'd have at least two plain-clothed officers from the London Metropolitan Police shadowing his every move.

At four in the morning, the police hunt for Holly and Sofia was suspended and soup, bread, and water were ferried out to the search party. It would be a fine day, if the first signs of the dawn were anything to go by, and everyone took time-out to put their heads down to catch a few moments rest.

The first of the mountain rescue teams had arrived and the news of their involvement gave everyone a lift. The helicopter would start a methodical sweep at sun-up.

Julieta Santiago, Enrique Castaño and Carlos Domingo were reluctant to delay the search, but even they recognised the need to take a breather. Pedra and Inocenta fell into a fitful sleep, propped up in the two fire side chairs in the Castaño sitting room.

Jacinta Estrada dozed in a white plastic chair on the terrace.

Four in the morning was also the time when it was agreed that the men who'd been helping to clear the rubble in the church should go home and get some rest - those who had work, could not afford to miss out on a day's wages.

At six, the day shift replaced the Guardia and Policia Local outside the church, keeping the media and anxious villagers at bay, whilst SOCO and forensics officers continued to search for José.

Ana-Marie lay on a pew, unable to sleep, her head resting on Father Gabriel's rolled up cassock.

Leo Medina went home and collapsed on the sofa. At nine he was scheduled to relieve Jacinta Estrada and let her get home for a few hours.

*

Fernández left the church and made his way to Rodrigo Perpiñán's.

'I've been expecting you,' Perpiñán said. 'The village is awash with rumour. They say the two girls have been kidnapped and José Castaño is buried in the church.'

Fernández pushed passed him, time short. 'Did the widow García leave any more pastries?'

'There's cold paella in the fridge. I'll put the coffee on.'

He slumped onto the large sofa in the sitting room. 'The kids haven't been kidnapped. Least ways, I don't think so...' his voice trailed off momentarily, a strident voice in his head reminding him that there was no sign of them, *was there*? He dismissed the thought - Paul Turnbull was in the UK and there was no one else he'd consider responsible for the girl's abduction. 'We've a suspect under surveillance.'

'For which investigation?'

'Both.' He felt oddly reassured as he said it.

'Same man?'

'Yes. Problem is, with all the speculation, someone in the village might try to contact him.' He looked at his watch. It was ten past seven. London was an hour behind - ten past six. In just under three hours Paul Turnbull would be boarding the nine o'clock at Gatwick - plenty of time for someone to warn him.

236

Once he'd arrived in Madrid he'd have over three hours before the connecting flight to Almeria - three hours in which to turn his mobile back on and collect any messages, three hours in which to engineer his escape from Spain's busiest airport and disappear into the capital city.

He closed his eyes.

Just after eight, he woke to find an omelette draped over a plate of steaming paella and coffee on the table in front of him.

'They're waiting for you.'

'Who?'

'You'd arranged to meet Juanita, Eduardo, and our illustrious Mayor?'

'Shit.'

'I told them you were taking a shower. Not a bad idea, after you've demolished that lot.'

He was an hour late by the time he got to the Town Hall. They took Vincente Cabrera's four-by-four and Fernández sat in the back studying documents Juanita had brought with her.

'Impressive,' he said, looking at the architect's drawings and site plan.

'This was the project that was going to make our fortune. A hotel with two hundred rooms, three pools, and five bars.' Juanita laughed hollowly. 'Nothing but problems from the moment they started excavating the foundations.'

'It's been a regular feature in several local papers,' Vincente Cabrera said, as they left the road and started down a rough track towards the coast. 'Objections from environmentalists, local residents, and land owners.'

'But it had been given the go ahead,' Eduardo Gomez prompted.

'Yes, but the regional government in Almeria has ordered an investigation into the local planning process,' Cabrera said. 'A final decision's due any day now.'

'They suspect corruption?' Fernández asked.

Vincente Cabrera shrugged. 'Could be, but it's much more difficult these days. Recent legislation has made the whole process much more transparent.'

'A few years ago, it was much simpler,' Eduardo Gomez said. 'A developer would buy land and submit plans to the local Mayor's office for approval. Money was paid under the counter, or one of the properties would be reserved for the Mayor, and the development went ahead.'

Fernández looked at Juanita. 'But what's this got to do with Juan Gonzales and your husband's murder? When you called me last night, you said you knew why your husband was killed.'

'It might be easier to explain when we reach the construction site.'

The track wound through a steep sided valley and deteriorated dramatically as it neared the coast. As they rounded the final bend a huge, unfinished hotel towered above the beach and surrounding land. It was a ghost of glassless windows and gaping doors, each floor as forlorn and empty as the one above.

They clambered out of the car and down to the beach, stopping just short of the sea as it sipped at rock pools and shingle. From there they could see the whole development.

'My husband had always been ambitious,' Juanita said. 'When he started out, he borrowed money from the bank, built starter homes in the village, luxury villas outside, and apartments along the beachfront. Business was good and we started making money.' She hesitated. 'It would be easy to blame the recession but the rot set in about ten years ago, when he went into business with an ex-pat who needed a Spanish partner.'

'To gain access to the town halls,' Eduardo Gomez said.

'To gain access to those Mayors who would be the most accommodating,' Vincente Cabrera added.

'My husband was a good man,' Juanita protested. 'Whatever he did, he did for his family. Just hear me out, before you start throwing your stones.' She paused, laying stress on her next few words, 'As far as I knew, the partnership proved to be a good move. Nothing was ever formalised, of course, just the word of two men, a handshake as good as any contract. Work continued to roll in, money was repaid to the banks and our reputation was second to none. Then, this happened.' She pointed at the hotel. 'His partner used him to get the plans accepted and then dissolved their partnership, cutting Bartolomé out of the huge profits they expected to make.'

'But, given the opposition to the hotel, his partner seems to have done him a favour,' Fernández said.

'On the face of it, I'd agree. But, last night, I found this.' She handed him a document. 'I just wish he'd told me what was going on.'

'*Rustico de Secano*,' Fernández said, glancing up from the document, suddenly realising what Juanita had meant when she phoned to say that she knew why her husband had been killed.

'Let me see,' Eduardo Gomez took the document, pulled out his reading glasses and skimmed through it. 'This is about the land the hotel is built on. It was bought eight years ago.' He paused, looking at the document again. 'The land was *Rustico de Secano* - farm land. It would have been illegal to build on it. Permission to build on this land should never have been granted. The whole process was illegal.'

'Corruption...' Fernández said.

'According to this document, the whole site was bought for fifteen thousand euros,' Eduardo Gomez said.

'Chicken feed. The profit would have been huge. But only if they could get permission to build,' Fernández said. 'And, by cutting Bartolomé out, he doubled his potential profit in a stroke.'

'Who's he?' Vincente Cabrera asked. 'Who bought the land with Bartolomé and then cut him out of the deal?'

'His partner, of course. Paul Turnbull.' Eduardo Gomez handed Fernández the document, pointing at the signature on the last page.

'But, what I don't understand is...' Juanita's voice caught as she uttered the next few words. 'Why kill my husband?'

239

Fernández looked at Paul Turnbull's signature alongside Bartolomé's. 'Turnbull is about to sign a multi-million Euro contract with the planning authorities in Almeria – part of the regeneration of the docklands and inner-city. Turnbull knew that Bartolomé could show the authorities this document and prove to them that he'd been involved in corruption.' Fernández hesitated. 'I don't know, but maybe your husband had threatened to tell the authorities unless Turnbull compensated him. The point is that, if the Almeria planning authorities caught wind of Turnbull's involvement in corruption, they would pull the plug.'

Juanita bit her lip, fighting back her tears. 'Why did all three men have to die?'

Fernández breathed out forcefully. 'Are you sure you want to hear this?'

'I need to know.'

'A few months ago, Juan Gonzales collapsed. Turnbull found him and took him to the doctors. We're not sure about what happened next, but presumably Turnbull found out about Alberto's part in the murder of Gonzales' parents, and told him. Juan Gonzales, of course, had no hesitation and we can only assume that Turnbull convinced him to kill all three men.'

'But, why?'

'He wanted Bartolomé removed, but knew his death might not be the end of the threat he posed. He had to kill Alberto and Matias. If they'd told the authorities about the corruption...'He took her hands, aware of the bewilderment in her eyes, and added a postscript to the events that had unfolded last Thursday. 'Turnbull got Juan Gonzales to do his dirty work and then shot him. But your husband was still alive. Turnbull had to be sure.'

*

Throughout the journey back to Los Mineros, Fernández sat in the back of the car mulling over the evidence with which he would confront Paul Turnbull and anticipating a long night.

Eduardo Gomez was certain that the mayor who would have taken Turnbull's back hander had died recently. He agreed to contact a few old friends and check out the extent of the corruption that had redefined the *Rustico de Secano.*

Vincente Cabrera offered to speak to political associates he had in Almeria to find out if the contract for the city's regeneration had been signed.

Juanita sat alongside Fernández, her face turned to the window, her eyes vacant, registering little as the car sped along the coast road, across the plain and back into the mountains. In her hand she clasped a small square of cloth that she'd cut from the shirt her husband was wearing when he'd been shot. She toyed with it, ringing it through her fingers, using it to wipe the silent tears from her cheeks.

Just before ten the car turned into the square at the Town Hall.

As he clambered out, Fernández's mobile rang.

'Yes?'

Jacinta Estrada. 'They've found them. The girls. The helicopter's located them.'

'Where are they?'

'Way up in the hills.'

'They're ok?'

'Yes, we think so.'

'You think?'

'They're with Pepe. The goatherd. He's carrying one of them, making slow progress.'

'That's great. Just great,' Fernández said, knowing that whatever he was feeling it would be nothing like the torrent of emotions that Julieta Santiago and Inocenta Castaño would be experiencing. He gave the thumbs up to Juanita, Eduardo and Vincente, before moving out of earshot and asking Estrada, 'Does Ana-Marie know?'

'Not yet. I'll go up to the church and tell her.'

'I'll meet you there.' He paused. 'I don't suppose they've found him?'

241

'No. SOCO have started on a fourth borehole. They've cleared the rubble from the first three, down to about two metres and found nothing.'

'No sign at all?'

'You're sure José's there?'

'No. No, I'm not.'

'The Madrid police have come back to us,' Estrada said. 'They've uncovered a betting scam that has defrauded hundreds of people in the Capital. José got caught up in it, borrowed and lost a serious amount of money.'

'How much?'

'Close to two hundred thousand.'

'But surely he could afford to take such a hit?'

'Thing is, Sir, he was leading the life of a super star but I've been looking back through the information sent to us by Real Madrid.'

'And?'

'His salary is linked to the number of games he plays and goals he scores for the first team.'

'And he'd only just broken into the big time.'

'The Aston Martin's on loan, the club picks up the tab for his accommodation, sponsorship clothes him and provides some of life's little luxuries, so coughing up would not have been as easy for him as it would be for some of his more illustrious team mates.'

'And loan sharks were after him.'

'It might explain why Laura was blackmailing Adam Wells and Javier Guzmán.'

'Not to help her father out?' Fernández rubbed the back of his neck and shook his head. 'But she wouldn't have wanted José to know she'd slept around.'

'No. No, of course not,' Estrada agreed. 'God, how stupid. She went to Turnbull and told him she was expecting his child, but it backfired because Ana-Marie's pregnant and they're about to start a family of their own. The last thing Turnbull needed was his brother-in-law's fiancée announcing she's carrying his child.'

242

'So, you're convinced that Laura had an affair with Turnbull?' Fernández was not persuaded. He was sure that the *dirt* Laura had on Paul Turnbull was something far more incriminating. 'Sofia must have told Laura she'd seen Turnbull follow Juan Gonzales into the campo last Thursday.'

'And you think Laura confronted Turnbull, told him she knew he'd been involved in the murders?'

'And demanded money in exchange for her silence.' He exhaled forcefully. 'And our only eye witness is a six year old kid.'

'Unless Carlos is right, and Pepe knows more than he's saying.'

*

It had taken an hour to bring the goats to heel after the scream of the helicopter had scattered them across the hillside. Pepe's dogs had worked overtime; barking and snapping at the goats, driving them back up towards the old ruin where Pepe had taken the girls to shelter over night.

As they made their way hesitantly down the mountainside, it seemed that half the village had turned out to watch Pepe shrug off offers of help from police and members of the mountain rescue team. He'd carried Holly this far and wasn't going to give her up that easily.

Julieta Santiago fell twice as she hurried across the campo, grazing her arm on a rock and collecting unwanted samples of coarse flora in her hair. She looked a mess – a jubilant, beside-herself-with-joy mess, tears streaming down her face. She didn't know whether to laugh or cry, combining both into a passionate outpouring of love, relief and anxiety. By the time she reached the man who carried her daughter as he would a stricken lamb, Julieta Santiago had discarded any pretense that her job was important or that she was important. The only thing that was important was the tired, frightened, brave little girl who struggled in Pepe's arms when she saw her mother stumbling towards her.

Inocenta Castaño watched from the terrace as Enrique hurdled the thickets of gorse and wild pampas grass, yelping with the vigor of a man half his age, his face alive with expectation. Inocenta smiled as Pedra put her arm around her and pulled her to her. They watched as Enrique swept Sofia into his arms, lifting her high above his head, crying out and then cradling her to his chest, almost hugging the life out of her. They watched as Julieta Santiago arrived and a tense standoff looked set to harden, as Pepe appeared reluctant to let Holly go. But, as Holly struggled to free herself, he relented. Julieta Santiago knelt down and Holly flew into her arms.

Jacinta Estrada stood alongside the two older women, not envying them their moment of relief. She knew that, if Antonio Fernández was right, this moment of elation would be no more than a respite for Inocenta Castaño. For the Priest's whore, the nightmare had only just begun.

*

He found Ana-Marie monitoring the excavation of the fourth borehole, her face lined with the twin agony of anticipation and denial. She had wrapped Father Gabriel's cassock about her shoulders to stave off the chill. She tried to phone her husband but there was no signal.

She stood watching every rock that passed from one crime-scene officer to another, their efforts supplemented by men from the Guardia. Rubble was dumped in a skip under the scaffolding outside the door to the southern nave.

As each rock was removed Ana-Marie would lean forward, holding her breath, scanning for traces of her brother. Nothing. But, nothing was good. Nothing meant that Antonio Fernández could be wrong. Nothing, gave her hope. Hope that she clung to. Resolutely.

When Fernández stood behind her and spoke gently, it was as though his voice was part of her nightmare.

'How have you been?' she heard him say. His voice seemed detached and even when he said 'They've found them,' his words didn't really register. It wasn't until he touched her shoulder and spoke her name, startling her from her trance, that she grasped what he was saying.

'They've found the girls,' he said.

'Yes, I know.'

'Both of them. Safe and sound.'

'Thank God.' She returned to her station, overlooking the borehole that grew deeper with each dredging.

'You didn't tell me you were a carrier.'

'A what?' she said, only half hearing what he'd said.

'When we talked of having children of our own, you didn't tell me.'

'Tell you what?' She turned round. 'What is it I didn't tell you? What is it that's so important that it can't wait? What is it that's more important than finding my brother? You're hoping he's here, aren't you? You're desperate to prove yourself right. Desperate to pin Laura's murder on my husband, just because of a stupid pendant, a stupid...' Her voice trailed off as though she was fighting off the stark truth: her husband had lied to her. He had told her that the pendant was for her, knowing it was Laura's gift to José - her engagement gift to him, for eternity. 'The child was José's?'

'We're not sure.'

'But the blood test?'

'At best, you're the baby's aunt. The DNA match was not as conclusive as it would have been if the sample had been taken from the child's father.'

'From José,' she said. 'Why can't you say it was his child?'

'We need to be certain.'

She pulled a tissue from beneath the sleeve of her blouse and wiped her eyes. He knew the timing would never be right, but pressed ahead. 'You didn't tell me you were a carrier. The blood test...'

245

'Because I didn't know. Not until...' Her hand settled on her stomach. 'They told me soon after they'd confirmed I was pregnant.'

'You know it's hereditary?'

'Haemophilia? Yes. I asked Mama. She was as surprised as I was. She said it must have skipped a generation.'

Fernández let it slide. He would need to run it past Julieta Santiago but, if his understanding was correct, haemophilia didn't skip generations. Ana-Marie clearly hadn't considered any other alternative, and now wasn't the time.

He walked towards the ramp, pausing to watch the forensic officers sifting through the rubble. 'I'll need to take your mobile,' he told her.

'My mobile? Why?'

'Have you contacted your husband this morning?'

'I tried earlier. There's no signal down here.' Her face registered alarm. 'What's going on, Antonio?'

'Your mobile, please, Ana-Marie.' He held out his hand.

'Antonio, you must tell me what's going on. I have a right to know.'

'Your husband will be arrested as soon as his plane lands this evening.' He looked at his watch: eleven fifteen. 'At the moment, he's on board the flight from London to Madrid. There'll be a delay before he catches the Air Nostram flight to Almeria.'

Ana-Marie stood, as if transfixed, struggling with the realisation that her husband may have killed Laura. Why else would he have lied to her about the pendant? And José? Had her husband killed him and buried him here, in this God-forsaken dungeon? She summoned up vestiges of defiance. 'If you're so sure, why didn't you have him arrested in London?'

'It's easier this way. We'll have seventy-two hours to interview him before we have to lay the evidence before a judge.'

'You were always so sure of yourself, weren't you?' She turned on him, her eyes ablaze. 'You're enjoying this, aren't you? Ten years you've had to wait.'

She was right; he had waited ten years, but not to see her suffer. He wanted to hold her, knowing that this would probably be his last chance to speak to her off-the record, but all he could summon was as a simple, 'I'm sorry.'

He called two Guardia officers over and said, 'Take Mrs. Turnbull to the Town Hall and place her in one of the holding cells. Confiscate her mobile.'

'Like hell you will,' Ana-Marie said as she pushed past him. Fernández nodded, and the officers held her. 'Get your hands off me. I will not be treated like this!' As they led her up the ramp, she struggled, crying out once more, 'For God's sake Antonio!'

He ignored her protest and followed, watching as she was manhandled out of the church. He phoned the Incident Room, updated Valencia Ramoz and was told that Leo Medina had just started debriefing Pepe.

He hesitated. With the media camped outside the church and the village rampant with rumour, he couldn't be certain that Ana-Marie had told him the truth about contacting her husband. He told Ramoz to alert the officers tailing Turnbull. 'Oh, and keep an eye on Ana-Marie. Make sure she doesn't come to any harm.'

*

The girls enjoyed sharing a bath and being fussed over by Holly's grandmother. Dressed in striped cotton pyjamas, they sat down to Sofia's favourite breakfast - honey pancakes and fresh orange juice. Julieta Santiago checked her daughter's ankle and wrapped it in a crepe bandage.

Jacinta Estrada waited patiently. It wouldn't be long before bed beckoned and she wanted to question the girls before exhaustion took its toll. As they cuddled up on the sofa, she reassured them that they weren't in trouble and then asked them to tell her exactly what they'd been up to.

They looked at each other and giggled, and then turned and started. 'Well.' They giggled again and stumbled over who would go first before Sofia said, 'We were only playing a game.'

They giggled once more, before the tale poured out of them: they'd climbed down the vine, chased each other across the campo and slipped under the tape the police had put round the new-build where the men had been killed last Thursday. They'd spent time peering in through the glassless windows, and then scampered higher up the hill. Holly had fallen and hurt her ankle. It was getting dark and they were scared. Holly tried to walk but her ankle hurt too much. Then suddenly hundreds of goats surrounded them. A man pushed his way through the goats, slapping their bottoms to make them move. He didn't say anything, but, as the girls huddled together, he'd stroked their foreheads with the back of his hand and brushed hair out their eyes. Sofia told the man what had happened to Holly and the man carried her to an old ruin, where he had water, some black bread and a soft blanket made of wool. It was dark, they heard people calling their names, and they asked the man to take them home. But he couldn't speak. He showed them the inside of his mouth. He didn't have a tongue. It was really scary! They'd begun to cry and Sofia had asked him if he was going to hurt them or kill them, like someone had killed Laura? Was he going to shoot them? The man shook his head and stroked their hair again. They asked him if he would take them home? He nodded. Now? He shook his head. In the morning? He nodded and smiled, patting the blanket. The girls had held onto each other, cuddling until they'd fallen asleep.

'Did he stroke you anywhere else?' Julieta Santiago asked.

'It's very important you tell us the truth,' Inocenta said.

The girls didn't need to consult. They looked, wide eyed, not understanding the significance of the questions or the concern of the three women who had unintentionally encircled them. 'He looked at my ankle and put that rag on it,' Holly said.

'First, he rubbed the rag over the back of one of his goats.'

'Then put it on my ankle. It smelt horrible!'

248

Both girls began to giggle again, unaware that Estrada had decided the time was right to ask the questions she'd been holding back.

'Sofia, who was Gloria paying hide-and-seek with?'

The room fell silent. Holly took Sofia's hand.

'We know who Gloria is, Sofia.' Estrada said. 'It's not a secret anymore.'

Tears filled Sofia's eyes and she looked at Holly.

'They're tired. Can't this wait?' Inocenta asked.

'Sofia?' Estrada said. 'Can you remember who Gloria was playing hide-and-seek with?'

'Señor Gonzales. The old man. He was carrying a rug under his arm.'

When was this?'

'Just before the fireworks.'

Sofia began to sob and Holly put her arm round her. 'I said it would be better if you told, didn't I?'

'Sofia?' Estrada got up and took two photographs down from the mantelpiece. 'Is Gloria in any of these photographs?'

Sofia nodded.

'Can you show me?

*

After raiding the duty-free for malt whisky, perfume and chocolates, Paul Turnbull settled in the business class lounge at Madrid airport. He'd only taken hand luggage and his Samsonite case had been neatly stowed in the locker room behind the reception desk. He'd been told that the Air Nostram flight had been delayed due to technical problems and if there was anything the airline staff could do to help make the delay more palatable, he only had to ask - nothing was too much trouble for such a valued, gold card customer. He'd thanked the tall, very attractive young woman who had made him the offer and said he was sure he'd think of something.

249

He flipped through a British tabloid and then checked several Spanish papers where he found references to two men being questioned in connection with the murder of Laura Domingo. There was also brief mention of Joaquin Alvarez's recovery, a column devoted to a 'bungled burglary' that ended in the death of Felipe Medina, and a profile of Juan Gonzales, 'fascist assassin'. The sports pages were full of football's summer transfers and the legacy of the Beijing Olympics, one year on. José Castaño seemed to have slipped off the radar.

Turnbull had lunch and then checked his iPhone. He was about to call Ana-Marie when he saw the air stewardess sashay towards him.

'I've got some good news.' She sat down beside him. 'The technical fault has been rectified and we'll be taking off as soon as everyone's onboard. You'll appreciate that there's no business class section on this Dash 8 twin prop, but I am sure we'll find a way of making your flight as comfortable as possible.'

'That's very thoughtful.' He grinned at her and glanced at her left hand, checking for a band of gold – less complicated if she was married.

'Is there anything else, Sir?' She raised one eyebrow slightly and smiled.

'You'll be accompanying the flight?'

'Of course. We want to make sure you're delivered safely, don't we? Now, if you could make your way to the departure gate. As soon as we have everyone onboard, we can taxi into position.' She pointed at his iPhone. 'You'll need to turn that off, I'm afraid.'

'No sooner said…' He was about to shut his mobile down, when he asked; 'I don't suppose you'd like to join me for dinner this evening? Say eight thirty?'

'A man with self-confidence. I like that.' She accompanied him to the reception desk where he collected his hand luggage.

'I'll see you later, then.' He smiled, paused and tapped a brief text message to Anna-Marie.

The air stewardess watched him take the escalator down into the main concourse. 'Oh, I'll see you later. You can bet your life on it.'

*

Fernández had just walked past the village bakery when he took a call on his mobile.

It was Jacinta Estrada. 'They need you at the church.'

'Send someone to fetch Doctor Santiago. She's at the Castaño's. Tell them to be discreet.'

'I'll go myself.'

'Yes. Good. Thanks. You'd better ask Father Gabriel to meet me at the church.'

He eased his mobile shut and stood quietly for a moment – even something as inevitable as that call still hit him hard.

The SOCOs had cleared as much of the rubble as possible, finally brushing away the layers of dust that had settled around the body. They'd removed the larger rocks and levered several boulders onto the granite floor around the borehole until, two meters down, they unearthed the unmistakable light blue of denim and the heel of a training shoe. Their choice had been stark - proceed with caution on the assumption that they were dealing with a corpse or throw caution to the wind in the faint hope that he might still be alive. It might have felt like an eternity to those looking down from the rim of the borehole, but the officer in charge had reacted almost immediately. 'Get down there and check.'

The young man was lying face down. A large rock had bridged across the crude burial chamber, protecting him from the rubble poured down on top of him. SOCOs winched the rock out of the hole before one of them was lowered down and began to tear at the rubble, filling several buckets and waiting patiently as each was returned to him. Suddenly, he stopped and moved an arc light to illuminate the body. He knelt and searched for signs of life – checking for a pulse in the neck, placing his ear close to the face. He looked up and shook his head.

251

'I'll let Inocenta know,' Father Gabriel whispered and hurried from the church.

Julieta Santiago arrived, unclasped her crime scene bag and asked to be lowered down. She spent several minutes checking. But José Castaño was dead.

Fernández told the SOCOs to take a break and waited until they'd left. 'You OK?'

She looked up at him, her body trembling in the cold. 'It's so sad, Antonio, so achingly sad. Moments ago, I'd held Holly in my arms and Inocenta had held onto Sofia as though her life would end if anything happen to her. Now she has this to face.'

He watched as she fought to regain her composure. He could not wait too long – time, as always, of the essence.

He lit a cigarette.

'This is a crime scene, Inspector.'

He stubbed out the cigarette and watched as she examined the body.

The SOCOs began to drift back and a uniformed officer arrived to report that Enrique Castaño was at the church doors, demanding to be let in.

'Don't let the press get to him,' Fernández said. 'Bring him inside but keep him away from here. I'll let you know when we're ready for him,'

'Antonio,' Santiago called. 'I can't do any more down here. I'll leave it for the SOCOs.'

'His father's here.'

'He'll have to wait. We'll need to remove the body soon anyway. Enrique can help us with the formalities.' She fell silent for a moment. 'Get me out of here.'

She was winched to the surface. 'It's not easy to asphyxiate a fit young man, but someone has…'

'He's been strangled?'

'None of the classic signs are present: bruising, fingernail marks, or damage to the larynx. But, there are signs of petechial hemorrhaging in the eyes and face. He'd been knocked unconscious, then hauled to his feet. Whoever did that, then crushed his chest, depriving him of oxygen.' She removed her gloves. 'The girls are safe.'

'Yes, thank God.'

'My mother's taken them into the City. They'll rest up at our apartment. Thought it better to get Sofia out of the village, away from all the press speculation and this…God knows what's going on in her mind. She's so young.'

'Let's hope we don't have to put her on the stand.'

'Can you secure a conviction without her?'

'I'm not sure her testimony will be accepted as reliable anyway. Pepe's a better bet…' He hesitated. 'I really am glad the girls came through ok.'

'Yes, I know you are, Antonio. Not your priority, though, were they?' She stepped to one side as forensic officers prepared to seal off the site and begin their painstaking examination. 'You want me to tell Ana-Marie?'

'Yes. Thanks,' he said, stung by her accusation, but as he stared down at José's body he knew she was right - Holly and Sofia had not been at the top of his list of priorities.

He headed out of the church, journalists tagging along behind, shouting questions and demanding answers. He looked at his watch. It was three-thirty. Paul Turnbull would be onboard the Air Nostram flight, bound for Almeria.

He stopped, turned and said, 'A press conference will be held outside the Town Hall at five this evening.'

'Oh, come on Inspector, you can do better than that, tell us what's going on,' shouted one of the TV news reporters, making sure his camera crew were in place. 'Give us something.'

Fernández lit a cigarette and dragged the smoke into his lungs. He glanced up at the barrage of cameras assembled in front of him, red lights betraying their readiness to record anything he said. He considered his options. He needed to keep them away from his next port of call and, knowing that the Guardia were in control at the church, he said, 'A body has been found in the crypt.'

*

253

He found Father Gabriel sitting with Inocenta Castaño. She was looking at photographs of her son. The Priest got up and whispered, 'I've told her about José. Enrique's gone to the church.'

'Thank you Father. Can you stay?'

'Of course.'

Fernández went over and sat beside Inocenta. She looked up at him, dry eyes not yet able to cry. He placed his hand alongside the framed photograph she held.

These had been happier days - the family on the beach before Sofia was born, a teenage Ana-Marie strutting her stuff, José more interested in the sand castle he'd constructed with his father.

Fernández glanced at Father Gabriel and shook his head. Now was not the right time. Any statement made under such circumstances would be judged inadmissible or ripped apart by a half-decent defence lawyer. She'd only just got Sofia back after twelve frantic hours. She'd only just been told that her son's body had been found and that he'd been murdered. But Fernández felt he had to be sure that Inocenta was just that – innocent.

'Antonio?' Her surprisingly strong voice startled him. 'Do you know who killed my son?'

'Yes. We think so.'

'It was him wasn't it? My daughter's husband?'

'Yes. It looks that way.'

'And it's all my fault, isn't it?' Tears, at last, began to trickle down her cheek. 'I was only trying to protect my family. Was that so wrong of me?'

'Now may not be the right time, Inocenta.'

'This may be the only time we have,' she said. 'It was when I heard that Juan Gonzales had killed Alberto that I realised…' Her voice trailed off. 'It all began to make sense - all those questions he kept asking me about the murder of Father Emanuel.'

'What did Turnbull want to know?'

'He seemed to know so much about that awful night. He showed me the photographs he'd bought from Rodrigo Perpiñán. He said he'd been drinking with some of the old men in the village and they'd told him about Alberto. He asked me if I remembered what happened that night, as if I could forget. He knew the names of everyone involved, including your father.'

'Did Turnbull know you were pregnant with the Priest's child?'

'Yes.'

'Do Enrique or Ana-Marie know?'

'Not yet.' Inocenta lifted her head and looked intently into the eyes of the man who had taken her daughter away from them more than ten years ago – they'd lived in sin, the neighbours had said, but that was nothing compared to what would be exposed during a trial. 'But, it's only a matter of time, isn't it? When this goes to court, everything will come out.'

'And you saw Paul Turnbull, last Thursday?'

'Yes. Sofia and I were on the terrace. We watched him follow Gonzales towards that new-build…'

'Did you know he was going to kill Juan Gonzales?'

'No, of course not. I had no idea. We'd found him a few weeks back. He'd collapsed and we took him to the doctor. I went to see him a couple of times, but he wouldn't take his medicine. Paul kept an eye on him.'

'Fuelling an old man's desire for revenge.'

She laughed hollowly. 'Sofia thought they were playing hide-and-seek.'

'Yes. She told one of my officers. Unfortunately, we didn't take her seriously.' He hesitated. He knew he had to press on with the interrogation. Paul Turnbull was hours away from custody and he needed to hear what Inocenta had to say. She reminded him so much of his own mother, fragile yet defiant, and wondered how his mother would cope if she'd just been told that he'd been killed?

He wasn't sure he could ask much more of Inocenta, but once again her resilience surprised him.

255

'I heard the rockets,' she said. 'Is that when he killed them?'

'Yes, we think so. The evidence suggests that Juan Gonzales killed Alberto and Matias. He also shot Bartolomé, but he didn't die immediately. Turnbull shot Bartolomé again, and then turned the gun on Juan Gonzales. Tried to make his death look like suicide.' Fernández paused, needing to clarify her version of events, but desperate to leave her to mourn her son. 'You told Turnbull the names of those involved and, in particular, the part played by Alberto?'

'No I didn't tell him. He'd got the old men drunk and they were brandy talking. They must have told him, but I suppose my silence simply confirmed what he'd been told.' Her tears fell unchecked and she looked at him as though pleading for understanding, for compassion. 'I'm so very sorry,' she said. 'For your family and for Rodrigo's.'

'Inocenta,' Father Gabriel said, 'you were fifteen years old. You cannot blame yourself for what happened that night thirty-five years ago or what happened last Thursday.'

She looked at him, shaking her head. 'I may have been fifteen, but Emanuel was not all to blame. Did you know they called me the Priest's whore?'

'Yes. It couldn't have been easy, for either of you.'

'We were in love.'

Father Gabriel took her hand. 'You were no more than a child.'

Inocenta pulled away from him, her face scarred by tears, her voice weary. 'I was carrying his child.' She fell silent, her eyes distant, as though watching images of the past. She pulled a handkerchief from her sleeve and dabbed her face. It was several minutes before she looked at Fernández and nodded.

He took her cue. 'And Turnbull knew Ana-Marie was Father Emanuel's daughter?'

'Yes.' Inocenta sighed heavily. 'When Ana-Marie became pregnant, she had all those tests. She had to explain to him that their unborn son was at risk.'

256

'That he would be a haemophiliac?'

'Yes. I'm not and neither is Enrique, so it didn't take long for Paul to work it out. The old men told him about Father Emanuel, about his illness and his trips to the sanatorium. He put two and two together. He told me he wouldn't tell Enrique, or the children, as long as I told him what he wanted to know.' She dabbed her eyes and blew her nose. 'But I didn't tell him, I swear.'

Fernández had one more question. 'And who's idea was it to take cake round to the Ramos women on the day their men were murdered?'

'He said he'd seen Juanita and that she'd invited me round. Sofia was playing up and I asked Ana-Marie to go instead.'

'Sounds like another one of Turnbull's lies,' Father Gabriel said. 'Keep the women occupied, out of the way, whilst he…' He hesitated and looked at Inocenta.

She looked at Fernández, her sorrow threatening to overwhelm her. 'Will you ever be able to forgive me?'

'Inocenta,' Fernández said, 'There is nothing to forgive.'

'You don't understand, do you? It was *me* who told Juan Gonzales what happened that night. When he returned to the village, all those years ago, it was *me* who told him who'd killed his parents.'

His breath caught in his throat. Tears welled up in his eyes. He was looking at the woman who had condemned his father to death. He wondered how she'd coped – hiding from the truth, living with the enormity of the lies she'd told, burying the secrets of that night, bearing their burden each day until the deceit finally caught up with her. He took her into his arms and held her close, shuddering as her sobs soaked into him, pulling her tightly to him.

'I was naked when they burst in,' she said. 'Your father and Pedro Perpiñán dragged Emanuel out of the house. Alberto sat with me on the bed and told me what they were going to do. When Juan Gonzales found out about the death of his parents he returned to the village with one thing on his mind. He recovered

257

the bodies from the old mineshaft and threatened to kill me if I didn't tell him who was responsible.' She paused, tears streaming down her face, her words punctuated by sobs. 'I was scared. I had no one to turn to. I gave him your father's name and Rodrigo's, but I didn't tell him about Alberto. I wanted to protect him. He'd been so kind.' She paused, struggling to compose herself. 'Juan Gonzales knew that someone else had been involved, but had to wait until last Thursday when he finally caught up with Alberto.' She pushed away from him, raised a trembling hand and stroked his cheek. 'I am so sorry, Antonio, so very, very sorry.'

*

The flight had taken an hour - just time for a couple of glasses of champagne with the man he'd met on his way from the business class lounge in Madrid to the departure gate.

Turnbull glanced out of the tiny portside window as the Air Nostram landed and taxied towards the terminal building. The sun seemed exceptionally piercing as it bounced off the tarmac and he slipped on his RayBans. He glanced round to see if he could catch the air-stewardess to confirm their date before they left the aircraft. She smiled at him from the crew seat, and then looked away.

The twin prop chugged towards the arrivals entrance and the pilot parked its nose facing the mountains in the distance. Turnbull slipped his seat belt off as soon as the sign was extinguished and stood up to retrieve his hand luggage.

'Mr. Paul Turnbull?' the air-stewardess said.

'Yes.'

'If you would accompany these two officers, please sir.'

'Something wrong?'

'Call it your very own Fast Track through customs.' Turnbull's business class companion pulled open his jacket, revealing a modified Glock17 self-loading pistol.

'I don't understand.' He looked at each unsmiling face. 'What's going on?'

The plane's front exit door eased open and two uniformed Guardia officers took the short flight of steps into the cabin. His head jerked round, looking instinctively for an escape route, but another passenger was standing in the aisle, baring access to the rear.

'The arresting officer will read you your rights.' The air stewardess smiled. 'Thank you for flying with us, sir. Have a nice day.' She nodded at the Guardia officers and watched as Paul Turnbull was cuffed and led into the main concourse building.

She turned to the two Special Operations officers who'd accompanied the flight and asked, 'Anyone know the Spanish for beer?'

*

After she'd arranged for José's body to be taken to the morgue, Julieta Santiago drove Ana-Marie into Almeria, where they sat overlooking scores of tiny craft moored in the fishing harbour.

After about an hour, Ana-Marie's mobile rang. A senior officer from the Policia National informed her that her husband had been arrested and taken to their headquarters, where he would be held until conditions for bail had been decided by a judge. She was informed that this process could take up to three days and that he was entitled to have a lawyer present and undergo any medical examination deemed necessary.

The police officer was apologetic – told her he couldn't discuss charges, nor would Ana-Marie be able to visit her husband until his case had been presented to the judge. She told him she understood and, as she ended the call, a text message arrived. It was from her husband...

Miss u - still in uk - c u sat xx

259

Ana-Marie closed her mobile.

He was lying.

Again.

Bastard.

But that was nothing compared with what he'd done to her brother.

*

'We'll give him something to think about overnight and then get some rest,' Fernández said, placing a tray of files and evidence bags on the table in the middle of the interview room and offering Jacinta Estrada and Leo Medina a coffee.

'How long can we hold him?' Medina asked.

'I'll talk to the Comandante, see if there's a case for an extension.'

'You think we've got enough?' Estrada asked.

'Never that simple, is it? We screw up and he'll walk. As things stand, the judge will probably grant bail.'

'And risk him killing again?'

'I want him off the streets as much as you do, Leo, but pulling him in when we did leaves us exposed. We need time to put the forensics and eyewitness accounts together. If his lawyer is half-decent, he'll make the case for bail. There'll be conditions attached, given the seriousness of the charges, but it's unlikely the judge will agree to a custodial remand. We have no proof he killed Felipe Romano, but the other four should stick.'

'Pepe's hard work,' Medina said. 'But I think he *did* see Turnbull kill Bartolomé and Juan Gonzales.'

'Let's hope the Judge plays ball.'

There was a knock on the door and a uniformed officer advised them that Paul Turnbull's lawyer had arrived and was conferring with his client.

They ran through the running order, then sat in silence for several minutes before Turnbull and his brief were ushered into the room. The formalities out of the way, everyone was reminded of the charges: the murders of Bartolomé Ramos, Juan Gonzales, Laura Domingo and José Castaño.

Fernández began by asking. 'How well did you know Bartolomé Ramos?'

'We'd together worked on a few projects. The partnership didn't last. He lacked the drive I need in an associate.'

'But, still, whilst it did last you were involved in several deals, one of which we have reason to believe involved corruption.'

Turnbull consulted with his lawyer. 'No comment.'

Fernández placed a document in front of him. 'For the record,' he said, 'Mr. Turnbull has been shown a document signed by him and Bartolomé Ramos in relation to the purchase of land.' Fernández drew on his cigarette as Turnbull glanced through the document. 'Even eight years ago the price you paid for this land was a bargain. It was so cheap, of course, because it was Rustico de Secano, land upon which it was illegal to build.'

Again, Turnbull consulted with his lawyer who spoke for him. 'My client fails to see what this has to do with the charges brought against him.'

'It's a matter of motivation,' Fernández began. 'Why would Mr. Turnbull put a bullet through the forehead of a man who'd already been shot through the throat? Could it be that his former partner had threatened to inform the authorities in Almeria that the land had been purchased illegally? The hotel in question hits the headlines every week, but it's not the objections to the hotel I'm interested in, it's the land.'

'No comment.'

Fernández glanced at Estrada.

She held up a plastic evidence bag. 'Is this your iPhone?'

'Not a crime, I presume?'

'No, no, of course not. Have you used it recently? To send a text message to your wife, for instance?'

'I may have.'

'Still in London, eh? That'll take some explaining.' She produced another evidence bag. 'And this?'

Turnbull looked at his old mobile phone. His face blanched momentarily. 'If I'd known you had this, I could have saved myself a small fortune. Where did you find it?'

'In the crypt of the church in Los Mineros, near where you'd buried the body of José Castaño.'

'My client,' the lawyer said, 'could have dropped it at anytime during the restoration.' There was something uncertain in his voice, as though he was beginning to suspect that Turnbull hadn't been straight with him.

Estrada smiled. 'Yes. Yes, of course. You're quite right.' She produced another evidence bag. 'But your client told his wife that he'd dropped this on the floor of the crypt.' She placed the gold pendant of the Indalo Man on the table. 'He told her that he'd bought it for her. We're checking retailers as we speak. Trouble is, if you turn the pendant upside down, you'll see that the initials JC have been carved into the souls of its feet. It belonged to José Castaño. Your client lied to his wife and tricked her into wearing it around her neck just days after he'd killed her brother.' She sat back.

Fernández changed tack. 'We're processing DNA taken during Laura's autopsy. Her own and the foetus she was carrying. A third sample found under her fingernails.' He hesitated and leaned forward. 'Now, if the was to match your DNA…'

'And, it may well, Inspector.' Turnbull's face broke into a smile and he stood up, removed his gold cufflinks and began to unbutton his shirt, easing it from his body. He turned to reveal fading scratch marks on his back. 'The stuff of erotica, eh, Inspector? A young woman unable to resist clawing at her paramour during the height of sexual ecstasy.' Turnbull smirked, replacing his shirt, not bothering to button it up. 'Laura needed money. I was glad to help. She paid me in kind. Been going on for some time. We had sex at my apartment last Friday afternoon and then she drove back to Los Mineros for dinner with her father. She was meeting up with Ana-Marie for the fiesta later that evening. Friday afternoon was the last time I saw her. I was shocked by the news of her death, but had nothing to do with it.'

The lawyer rose and began to pack his brief case.

'Will that be all, Inspector?'

'Not quite.'

Leo Medina folded his arms, leant forward and asked Turnbull, 'You like bull fighting?'

'Cruel and barbaric.'

'I'm a huge fan. I'd provide a demonstration, but I'm sure you know how it goes?' He slid a copy of the bullfighting poster across the table. 'The Matador infuriates and frustrates the bull, making it turn and turn again. There are many different passes, collectively known as the Pases de Gloria.'

Paul Turnbull looked at the poster and then at his lawyer, rolling his eyes and shaking his head.

'Inspector,' the lawyer looked at Fernández. 'We are grateful for the insight into Spain's heritage, but…'

Fernández ignored him and asked Turnbull, 'Were you aware that Laura had given you a nickname?'

'Nickname?'

'Gave most of us nicknames, apparently.'

'Humour me.'

'She called you Gloria.'

Turnbull shifted in his seat. 'I'm sorry, but what has this got to do with..?'

'Pases de Gloria: the turning of the bull.'

'Inspector, this is not making any sense.'

'The turning of the bull: Turnbull.'

It was his lawyer's turn to laugh. 'Is that the best you can do? I really must insist that this interview and my client's detention are terminated immediately.'

Fernández ignored him. 'And you know, at first we couldn't work it out. Last Thursday, *Gloria* was seen playing hide-and seek with an old man carrying a rug under his arm. Laura had arranged for *Gloria* to take her to the airport. Laura was about to dish the dirt on *Gloria*.'

'Are you telling us you have eyewitnesses?' The lawyer asked.

'Two, actually. One helping us with our enquiries as we speak.' Fernández extinguished his cigarette and lit another. 'We don't believe you killed Laura because of the money, or because she threatened to tell Ana-Marie about your affair. You killed her because she knew you'd killed Juan Gonzales. She'd spoken to one of our eyewitnesses.'

Three days later

Day Twelve

Monday 29th June 2009

When Ana-Marie suggested that they hold a joint funeral service for José and Laura, both fathers had merely shrugged. The nature of the service was irrelevant to them.

It had been ten days since Laura had come home from the fiesta, packed, and left around two in the morning. Since her body had been found, she'd been locked in a refrigeration unit in the morgue and Carlos had had to cancel her funeral several times.

Enrique hadn't seen José for months, not since he'd played in a reserve match in Malaga, or was it Almeria? He couldn't remember. But he'd never forget watching the forensics officers pull his son's body from the rubble. He'd been asked if it was his son? He'd nodded, but when he'd asked if he could hold his son in his arms for a few moments, they had refused. They'd told him he might contaminate the site.

No, as far as Carlos Domingo and Enrique Castaño were concerned the funeral arrangements were not uppermost in their minds.

Fernández drove into the village and was pulled over by officers from the Guardia Civil. He produced his police ID card, was waved through and parked outside the bar.

The Policia Local had cordoned off the square and two coffins were unloaded from hearses and carried straight into the church. Flowers had been arriving all day - placed against the church wall, together with messages pinned to cellophane. There were teddy bears dressed in Real Madrid's all-white first team strip for José, and blond dolls or cuddly toys for Laura. Everyone understood that it was to be a private service, restricted to immediate family and close friends. Those villagers who had been invited were already inside, standing, glancing around, watching the cortege make its way towards the altar. There was a single wreath on each coffin.

Fernández watched as Inocenta and Enrique stood alongside José's coffin. He watched them holding hands, as they might have done early in their courtship, bearing the death of their son together.

Carlos Domingo, stood alone, his head bowed, his face impassive.

When he saw Ana-Marie join her mother and Enrique, Fernández wondered if Inocenta had confessed everything? Whether she had told them about her affair with Father Emanuel and that he was Ana-Marie's biological father? He wondered whether such a confession would have drawn them closer together or whether this display of family unity was for José's sake?

He caught a glimpse of Julieta Santiago, her hair ruffled by a breeze filtering through the church doors. She was near him, at the back of the church, intent on the service, her face bearing her heartache.

He turned and watched as Ana-Marie slipped her hand through the arm of the man she had known all her life as 'Papa', and, as the service began, he saw Enrique draw his daughter and his wife closer to him.

*

Alone in his apartment, Turnbull phoned for a pizza, poured himself a malt whisky, took the bottle out on to the balcony overlooking the marina and ran through the case against him:

Pepe, phone records. My nickname!

266

He laughed, refilled his glass and took a moment, holding it up to the evening light, admiring the whisky's depth of colour, running the glass through his hands, taking a long draught, swilling it around his mouth, and enjoying the sensation of its complex distillation.

Forensics, DNA, fingerprints. Waste of time.

The pendant had been the one thing that troubled him. A local jeweller had provided a replacement and a backdated receipt, but he wasn't sure he could rely on him to keep his mouth shut.

Maybe I should make sure he'll never be able to testify?

His lawyer had insisted they disclose the names of the eyewitnesses.

Of course they'd refused. Eyewitnesses? Lying bastards.

He took another sip of whisky, put his glass down, tired suddenly, and sat back, closing his eyes.

Pity about Bartolomé. He was stupid. Threatening me like that. Doesn't matter now, of course, the contract's as good as mine.

He went through to the lounge and flicked through the Spanish TV channels. The evening news included highlights of Felipe Romero's funeral, held on Saturday morning, and the day's main event - the funerals of Laura and José. Turnbull shook his head as he watched his wife and her family follow the coffins into the church. If his case did go to trial, he would make sure they suffered - the Priest's whore, the bastard child and the cuckold husband. He would expose their hypocritical lives.

267

He poured himself another drink and watched an update on the investigation into the murders for which he had been arrested. He raised his glass when he saw shots of his lawyer defending the judge's decision to release him on bail and cutaways of the detectives leading the investigation. He wouldn't need a hotshot lawyer, not with the prosecution case resting on evidence provided by an Inspector who'd been too busy trying to bed a scrawny pathologist and whose judgment had been clouded by brandy and a lack of detachment. Any decent brief would tear holes in what they had against him. He smiled and wondered if the best that Inspector Antonio Fernández could come up with was that he'd killed Laura because she'd called him *Gloria*?

The shrill of the intercom buzzer cut short his solitude. Someone wanted to talk to him from the street below. He pressed the communication button and was momentarily unsettled to hear her voice.

'Let me in.'

'Yes. Yes, of course. I wasn't expecting…'

'No, but I am.'

He heard her push her way into the lobby, opened his front door and waited for the lift. Within moments the doors slid open and Ana-Marie stood before him.

She removed the headscarf that had hidden her face. She didn't say anything, but brushed passed him and poured herself a whisky.

'How are you?' he asked.

'How the hell do you think I am?'

'I'm sorry I haven't been in touch.'

'I'm not.'

'I'm innocent, you know. I didn't do those awful things.'

'What else would you say?' She paused and waited until she was calm before she added, 'My father was right. He knew there was something going on between you and Laura.'

Turnbull laughed, drained his glass and placed it on the coffee table. 'Enrique is not your father.'

'I know, but I can't afford to let you to have your day in court.' Her voice was ice cold. 'Inocenta has told us everything - from the moment you found Juan Gonzales lying in the gutter, took him to the doctor, and bullied her into betraying Alberto Ramos.'

'It'll never stand up in court.'

Ana-Marie continued as though she hadn't heard him. 'I had an interesting chat with Antonio Fernández after the funeral today.'

'Recalling old times, no doubt.'

'You persuaded an old man to kill Alberto, Bártolome and Matias, and then you blew his brains out. You killed Felipe because the police were about to arrest him. You killed Laura because she knew what you'd done.' Ana-Marie started to sob, finally giving way to her grief.

'You can't believe..?'

'You lied to me!' She spun round and threw the glass. It shattered against the wall. 'You lied to me. How the hell do you expect me to believe anything you tell me? You told me the pendant was for me, you'd wanted it to be a surprise, but you'd lost it.'

'But, I did buy one for you. Look,' he went over the sideboard and took a sheaf of paper from a plastic folder. 'The receipt.'

'Liar. It was José's. My brother's. And I wore that fucking thing round my neck. But what I don't understand is why you had to kill him?'

Turnbull moved towards her and she flinched. He grabbed her jaw, his hand clamping into her cheeks. 'If you're so sure I'm such a fucking monster, what are you doing here?'

Ana-Marie knocked his hand away. 'I can't afford to let you have your day in court,' she said again, calmly, as though she'd run the words over and over in her mind.

'And what's that supposed to mean?'

'I won't allow my family to be publicly humiliated.' She forced a smile. 'Besides, there are others who want to talk to you.'

Turnbull heard the door to the apartment close and turned to find a shotgun pointing at him.

'Time to take a stroll, Gloria'

They bundled him from his apartment, down the rear staircase, out through the emergency exit and into Carlos's old 4 x 4. Ana-Marie behind the wheel, Carlos and Enrique riding shotgun, Turnbull protesting his innocence and threatening reprisals, the twin barrels pressed deep into his ribs.

They drove through the open five bar gate, across the farm yard and drew up out side the barn. Ana-Marie and Enrique hurried to open the barn door whilst Carlos pulled Turnbull from the car and, easing back the twin hammers, forced the shotgun into his neck. 'Don't give me an excuse to use this, because I won't hesitate. Now, get inside.'

Carlos handed the shotgun to Ana-Marie and then tied Turnbull's hands behind his back. Enrique took a rope attached to a series of pulleys, looped it through the knot and pulled sharply, forcing Turnbull's arms upwards behind his back, pushing his head and torso forward.

'We'll be back in a moment,' Carlos said. 'We've got company for him.'

Ana-Marie watched as they walked out of the barn, before she turned to her husband. 'You want to tell me why?'

'Ana-Marie. You must believe me. I didn't kill Laura. Why would I do that?'

'You were fucking her. I'm carrying your child and you were fucking another woman.'

'She flirted. I was flattered. But I didn't sleep with her.'

'That's not what you told Antonio Fernández.' She walked behind him. 'During your interrogation, you said you were with her on Friday afternoon, hours before she joined us at the fiesta. You boasted she'd left marks on your back.' She

270

laughed, hollowly. 'Your sex was always about as subtle as a donkey's.' Suddenly, she struck him between the shoulder blades with the butt of the shotgun. 'You stupid bastard!'

'Ana-Marie, you've got to believe me.'

She stood in front of him and spat in his face. As he screwed up his eyes, she stepped back, held the shotgun high in the air and punctuated her next four words with strikes to his face and head. 'Don't lie to me!'

She watched as blood ran from his nose and cuts above his eyes. Suddenly, she felt a twinge in her womb and a sharp pain cut across her abdomen, making her gasp and drop to one knee.

The door opened and Carlos and Enrique herded a large pig into the barn, hitting it with a crook and kicking out at it when it tried to escape.

Enrique took the shotgun from Ana-Marie and helped her to her feet. 'You all right?'

'It's nothing, Papa. It'll pass.'

Enrique nodded, searching her face for the truth.

Ana-Marie smiled, trying to reassure him. 'I'm OK.'

Carlos tied a rope around the pig's neck and hooked it up to another set of pulleys next to Turnbull.

'Carlos.' The injuries Ana-Marie had inflicted had distorted Turnbull's face and he spat blood from his mouth. 'Carlos. You must believe me. I didn't have anything to do with Laura's death.'

'Thought that's what you'd say. I didn't expect you to come clean.'

Carlos was examining Turnbull's injuries. He stood so close that he could smell the trickle of urine that stained the dirt floor at Turnbull's feet.

'Carlos, you've got to listen to me.'

'I know you killed her.' Carlos took the shotgun from Enrique and lashed its twin barrels across Turnbull's face, opening fresh wounds, blood running freely from each cut.

Enrique stepped forward. 'You killed my son.'

271

'No, no. I swear.'

'He knew you'd killed Laura, so you killed him.'

'No.' Turnbull's mouth was filling with blood. 'Enrique, please believe me. I didn't kill José, and I didn't kill Laura. Please help me.'

'You killed my son and threatened my wife. You have to pay for that.'

'Let's get on with it,' Ana-Marie said, her voice detached and calm.

Carlos looked across at her. 'I want you away from here. As I see it, there's no point either of you being here. I'm done for, anyway. The cancer will come for me any day.' He smiled and added, 'You've got your old man here, your mother and that young sister of yours. They've been through enough. Having you arrested and sent to prison ain't going to help them, is it?'

Ana-Marie stood her ground. 'Killing this bastard was my idea.'

'Maybe that's so, but I have to kill him. He took my Laura from me.' He lowered the shotgun. 'Beside, you've got your own little one to think about.' He paused. 'Is it a boy or girl?'

'Little boy.'

'They're all little when they come out.' Carlos smiled unconvincingly, sadness coursing across his face. 'Go on, both of you, be off. I can handle things from here.'

'It's for the best, Ana-Marie,' Enrique said, offering his hand.

'Papa?'

'It's for the best.'

She hesitated, took one last look at her husband, and allowed Enrique to lead her out of the barn.

In the calm that descended, Carlos lifted a large, solid plank of wood and slid it through metal guards on each side of the barn door, securing it.

'Carlos! Please, I beg you,' Turnbull cried again, blood seeping into his eyes, clogging his vision.

Carlos ignored him and disappeared behind a curtain of old sackcloth. Moments later, he dragged a small table in front of the curtain and placed a digital recorder on top of it. He pressed a button and then disappeared behind the curtain again, returning with a length of thick hemp rope. He loosened the lasso round the pig's neck, tied its hind legs together, knocked it to the floor and then tied its front legs. He spoke as he worked. 'That man you killed, the fascist bastard who carried out all them assassinations? He used to explain to his victims why they had to die.'

'I didn't kill Laura. Carlos. What can I say to make you believe me? I shot Juan Gonzales. I shot Bartolomé and killed Felipe…' He paused, sucking in breath through a nose that felt badly broken and was haemorrhaging freely. 'José turned up at the church. He'd heard about Laura. She'd told him I was going to take her to the airport. He'd put two and two together and came up with the wrong answer. We argued, he attacked me and I struck him in self-defence.'

'You're a liar.'

'Laura sent me a text message, asking me to take her to the airport, but I swear…' Turnbull hesitated, his mind racing, desperate to buy time. 'Carlos, I was with another woman, someone I've been having an affair with for the last three years. You can ring and ask her. She'll tell you I was with her. I didn't find Laura's text message until I switched my phone on, on Sunday morning. You've got to believe me. I didn't kill her.'

Carlos continued as though he was immune to any further protestations, but wanted to explain. 'You have to die because I can't wait. I can't wait to see how many years in prison your going to get for killing my little girl. The cancer will take me long before they fix a date for a trail. And, even if I did last until the end of the trial, I won't be here in twenty years time when you get out.' He took a long bladed knife from its sheath. 'They say,' he said, placing the knife against the pig's throat, 'that the pig screams when its throat is slit, but it's only air

273

gushing out.' He ran the blade gently along the length of the animal's neck. 'It don't die immediately.' He took a rope, attached it to the pig's hind legs and slipped the other end through pulleys attached to a rafter.

'Carlos! Please!' Turnbull was sobbing. 'I'll go to the police. I'll tell them everything. But you have to believe me, I did not kill Laura!'

Carlos began to haul the pig off the ground until it hung, squealing and struggling, its head and neck pressed into the floor by the weight of its body. 'When I've slit its throat,' he said, 'I like to hang the pig up. It helps the heart pump all the blood out. It'll spasm for several minutes. Even when it's dead, it'll continue to spasm, as though it was still alive. It's the muscles. They keep working. Amazing really, isn't it?' He paused. 'It don't take too long before it's all over.'

'The woman's number, Carlos, write her number down.' Blood flowed freely from Turnbull's mouth, nose and from the gashes above his eyes. 'It's the woman I was with. She'll tell you.' He began to recite a number.

'I don't believe you,' Carlos said, taking the knife, and twisting it in his hand. 'You'd say anything to save your own skin. But I ain't listening.' Suddenly, in one swift, violent movement, he plunged the knife into the pig's throat. Its shrill scream filled the barn and the old farmer stood back as blood pumped out and soaked into the dirt floor.

'Carlos!' Turnbull wept. 'For God's sake. No. The number, you must write down the number.'

Carlos dropped the knife, grabbed the end of the rope, hauled the pig's carcass off the ground and stood back as blood continued to spout with each beat of the pig's heart. Within moments, its body began to spasm. He turned, picked up the knife and walked towards Turnbull.

'It didn't suffer too much, did it?' He ran the blade along Turnbull's throat. 'Now it's your turn.'

*

'Going somewhere?' Julieta Santiago asked, standing in the open doorway to his apartment.

'I'm due a few weeks leave.'

'Not the real deal, eh? You and me?'

'Thought I'd blown it.'

'The girls?'

'Not my priority, you said.'

'That wasn't fair of me, given the circumstances.'

'But I'm not sure you were far off the mark.'

They fell silent. Fernández finished packing his suitcase and then sat heavily on the sofa. 'How long can you stay?'

'Not long. I'm taking Holly down to the harbour. I want to show her where I nearly stowed away and ended up in Rio.' She smiled and picked up an empty bottle of red wine. 'But, I've got time for a glass.'

'In the fridge.'

'I'll get it.' She made her way into the kitchen.

He laid back on the sofa, staring at the ceiling fan and listening to the noises in the square outside, still uncertain about his feelings for the woman who'd removed his cigarette and taken charge of the crime scene the very first time they'd met. Each time they'd inched closer, work got in the way, or Holly. Not that Holly *got in the way. Oh, God, will it always be this complicated?*

She returned from the kitchen holding two glasses in one hand and an open bottle in the other. She set the glasses down and poured two generous measures of Rioja, but as she handed him a glass his mobile rang. He shook his head and looked at her. 'I'm sorry.'

'Don't be.' She got up and left.

He sighed, cursed and flipped open the phone.

It was Valencia Ramoz. 'Policia Local have traced the laundry bag and ticket that was recovered from the beach to an outlet in Almeria. Cientifica have found traces of Laura's blood in the car.'

'Turnbull's?'

'No. The car belongs to Doctor Guzmán. It was Guzmán who picked up his laundry…'

'On the day he killed Laura.'

'We've got CCTV footage showing him with Laura in a beach bar at three-thirty on Saturday morning. Turnbull didn't responded to her text so she must have phoned Guzmán.' She paused, as though waiting for a reaction, but Fernández was too busy calculating the cost of this latest bombshell. 'There's something else.'

'Go on,' he said.

'I've just had a call from Policia Local in Almeria. The concierge at Paul Turnbull's apartment contacted them. Turnbull ordered a pizza but when it was delivered no one responded. The delivery boy complained to the concierge, who opened up and found glass smashed over the floor.'

'And Turnbull?'

'Wasn't there. The in-house CCTV has been checked.'

'Anyone we know?'

'The concierge accounted for several, but two others were unrecognisable - a woman in a headscarf and a man shielding his face …' Ramoz hesitated.

'And?'

'Carlos was with them. He was carrying his shotgun.'

'Jesus Christ, that's all we need. Get the Guardia to check Guzmán's apartment.'

'He could be at the surgery in the village,' Ramoz suggested.

'I'll send Jacinta and Leo to check.'

'Where will you be?'

'My guess is that Carlos has taken Turnbull to the farm. I'll let you know. Put an ambulance and back-up on standby.'

*

276

Jacinta Estrada glanced through the glass-panelled door of the waiting room and snatched her head back. Leo Medina had taken up position on the other side of the door.

'We have a problem,' she said. 'One of your kids is in there. The eldest…'

'Pablo?'

'He's talking to one of the old women from the village. Which means…'

'That Roz and Rafe are in with Guzmán.' Medina pulled his Berretta from its holster beneath his jacket and pushed past her.

She grabbed his arm, stopping him in his tracks, struggling to hold on to him. 'Leo, wait…'

'That's my kid in there.'

She forced him away and stood between him and the surgery door, placing her left hand flat against his chest and insisted he listen. 'For God's sake, Leo. Guzmán's not some armed terrorist holding hostages. He's unaware we're here. He's with your son - just another patient at yet another evening surgery. If we play this right, no one need get hurt. Go in brandishing your gun and God knows what might happen.' Medina hesitated just long enough for her to attempt to reason with him once more. 'Help me clear the waiting room and get Pablo and the rest to safety…'

'And then, I go in.'

'Let me call for back-up.'

'Fuck the back-up. We have a deal, or I'm going in now.'

'I'll take that.' Estrada pointed at his handgun. 'Unarmed, the risks to your family are reduced.' She looked at him, sensing they understood each other, but not sure what she would do if he refused.

He looked at her, balancing the Beretta in his hand as though weighing up his options and struggling to know what to do. She watched him run his hand over the cold steel of the barrel before turning the grip of semi-automatic towards her and

277

unbuckling his shoulder holster. Estrada slid his handgun under her jacket, between her shirt and trouser waistband at the base of her spine. She stepped to one side of the surgery door, and nodded at him. 'OK – we clear the surgery first. Then you get Roz and Rafe out.'

She took out her warrant card and stood at the door, waiting for Medina to open it. As he did, she slipped silently inside, pressing an index finger against her lips and holding her warrant card high in the air. He followed her, reinforcing the command to be silent and beckoning to his son. Pablo got up slowly, confused. Medina waved him over, took his hand and led him outside as Estrada cleared the rest of the patients.

Deserted, the waiting room looked drab and bare, its whitewashed walls covered in posters that were out of date, its woodwork peeling from years of neglect. The muffled sound of Guzmán's voice drifted through the frosted glass panel of his surgery door and was joined by the sound of Roz translating the medical diagnosis into child-speak for Rafe. Everything seemed calm, commonplace. The normality gave Estrada valuable seconds in which to assess the situation and she pulled Medina away from the surgery door and whispered. 'You go in and you play the anxious father coming to check up on his kid. I'll stay out of it until Rafe and Roz are clear.'

'OK.' He hesitated, trying to stay calm, trying to regulate his breathing. 'Watch my back.'

He knocked and eased the door open. Guzmán looked up from examining Rafe's chest, his stethoscope still hooked around his neck. Medina forced a smile and asked as light-heartedly as he could muster, 'Will he make it, doctor?'

Guzmán ignored him, curtailed his examination, told Roz to get her son dressed, and then turned to his computer to print out a prescription.

Roz pulled Rafe's t-shirt over his head and Medina swept his son into the crook of his left arm. 'I've come to apologise,' he said, addressing the doctor.

At first Guzmán didn't react, but continued to concentrate on the paper work.

'I had it all wrong. You and Laura Domingo.' Medina hesitated as Roz looked at him anxiously. He rocked his head to one side, indicating that she should leave. He placed Rafe on the floor and the boy took his mother's hand.

Roz took the prescription from Guzmán and led Rafe through the surgery door.

'We've made an arrest,' Medina said, watching Roz cross the waiting room. She'd paused, no doubt looking for Pablo and he imagined Jacinta Estrada smiling reassuringly, her index finger planted firmly against her lips.

Guzmán walked from behind his desk and pulled open the top drawer of a cabinet. 'Doesn't make your harassment of innocent people any more excusable. I shall be filing a complaint with your superiors.'

'We've arrested Paul Turnbull.'

'Another travesty of justice, no doubt. Don't mind trampling through people's lives do you detective? First Adam Wells then me and now Turnbull. Doesn't matter, does it? Getting the right man isn't a priority…'

'We don't believe Turnbull killed Laura.'

Guzmán walked back behind his desk, looked up at Medina, and shook his head. 'My point entirely. Now, if you don't mind, I have work to do, saving lives, not ruining them.' Agitated, he began to clear his desk.

Medina took one last glance back towards the waiting room and satisfied himself that Roz and Rafe were safe, before he said, 'The boys at forensics have found blood. Laura's blood. In your car.'

Guzmán laughed. 'Evidence that's been planted.' He leaned heavily on his desk. 'You know, Leo, this whole charade would be laughable if it wasn't so sick. Fine, healthy young kids you have there. It's a pity you'll struggle to support them. Even construction work's hard to find these days, especially for a disgraced cop.'

'I apologised earlier,' Medina said, 'because although I always knew you'd killed Laura, I thought it might have been a crime of passion, a fit of anger - killing her after she tried to extort more money from you. But it wasn't, was it?' He paused. 'It was cold, calculated, and quite deliberate. It's my guess you decided to kill her when you were sipping cocktails at that bar on the beach. What did you do? Slip into the kitchen, select a boning knife and hide it under your shirt?' Medina rested his hands of the other side of the doctor's desk and lent forward. 'You see, if you did steal a knife, that would make Laura's murder premeditated, and you'll go down for a very, very long time.'

Guzmán pushed himself away and collected patient files from the top of his desk. 'If you'll excuse me,' he said, his breathing shallow. 'I have a waiting room full of patients.'

'Was full of patients, doctor.' Estrada was standing at the surgery door. 'Now, it's just the three of us.'

'Ah, the cavalry arrives yet again.' Guzmán laughed and shook his head. 'What can I say to make you believe me?' He thumped the desk with both hands, scattering files to the floor. 'What do I have to do to make you understand? I did not kill Laura!'

Estrada looked across at Medina and nodded. He moved forward and said calmly, 'Doctor Javier Guzmán I am arresting you on suspicion of the murder of Laura Domingo. You do not have to say anything, but anything you do say…' He completed the caution, moved towards Guzmán and placed a large hand on his shoulder. 'If you'd come with me, sir.'

Neither of the detectives saw the glint of fluorescent light on the blade of the scalpel. Neither did they react in time when Guzmán lunged forward and pressed it into Medina's neck.

'Sargento, place your gun on the desk and step away.'

Estrada pulled her handgun from her shoulder holster and levelled it at Guzmán's head. 'This is not one of your better ideas, doctor. Don't make me use this.'

Guzmán pressed the scalpel deeper into Medina's neck and a thin trickle of blood seeped from the wound. 'Put the gun down, Sargento. I will not repeat myself.'

'Shoot the fucker.' Medina's eyes glared at her.

'Your call, Sargento.'

Medina struggled.

'Sargento?'

She lowered the handgun. 'As you wish, Javier.' She used his first name, distracting him momentarily, and placed the semi-automatic on the desk. 'I've done what you asked, doctor. Now, let Leo go.' She stepped back; hoping Medina understood the glance she'd shot at him. His life could depend it. It might buy them precious seconds.

Guzmán forced Medina's head back, lent forward and grabbed the Beretta. 'Smart move Sargento.' He switched the scalpel to his left hand and pressed the handgun into Medina's neck, and then opened the young detective's jacket. 'Where's your gun?'

'Probationers don't carry weapons. When I'm fully trained…'

'Not going to get that chance, are you?' Guzmán laughed. 'You're as impotent as ever. No wonder you had to settle for that mouse of a woman and couldn't satisfy Laura.'

Medina snapped, turned on him, pushed the gun to one side, bulldozed him backwards into the waiting room, caught him around the neck, lifted him into the air and slammed him against the wall.

As he crashed to the floor, Guzmán levelled the gun at Medina and pulled the trigger.

Nothing happened.

He fumbled to disengage the safety catch.

At the same moment, Estrada pulled Medina's Beretta from between her shirt and trouser waistband.

Guzmán struggled to his feet and raised his gun.

Both exploded at the same time.

Guzmán's body sagged and collapsed onto the floor. Estrada was thrown against the wall, her left arm searing.

She screamed, scrambled across the room and kicked out at him, rolling him onto his back. As he came to rest, his gun was pointing directly at her.

She didn't hesitate, firing once more. She felt faint, blood pouring from her arm, the pain intensifying but she managed to stagger over to where Guzmán had fallen. She stood over him and waited. He lay motionless, but she felt she had no choice. She fired again, then turned her back on him and hurried over to Medina.

He was slumped against the wall, both hands clutching at his gut, shock spilling from his eyes as blood from his stomach began to trickle between the scalpel and his fingers. He sank to the floor.

Estrada stowed her gun and took out her mobile and waited a few agonising seconds before Valencia Ramoz answered. 'It's Leo. Get an ambulance.' She watched Medina slip into unconsciousness. She grabbed a handful of lint bandages and packed the sleeve of her shirt. 'Where's the Inspector?'

'No idea. He's not answering his mobile.'

'Well, find him. And for God's sake, hurry.'

*

Fernández steered his Seat through the open gate and into the yard. A few days earlier, geese had attacked him, as though sensing he'd brought the worst news any parent could hear. This evening, the farmyard was quiet. A few chickens scratched at the earth, but the geese had been penned up for the night. From inside the house, he heard the dogs bark at the sound of the car, but even they fell silent.

He climbed from the car and stood, listening for sounds that might indicate where Carlos had taken Paul Turnbull. He called the old man's name several times as he walked over to the farmhouse door and pushed it open. The dogs barked furiously at him, snarling as he stepped into the main parlour. 'Carlos?' he called, offering a clenched fist for the dogs to smell, hoping they would back off. 'Carlos!' He stepped cautiously up the narrow staircase and checked the two bedrooms. 'Carlos!' he called once more before retreating, closing the farmhouse door and standing on the stone step, surveying the yard and shuddering as cool air swept down from the mountains.

Suddenly, a sickening scream shattered the silence. Fernández froze momentarily then hurried across the farmyard to the large barn. He tried to force open the doors, but only managed to prise them apart. In the thin shaft of light he saw the carcass of a pig hanging upside down. 'Carlos!' He cried out. 'Carlos! Turnbull didn't kill Laura. Carlos! Listen to me!' Again, he tried to force open the barn doors, but failed, hurried back to his car, turned the ignition, revved the engine and slammed it into first gear. But before he could move, he heard the unmistakable explosion of a shotgun.

He slipped the clutch and accelerated, careering towards the barn doors, crashing into them and forcing enough of a gap to enable him to scramble through.

The late evening sunshine streamed through the opening, falling on Carlos's lifeless body slumped on a chair, his shotgun on the ground, the back of his head showered across a crude cloth screen behind a table. Fernández stood before him, fighting back the tears. 'Dear God, Carlos.'

He glanced over at the pig. It was still, its life-blood drained into the parched soil, its head hanging grotesquely to one side, a huge gash in its neck moist with fresh blood, flies gathering.

Alongside the pig, Turnbull's body hung upside down, blood pooled beneath him, his face horribly beaten, disfigured and swollen. Fernández crouched and studied Turnbull's face. The flow of blood had slowed, trickling from a body that continued to spasm. Turnbull's eyes stared back at him. He blinked.

Fernández shook his head, moved back to the table, and pressed the stop and rewind buttons of a digital tape recorder. He listened to the conversation between Carlos and Turnbull several times before he turned the machine off, carried it over to Turnbull, sat down on a pile of logs and lit a cigarette.

'You should to listen to this,' he said. 'It would be inadmissible, of course, but Carlos wanted to make sure we knew.' He played the tape. He looked into Turnbull's eyes as his confession filled the barn. 'Carlos used to help Laura and her friends record music. He obviously remembered which button to press.'

Fernández turned the machine off and pocketed the cassette. 'You know,' he said, each of his sentences measured and punctuated by long pauses. 'I could thank you for bringing me closer to my father. I may never have known what he did, or what drove him to kill a man.' He paused, dragging on his cigarette, exhaling the smoke forcefully towards Turnbull's bewildered eyes. 'I might never have known how he died, or what my mother has had to live with all these years. And I've been so wrapped up in myself and in my career...'

He stubbed out his cigarette and lit another. 'I might have been tempted to justify what you did when you killed Bartlomé: trying to provide for your wife and unborn child; making sure you put food on the table; securing their future; removing anyone who put that at risk.' He dragged smoke deep into his lungs and lifted his head, exhaling towards the rafters of the barn. 'But, you weren't concerned for anyone but yourself, were you?'

Turnbull's body shuddered. Final spasm? Fernández wasn't sure, but several coins fell from the pocket of Turnbull's trousers, dropping into the pool of blood beneath his head.

Fernández lent forward, dipped his fingers into the blood and picked up the coins. 'This is what it's all been about. Hasn't it? Money. Driven by your greed, and to hell with everyone else.'

He threw the coins across the barn and, as he wiped his fingers on Turnbull's shirt, he checked for signs of life - fainter now, almost indistinguishable from the final throws of death.

'But d'you know what sickens me more than anything?' He paused, watching and waiting. 'The callous disregard you had for those left behind. Alberto, Bartolomé, Matias. Their widows condemned to life-long sorrow. Felipe may have been a drunk and dirt poor, but he was someone's son, brother, friend.' His breath caught in his throat, his sorrow threatening to overwhelm him. 'And Ana-Marie and her family?' He gulped in air, his voice wavering as he spat out each word. 'I hope to God you rot in Hell.'

Day Thirteen

Tuesday 30th June 2009

Fernández stayed at the hospital for most of the night. Surgeons had performed a second operation on Leo Medina to repair internal damage caused by the scalpel and he was waiting for an update.

Estrada joined him at three in the morning, her left arm supported by a sling. 'How is he?'

'Touch and go.'

'He'll pull through?'

'God willing.' He paused. 'How's the arm?'

'Flesh wound,' she said. 'Good as new in no time.'

'There'll be an independent inquiry. Circumstances surrounding both arrests: Guzmán's and Turnbull's.'

'Thought as much.'

'It's routine, but you might want to think through what you'll tell them.'

'I've got nothing to hide.'

'They'll want to talk to Leo when...'

Estrada dropped her head, shaking it gently, tears marshalling.

'You did all you could.'

'I know, but if we'd handled it differently...'

'You should be proud of the job you've done; both of you. You had Guzmán in the frame for Laura. It was me who got it wrong. Me who thought Turnbull had killed her.'

'Leo's got good instincts. He'll make a good detective. Please God, he pulls through.' She looked up at him. 'You want to go home, get some rest?'

'No, no thanks. There's a couple of benches down the corridor. I'll take my chances on one of them.'

They dozed for several hours, the hospital eerily quiet most of the time, lighting at a minimum, nursing staff calm and efficient, but as dawn broke the pace picked up and it wasn't long before the business of caring was back in full swing.

At eight, he fetched two coffees from a vending machine and they sat, blurry eyed, sipping the insipid espresso.

At nine, Roz arrived, two sons walking behind minded by an elderly woman who sat them down next to Estrada. They watched as a consultant came out of Medina's room, spoke to Roz, and then walked along the corridor towards them.

'Would the boys like to see their papa?'

They didn't need a second invitation, scampering along the corridor.

'Well?' Fernández asked as soon as the boys were out of earshot.

'Leo's condition remains critical, but there are signs of improvement. It's too early to call but, unless there's a relapse, we're confident he'll make a complete recovery.'

'Thank God.'

'You want to see him?'

'Yes. Yes, of course.'

Medina smiled at the two detectives and then lifted his hand and caressed his wife's face.

The boys were hoisted onto the side of the bed, their eyes staring fearfully at the plethora of medical equipment hooked up to their father.

'You look after your mother, until I get out of here, won't you?' Medina's voice was weak.

They nodded and Rafe began to cry. 'Are you going to be all right, daddy?'

'Yes. Everything's going to be just fine.' He looked across at Estrada. 'I owe you.'

'It was nothing.'

He tired suddenly and closed his eyes. His boys looked anxiously at Roz.

'Best let him rest,' a nurse said to the children. 'He's in safe hands.'

As Roz led her two boys from the room, Fernández and Estrada turned to follow.

'Inspector,' Medina's voice scratched across the room. 'How's that cocky pathologist?'

They retreated to his local bar and ordered a couple of coffees and a selection of tapas.

'Word is you're on the move,' Estrada said as she broke into a slice of fresh tortilla.

'I'm taking a couple of weeks leave. When I get back, the Comandante has arranged for us to spend a month with the London Metropolitan Police - training with their armed response unit.'

'Us?'

'You and me. When we return, we'll be part of a revamped Serious Crimes Unit. It'll be based in Almeria, covering Andalucia and neighbouring provinces.' He paused. 'We'll be responsible for putting a team together. Interested?'

'A couple months in England?'

'Training's outside London. Place called Gravesend.'

'Unfortunate name.' Estrada smiled. 'Yes, count me in.' She hesitated before asking, 'What about Leo?'

'Assuming he's interested.'

'Can't see him turning down the opportunity.' She slid off the stool, gathered her jacket and said, 'Have a good holiday, wherever.' She didn't wait for a response, but walked out of the bar and into a day that was already stifling.

Fernández turned to the TV and watched a feature on close-season activity in the football transfer market.

'You going to settle your bill?'

'When you learn to smile.' He pulled a fifty-euro note, collected his change and glanced at the television.

'You want to come to tea?' He felt a tug at his jacket and looked down to see Holly and Sofia grinning up at him. 'We're going to make chocolate muffins,' they chorused.

'The girls are planning to poison us all before we take Sofia back home this afternoon,' Julieta Santiago said.

'Can't I stay one more night? Mama won't mind. She says it's good for us to play together.'

'As long as we remember to behave ourselves,' Holly reminded her and then grabbed Sofia by the arm and pulled her. 'Come on. Let's play chase.'

'Nothing much has changed there, then.' Fernández watched the girls dash about the square.

'How's Ana-Marie?'

'Settling back in the village. Going through with the pregnancy.'

'You'll be by her side?'

'It's a few months away, but yes, if she wants me there.' He searched her face for a reaction.

'I'm sure she'll appreciate that,' she said. 'At least we've been able to confirm that José was the father of Laura's unborn.'

'Yes.' He sighed and lit a cigarette. 'Look, I'll give tea a go but only if you'll let me buy you dinner this evening.'

'Dinner?' she asked, watching the girls hiding behind a ficus tree. 'I might enjoy that.'

'Good.' He pulled an envelope from the back pocket of his jeans and pushed it towards her. 'Will Holly be ok for a couple of weeks whilst her mother's away?'

'Whilst I'm away?' Santiago looked puzzled.

He tapped the envelope. 'Two tickets for Rio. Wondered if you'd like to join me?'

Santiago ignored the envelope, took a sip of her coffee and then removed a plastic evidence bag from a pocket inside her jacket. 'I found these on the barn floor, near where Turnbull had been strung up.'

He looked at the remnants of three spent cigarettes.

289

'They're yours,' she said. 'You phoned for an ambulance. One was on standby in the area. It took less than ten minutes to reach the farm, but it was too late, they couldn't do anything for him.' She tilted her head, raising an eyebrow slightly. 'You want to tell me why you waited so long before making the call?'

He exhaled forcefully, looked at her and took a small cassette from his jacket pocket. 'Carlos made sure we had this before he turned the shotgun on himself. When you have a moment, doctor, listen to it. Listen to it several times, as I have done, and tell me whether you think Turnbull gave a shit about anyone but himself?'

He stepped down from his bar stool. 'I'll see you here at eight this evening.' He walked towards the door, hesitated, and turned round. 'Oh, and don't be late.'